PIECES Of A Man

PIECES Of A Man

Cas Sigers

urban soul

URBAN BOOKS

http://www.urbanbooks.net

URBAN SOUL is published by

Urban Books
10 Brennan Place
Deer Park, NY 11729

ISBN-13: 978-1-59983-026-1
ISBN-10: 1-59983-026-4

First Printing: June 2007

10 9 8 7 6 5 4 3 2 1

Printed in the United States of America

Chapter 1

Is Romance Enough?

I don't know when or how it started, but one night, dinner and a movie became "Dinner and a Movie." Two years later, I'm madly in love with this person who I know is not the one for me. Yet I can't walk away. Therefore, I choose to stay and make this love, or as my friends call it "emotional instability," work. They just don't understand that I have a good thing. Even if I say he's not the one for me, that's only my mind speaking, and for the last two years my mind and my heart have been in a battle. Every time my mind ties the score, I read one of his love poems or open a surprise gift, and *score!* The heart leads again. My problem is, I am a sucker for romantic gestures and my man is the king of romance. For example, the other day I came home to a trail of square pieces of paper scattered on the floor. Each square had letters on the front and numbers on the back. So I sat for an hour pondering this homemade Scrabble game. Finally, I decided to put the numbers in numerical order. 1, 2, 3, 4 . . .

I WANT TO SPEND 4 EVER WITH U.

See what I mean? He does the sweetest things all of the time. Even though this gesture is to make up for an argument last night, I must admit he has a special way of treating me and I just love it. I even love his name . . . Romance Williams. His mother had a one-night rendezvous with a romantic stranger. She named him after this elusive man, and fortunately for me, he constantly feels pressure to live up to his name. Since Romance sounds a bit fictional, I call him Ro for short.

Tonight is our two-year anniversary. I take the time to create a special gift because I want to show him that I can also be very romantic. I take a classic beach picture that we took three years ago and place it in a wooden, double frame. Alongside the picture, I place one of my original poems. Oh yeah, I write; not professionally, although Ro is always saying I should. Therefore, I know he is going to like the poem. It's a perfect combination of tenderness and adoration. I wrap the frame in a blue box and wait. My excitement is building. Ro said to wear my favorite black dress because he is taking me somewhere special. So in my living room I am sitting dressed in sexy attire and waiting for our special evening to begin. Six o'clock, then seven comes, and I am still waiting. Finally, ten rolls by and the phone rings.

"Lily, baby. I just finished playing ball. Maybe we can do dinner tomorrow," says Ro with no regret in his voice.

Now, usually I don't sweat the small stuff. However, he asked me out to dinner and then he casually breaks it as if tonight is not our two-year anniversary.

"What did you say?" I calmly ask.

"I just finished playing basketball. I'll see you tomorrow," he repeats.

I sit and listen to him again, and I can feel the rage building up in my chest. I am going to let him have it.

"Okay, I'll see you tomorrow," I state with disappointment.

He hangs up and so do I. What just happened? Why did I say okay? It is not okay and I need to let him know that it's not okay. This evening is important to me. He is going to have a peaceful, good night's sleep while I sit up most of the night angry. Why couldn't I communicate that? Have I lost my touch?

As a test, I call my girlfriend Tam to explain what has happened and my feelings about his response. What can I say? A girl needs a little emotional validation at times. As Tam listens intently, I express myself very well. She agrees with my position and this is when it hits me: I cannot tell Ro how I feel because I do not want him to be upset with me. If he gets angry enough, he could leave and I do not want to lose him. Therefore, I suppress my true feelings in order to keep the peace. Unknowingly, I have done this for years. So much, it has become second nature.

At that moment, I realize that all of the gifts, cards, and surprises meant nothing. They hold no merit because he did not give them to me; he gave them to an impostor. The impostor who is afraid of what will happen if she speaks her mind. I immediately open his gift, remove the original poem, and replace it with a new one.

The very next day, as promised, Ro comes over to celebrate our anniversary.

"Happy anniversary. I'm sorry it's a day late, but I know it will be okay once you see what I have in my hand," he boasts with a huge smile.

Ro leans over, wraps his hand around my waist, pulls me into his chest, and kisses me. I keep my lips closed as I indulge his affection for a second. When I move away, I speak anxiously.

"Open mine first."

Ro graciously takes the little blue box from my hand. Sitting on the edge of the futon, he smiles at the picture and begins to read his poem. As one eyebrow lifts, he smirks. By the tenth line he begins to read the poem aloud, as if I am unaware of its content.

"Are you strong enough to be my man?" he reads.

Ro slowly lifts his head and rolls his eyes toward the kitchen where I am standing.

He speaks, as his tone rises a pitch. "Am I?"

"Well, are you?" I say as I roll my neck and bat my eyes.

No answer. Instead he walks over and rests his gift on top of my hands. Although my eyes follow him to the refrigerator, he doesn't focus on me. He opens the fridge door, removes a beer, and walks back to the futon. I know I could have explained myself better, but I express myself best through writing. Instead of writing a sarcastic poem, questioning his manhood, I could have said simply, "You do not always treat me fair. You are insanely jealous, which causes you to act like an idiot. You are disrespectful at times and rarely do you consider my feelings. I am not going to take it anymore. So when I tell you how I feel, I pray that you are man enough to handle it."

"I don't think he got the point," I whisper to myself.

Okay, we all agree. I need to work on my communication skills. But it's so hard, especially when he looks so cute. I promise to explain myself better as soon as I open his . . .

"Oh my God!" I scream while jumping up and down.

No, it is not a diamond. It is a music box. However, it is not just any music box. With Ro, every gift has meaning. When I was six years old, my grandfather made me a wooden music box and topped it with a ballerina, in arabesque. The music box played "My Funny Valentine." Although I was told not to take it outside, I wanted to show my friends, so I took it out to the corner, set it on the pavement, and turned the key. We all watched in awe as the tiny ballerina twirled to the tune. Suddenly, out of nowhere came Tommy James hurling on his Big Wheel. He turned the corner and crushed my music box. I cried until my eyes hurt. I was so upset that I didn't even get a spanking. My parents knew I had suffered enough.

But now in my hand I hold a music box identical to the one I held over twenty years ago.

"Please don't let it play 'My Funny Valentine,'" I pray.

I know if it plays this song, I will not be able to contain my tears and my anger and frustration will reduce to a mere "Oh well." As I wind the box, I feel myself getting weaker and weaker.

"It plays 'My Funny Valentine,'" I squeal.

I begin to cry as if I were six years old all over again and I can't remember what I was going to say. I look at him as he pretends not to look at me. Quickly, I see a grin come upon his face.

His smile suggests, "Yes, I have done it once again."

With my arms spread, I walk over and embrace Ro. Grabbing his arm, I give him a slight nudge toward the bedroom and we retire for the rest of the evening.

P.S.: No, I have not forgotten that I still need to give him a piece of my mind. . . . It can wait . . . I'll do it tomorrow.

Good night.

Chapter 2

Newfound Courage

This morning I lie in bed, for close to an hour, listening to the songs of the chirping birds. Spring is quickly approaching. When I finally rise and look out of the window, my nose is lured into the kitchen. I change directions and make my way to the oven.

"What is that smell?" I whisper. "Could that be breakfast? Ro, did you cook breakfast?"

"Ro. Romance!" I yell.

I stand in the center of the kitchen, but instead of seeing my boyfriend, I see a pink Post-it stuck to the front of the microwave.

Baby,
Sorry about the mess. I cooked breakfast.
See ya later tonight.
Love, Ro

"That's sweet, he cooked breakfast."

Eager, I open the oven to see what my man has left me for

breakfast. Peering into the dark, cold oven, I am surprised. He leaves me absolutely nothing. The oven is empty. For breakfast, Ro leaves me his dirty dishes. The anger is now coupling with the hunger pains in the pit of my stomach. I know this might be petty, but I am getting tired of his mess. This is what happens when I let things slide. Pretty soon, everything that man does is going to get on my damn nerves. Before long, the tiniest thing is going to send me over the edge. As soon as the phone rings, I know it's Ro.

I answer, "Hello."

"Did you get my note?"

"I sure did. I also got the delicious breakfast you made," I mention with overt sarcasm.

"I didn't have time to fix you anything. You don't eat eggs."

"Whatever, Ro," I mumble with obvious irritation.

"I'll make it up to you. Let's go to the movies tonight. I want to see that new Spike Lee joint."

"I don't want to see anyone's joint. Besides, I have plans."

"Well, break them and go to the movies with me," he says. "No!"

"Fine. I'll talk with you tomorrow." He abruptly ends communication.

"He makes me sick!" I say aloud.

He wants to make up his breakfast mistake with a movie that he wants to see. That is so inconsiderate and I am not falling for it. I told him I have plans and now I must create some. I've got to make evening arrangements with Tam because I am not sitting in this house tonight.

"What's up, girl? What are we doing tonight?"

"I don't believe it. You are actually going to spend time with your girlfriends? How exciting," she says cynically. "What happened? Ro pissed you off?"

"Nah, girl, I miss you. Let's go to that new jazz spot tonight. It's called the Blue Room, right?"

"Yeah, sounds good. I'll call Evelyn. Do you want to meet there around eight?"

"Eight is perfect. I'll see you tonight. Bye," I respond before hanging up the phone.

"I'm going out tonight. I'm going out tonight," I sing, dancing around the room.

I really need to get out more. What will I wear? Maybe I'll treat myself to a new dress and a new pair of shoes. Sure, Ro is expecting me to break my plans, call him back, and ask him about movie arrangements. However, that was the old me. The new and improved me is going out to have fun with my girls.

I sing and dance because, hell, I'm going out tonight and I'm going to have fun. "I'm going out tonight. I'm going out tonight."

My watch says 8:19 as I hand the valet my keys. Strutting into the Blue Room, I am taken aback by the lavish furnishings. I can tell by the décor I will definitely be back. Candles and lanterns dimly light the large open space. The "Bedrock" tables, made from oval-shaped, flat pieces of marble, sit atop huge black stones. At each table and throughout the room are bright-colored, plush chenille pillows. Oriental rugs garnish the concrete floors and long, rectangular mirrors adorn the burnt-orange walls (very feng shui). This is definitely a place where beautiful people hang out, and I love it. In my new dress, I am a perfect fit. I carefully sit on one of the pillows and greet Tam and Evelyn. After delivering a brief speech about neglecting her for Ro, Tam hands me a mango daiquiri. We toast, but just as my glass clings with hers, my mouth drops open as I watch this heavenly figure glide across the room.

"Do you see what I see?" I sing to the Christmas melody. Tam and Evelyn turn and notice the beautiful stranger.

"He is fine," says Tam.

"The displaced Afro is so dated, and where are his shoes?" says Evelyn as she frowns in dismay.

Now, Evelyn is a different sort. If a man is not clean-shaven, wearing Gucci, and stepping out of his BMW or Range Rover, she has no attraction to him. Too bad . . . her loss. This man is absolutely delicious; as though God dipped Maxwell in dark chocolate, graced him with Denzel's smile and Wesley's ass, and there he walks. I stare in awe as he makes his way to the stage and sits Indian style on a small purple pillow.

"Greetings, everyone. We are SoulTyme and we will be this evening's entertainment."

"Wow, he plays an instrument too. I'm entertained just looking at him. I didn't know he came with music," I whisper.

Tam shouts while snapping her fingers in my face. "Hello! Can you get your eyes off that man? You have a boyfriend! Remember?"

Tam might as well be talking to the people in India, because I cannot stop staring. As he strums his guitar and sings a sweet tune in a low tenor, I begin to daydream about this man. I can just imagine, I bet he is better than chocolate. Light-headedness is setting in due to the lack of air intake, for he is undeniably breathtaking. I have to get a hold of myself, but it is too late. I think he has seen me gawking, and now he is staring at our table.

"Is he staring at me?" I ask Tam.

"Either that or he's staring at me," she hints while sipping her drink.

However, once he finishes his set, he walks over, grabs my hand, and pulls me to the bar. It becomes apparent; he was not staring at Tam. I turn and stick my tongue out at her as I float away with this gorgeous musician. When we get to the bar, he leans over and whispers in my ear. As his sweet breath hits my earlobe, I could melt.

"I want to let you know that I could see your panties the entire performance. I didn't want to embarrass you in front of your friends."

Oh no! I really could melt into a puddle of mud and slither my way back to the table.

"Really?" I say with gross shame.

"Yeah, I think it's sexy when a lady matches her panties with her outfit," he whispers seductively.

What do I say? Is that a compliment or does he think I'm slutty?

"Thanks, it's just a little something I like to do."

Matching my underwear is something I never do. Thank God I need to wash clothes. It was either these olive panties or a pair of Ro's boxers.

"My name is Will Dickson. However, my friends call me Dick." Extending his hand, Dick formally greets me.

"Well, hello there, Dick," I say with blatant sexuality.

Leaning against the bar, we continue light, intimate conversation until the second set. Thirty minutes later, I return to our table only to greet the disapproving eyes of both Evelyn and Tam. Yet I cleverly convince them to move closer to the stage during the band's last performance. I mention to Tam that one of the band members is interested in her. The truth is I don't want Dick to strain his eyes looking at my underwear.

After the performance, Dick and some of his bandmates join us on our red, oriental rug. We all sit and laugh for hours. I cannot take my eyes off Dick's face and my hands off his legs. Along with a great personality, he has great teeth and the sexiest lips you ever want to see on a man. It's exciting to watch him speak. Around 2:00 AM, Tam and Evelyn nudge my side to indicate they are ready to leave.

"I'll see you later." I wave, scooting closer to Dick.

"Excuse me, gentlemen. I need to see her in the ladies'

room," Tam expresses as she pulls me up and pushes me toward the back.

With my arm clutched within her hands, she murmurs, "You will leave when we leave. Get his number, say good-bye, and take your ass home to your man. Better yet, don't get his number, just go home."

After a bit of hesitation, I eventually whisper, "Fine."

I scuffle my feet back to the area rug where Dick and I exchange numbers. Sitting in my car, I wait for my friends to leave. I have reverted to high school, sneaking to meet a boy whom I have no business being with. Yet, as I sit here waiting, Ro floods my mind. He is my man and how would I feel if he were doing the same thing? Therefore, after a long sigh . . . and I mean a really long sigh . . . I realize that I have had my fantasy and it is time to go home to my reality.

After a slow ride home, I walk into the house, throw my keys on the coffee table, and walk into the bedroom. Sprawled across the foot of my bed lies Ro with his feet dangling to the floor. I lean against the door frame and watch him sleep. Although it took some serious consideration, I am glad I came home. But I do not want to be questioned about my where-abouts tonight. Therefore, knowing he will awake as soon as I lie down, I quietly jump in the shower and fall asleep on the futon. A few minutes into my sleep, I immediately begin to dream about Dick.

"Wake up."

I think Ro is trying to wake me up. Maybe if I lie still, he'll go away.

"Wake up," he says, tapping me on the stomach.

Damn! It is as if he knows I'm dreaming about another man.

"What do you want, Ro?"

"Where have you been?"

"At the Blue Room with Tam and Evelyn. May I go back to sleep?"

"What do you mean, 'Am I strong enough to be your man'?"

Hmmm . . . I guess he got the point better than I thought. After taking a few seconds to gather my thoughts, I slowly open my eyes to face the music. Without more ado, I start explaining.

"I was wrong for not explaining myself better. I have been unhappy with your disrespectful behavior. You never ask me anything, because you are too busy telling me everything. You are insanely jealous and it is unnecessary. I should have told you this a year ago and I am sorry. I was afraid of losing you. However, I am tired of it. Things have to change and I hope you are man enough to handle it. Hence the poem."

There, I said it. It is amazing how interest from a new man can give a woman the courage to stand up to her current one. Staring at the floor, Ro sits on the edge of the futon. I can only assume he is contemplating his retort and it seems as though he is going to take a while. Thus, I close my eyes and lean back against the pillow.

Just as I doze off, he speaks. "I think you are wrong. You need to get over it. Everything I do is for you. What about the things you do that get on my nerves? I overlook them, because relationships are about compromise. Of course I get jealous when men approach you. I love you and I don't recall being disrespectful. Unless you can sit here and name the times and the places, I'm not even going to acknowledge that comment. You need to decide if you want a man or a dog that jumps at your command. Until then, I am gone."

Grabbing his hat, Ro storms out the door without looking back. Man, he is angry, and come to think of it, he is crazy. I never said I wanted a dog to jump at my command. I just want him to be more considerate. Oh well, I am not going to lose a minute of sleep over this argument. I guess there is a first time for everything. As a matter of fact, I am going right back to sleep. I only hope I can pick up my dream where I left off. Dick and I were playing strip poker and he cannot bluff worth a damn.

Good night.

Chapter 3

It's a New Dick . . .
I Mean New Day

Ring, ring.

This better not be Ro calling me to argue.

"Hello."

"How would you like breakfast?" says the mysterious voice.

"What? Who is this?"

"We met last night. Have you forgotten about me already?"

"Dick?" I question.

"Look here, I know we just met and I know you aren't going to let me pick you up and take you to breakfast. However, I am going to be at Rita's Café in about twenty minutes. If you come, breakfast is on me. I hope to see you. Peace."

That is so sweet, asking me to join him for breakfast. What should I do?

"You should go and enjoy a free breakfast," says the red guy on my left shoulder.

"No, if you go to breakfast, it might lead to other things and that could be trouble," claims his winged nemesis on my right.

"At least he wants to take you to breakfast," retorts Red. "Ro left you with an empty oven. Remember?"

"And he left me with dirty dishes," I add.

No one has treated me to breakfast in years. Therefore, concurring with Red, I am going to eat and enjoy myself. If it leads to something else, I will deal with that issue at that time. I rise, brush my teeth, wash my face, and throw on my fitted blue sweater and indigo Joe's Jeans.

I arrive at Rita's Café and immediately notice Dick wearing large, light-colored sunglasses with a blue bandana tied around his wrist. He is sitting with his legs stretched across the booth seat, and I can see his black motorcycle boots hanging off the edge. With his head leaning against the window, he makes Lenny Kravitz, who is the epitome of rock stardom, look like a bum. He was gorgeous last night, but I swear he looks twice as nice in daylight. Noticing me, he rises and gives me a long hug. He holds his arms around my back and kisses my neck gently as if I had not seen him in months. Together we sit and I order juice as he sips his water. Reaching across the table, he begins using his thumb to draw invisible music notes on my arm. Maybe the angel was right, this could be trouble. Yet this dilemma is very inviting. He removes his shades and stares into my eyes. Placing his full lips on the tips of my fingers, Dick begins smiling. I can tell with the curl of his top lip, he is in full thought, and of course I am curious.

"What are you thinking?" I ask.

"I'm wondering if you have on light blue panties to match your sweater."

"I guess you'll have to find out," I say in a tone slightly below my normal octave.

What did I just say? It is like my flirt switch is jammed in the on position and I can't control my answers. Maybe he didn't hear.

"I can't wait," he replies with obvious motive.

Damn, he heard. I must make a conscious effort to be quiet

the remainder of breakfast. Therefore, I smile bashfully and gaze out of the window.

After we eat, he invites me back to the studio to listen to him rehearse a new song. I give it thought for a second; it seems innocent. Besides, I love his music. The band members are nice guys, and I should enjoy myself. Dick holds my hand and leads me into the dark studio. As he flips on the light switch, I see we are alone. The other members are not coming, and I quickly become nervous. Not that I am afraid of him, but I am afraid of what might happen if I spend time alone with him. Dick walks into the sound booth, plucks his guitar, and hums a seductive tune. He is drawing me into his world, as I swiftly weave my own tangled web. I sit in a dim studio, listening to one of the most beautiful men I have ever met serenade me with sweet music, and I am getting excited. This moment, which once seemed so innocent, has evolved into the quintessence of eroticism. I have to go. I walk from the control room into the sound booth next to Dick. I really have to go. Okay, enough practice, I must formulate these words aloud.

"I . . . have to go."

"The bathroom is down the hall."

"No, I have to leave. I can't stay here."

"Are you not enjoying the music?"

"A little too much," I admit.

"Fine. We can go somewhere else. I just want to spend time with you."

He just wants to spend time with me. I have not heard these words in so long. Maybe if we go somewhere around other people, I'll be okay.

"We can go to the movies. Is there anything you want to see?"

He wants to know what I want to see. Ro never asks me;

instead he tells me what we are going to see. Little things mean so much, and Dick realizes that.

"I want to see Halle Berry's new movie."

Dick frowns as he asks, "The love story?"

"You know what, that's okay. I need to go home anyway," I respond, quickly changing my mind.

"No, we can go see it," he says, holding my arm. "Today is your day."

"Today *is* my day," I softly reiterate.

This man is saying all the right things. He seems perfect. That's because he's trying to sleep with me. Once we sleep together, he will probably start acting like Ro. Hold up. I just said once we sleep together? I am considering sleeping with this man? I have a boyfriend and I've been faithful for two years. I cannot believe I am contemplating having sex with someone I have known for less than twenty-four hours. I need to just go home right now. Well . . . after the movie, I must go home . . . alone!

Seven hours later we arrive back at the studio; so much for going home after the movie. The entire day has been spent with Dick. While walking around the park, eating dinner, and talking over dessert, I am growing very fond of my new friend. Now we stand beside my truck in that awkward first-date silence. I know he is going to try to kiss me, but I cannot let him kiss me on the lips. In this moment, he thanks me for the wonderful date, slowly kisses two of his fingers, and softly presses them upon my lips. Leaving me dazed, Dick turns and walks away.

"I don't believe it. He didn't try to kiss me."

He does not give me a hug. He simply walks away. Beside the car, I stand dumbfounded. Although I did not want him to kiss me, I need to know why he didn't make an attempt. Just then, he leisurely turns his head over his left shoulder, licks his lips, and speaks.

"I guess I'll have to see the color of those panties some other time, unless . . ."

Then, in the same laid-back manner, he turns back around and walks into the studio, intentionally leaving the door cracked open, just in case I decide to follow.

"Oh, he's good," I murmur.

During our date he must have learned something about me, and that is, I don't fare well with temptation. Thrown, I know I should not go in, but I want to, desperately. I look to my right shoulder praying to hear an angelic voice, but I hear nothing. I assume my friend in white is weary of giving advice in vain. Consequently, I am on my own. If I go in, I know I will cheat on Ro. However, I have had an intimate date with this man. I shared an intimate walk and engaged in intimate conversation. Therefore, the cheating has already begun. I debate with myself for what seems like hours. Finally, leaning against the hood of the car, I make a decision I can live with.

"They're light blue, just like my sweater."

"It's about time," he flaunts.

For the next six hours—that is correct, six hours—the only music coming from that sound booth is the melodious moans and sighs of my new song. With Dick singing backup, I hit pitches never thought imaginable. After our intimate duet, we lie wrapped tightly in a blanket like a sexual taco, filled with sin and lust. I stare at the foam ceiling hoping to feel an ounce of remorse. However, I feel nothing. I am numb. I have slept with a man I hardly know, and the only thing I feel is the inclination to do it again. I close my eyes and pray that I come to my senses, yet common sense fails. Dick stands, turns on the music, and reaches for my hand.

"May I have this dance?" he whispers.

I gaze upon his naked body and realize that he is unscathed. He has no marks, no tattoos, and no scars. He is dark chocolate from his head to his toe and all parts in between. I have never seen such a sight. His body looks like a sculpture, courtesy of Michelangelo. Damn! He *is* fine!

"I would be honored."

He pulls me up and into his body. I cannot control the incessant smile on my face. I should not be so happy. I hope he doesn't look at me. He will think I am a nutcase, for no normal person smiles consecutively for more than two minutes. Therefore, I bury my head into his chest as my mind explodes with thoughts. I have not slow-danced like this since my junior prom. It is so innocent, as if we were not rolling around on the floor having raunchy sex just minutes ago. As I softly kiss his chest, his body becomes excited and I can feel him pulsating against my lower stomach. With my arms draped over his broad shoulders, Dick lifts me off my feet and I start to worry that my weary body will not make it through another six-hour sex-fest. However, as his warm tongue caresses my alert nipples, my body perks up and takes an interest in what he has to say.

This man is the devil, I say to myself.

His exterior is perfection, but he makes me want to do nothing but wrong. He presses my body up against the one carpeted wall and with my legs interlocked around his back, he enters me. Again and again he strums my body while composing his new aria. I have never felt so secure with a stranger inside me. What in the hell is going on?

Exhausted, I walk through my door four hours later. I want to fall asleep, but I must check the machine to see if Ro has called.

"You have one message," says the service voice.

Tam blares over the voice mail, "Girl, where have you been? I have been calling and paging you for the last twenty-four hours. You better not be with that singer boy. Call me."

"Whatever, Tam. You wish someone that fine would take you out," I sass to the machine while removing my clothing.

I jump in the shower and toss my weak body across the bed and fall asleep.

Good night.

Chapter 4

Playtime Is Over

I have a great day at work. Humorously, Tam calls three times to cross-examine me about my missing twenty-four hours. On her third attempt, I finally decide to speak with her. In brief conversation, I lie and say I needed time alone for meditation. I want to be honest about Dick, but I cannot face her shameful comments and sincere criticism. It's pitiful when you do something so inappropriate that you can't admit it to your best friend. This is a new low. I'll eventually tell her the truth about Dick. However, I don't think I will mention that our escapade took place the same weekend we met. She knows I'm not virtuous, but I can't have her thinking I am a ho.

Close to six that evening, I walk into my house, throw down my purse, and rush over to check my machine.

"You have no messages," taunts the voice.

Oh well, I suppose Ro wants to play hard, so I will give him a few more days. I am sure he will come around. In the meantime, I will enjoy my time with Dick. And if Ro really wants to act tough, he might be replaced. Besides, there is nothing like a new Dick to get over an old Romance.

For the next three days, I consume myself with work. Nonetheless, today is Thursday, six days since our argument, and Ro still hasn't called. This is upsetting me more than I thought. Why has he not called? Perhaps he is waiting for me to call. Yet he's the one who walked out; he's the one who should call. Is he playing tough or has he found his own Dick? Frustrated with this notion, I refuse to sit here any longer and worry about Ro. I am going to take Dick up on his dinner offer. He gives me directions to his house and we agree to meet at eight.

Dick lives about twenty minutes from me. Funny thing is, he only lives five minutes from Ro, and I must pass Ro's house on the way to Dick's place. However, this doesn't deter me from dinner. I pull up to Dick's building and sit in the car listening to the final chorus of Faith Hill's latest song. This is the first time I have felt an ounce of regret. The moment I entertain the idea that Romance may have found another, I become remorseful. It is so easy to deceive when we don't consider the boomerang effect of our actions. Nevertheless, as soon as we step into the reality of karma, we want to analyze our wrongdoings. However, at that point, is it too late?

Dick greets me at the door with a kiss on the cheek and invites me into his spacious condominium. All of the walls are white, a perfect disguise for a devil. His modern furniture is sage. He has one sage wall hanging to the left of the fireplace that holds a beautiful silver frame containing Salvador Dali's *The Last Temptation of Christ* and the irony continues.

Smiling, I comment, "Although this is not my favorite of his works, I like Dali. No matter how many times I look at his paintings, I continue to see different things."

Moving closer to study the picture, I see a book on the glass table in front of the print. It is *The Prophet* by Kahlil Gilbran, one of my favorites. Well, well, it seems Dick and I have more in common than our desire for great sex. As I place the book back on the table, Dick leans over his bar and sings a sweet melody, calling me to dinner. His table setting looks like the front of a Martha Stewart catalogue. Unlike my place, his decor is quite meticulous. We eat salad on small brown square plates and spinach manicotti on the larger matching set. I can now add culinary connoisseur to Dick's list of qualities. However, Ro is heavily on my mind and by the time I finish the main course, I have a nasty taste in my mouth.

Dick questions, "Is everything okay?"

"I have a boyfriend," I blurt out.

"I know," he admits. "Tam mentioned it several times that evening at the Blue Room. I assumed you didn't want to be with him anymore or that your girlfriend didn't want you to be with me."

Laughing, I reply, "It's a little of both. I just want you to know."

"It's okay, I have a boyfriend too."

Did he just say what I think he said? "What in the world did you just say?"

I stand with deep concern as he bursts into laughter.

"I'm joking. I want to see that pretty smile of yours."

The only thing he is about to see is my ass walking out the front door. I am no expert when it comes to men. However, the one thing I know about most heterosexual men is that they do not joke about being homosexual. As usual, deceit begets deceit.

"Seriously, I am joking. Please don't be upset. I love women. I have never dated a man," Dick insists.

He rushes into the bedroom and brings out his little black book. Opening it, he shows me the numbers. "Look, nine out of ten of the names are women."

He sees by my expression that I am not convinced. Why would he joke like that?

"My ex-girlfriend decorated this condo. I'll call her and you can talk to her if you want."

"That's okay. I believe you," I say, looking away.

I don't believe him. I knew he was too good to be true and I am ready to go.

"Thanks for dinner. I have an early morning. I need to leave," I quickly retort while moving away from the table.

He begs me not to leave, but it's too late. My spirit is already gone. To Dick's disappointment, I leave quickly after dinner.

I walk into my home and, of course, no call from Ro. As I mull over this week's activities, I become depressed. Not only has Ro not called, but I have comforted my frustration by sleeping with another man, possibly a gay one. If this is a test, I made an F–. I love Romance and although most times I don't like him, I don't want to lose him. This situation is a stinking mess. Here I am, concerned about losing him, when I need to be concerned about finding myself—the girl I lost a long time ago. Maybe losing Ro is not the problem. Perhaps I just don't want to be alone. People always speak about the thin line between love and hate. What about the very fine line between love and dependency?

Ring, ring.

Who is calling me at this hour? I hope it's not Dick. I lean over to check the caller ID and see that it's Tam. What does she want? I place my hands over my ears as I block out the third ring. Yet I might as well pick up the phone before the cell starts ringing.

"Yes, Tam, what do you want?"

"Something in me said call to see if you were okay."

Funny, when I answered the phone I was okay. However,

as she says these words, my eyes begin to water. It is as if I was waiting for someone to say it's okay to cry and so I do.

"I miss him," I wail.

Tam listens quietly and says nothing. This is what I love about her. She doesn't try to fix the problem; she just lets you blabber on until the solution rises to the surface. Thus, I continue.

Have you . . .
ever become nauseated with anticipation of seeing those
    eyes
Or changed clothing twelve times to create that look to
    light up his face?
Found yourself giddy with delight being in the same room.
Have you . . .
Ever felt heartbeats pound in unison as arms embraced
    entangled bodies?
Become engrossed into that silent stare that whispered
    a thousand I-love-yous?
Tenderly danced cheek to cheek, chest to chest, hips to
    hips, thighs to thighs, on a humid summer's eve?
Have you . . .
Ever stared out of the window on a rainy day until the
    raindrops on the glass evolve into the teardrops on
    your cheek
Or found yourself staring at the phone, impatiently
    checking the ringer, making sure you haven't missed
    that call
Unable to move from bed all day, because all of your
    energy was spent on wondering WHY?
Have you . . .
Ever known if given the chance you would make it last
    forever
and spent days upon days wondering if that chance
    would ever come

> *Wondered if that piercing pain that comes with every breath will cease only when the heartbeat is no longer?*
> *Have you . . .*
> *Ever loved?*

As I finish, she responds simply, "Yes, I have. I love you. Good night."

Good night.

Chapter 5

Decisions, Decisions

I awake to a pair of swollen eyes. I know better than to cry like this during the week. I now have to go to work with a puffy face. As I brush my teeth, I begin thinking about my great friendship with Tam. Then as I think a little more, I replay her last words in my head. Did she say yes, I have, period? Then I *love* you and good night? On the other hand, did she say yes, I have, comma, I love *you* and then good night? Who knew a little punctuation and intonation could change a relationship? Perhaps I am a tad bit paranoid from Dick's boyfriend comment. I have known Tam for years and she has had many dates, none with women. Besides, she is not the dating type. She would rather put her time and energy into her catering business. Tam is a chef with expert Caribbean culinary skills.

"She's a chef, not a lesbian," I say to my twin in the mirror. "A lesbian chef perhaps? Ughh! I have to go to work!"

Once I get to the office, I decide to call Tam and ask her to dinner. During our meal tonight, I will watch how she watches me and I see if I detect any signs of funny business. Surely I will find out what is going on in that head of hers.

Today, I receive several calls on Dick's behalf. Including a call from his ex-girlfriend, who assures me he is not gay. She seems honest, but for all I know that could be his mother. As tempting as it is to check my messages, I do not allow myself to call. I want to come home to a surprise message from Ro.

Five o'clock comes and I quickly rush home, walk in the door, use the restroom, and walk into the kitchen. Finally, I can't tease myself any longer. I hurry to check the voice mail and surprise! Ro did not call. It's been seven days since we argued. I give up; he wins. I'm going to call him. I hesitantly dial his seven digits. Three rings and he has not picked up. Maybe he's not home. It is a good thing that I blocked my phone number. I will not give him the satisfaction of knowing I called first. Then just as I am about to hang up, he answers.

"Hello."

At first I am silent. Then after a ten-second pause and a one-second hello I speak. "Hi, Romance. How are you?"

He coldly responds, "I'm busy. Can I call you back?"

"Yeah, I'll be here," I mumble. "He makes me *sick*!" I yell, slamming down the phone.

I am positive he has been planning that slick response all week. Unfortunately, I am back where I started, waiting for his call; only this time he has the upper hand because I called first. Now our relationship has become a warped game of chess. But unlike chess, there is no intellectual thought process calculating each move. This is a game of power, or lack thereof.

As I get ready for dinner with Tam, I stop and contemplate my dress. I can't believe I am contemplating anything. What is wrong with me? Her little comment has me all in a tizzy. I don't want to dress too sexy, yet I don't want to be too drab. Therefore, I throw on jeans and a blouse. When in doubt, fitted jeans and a dressy blouse fit almost every casual occasion. Grabbing my purse, I walk onto the porch and nearly trip over the guy sitting at the edge of the first step. I look down and see that it's Ro.

"What are you doing here?"

"This is my third time over here this week. I never made it past this step," he admits.

Oh, he misses me as much as I miss him. Beaming inside, I sit down beside him and apologize.

"I am sorry for the way I approached this situation. I should have sat down and explained myself. But, baby, you have hurt my feelings so many times that I became angry."

Confused, he looks at me and speaks sincerely. "I don't know what you want. I thought I was doing the right things. You told me you liked men who took control of the relationship. You said you liked assertive men. I promise to work on the jealousy, but what more do you want?"

I pause with my head on his shoulder, then whisper, "I don't know anymore."

I sit contemplating my vague answer and realize I'm not sure about anything. The man I love finally asks me what I want, which is exactly what I have been desiring. Yet the only answer I can come up with is "I don't know." Before Ro, I dated a guy who could never make a closing decision without the help of others. At that time, Ro and I were friends. I knew he was headstrong and independent and I thought he was what I wanted. It's amazing how we can want something so bad, until we finally get it. Then, once it's ours, it's not as appetizing.

When I was thirteen, I begged my dad for a pair of pink high-top Converse. I wanted to be a professional break-dancer. What was I thinking? When I was fifteen, I cried to get a perm in my hair. Now I would not touch a perm with a

ten-foot pole. When I was eighteen, I wanted three holes in
my right ear and five in my left. Currently, I have not a single
piercing and the list goes on. I recognize that all of these
things were fads. Have all of my relationships been fads as
well? What *do* I want?

Moving his shoulder from underneath my head, Ro speaks.
"I want you to do me a favor. Since you are into writing these
days, maybe you can write down what you want and give it
to me."

"Write it down? " I ask.

Just then my cell phone rings, interrupting our conversation. It's probably Tam calling to see if I am en route.

"Excuse me, Ro. Hello."

"Hi, beautiful. How are you?"

Oh no, it's Dick. I don't know what to say. I can't pretend
it's Tam; Ro is sitting too close and I know he's listening.

"I'm fine," I quickly retort.

"What are you doing this evening?"

"I'm going to dinner with Tam."

"What are you doing after dinner?" he persists.

"Um, I'm busy. Can I call you back?"

I don't wait for his response. I quickly hang up the cell
phone and continue my conversation with Ro.

"Who was that?" he says curiously.

"Dick," I whisper. "Do you want a poem or what?" I
quickly continue in attempt to deter his questions.

"I don't care, I just want you to write."

Although I wish he wouldn't, I know he is going to eventually ask me about Dick. I only hope I have time to come
up with a story. I can't tell Ro that Dick is the man I have
been sleeping with since our argument last week. How would
that sound?

"Well, I don't want to hold you up, I hear you have dinner
plans with Tam."

"Oh yeah, I do," I say, standing.

"So that was not an excuse you used to get rid of Dick," Ro says, placing an emphasis on the D.

I can tell by his expression, he's surely going to ask about ol' Dick, and it will be sooner than I think.

I arrive at the Italian eatery and greet Tam at the bar. This place is known for its homemade sauce, and I can't wait to dig into the bottomless bowl of spaghetti. The host seats us immediately and once we sit the conversation is minimal. I know what I am having for dinner, so I immediately grab the dessert menu. As I look over the sweets, through my peripheral I see Tam staring at me. If I am not mistaken, I think she's looking at my breasts.

"Are you looking at my breasts?" I ask.

She replies with a puzzled look on her face, "What? I am looking at the guy behind you."

Okay, maybe she wasn't looking at me, but something is on her mind or she wouldn't be so quiet.

"Oh," I say casually.

My mind is in overdrive; therefore, I try to avoid all eye contact with Tam. To keep myself busy, I begin observing each couple in the restaurant. Noticing that only three of them are making eye contact with one another, I wonder why the rest of them look miserable. They are simply going through the motions of eating dinner together because that is what couples do. It's interesting how couples get so caught up in daily routine that we sometimes neglect to see that our view has changed. Next thing we know, we are on a different street, in a different town, and we have no idea how we got there. Therefore, we have no idea how to get back.

I take the box of crayons that sit beside the salt and pepper shakers. Opening the box, I scatter the colors onto the brown paper tablecloth. I assume the paper and crayons are for the kids to entertain themselves, but I cannot help myself. I spread all of the crayons on the table and study the colors. Red is passionate, blue is calming, and black is strong. It's true. Never put kids in a red room to go to sleep, and wearing black empowers confidence. However, if you're depressed, black can be suicidal. Colors definitely suggest or enhance our emotional state. They are very similar to love; as a matter of fact, love is color and this is the subject of my poem. I finish writing on the paper, just as dinner arrives. It looks mouthwatering. Yet, just before I plunge into my spaghetti, something possesses me to ask Tam what she meant by her love comment.

"When you said you loved me the other night, what did you mean?"

"I meant I love you," she responds.

"I love you, like you love your sister? Or I love you like you love your man?"

"What is wrong with you? Love is love. I love everyone in my own special way. I don't want to sleep with you, if that's what you mean."

"Oh, okay. Sorry, I'm tripping," I say, reading over my poem.

Now she thinks I am crazy, but at least now I can enjoy my dinner. During our meal, she doesn't ask me about Dick or Ro, which is a smart move because I don't want to hear her negative comments when I mention seeing Dick again, this Saturday. It's not my fault I thought Ro was gone for good, and though I keep reminding myself that it's over, I did agree to meet him once again at the poetry spot. However, this time I plan to beat him there in order to do a little investigating. I pray I don't find any evidence of him being gay. He repeatedly says it was a joke. But you know what? It doesn't matter, because I am certainly not sleeping with him again.

According to plan, I arrive at the Blue Room twenty minutes ahead of Dick. Casually, I ask around to find out if anyone has seen him. Everyone here knows him, and the way women light up when speaking about him assures me that his little comment is surely a joke. Therefore, I take a seat near the back and wait for his entrance, which is always a treat. I engage in conversation with a cute guy at the next table; however, I can feel Dick's presence as he walks in. I look toward the door and see him standing by the bar, wearing his leather vintage coat, baggy jeans, and brown Timberland boots.

Suddenly, as if she is participating in a fifty-yard dash, this girl runs from the corner of the room and jumps up into his arms. I carefully watch their interaction as she kisses his neck. She is all over him. Who is she? She could be a decoy to throw me off his gay trail, and if so, it is working because I can tell by their contact that they have had the same intimate relationship we have had. After she slowly peels her body away from his, Dick sees me sitting at the table and acknowledges my presence with a slight nod of his head. A few minutes later, he strolls to the table and sits. Apologizing for his delay, he explains that the girl is an old acquaintance he had not seen in a year. Within my veneer, I shrug my shoulders as if I couldn't care less.

"I miss you," he says.

"You do?"

"I don't know what's going on with you and your man, but I hope he realizes that you are a very special lady," he continues.

Blah, blah, blah is the literal interpretation by the time these words reach my eardrums. Assuming he's being tuned out, Dick moves to my side, pulls out my chair, lifts me up, and takes me to the back by the restrooms. It all happens so quickly that I do not have time to ask what he is doing. He thrusts me against the wall and kisses me. Pressing his lips against mine, he gently opens my mouth with his tongue. It is the most passionate twenty seconds I have ever experienced. Suddenly I realize that Dick and I have never kissed, not even during our moments of heated sex. Perhaps because kissing

opens certain vulnerabilities that sex does not. Isn't that a
shame? Sex has become so commercial and tainted that
strangers would rather enter each other's body than swap spit.
Think about it. Most couples on the verge of breaking up still
have sex, but rarely do they kiss, because kissing would
expose their exact feelings. We have corrupted the original
purpose of intimacy.

"What was that for?" I ask as I wipe my lip-gloss off his lips.

"I want to assure you that our connection is not about the
sex. I would have done this at the table, but I never know if
you have spying eyes."

I smirk. Yet I say nothing. I turn and walk back to the table.
As I am walking, the stage host greets me and informs me
that it is my turn to read. I look over and smile at Dick as I approach the stage. Once positioned, I close my eyes and begin
to speak about the . . .

The Rules of Dating
So when am I going to see you again?
Not that I'm excited or anxious. I just want to see you
    again.
So who am I fooling, you or me?
Damn, I dig you, I like you, and I feel you.
I'm excited about the possibility of sharing experiences
    with you.
I'm anxious about future memories I will have of you.
So when you don't hear from me in a day or two
It's not that I don't want to talk to you. I just can't appear
    that way.
Understand what I say. It's the game.
The game that no one admits they play, but all play, just
    the same. . . .

I walk off the stage and return to the table where Dick awaits.
"Stay with me tonight," he whispers.

Everything in my body says don't do it—everything, except for my mouth.

"Okay," I respond, staring deep into his light brown eyes.

After a few more poets, we leave. He stops by the twenty-four-hour grocery for chocolate chip cookies and condoms, and then we journey to his house. Like nights before, I am determined to get through an entire evening and not have sex with this man. And like nights before, my mission goes unaccomplished. Even so, our passionate evening is heightened when we sit up all night reading our favorite passages from the collection of Kahlil Gibran and reciting our favorite quotes from black cinema. This may sound corny, but I am turned on when he reads to me. Throughout the night as I laugh with Dick, the thoughts I want to express with Ro come rushing to my head. Why is it that I am so at ease with Dick and so unnerved with Ro? Possibly because I have yet to discover Dick's irritating habits. Thus, I excuse myself, rush to the restroom, and scribble my wish list for Ro on a paper towel. Once I get home, I turn it into a poem about the things I desire.

On my way to church Sunday morning, I drop off Ro's letter. I am determined to have a beautiful day. The sun is out and the weather is gorgeous. So after church, I decide to take a long walk in the park—alone. I remove my heels, slide on my sneakers, and walk along the path normally crammed with bike riders. I pause to notice a single squirrel making his way down a very broad tree trunk. Squirrels, unlike people, usually travel alone. I think they are on to something. I have not spent time alone in an extremely long time. During this moment, I realize that we have to like ourselves to spend time by ourselves. Because when we're alone, there is only one person to talk with and there is nothing worse than being stuck talking to someone you don't like.

Spending time alone is a true reality check, and during my

self-examination I realize that the same mistakes I made with
Ro I am now making with Dick. Have I not learned a thing?
If I start this relationship on a sexual basis, can it ever be anything more than a sexual relationship? Does he respect me?
I am not sure. Yet I only have myself to blame. However, hindsight is twenty-twenty and I can't obsess over Dick because
I still have a boyfriend, and Ro deserves better. Pondering my
situation, I'm sure if I leave Ro and begin seeing Dick, he will
always remember how we got together. He may not admit it
aloud, but in the back of his mind, he will know I cheated
once and that I may do it again. I should know; that is how I
started dating Ro and that is partially why I cannot fully
commit to him. I know in either relationship, I will never get
the respect I deserve and I refuse to remain in a relationship
with a man who will not give me the utmost respect. However, what can I expect? I can be the queen of Egypt, but no
one will ever treat me as such if I run around the streets like
a harlot.

I need to be honest with Ro, but let's take one step at a
time. First, I have to stop dating Dick. No matter how much
he insists we remain friends, that concept is a delusion. With
Dick, the temptation is always there. Him and me having a
platonic relationship compares to giving a recovering drug
addict a job in a pharmacy. It does not matter if he is there to
work, he will eventually find a way to get high. It's the same
theory. Therefore, I have to walk away, cold turkey.

The addiction of a relationship can be very draining, and
all of this thinking has me tired. I make my way home and an
hour later I lie here on my futon with my mind overflowing
with confusion. I have walked, thought, and walked some
more, and it is time to go to bed. Tomorrow is a new day, and
I pray I have new outlook for my old problems.

Good night.

Chapter 6

Yes, I Do . . . Don't I?

Overdue for a break, I make a conscious effort to spend a week without seeing or talking to Ro or Dick. I am going to have a week of peace and quiet.

Ring, ring.

I think I will even cut the ringer off my telephone.

Ring, ring.

I lean over and read the caller ID. Tamela Jones. What does Tam want? I told her not to call me. I'm sure she will leave a message. In the meantime, I'm going to the kitchen to blend myself a fruit smoothie.

Ring, ring.

Why did she hang up and call right back? What is wrong with this girl?

"What in the hell do you want?" I answer jokingly.

"What's up, girl? It's Evelyn."

"Are you at Tam's house? What are you two doing?"

In a serious tone she says, "You need to come over immediately."

"Stop playing, let me speak with Tam."

Suddenly, Evelyn begins to sob and so I immediately begin to sob. Something terrible has happened. I know it. But I cannot formulate my words to ask what.

"I'm on my way."

Hanging up the phone, I frantically throw on a T-shirt and scramble around looking for my keys. My tears begin to flow heavier, making it impossible for me to keep searching, so I call Ro. Wiping my face with my right hand, I quickly dial his number with my left.

"Hurry and answer, Ro," I whisper before he picks up. "Something has happened, but I don't know what."

"What are you talking about?"

"Evelyn called. Something has happened. Please come over."

"I'm on my way."

Fifteen minutes later, Ro is walking through my front door, extending his arms to comfort me. We get in the car and arrive at Tam's in ten minutes. As we pull up to Tam's house, I notice the driveway is filled with cars.

"Something has happened to Tam," I yell hysterically.

My body will not move. I am frozen as Ro gets out, opens my door, and pulls me from the passenger seat.

"You need to calm down and find out what is going on."

Ro is wiping my tears as we walk toward the front door. I pause for a moment and attempt to get myself together. Evelyn comes to the door before we can ring the doorbell. She steps out onto the porch and gives me a long hug. Evelyn is not the emotional type, so of course this hug confirms that there is something terribly wrong and I begin to cry all over again. She kisses my cheek, wipes my tears, and guides me into the house.

"I need to use the restroom," I utter.

Luckily, the guest restroom is by the front door. I walk in and lean against the sink.

"Whatever it is, I can handle it," I say into the mirror. "I am sure Tam is okay. Oh no! Maybe it's her mom. She has been struggling with cancer. That's it. I have to be strong for Tam."

Still looking in the mirror, I take a few deeps breaths. Wiping my face, I gain some composure and slowly open the bathroom door.

"Surprise! Happy birthday!" everyone shouts as I enter the dining room. Flabbergasted, I cannot believe they surprised me. No one has ever surprised me.

"Are you okay?" asks Tam.

"I thought your were dead," I cry.

She runs over and consoles me. "I'm okay. Everyone is okay. We knew the only way to get you over here was to pretend that it was something serious. It's okay, stop crying."

My friends give me a surprise birthday party, and I sit in the dining room crying. Once the floodgates open, they are extremely difficult to close. After five minutes of weeping, I finally join the party and have a great time dancing, eating, and drinking until three in the morning. I am going to be bushed at work tomorrow and it will be well worth it. It is wonderful to have friends who love and care. And it is more wonderful to have friends who buy you nice gifts on your birthday.

Around noon the following day, the lack of sleep suddenly hits and after several attempts to sleep sitting upright in my chair while pretending to work, I call it a day and leave the office. This twenty-nine-year-old body cannot cope with exhaustion like it could when it was twenty-one. Ro and I didn't get home until almost four this morning. I didn't want him to drive home after watching him put away four beers, so I invited him to sleep on the futon last night.

I stick my key in the lock, walk in the door, and the sweet aroma of rosemary chicken greets me. Not only is Ro still here, but he has prepared dinner. This is supposed to be my

week of seclusion. However, last night's party ruined that
attempt. So I obliged his invitation to hang out. Besides, I
would be a fool to turn down Romance's rosemary chicken.

"Dinner and candles? What are you up to?"

"Just sit down and relax."

I change into my normal after-work attire—a tank top and
boxers—and then sit at the table.

"We really got you good last night."

"Yeah, yeah. So what? I can't believe you were in on it.
How did you know I would call?"

"We all know how nervous you get when you think something is wrong. Who else would you call?"

Looking at Ro with a blank expression upon my face, I
can't help but think how interesting it would have been had I
called Dick.

"I guess you all know me very well," I reply.

We sit quietly and eat dinner. Not much is said, but we
make lots of eye contact. There is an amazing amount of flir-
tatious energy passing across the table. Oddly, this dinner is
very similar to our first date and I feel giddy. Across the table
sits a new Romance, not the same Romance I was tired of a
few weeks ago.

"Would you like dessert?" he asks.

"What is it?"

"Just say yes or no."

"Yes or no," I taunt.

I move away from the table, walk over, and sit in Ro's lap. "I
am so happy you are here. Thank you for a beautiful dinner."

"What about dessert?"

"Sure, why not?"

He cleans the table and walks into the kitchen. Removing
the ponytail holder from my hair, I stretch across the futon listening to Joshua Redman. Closing my eyes, I think to myself.
In the last few weeks, I thought I had lost Ro and last night I
thought I had lost Tam. When we think a relationship is over,

whether it is a lover or a friend, it makes us reevaluate that person's importance. Why does losing someone do this? Last night, all I could think about is how I never told Tam I love her. Punctuation and intonation did not matter as long as she knew how I felt. It's the same with Ro. Sure, he gets on my nerves, but I really do love him. Sadly, I rarely tell him. From this moment on, I pledge to make a point to communicate my feelings better. I will no longer assume that my friends know what is on my mind. If anything ever happens to any of my loved ones, I want them to know how much I care.

Interrupting my random thoughts, Ro sets a platter on my lap. "Dessert has arrived."

Gazing into the sterling cake cover, I ask, "You made a cake?"

Ro simply points to the platter and, smiling at my reflection within the silver cover, I slowly remove it and stare at the plate. I glance over at Ro, who is on one knee. Then cutting my eye back to the plate, I gawk at the two-carat, princess-cut diamond ring placed within a brown velvet ring box.

"Will you be my wife?"

His words resonate through my ears in slow motion. Still, I say nothing.

"Will you?"

As I am about to speak, my mouth becomes arid and sexual mirages of Dick flash across the desert of my mind. It's the strangest feeling as I stand outside this picturesque moment and watch Ro propose.

In this other dimension, I faintly hear him speak. "Baby, what's wrong? Your mouth is moving but nothing is coming out."

This out-of-body experience continues for more than a minute, because my outer spirit observes me watching him as he walks into the bedroom. Gradually my two bodies merge and I wake from my coma.

"Yes! Yes!" I scream.

Ro returns to the bedroom doorway. Peering out, he speaks. "Is yes your answer?"

I nod my head repeatedly.

"You scared me. I thought you were going to say no."

"Why would I say no? I love you," I respond.

"I don't know, for a split second, I thought there was someone else."

Gasping, I am astounded by how the subconscious speaks at times of poignancy. But do we listen? No. We would rather ignore the voice of a higher consciousness and roam about earth aimlessly. My sudden imagery of Dick says, resolve these issues, or you can't marry this man. Simultaneously, Ro's inner voice speaks to him saying, her hesitance suggests there is someone else; confront her. However, he does not. We should be sitting down having a long discussion about our past and present relationship. Instead we make love and go to bed with plans to become husband and wife.

I awake early after a restless night of sleep, for my subconscious was very busy last night repeatedly reminding me of my troubles. I hate to admit it, but I do care about Dick. Nevertheless, I knew before Ro's proposal that I must end things with him. Now I must expedite the process. I look over at Ro, while softly stroking his face. He is so beautiful when he sleeps. He looks like a peaceful baby. I'll leave him a note. I don't want to wake him.

Jubilation, my expression
Elation, my complexion
My demeanor; beautiful
Because you Love Me
Motivation, my spirit
Satisfaction, my temple
My composure; beautiful

Because you Love Me
Elevation, my mind
Exhalation, my soul
My entity; beauty
Because you Love Me

Friday finally arrives. This has been an extremely long week. Today is the actual date of my birthday. My friends gave me the party five days earlier to ensure that it would be a surprise. I haven't spoken to Dick all week; however, he calls and leaves me the sweetest message. Playing his guitar over the phone, he sings his sexy rendition of "Happy Birthday." I am regretting it, but I must talk with him tomorrow.

As the day progresses, I become extremely nervous just thinking about seeing Dick. Perhaps I will write him a note. A letter is such a callous way to break it off with someone, but it is safe. I want to be sure I get my point across, and I am going to have a hard time saying what I need to say in person. He is so gorgeous. The only way I will not yield to temptation is to go over there blindfolded. Even then, he'll try to turn that into a sexual episode. I have to give him the letter and follow up with a phone call. He has no choice but to understand. This whole situation has my stomach in knots. I finally confess the entire chaos to Tam.

"I want to tell Ro about Dick," I say.

"Don't do it," she suggests strongly.

"But if we start a new relationship, it should be based on honesty."

"If you tell Ro about Dick, there will be no new relationship."

After thinking about what Tam says, I realize she is right. I should have said something by now. It is too late. I am wearing his ring. He will never forgive me.

"Are you going to stop seeing Dick?"

"Of course. I have already written him a letter."

"A letter?" She raises her pitch.

"It's the only way I could do it. I know it's not right but I almost want him to be mad so that he doesn't try to be friends. I'm such a chicken."

"Sounds like you are a chicken that is not ready to become a wife. If you were confident about your relationship with Romance, you would have no problem ending things with Dick," Tam analyzes.

Once again, she is right. But I am marrying Ro. It is decided. I will gain more confidence once Dick is out of the picture.

"Is Dick really that good in bed?" she asks.

"Please stop. The vivid, mental pictures are too much to deal with right now. It is over!"

"Good! Give him the letter and be done with it. Do not call him and tell him not to call you. Make sure he knows that you are getting married. He isn't the stalker type, is he?"

"No. He's a decent guy. I hate to end things this way, but it has to be done," I say, sighing.

"Let me know what happens. Stay strong. I'll talk with you later. Love ya, bye."

Leaning across the bed to hang up the phone, I roll over onto my stomach and finish Dick's letter. After signing my name, I lie on my back and begin to pray aloud.

"Please let me dream about Ro. Please let me dream about Ro."

I open my eyes and gaze at the ceiling.

"Damn you, subconscious! Stop teasing me. I am ending things with Dick. Isn't that enough?"

I lean over and pick up a picture of Ro. Holding it close to my heart, I close my eyes and go to sleep.

Good night.

Chapter 7

The Dick Hits the Fan!

The weekend is past. Two days is not enough time to clean up the mess we create during the week. Due to time, I fail to drop off Dick's letter. I promise, it was only due to time. Good news, though: I did dream about Ro all weekend long. I even take the time to write a little something for him; I title it "My Stimuli" because he stimulates every part of me. I hope he likes it. He will be surprised when he gets home from work tomorrow.

Monday mornings are always rough. I do manage to leave the house early enough to go by Dick's condo and leave his good-bye letter with the doorman. In the letter, I apologize for everything and ask him not to call. We'll see if Dick respects the fact that I have rekindled my old relationship. After work, I stop by the grocery store, because I want lasagna for dinner. Plus, I have a feeling Ro will come over after reading my poem, and he loves Italian. I rush home to cook and my phone is ringing as I walk through the door. With groceries in my arms, I grab the phone, not thinking to check the ID. I am sure it is Ro.

"Is this really how you feel?" says Dick.

I should have checked the ID.

"Why are you calling me?" I ask.

"I got my package you left with the doorman. I can't believe you wrote this."

"Please believe it," I respond.

"You stimulate my mind, when your eyes stare into mine," he begins to read.

"What . . . what . . . did . . . you . . . you say?" I stutter.

"Your poem is so beautiful. I have to see you tonight."

My grocery bags fall from my arms to the floor. Without hesitation, I hang up on Dick.

"What did I do?" I shriek.

I must have placed Ro's poem in Dick's envelope. Which means I placed Dick's good-bye letter in Ro's envelope.

"Shit!"

Like a woman gone mad, I charge through the door, hop in the car, and begin peeling out of my driveway. However, I rapidly halt due to the red Jeep pulling in. Forcefully honking the horn, I yell out of the car window, "I need to get out."

Looking in my rearview mirror, I notice a man getting out of the Jeep and coming toward me. Oh no, it is Ro. His friend Todd is driving. This means one of two things: Either Ro is having car trouble or Todd is here to help him get rid of my body. My heart begins to pound out of my chest as he approaches my car window. I can't look at him, for I know he has read the letter. My skin breaks out into a cold sweat, I can't swallow, and my hands are glued to the steering wheel. Ro stands at my door waiting for me to address him, but I am too embarrassed. Even if I were a politician, I couldn't lie myself out of this dilemma. The letter I intended for Dick held the intimate details of our sexual relationship. Although I ended things, the letter reiterated how much I enjoyed his attention and his affection.

"I believe this is yours," he states as he reaches his hand into the window.

He holds the letter in my face so that I am forced to face my shame. At last, I pry my hands from the wheel, look him in the eye, and extend my hand to grab the letter. As I look at him, he looks away. Infuriated, Ro bites his lower lip. He can't bear to look at me, and I am mortified. He lifts his head just above my window and places his chin on the roof of the car. I am so nervous; I don't know what Ro is going to do. My heart will not stop racing. This one minute of silent confrontation seems like hours. Finally, he leans over and sticks his head into my window. Looking me straight in the eye, Romance softly but firmly speaks.

"Good-bye."

Through the rearview mirror, I sit in my car watching him walk out of my life. There is nothing I can say. There is nothing I can do to make him turn around. He hops into the Jeep and they drive away. I sit in my car for thirty minutes, praying that he will come back just so that I can explain myself. If only he were angry enough to argue, then I would know he still cared. But he only had one word to say and that one word said a thousand more.

Feeling like sludge, I slither out of the car and slump into the house only to fall out onto the futon. Staring at the ceiling for hours, I replay all of the laughs and tears Ro and I have shared. I compare his past facial expressions to this last one. He has never looked at me like that and he has never spoken in that tone. It was in a manner of disgust. My behavior has repulsed him and he is hurt. Consequently, I am sick. My stomach and my head are having battles as to which hurts the worst. I never wanted to upset Romance. Honestly, I never thought he would find out. I assume my subconscious wins the battle after all. I still can't believe I mixed up the letters. I grab Dick's letter off the floor and begin reading it. Perhaps it is not as explicit as I think and maybe I can salvage this broken Romance. I begin with the first line.

"I am sorry I have to write you a letter to tell you this but I didn't know how else to do it."

Okay, not so bad.

"You are an incredible man and when I am with you, I feel like an incredible woman."

It's still all right.

"Mentally we connect, spiritually we connect, and sexually, our connection is unbelievable."

I shouldn't have said unbelievable, but maybe I can tell Ro it was one time.

"Every time you entered me, I felt an explosion of energy I have never felt before."

"Damn! It's over!" I sulk.

I feel my eyes begin to water, but I will not allow the tears to fall. I cannot spend the next few days crying about this man or this situation. I brought this upon myself and now I have to deal with it. Besides, crying is not going to make this situation better and it is not going to make me feel better. There is a time to purge, and there is a time to get up and keep walking. This is the time to keep my head up and walk. As I cover my face with my hands, I realize I am still wearing the engagement ring. If it's over, why didn't he ask for the ring back? I have got to call Tam and tell her what just happened. I lean over and grab the phone off the floor.

"What's up, girl? You are not going to believe what I did. It's so crazy. I can't tell you over the phone. You have got to come over here tonight. Call me when you get in."

Where is she? She should be home. Just then, my phone rings. This is probably her. She's at home screening her calls again.

"Girl, you are not going to believe what I did," I begin.

"What did you do?" asks Dick.

"Dick? I thought you were Tam returning my call," I reply, surprised.

"Sorry, it's just me. You hung up the phone earlier. Can we talk or is it a bad time?"

"I'm glad you called, I need to talk to you. Would you like to come over?"

"What? You are inviting me to your house? I thought your place was off-limits," he says.

"Not anymore. I'll give you directions."

I give him directions and Dick makes plans to come over in an hour. That is just enough time to finish dinner and freshen up. I am going to tell him the truth; that the poem is not for him, but for Romance. Then I will give Dick his letter, which will end things with him. After tonight, I will start over as a single woman.

I swear that hour passed like ten minutes. I look out of my window and Dick is getting out of his Jeep. He is wearing his hair in braids. It's a new look for him, but I like it. He has on a white tank and a pair of baggy jeans. He is looking mighty fine. Breaking up with him will be a little harder than I thought. I brace myself. Opening the door, Dick greets me with a kiss. He grabs the back of my head and pulls me into his lips. Lifting me up, Dick walks with me in his arms and sits on the futon. He kneels between my legs and initiates small kisses on my neck and my ears.

"It's so good to see you," he says between the kisses.

"It's good to see you too. We need to talk," I insist, pulling myself away from his arms.

"I would much rather talk after sex," he says, attempting to lift my shirt.

"That's what we need to talk about. I can't keep having sex with you. I dig you, you know that, but we can't keep seeing each other."

"I don't understand. I mean, your poem was so—"

"Let's talk over dinner. I cooked Italian," I interrupt.

I begin to tell Dick the story. Immediately, laughter sets in. He thinks the entire incident is hilarious.

"That is what you get for trying to break up with me using a 'Dear John' letter," he states, laughing.

"It's not funny. It backfired."

"So since you don't have a man anymore, what are you going to do? You seem to be okay with it," says Dick.

"I don't think it has hit me yet," I respond.

"Well, do you still want to end things with me?"

I was hoping he would not ask me that.

"I have to end things with you," I confess.

"Why? You were ending things because of your man—the man you don't have anymore. So if you are single, why can't we be together?"

Why did he put it like that? His word phrasing throws me completely off course. Before, it made so much sense to leave Dick. Now I am not so sure.

"You say you dig me," he continues.

"I do," I admit.

"I dig you, and I want to date you. Although the poem wasn't meant for me, you cannot say that I don't make you feel all of those things and more," he brags.

"I need time to think about everything. I haven't given him his ring back. Give me time to clear my thoughts," I say.

"I understand how it is to get over someone. Enough said. When you are ready, I will be here," he says as he leans over and kisses my forehead.

Dick is so cool. Maybe we will be able to be friends.

"You know if we are friends, we cannot have sex," I say with a smile.

"I want to be more than your friend, but if our relationship is platonic, I will respect that."

We retire to the living room and play a few games of Scrabble. Afterward, we lie on the floor, head to feet, and watch a boring made-for-television movie. I don't recall how it ends, because somewhere toward the middle I fall asleep.

I awake in my bed hours later. Not knowing how I got here, I sit straight up and look at the clock. It's 3:00 AM. I glance over and see a note on my pillow. It reads: "Thanks for the wonderful meal and the great conversation. I only hope that we can grow closer as time passes. I know you need time, so call me when you're ready. Have a good morning. Luv ya, Dick."

I lean my head against the headboard, smiling from ear to ear. But just as my smile hits my left earlobe, I realize that I am single. Ro is not going to call me, and although Dick wants us to date, I don't feel right jumping into another relationship. I slink down into the covers. My mind is flooding with thoughts, and I can't sleep. I wonder what Ro is doing. I wonder if he is asleep. I'm going to call him. It's 3:00 AM, he won't answer the phone, so I'll leave a message.

Ring, ring. Ring, ring. Ring, ring.

"No one is here, leave a message," says the voice mail.

I quickly hang up, for I don't know what to say. Maybe I shouldn't have called.

Ring, Ring.

Oh no. He is calling me back. I hate this stupid technology.

Ring, Ring.

"Hello," I answer as if I am asleep.

"What do you want?" he snaps.

"What are you doing?" I ask in a soft whisper.

"What the fuck do you want, Lily?" he yells.

Oh no, he is cursing at me. I don't know what to say. Stuttering, I come up with a lame response. "Do you want me to bring the ring over tomorrow?"

"I don't want to see you, just leave it on your dresser. I'll come and get it tomorrow while you are at work, and I'll leave your key," he suggests coldly.

"But I want to see you—"

He hangs up before I can finish my sentence.

"He hates me," I whine.

It's really over. I said I wasn't going to cry but I don't think I can contain my tears any longer. Therefore, as my tears well up, I allow them to fall and then become a tidal wave. I couldn't care less about being strong and keeping my head up. I just want to cry.

I awake late with a strong desire to call out of work today; however, I don't want to run into Ro when he comes over to get the ring. The thought of seeing his disgusted expression makes my stomach ache. Therefore, I have to quickly get dressed and leave the house. My day creeps by. I do nothing at work today, except think about Ro. I would love nothing more than to walk into my house and see Ro kneeling on one knee and proposing all over again. However, when I get home and open the door, there is no Romance. There is only a key in the place of my ring. He leaves no romantic good-bye notes, no flowers, and no candy. I sit on the foot of my bed, holding the key to my supposed future with Ro. Taking a deep breath, I throw the key in my drawer and walk into the kitchen to prepare dinner. Although I come home to an empty house plenty of days, my house has never felt so desolate.

The next few weeks, I decide to absorb my days in paperwork and my nights in a good book. The last month has been so consumed with my love relationships that everything else has been slipping. I look at my calendar and notice my spa appointment tomorrow morning at seven. I am getting a facial, a wax, and a full-body massage. Tam and I always have a ball whenever we go to the spa, and considering the last few events taking place in my life, this visit will be no different. Before turning in, I decide to write Ro a poem. It may not do any good, but I choose to write and mail it anyway. For me, writing is cleansing, and I am still purging. If he doesn't want to read it, well, he doesn't have to open it.

If I could fly, then I would soar.
I would soar into your mind
Just to see what's on your mind
and hope your thoughts are filled with me.
If I could stream, then I would flow.
I would flow into your heart
Just to run all through your heart
and consume your love with me.
If I could burn, then I would melt.
I would melt into your soul
Just to be one with your soul
and live there eternally.

Good night.

Chapter 8

My Loss . . . Her Gain

As I lie here trying to enjoy my massage, I am fervently harassed by a continuous giggle.

"I wish I could have seen your face when Dick called you reading Ro's poem," laughs Tam.

"Ha, ha. Must we all have a laugh at my expense?" I say, rolling my eyes.

"Yes!" tease Tam and Evelyn.

"Forget you two."

For the next hour, these two cackling hens continue to badger me, but I block out their noise and enjoy my massage. In minutes, friendly girlfriend banter can turn a serious situation into a juvenile high school occurrence. After a few jokes, I can't help but join in on the repartee.

Although I shouldn't, I decide to stop by Ro's house to leave his poem in the mailbox. I was going to mail it, but I have to pass his house on my way home from the spa. As I pull up to his home, I notice an unfamiliar car in the driveway. The license tag says QTPIE. Whose car is that? I find myself sitting outside the driveway for an hour as I contemplate knocking on his door. However, I refuse to further embarrass myself. Therefore, I place the poem in the mailbox and drive off. I nearly run off the road trying to grab my cell phone to call Tam. Before she can say hello, I start in.

"Tam, Ro had some girl over to his house."

"Crazy girl, why did you go to his house?" she asks.

"I stopped by there to give him a letter."

"Haven't you delivered enough letters, mail lady?"

"Hush. We need to find out if he is seeing someone," I whine.

"You have lost it, and you need to get a hold of yourself. I will do some investigation, if you promise not to go back over to the house."

I am not ready to see him with another woman. I never thought he would start dating someone else. Maybe she's just a friend. Maybe it's one of his boys driving his mom's car. Maybe I am a fool who lost a perfectly good man because of stupidity.

"Okay, I promise I won't go back to his house. Let's go out tonight. How about the Blue Room?" I suggest. "It will help ease my mind."

"Are you sure? Our little trip to the Blue Room is what started all of this mess," Tam reminds me.

"So what? Let's go back."

"Fine, I'll pick you up at eight. See you tonight," says Tam.

Around nine that evening, we walk into the Blue Room and once again it is filled with nothing but beautiful people. Tam and I spot a rug on the right side of the stage and have a seat. After a few drinks and laughs, we spot a few of my coworkers. I hope they do not come over and sit with us. I like to keep pleasure and work totally separate. However, as soon as they see me they make a beeline to our rug. I guess my friendly coworker smile and hand wave weren't enough.

"Hi, I didn't know you come here," says my coworker.

"It's only our second time, but it's nice," I say with little enthusiasm, hoping she will walk away.

"Tam, this is Veronica and Sam. This is my good friend Tam."

Veronica keeps standing here looking at our rug. I hope she does not ask to sit down.

"May we sit down?"

"We're expecting some others," I quickly retort with false zeal.

"Well, maybe we'll see you guys later on tonight," she replies as they turn and walk away.

As Tam taps me on the arm she whispers, "I cannot believe you blew them off."

"Well, I'll be damned," I say, looking at the door.

"What?" Tam asks.

I place my hands upon her chin and point her face toward the door.

"Oh no! What are you going to do?"

"I'm going to sit here and enjoy myself," I say. Yet I can't help but stare as Ro walks in with this "QTPie" on his arm.

"I guess he is over you, huh?" says Tam.

Reality is so unsettling, yet leave it to Tam to make it even more depressing. Face forward, I fall onto the rug. This is going to be difficult. After they sit, the girl leaves Ro's side and walks to the restroom. Of course, I assume the ex-girlfriend role and stand to follow while Tam vigorously tugs on the bottom of my shirt.

"Where are you going?"

"To the restroom, do you mind?"

"Do not start anything with her."

"Please, that's not my style. I just want a closer look," I whisper.

I stand looking in the mirror, playing with my hair, until she comes out of the stall. I smile and she smiles.

"I like your shoes. I never look good in that type of sandal, my feet are too large," she comments while giving me a quaint smile.

"Indeed, they are large," I murmur.

"Did you say something?"

"They look good in large sizes too," I say with a slight smile.

She nods and leaves the restroom. I follow her and make my way to my rug.

"She's not that cute," I say to Tam as I sit.

The female psyche can be so catty. I pride myself on being mature, but sometimes the feline just slips out.

"Look at her. She is all over him."

"Suck it up. The last time you were here you were all over singer boy Dick. He has the right to have some 'QTPie' all over him. We are staying here because you need to get over this."

"But I signed up to read. I am not going to be able to read with him here."

"You can and you will."

I sit nervously on the rug, waiting for them to call my name. I should have stayed home tonight. What am I going to say?

"They called your name," says Tam as she scoots me off the rug.

I grab my pillow and begin walking toward the stage. Waiting for someone to shout "dead woman walking," I finally step onto the stage. I pull the microphone off the stand and sit on my pillow. Closing my eyes, I take a deep breath and freestyle my thoughts, making up the piece as I go. I'm not sure what I am going to say, but I start with "I feel I have swallowed my heart. . . ."

As I finish, I feel moisture on my cheek. Surely, I can't be crying in front of all of these people. I open my eyes to see many empathetic faces, realizing that I am not the only one using this place as an escape from love's reality. Suddenly, the beautiful people mutate into a bunch of people with underlining issues. Amidst the claps and snaps, I walk over to Tam. She has our purses under her arm, for she knows that it is time to go.

Unfortunately, I have to pass Ro's table on the way out. I am too weak to make eye contact with him. If I look into his eyes, I am sure to break down, so I keep my focus straight ahead and I walk fast.

It is a quiet ride home tonight. When we arrive to my door, Tam finally speaks.

"Do you want me to come in?"

I look at her and shake my head and give an unsure no.

"You'll be fine. It's a twelve-step program. A few more steps to go and you are in the clear." She smiles before kissing my cheek.

I step out of the car and Tam waits in the parkway until I open the door. I don't turn back to say good-bye, I simply hold up the peace sign as I walk through the door. She honks the horn and pulls away. Before I can shut the door, I am bawling. I make it to the bedroom and fall out across the bed. I continuously wipe my face with the pillowcase. Yet I cannot stop crying. I am not sure if I am crying over the loss of Romance, my disappointing behavior, or the fact that he dumped me before I could dump him. All the same, I still can't stop crying.

Good night.

Chapter 9

Isn't the Beach Refreshing?

Surprisingly, the next day I feel so much better. It is like I cried Romance out of my system. After church, I decide to go to the movies, alone. I used to scoff at people who went to movies alone. I thought they were pitiful and lonely. Now here I am at the movies by myself and it is not so bad. Of course, there is no one to talk to or share popcorn with, but movies are better with no talking. And I don't like to share my popcorn. This is a good feeling. I make a mental note to start doing more things alone. No more pity parties, I am going to start my week revitalized.

Monday and Tuesday breeze by. However, by Wednesday the office gossip usually makes its way to my floor and guess who is this week's hot topic? Me. The word is I am having a mental breakdown over my breakup with Romance. This is exactly why I keep business and pleasure separate. My coworkers' lives must be pretty boring if I consume their daily conversation. It's quite funny. I think I will add something to the gossip—just to give the story a little more zeal. Furthermore, when they confront me, I am going to play along. Hell, I might get a few days off work if I play my cards right.

I make it over hump day. Friday is here and I couldn't be happier. This evening, Tam and I are going with Evelyn to her time-share on the coast. It is a stunning beach condominium on the shores of Hilton Head. A delightful weekend away with the girls is just the thing.

Ring, ring.

"Marketing," I answer.

"I thought you were leaving work early," Tam says.

"If you hadn't called I would be walking out the door."

"Well, we want to leave around six this evening. Stan and I are going to meet at your house."

"Hold up. Who is Stan?" I question with irritation.

"Oh yeah, Stan is my date. He's coming with us this weekend."

"No, he's not. I thought it was just the girls. Why are you bringing Stan?" I ask.

"When I spoke with Evelyn yesterday she mentioned her date, so I had to get one."

"What?" I yell. "If you two are bringing dates, then I have to bring a date or I am not going."

"You have to go, you don't need a date," insists Tam.

"Are you crazy? I am not going to be the fifth wheel. I'll see you at the house with a date on my arm."

I cannot believe my girls sold me out like this. They know I am going through a dating crisis. This was supposed to be a girls' getaway weekend and they have turned it into a sexy beach rendezvous. Now more than ever I wish Romance and I still dated. We would have so much fun. I suppose I can go through my old black book, although I hate to call up ex-boyfriends for weekend dates. It makes me look desperate. Of course, there is Dick. He would be fun. But if I take Dick with me to the beach, it is going to be damn near impossible to stay a safe-sex distance from him. Maybe my best bet is to stay in town this weekend. Dejected, I grab my purse and walk away from my office. I get a few feet away when my perky assistant leans around her cubicle and speaks.

"I hope you have a great time this weekend."

"Forget this, I am going to the beach this weekend, and I will have a date," I mumble under my breath.

I rush downstairs to the parking deck while reaching for my cell phone.

"Hello, Dick, please call me when you get this message. I need to ask you something important."

Maybe he's at the studio. I'll try his cell phone.

"Hello."

"Hello," says the female voice on the other line.

"Uhm, is Dick around?" I ask.

"He's rehearsing. Can I take a message?" she asks.

"It's important, can you go get him?"

"Hold on."

I know we are not seeing each other, but I am very curious to know who is answering his phone.

"Dick? Hi, sweetie, how are you?" I ask.

"Hi, beautiful, how are you?"

"I will be wonderful if you go with me to Amelia Island this weekend."

"Are you asking me to go away with you this weekend? What about our new platonic relationship?"

"We can't go to the beach as friends?" I ask.

"We are adults and there is no need to joke about adult situations. I would love to go away with you this weekend. But I am not going to spend two days and two nights with you on the beach and not have a desire to sleep with you. In fact, if I can't have you, I don't want to be put in that situation."

"Wow. That was eloquently put," I answer.

"I respect the fact that you want to be friends. You have to respect the fact that I am attracted to you, and I am a man. I don't want to put you or myself in an uncomfortable situation."

"Well, okay. You make a lot of sense," I say, discouraged.

"Think about it and let me know," he adds before hanging up.

I toss the cell phone into the passenger seat.

"Damn! I want to go the beach!" I whine.

I pull into my driveway and contemplate calling Tam. I guess I won't be going with them to the beach after all. I want to go with Dick, but he is right. I cannot ask him to spend that time with me and then turn right around and ask him to just be friends. This is definitely not a "just friends" weekend. However, I don't want to spend another weekend here alone. This single life is not so much fun. What do single people do? There are only so many movies we can see alone. I cook too much to eat alone and who wants to spend every night reading books? Single life is boring, and I don't like it.

I pace the hardwood floors, thinking about Dick's comments. He is a good guy. There is absolutely nothing wrong with dating him. Ro has moved on and so should I. Therefore, I am going to call him back. The brain is such a powerful tool. If we think about situations long enough, no matter how insane, our mind will legitimize our every thought.

"Hi, Dick."

"I didn't think I would hear from you any time soon," he answers.

"I still want to go away this weekend. We are leaving in about an hour. Would you like to go?"

"If you can wait an extra half hour, I'll see you at your house."

"I can't wait."

Well, I invited him. This means I am going against my decision to maintain this platonic friendship. I hope I know what I am getting myself into. Meanwhile, I'd better run to the store for condoms.

We arrive at the condo around 10:00 PM and everyone is exhausted. The ladies rush in to pick out the rooms for the weekend as the fellas haul the luggage out of the Jeep. We draw straws to see who will get the ocean-view bedroom. I win. Dick and I place our things in the open-spaced, upstairs bedroom. I open the patio door and let the breeze of the ocean brush against my face. The ocean is breathtaking. How can something so vast be so peaceful? As I sit curled up in the rocking chair, Dick strolls onto the patio and gently positions a blanket across my legs. Sitting down in front of me, he places his head in my lap. We sit in silence for hours staring into the immense body of water. Finally, he breaks the silence.

"We are such a tiny piece of the puzzle."

I look down into his eyes while running my fingers through his hair. "Indeed we are."

I slide onto the balcony floor and we wrap ourselves in the blanket. Grabbing the pillow from the chair, Dick leans back onto the deck. We lie there listening to the harmonies of the ocean water. Using his chest as my pillow, I close my eyes. As he tenderly massages my scalp, we fall asleep to the sounds of nature.

I awake the next morning to Tam banging on our bedroom door.

"Wake up, sleepyheads."

Slowly, I rise to the aroma of salt water and fresh fish. I kiss Dick on the forehead and cheek, before rising to open the door.

"Wake up," I say softly, nibbling on his ear.

I rise, go inside the room, and open the door to find Tam standing there with her hands on her hips and a curious look on her face.

"How was your night?" she asks anxiously.

"It was lovely, and yours?" I answer politely.

"We're going down to the beach. You guys want to come?"

"We'll be down."

She slowly turns around, leaving her eyes fixed upon my expression. I know she can't wait to ask what is going on with Dick. She couldn't ask in the car because everyone was into our conversation and she didn't have time to ask last night. But I know her questions are soon to come. Thus, to annoy her further, I simply close the door in her face and retreat to the balcony.

"Thank you for your invitation," says Dick as he stretches his arms to the heavens.

"Thank you for agreeing to come."

Then suddenly, he jumps up with instantaneous energy and claps his hands.

"Let's hit the beach!" he exclaims.

Rushing into the bedroom, Dick turns on the radio and begins carelessly dancing around the room. As I watch him, his moves become hilarious. Either he is joking or he really can't dance, and I seriously hope he is joking because he is too handsome to be a bad dancer. However, at this point it doesn't matter because his dancing skills are not what have my attention. Sometime during the night he has slipped off his jeans and boxers and they are lying beside me on the blanket. His body is so magnificent, I ogle it any time I get the chance.

"Put some clothes on and let's go," I say as I ruffle through my luggage to find a bathing suit.

We walk down the stairs leading from the balcony and onto the sand. It is close to eighty degrees with an occasional breeze. Perfect weather. We find the gang sprawled out on their towels basking in the sun. The condo, built on a private beach, has minimal traffic. This is an excellent vacation getaway.

"Good morning," says Evelyn.

"Good morning," we say in unison.

Dick places our huge towel next to Stan and Tam, then immediately heads toward the water. The other guys soon follow suit. I know the questions are about to start, so I prepare myself for debate. As soon as the men get a few feet away, the badgering begins.

"I thought you were going to stop seeing him," says Tam.

"Have you and Ro ended things for good?" follows Evelyn.

"I didn't know what to say when you stepped into the Jeep with Mr. Dick. Did you sleep with him last night?" berates Tam.

I do not say a word. Instead, I sigh, watching our dates play like twelve-year-old boys in the ocean.

"Girl, do you hear us talking to you? Do not ignore us. You have got to tell us something," Tam yells, hitting me on the shoulder.

Leisurely, I turn toward them, smile, and speak in a calming manner. "Behind each Winter there is a quivering Spring, and behind each night there is a smiling dawn."

I then turn away in the same relaxed manner and continue watching the men play.

"What in the hell does that mean?" mocks Evelyn.

"It means she is not going to tell us a thing. It also means she likes him a lot," replies Tam.

"Let's go play with the guys," Tam continues as she begins to rise.

Tam and Evelyn pull each other up and walk into the ocean. Evelyn stays back away from the waves. I can tell she doesn't want to get her hair wet. But soon, as a large wave comes along, Stan and Dick grab her legs and dump her into the water and she is furious. Laughing, I think about what Tam said to Evelyn. Am I falling for Dick? He is a wonderful man, but it is too soon. I have to be careful and keep my emotions under control. Standing, I run my foot across the sand to clear off a large area. Using a stick, I begin to write a short poem in the sand. As I finish, Dick runs up behind me, grabs my waist, and hoists me up onto his shoulders.

"What are you doing? Come into the water," he suggests.

"Okay."

He pauses for a moment to read my sand poem.

"Stop reading it," I gripe.

"You are a trip. What's the point of creating something beautiful if you are going to horde it?"

I shrug my shoulders and place my shades on the towel.

"Oh my God!" I shriek.

"What?"

"That man is naked and so is that woman."

I rush to the ocean to tell Evelyn.

"Evelyn, those people are naked."

"Oh yeah, this is a clothing-optional beach," she answers casually.

I gasp as Tam bursts into high-pitched laughter.

"Are you serious?" I ask.

"Great!" replies Dick as he leans into the water and removes his shorts.

"What are you doing?" I whisper frantically.

"Stripping," he mentions while walking out of the water to place his shorts onto the towel. My eyes cut toward Tam and Evelyn as their mouths agape. Gazing at my chocolate Adonis, they drool as the ocean drops trickle off his silky skin.

"My, my, my!" oozes Evelyn.

"The displaced Afro is so dated. Remember?" I say with apparent jealousy.

"Please, girl, do you really think I am looking at his Afro?"

I quickly run out of the water and deliberately behind Dick to curtail the girls' view. I must catch up with him before he turns around and heads back into the water. His back view is amazing, I agree. Yet his front view has the potential to delightfully send a girl into shock.

"Sweetie, do you really want to be naked? If you wait until the night, we can both bathe nude on the beach," I entice.

"What's wrong? The body represents beauty and I am not ashamed of it."

"And you shouldn't be, but I don't want everyone seeing how beautiful your body is."

Oh no, he is turning around. I must remain strategically placed in front of him as we walk back toward the water. Getting closer, I can hear Evelyn begging me to move an inch to the right.

"My friends are staring at your body, and it makes me uncomfortable."

"Why? You never struck me as insecure," he says, tussling my hair.

"Please," I whimper.

Huffing, Dick turns back around and grabs his shorts off the towel. Facing away from the water, he quickly puts them on.

"Thank you," I say, sweetly kissing his chest.

"You owe me a midnight skinny dip," he says, kissing my nose.

Whew! That was close. I know he is uninhibited, but this is a new thing for me. In Jamaica, I once visited a nude beach. But the only people taking their clothes off were the older, overweight men. There is no way I could have my man being gawked at by my girlfriends.

"Let's go swim. I'll race you," he teases.

It's funny how the beach brings out the youthfulness in each of us. Once we get back to the ocean and I start enjoying myself, another jolt hits the waters.

"I think I will take my bathing suit off. Do you guys mind?" asks Evelyn.

"Of course not," respond the men with bulging eyes.

"Personally, I don't want to see your half-naked behind," shouts Tam.

"I second that," I yell, raising my hand.

"Well, you two are outnumbered," she says, tossing her swimsuit on the shore.

Now, I don't talk about Evelyn too much, because she and

I have a fickle relationship. A few years ago, she and I were introduced to each other by Tam. Evelyn Hampton is a true socialite whose family belongs to a country club. This former beauty queen is very materialistic. If it were not for Tam, our circles would never have collided. Although she has a good heart, Evelyn has been sheltered. Therefore, she is somewhat naive. Now, like many socialite beauty queens, she is gorgeous, I must admit. Standing five eight, with long legs and measuring 38-28-36, she makes men lose speech in her presence. She has a golden bronze complexion, beautiful teeth, pouting lips, and light brown eyes that slightly slant upward due to her mother's Asian ancestors. Although she is quite a looker, her personality falls way short of her beauty. She reels in men hand over fist, but they usually lose interest after she pulls a whining episode. Once, she started crying loudly in a department store after her man refused to buy her a pair of four-hundred-and-fifty-dollar Manolo Blahnik strappy sandals. In other words, she is a spoiled brat. Nevertheless, with a swift call to her daddy or a swift sweep of the credit card, she eventually gets what she wants. Now, something tells me that she wants my man; and that's a problem.

"I love when the water swooshes between my legs," she giggles as her perfectly round breasts sparkle in the sun.

Pulling Tam away from the group, I question, "Why doesn't her man mind her being naked?"

"That's not her man. That is some guy she's been sleeping with the last month just so she can get a free membership to his father's spa. There is no love involved, so he couldn't care less if everyone sees her butt-ass naked."

"Well, I hope a crab lays eggs in her vagina while the ocean is swooshing between her legs," I scorn.

We walk over to the men, who suddenly have no interest in playing Frisbee. Instead, they are circling Evelyn like shark rounding their prey.

"I'm going back to the house," I say loudly, with intentions for Dick to follow.

"Yeah, me too," adds Tam.

The guys act as if we are invisible. We could be walking out into the ocean depths to commit suicide and they would be oblivious until they saw it on the six o'clock news. It is amazing how a pair of perky breasts and round buttocks can shut down a man's mind.

"What did you say?" asks Stan as he swims into Dick.

First, their hearing becomes faint. Next, their vision becomes blurry.

"Um, huh?" mutters Dick.

Lastly, their speech reverts to baby talk. Shaking our heads in disappointment, Tam and I look at each other and retreat to the house. Dick and Stan waddle behind minutes later.

As dusk arrives, Tam and I begin preparing dinner. The men decide to rent fishing poles and catch tonight's feast. Having little faith in their fishing skills, we run to the store to purchase salmon steaks. As Tam and I return to the kitchen we find scantily clad Evelyn propped on top of the counter tossing the salad. Tired of her catty antics, I roll my eyes as I approach the kitchen.

"Will you put on some clothing?" I say with an attitude.

"I have on a bathing suit. This is the beach. Tell her, Tam," she replies.

"Evelyn, we are in the house, and I am not going to eat dinner with your half-naked behind poised across the table."

Mumbling to herself, she goes into the bedroom to put on a tank top and linen pants. Suddenly, Dick bursts through the door.

"We are men and we bring you dinner," he boasts while beating upon his chest.

We run over to the ice chest filled with fish.

"What are we supposed to do with these?" I ask.

"Clean them," he says.

"Oh no. You catch the fish. You clean the fish. I am not cutting off fish heads or cleaning out fish guts. Look, a few of them are still wiggling."

"That's right, you men, go back outside and come back in with fish fillets," agrees Tam.

"It's just fish. We can clean them," yells Evelyn from the kitchen.

"Okay, June Cleaver, you clean the fish," I tease.

I grab one of the living fish by the tail and toss it into the kitchen at Evelyn. Landing right against her neck, the fish slides down her arm, causing Evelyn to squeal as it flaps around on the floor.

"It's still moving! It's still moving!" she yelps while jumping around the fish.

We all have a great laugh at her expense. As usual, it feels so good to unnerve the poised and proper. Dick takes the ice chest around the back to clean the fish and Evelyn runs to the room to change clothing. Still laughing, Tam and I finish the corn, broccoli, and salad.

During dinner, I observe Evelyn staring at Dick from the corner of her eye. Knowing Evelyn always covets what others have, I decide to ignore her pitiful behavior. When Tam purchased a new car, she purchased a new car. When we go shopping, she must buy as many items as each of us or more. Furthermore, she must be the center of attention. I never thought about it before, but Evelyn always enters the room after or before us, she never walks in with us. When we get home, I will draw this to Tam's attention. I think Evelyn is trouble, and I don't trust her.

After dinner, we all retire to the living room to watch a movie. Evelyn sits in the lap of her handsome date, Marion. He is six feet and some odd inches with a chiseled face, bedroom eyes, and a great physique. Evelyn never strays far from this prototype. Most of her men are athletes.

"So, Marion, what do you do for a living?" I ask.

"I just finished my last season of basketball over in Italy."

"My baby speaks fluent Italian," boasts Evelyn.

"And that would be wonderful if only you spoke Italian," I respond in Italian.

Evelyn fumes as he and I share a moment of laughter. Not only does she not know what I said, but he and I share a second that excludes her, annoying her further.

"You speak the language well. Did you live in Italy?"

"No, I worked with an Italian client for six months. I learned a lot from him and I listened to tapes to practice."

"Very impressive." He smiles.

Brains eventually conquer beauty almost every time. Dick moves in between my legs and leans his head against my stomach. His hair is placed in two pigtails to the sides of his ears. He looks like a young girl.

"Will you braid my hair?" he asks, batting his long eyelashes.

Chuckling, I look down at his quirky hairdo and nod yes. Tam scoots close to the television and pulls out the videotapes. Everyone was told to bring his or her favorite movie. I bring *Uptown Saturday Night*, a comedy classic. Tam brings *Eat, Drink, Man, Woman*, which is a great foreign film. However, no one wants to sit at the beach and read a foreign film with five other people. Stan brings *Sleeping with the Enemy*, which leads me to question his involvement with my friend Tam. Dick forgets his movie. Marion, on the other hand, brings *Purple Rain*, which is no Academy Award winner but definitely a cult classic. Lastly, Evelyn brings *Breakfast at Tiffany's*; great story, great fashion—wrong crowd, wrong setting. What is she thinking? We are definitely not watching that, therefore, we agree to watch *Purple Rain*.

Thirty minutes into the movie, as I am braiding Dick's hair, he starts kissing the inside of my thigh. Trying to keep my composure, I let out a girlish giggle.

"Go upstairs with that crass behavior," teases Tam.

"I think we will," says Dick.

Picking me up, he places me on his hip and rushes upstairs. Before we can get the door closed, Dick is pulling off my pants and laying me down. He lifts my shirt, places a firm grip around my waist, and pulls me to the edge of the bed. Kneeling, Dick wraps each of my legs around his shoulders and buries his head in between my thighs. With his moist tongue working overtime, my body overflows. My legs stiffen and my toes spread. Finally, when I see his face again, my eyes are teary from the tidal waves of convulsions. Lying on the edge of the bed, I attempt to regain full consciousness as he strolls into the bathroom.

"Are you ready for our midnight skinny dip?"

"I can't feel my legs. I might drown," I mutter.

He laughs as I slither from the edge of the bed down to the floor.

"Get up," Dick insists, reaching his hand down to assist my weak limbs.

"Hurry up."

"I'm coming."

Swiftly wrapping my towel around my body, I meet him on the balcony. I leave on the bottom portion of my swimsuit, due to my paranoia with sea creatures creeping into body orifices. Dick grabs the large beach ball from the house and runs to the shore.

After playing in the water for about an hour, Dick and I drip back to the balcony. As we are approaching the house I notice a dim light on the patio. Getting closer, I see Evelyn peering through a large telescope pointing directly at us—correction, pointing at Dick. She will not stop until she sees everything that she is missing. With my focus on Evelyn, I fail to realize Dick has stop walking beside me. He has disappeared into the darkness.

"Where are you? Come on, it's cold," I yell into the night.

Catching up with me, he tucks his head between my legs

and tries to heave me onto his shoulders. I, unaware, and still weak from his oral gratification, lose balance and fall backward onto the sand.

"Are you all right?" he asks with a tiny chuckle.

Dick kneels by my side, as I lie dizzy in the sand.

"You play too much," I say, hitting his chest.

He cautiously lifts me up and carries me back to the balcony. Carefully sitting me in the rocking chair, Dick enters the restroom to run my bathwater. "Would you like me to wash the sand from your hair?"

"Uh-huh," I say, softly with a childlike expression.

Oozing down into the large, oval sunken bathtub filled with bubbles, Dick squeezes behind me to wash my hair. "What did you write in the sand today?"

"Just a few thoughts. I don't remember."

"You mean once the tide washes it away, it will be gone?"

"Pretty much."

"Well, what was it about?" he continues.

"What is so interesting about that poem?" I question.

"It's not the poem, it's you. I want to know what's on your mind. I figure your poetry is the best way to find out."

"The best way to find out about me is to ask."

"Okay, so what is on your mind?" he asks.

I shyly look at him and whisper, "Nothing."

He dumps a handful of water over my head and steps out of the tub. When I come into the bedroom, Dick is sitting, naked, on the bed strumming his guitar. The one thing I can say about this man is, he does not like clothing.

"Let's write something," he says.

"Cool. I would like that," I consent.

Scooting close to him, I grab my book, tear out a sheet of paper, and stretch across the bed.

"What is this masterpiece going to be about?" I ask Dick.

"Love," he answers with a definite expression.

"No, let's write about something else," I quickly retort.

"Well, write what you want, I'm going to play along."
I scribble a few lines on the paper as he makes up a tune.
"I don't want to write anymore. I'll just make something up."
"Whatever floats your boat," he comments.
"This is called . . ."

Yeah, Right.
Nah, nah, baby, this ain't no love thang
What's up, baby? Hi, sweetie . . . just slang for those
    dear to me.
By no means does it mean you're my man or anything
    like that.
I know we are kicking it almost every day.
But I say, we are just enjoying each other's company.
Nothing wrong with that . . . right?
We hook up, we chill, we laugh, we converse, we fulfill
    each other's desires.
You understand me and I understand you too.
So together we hang, that don't constitute no love thang.
But, hey, I must admit the sex is the shit out of this world.
The way my back arches as you enter me. Giving you
    just enough space to place your arms underneath
    and hold me close.
I love that. I often find myself falling into a daydream of you,
Often a night dream and sometimes a wet dream.
But what does that really mean?
It means you sexually satisfy me.
So what, a little conversation, a little sex, we sit,
we laugh and all of the above.
That don't mean this thang is love.
We vibe, we kickin' it.
And I don't mind saying I don't want it to end. No time
    soon anyway.
You and me are cool and I hope we stay cool like this.
So no worries, man, I go nowhere.

Not the way your eyes stare into mine.
And, baby, oh, baby, you are so fine,
The whole package complete.
And though they say that love jones can be a motha
I ain't a sucker. I like things the way they are.
No ties, no commitment, no strings.
See, baby, this definitely ain't a love thang.
We just kickin' it . . . right?

Dick laughs. "Yeah, okay. I hear you loud and clear," he says, whispering the last phrase over again.

Sharing kisses here and there, we laugh and sing until we both fall asleep on top of the scattered pens and paper.

Early the next morning, I awake after only a few hours of sleep. I can't wait to ask Evelyn why she was watching us last night. Scurrying downstairs, I hear Evelyn and Tam moving about in the kitchen. Leaning against the couch, I confront Ms. Hampton, the coveter.

"I saw you watching Dick and me swim last night." I waste no time.

"So what?" She smirks, then continues to speak. "I like watching the stars at night. I didn't realize anyone was on the beach until I spotted you two walking toward the house."

"Since when did you become interested in astronomy? You can't even spell astronomy," I tease.

"You two cut it out," interrupts Tam.

Gently, Evelyn puts down her eggs and saunters into the dining room. Looking directly at me, she confidently speaks. "I want to fuck Dick. I don't want a relationship with him. I don't want to date him. I simply want to sleep with him."

Nervously, I tap my nails against my teeth as if I am pondering her request. However, I think the ocean water is lodged in a canal of my eardrum and surely I did not hear Evelyn clearly. Yet when I peep her facial expression as she tilts her head and raises her left eyebrow, I know there is only one thing to say.

"Bitch, you must be crazy!" I rise from the couch and stand amazed at her audacity.

Tam rushes into the dining room for fear that I will hurl the nearest sharp object at Evelyn's face. And, to my disbelief, Evelyn continues to rationalize her statement.

"It's not like he's your boyfriend. He's just someone you are sleeping with. If it makes you feel any better, you can sleep with Marion. I saw you looking at him during dinner."

With an odd stare, Tam looks at Evelyn and responds, "You really are crazy. There will be no switching men, this weekend or any other weekend!"

"I don't want Marion. I have Dick and you can't have him," I sing to the schoolyard tune. Then, whipping back around, I change my tone and continue to speak. "However, what you need to have is a vasectomy, because you have one pair of *cajones de grande*."

I hasten to leave the room. Opening the bedroom door, I find Dick basking in the early morning sun, naked, of course. I walk onto the balcony and kiss him on the neck. Perhaps I shouldn't tell him about my previous conversation with Evelyn, but I am so appalled by her behavior, I have to share it.

"I was just in the kitchen speaking with Evelyn and Tam when Evelyn informs me that she wants to sleep with you. She does not want to date you, she just wants to have sex with you. She even says I can sleep with Marion if I like."

"Cool," he says calmly.

"What?" I shriek.

"I mean, are you down with things like that? Some people are," he says in the same soothing manner.

"What the hell kind of fish did you two eat yesterday? Jellyfish? Both of you are hallucinating. No, I am not *down* with things like that," I shout.

"Okay, calm down. I didn't know. It seems odd she would say something like that if you hadn't done it before."

"You damn right, it's odd. Have you ever done it before?"

"Twice, but with the same couple."

I really need to ask more questions. "What's your name, sign, and occupation?" Doesn't cut it these days. Dumbfounded, I sit at the foot of the bed. Although it shouldn't be that surprising, Dick is a free spirit. I am sure he has done many things that I have not. Suddenly, this thought prompts me to ask. "Have you ever been tested for HIV?"

"Yes. I have been tested every year since 1996, and you?"

"Yes, but only twice."

He gives me an appeasing grin. This is a conversation we should have had the night after we met. Although we have protected intercourse, Dick and I have been very intimate. Sadly, intimacy can give us the illusion that we know our mates, when in reality we don't. This is just one of the reasons why we should be well acquainted with our sexual partners, and there are many more reasons why partners should not end in an *s*. Sex is too complex an issue to share with someone we are not prepared to be with.

"I don't want to sleep with Evelyn," Dick says.

"Sure you don't," I say with little conviction.

"I don't like her. I think she is pretentious."

In disbelief, I continue to look at him from the corner of my eye.

"Sure, she is fine. But I don't sleep with women just because they look good. I have to desire them in more ways than one. I want to talk, laugh, and share with them."

I think to myself, *Dick must think I am the village idiot.* Covering his mouth with two of my fingers, I silence his dissuasive chatter.

"Have you forgotten that we slept together the day after we met? I know I have a great personality, but you, Mr. Dickson, were not sexing my sense of humor," I retort wittingly.

His chuckles grow into robust laughter, only further proving my point.

"It's okay, Dick. This entire trip has been a learning experience. I am glad we can communicate openly with each other. But if I catch you looking in the vicinity of Evelyn's breasts, I am going to have to cut you . . . deep. Now stick that in your little guitar and strum on it."

Continuing to laugh, Dick pulls me into his chest and covers my upper body with his broad shoulders.

Quiet and peaceful is the remainder of the day. With each couple lingering in their separate corners, it feels like Dick and I are here alone. While horseback riding, we see Tam and Stan strolling on the beach. Happily, I don't see Evelyn all day. As dusk sets in, we return to the room to pack up our things. Alas, we have to leave this beautiful island in the morning. Tam and I have to return to work on Tuesday. Dick, on the other hand, only has to return to pick up his tenants' rent. He purchased a nice fifteen-room building with his father's insurance money. He turned the fifteen small rooms into eight spacious lofts. With the money he makes from rent, he can work on his music full-time. See, not only is he fine, he is smart and investment-savvy.

Early the next morning, each of us pile into the Jeep and head for home. The ride is quiet for the first hour, but as the sun rises so does the conversation.

"Evelyn, thanks for the invitation. My girl and I really enjoyed ourselves," Dick says as he kisses me on my cheek.

Tam whips around and speaks. "You and your girl?"

"Yes, my girl and I . . . us . . . we had a great time," says Dick with more conviction.

"No problem, you can call me any time you want to use the place," flirts Evelyn.

Though Evelyn works my nerves, I will not let her steal my

joy today. My attention is focused on Dick's comment. When did I become his girl? He said it twice, which means the comment was intentional. I look up at Tam, who is still staring into the backseat waiting for my response. However, I don't care to entertain her series of questions; therefore, I change the subject by talking to Stan.

"Stan, you have been very quiet the entire trip. What's on your mind?"

"I loathe going back home to my wife."

Nearly choking on my bottle of Evian water, I shriek.

"Your wife?" I say loudly.

Quickly coming to his and her defense, Tam interrupts. "Yes, Stan is married. He needed a getaway, so I invited him to come with us."

"And I really appreciate it," he says before kissing her hand.

This is unbelievable. Tam has interrogated me this entire trip. Clueless, I could have been on her ass about ol', married Stan. I knew there was something strange about him. Physically, he is her type, muscular build, short and stocky. However, he is too quiet. Tam dates garrulous men who liven up the party.

"How did you two meet?" I ask, piercing my eyes through Tam's tough exterior.

"We had a special event for the PTA at my school. Tam catered the affair. We met that night and we have been friends ever since."

"That's nice."

With me displaying my villainous fake smile, Tam knows she is going to have some explaining to do when we get home. Consequently, she is silent the remainder of the trip. And thank God, Evelyn shares that moment of silence. As we hit dry land and the ocean is no longer in view, I begin pondering Evelyn's crass behavior. "Let me try yours and I'll let you try mine" is what she might as well have said, I think to myself while staring at Marion in the rearview mirror.

Embarrassed, I quickly look away as he notices me. I admit, he's cute, but not nearly as fine as Dick. Yet I cannot believe she offered him to me like a piece of dessert. My mom always said that folk with money do things different than the average working man. I'm starting to believe her. I desire to become one of the wealthy elite over the next few years, but I hope to always maintain my decency. With that notion, I need to start practicing, because my ethics are already in question.

Laying my head against the window, I reflect. One day in the eighth grade Tim Booth pulled me around the side of the school building to show me his "thing." I thought it was the most grotesque thing I had ever seen. I was afraid to look at it. Yet he was so proud, he just whipped it out for all to see. Insulted, I yelled for him to put it away. I remember thinking, I would never in my life touch such an ugly object. Plus, I knew I was too precious and too important for him to put it on me. What happened? Sure, puberty has its place, but have I devalued myself along the way? Although my view of a man's penis has changed, I need to realize that I am still important and my body is still precious.

My grandmother used to say the body is a temple and everyone is not worthy of worshipping in your temple. She couldn't have been more correct. For the remainder of the ride, I close my eyes and continue to reflect. When we get to town, Marion stops by my house first. Dick grabs our bags and helps me out of the car. I lean my head into the window and whisper into Tam's ear, "You know we need to talk. Cook dinner tomorrow. I'm coming over."

She keeps her focus forward as she nods okay. Waving bye to the gang, Dick and I walk into the house. Although my relationship with Ro is over, I would love to walk into a house filled with red and white roses. This would be one of Ro's stunts if he were trying to make up for a stupid argument. But there are no roses, only the smell of old cabbage left in the garbage. I hate when I forget to take out the trash.

"Baby, the trash stinks. Will you please take it out?"

He grabs the bag and walks down to the Dumpster. While he's gone, I run to the phone and check the messages.

"You have one message," says the operator.

"Hi, baby, where are you? I have not talked with you in a week. I hope everything is okay. Call me when you get in. I love you."

"My mommy called me," I say aloud.

It is always soothing to hear Mom's voice. She and I have a great relationship. Although she still thinks I am her little baby, she respects my adult decisions. However, she still thinks Ro and I are engaged. I am too ashamed to tell her what happened. She will be extremely disappointed in my behavior and I don't care how old we get, we never want to disappoint our parents. I'll eventually tell her we broke up, but I will never tell her it was my fault.

"Are you hungry?" Dick says as he walks in the door.

"Are you going to start introducing me as your girl?"

"That depends."

"On what?" I ask.

"On you. How would you like me to introduce you?"

Confused as to how I should answer that question, I forcefully chew my gum. It's funny how my small habits go into overdrive when I get nervous. Why do we have to define the people in our lives? Is it so important to say my girl or my man after an introduction? Is it said because we are proud, or to inform others that this person is off the market? Maybe it is both. Yet people are curious by nature, and if we don't define who our partners or peers are, others around will always ask. I remember when Tam dated this older man; when they were out together, he only introduced her by name and people would always ask, "Is that your daughter?" Embarrassed, she stopped dating him. Which is unfortunate because he made her happy.

"You never answered my question," Dick pursues while tugging on my arm.

"You can introduce me as your lady," I say with a proper English accent.

He bows with a sweet smile and responds, "My lady it is."

"Well, it's decided. Now it is time to take your lady out to dinner," I say, smiling.

Grabbing my purse, I hop onto Dick's back and we skip to the car. I enjoy the playfulness in our relationship. After back-and-forth discussion, we decide to eat at a small café near the house. The crowd is minimal; therefore, we are back home in an hour. After politely asking, Dick stays the night.

And this becomes the scene over the next couple of weeks. Dick and I see each other almost every day. Either I go to the music studio after work or he comes over and cooks dinner. A few days during the week, Dick tries to surprise me with lunch. But when the girls in the office see him coming, the gossip hits my floor before he can make it up the elevator. Regardless, I pretend to be surprised, because he loves to catch me off guard. And he succeeds when he comes over one night with four tickets to *Carmen*, my favorite opera. I invite Tam and she invites Stan and tonight the four of us are going to the theater. I am wearing a scarlet red dress with spaghetti straps and a fitted bodice, trimmed in tiny clear bugle beads. I want his mouth to hit the floor when he sees me in this dress. Therefore, I request he gets dressed at his home, and pick me up at seven for our date. At 6:50 he rings my doorbell, and ironically receives the effect from me that I desired from him. I nearly faint when Dick walks through my door. There is something about a man in a suit, and this man looks incredible, wearing a tailored four-button ecru suit with a crisp mauve shirt. Against his dark skin, that ecru is ravishing. He stands in the mirror and fixes his shirt as I gawk. Soon, he stops fidgeting and begins to stare at himself.

"Why the pensive look?" I ask.

He takes a moment, then looks at me through the mirror and speaks. "Do you think that I am beautiful?"

Wow. I have never heard a man ask that.

"Yes. Why do you ask?"

"Women are always telling me I am beautiful. I wonder what they see. They don't know me, so they could only be looking at my shell. If I were to get burned or maimed, would I no longer be beautiful?"

"I can't speak for them, I can only speak for myself."

"That is why I asked you," he states.

I run and get my book, flip through the pages, and let him read one of my poems on beauty.

"I don't care if beauty is in the eye of the beholder, if it's not in the hearts of those we behold as beautiful," I say just before he begins to read.

As he finishes, Dick places the book in my hand and asks, "You wrote that?"

"Of course," I say, rising to place my book on the dresser.

"You ought to publish your writings."

"Yes, Ro, I know."

I nearly choke attempting to swallow my own words. Damn, I just called him Ro. I hope he didn't hear it. I meant no disrespect, and I certainly don't want to argue before the opera.

"Are you ready to go?" he asks.

Thank God, he didn't hear me. Since Ro was always telling me to publish my work, his name just slipped out. Nonetheless, it is not cool to call your current man by your ex's name. I have got to be more careful. Grabbing my purse, I walk toward the door as Dick stands there waiting. Leaning over, he lifts my chin, gently kisses my lips, and speaks. "It's okay, I know you miss him."

Then slipping his arm through mine, Dick escorts me out and closes the door behind us. That is all that is said and we head to the opera.

Our dates drop Tam and me off at the door and continue toward the parking garage to park the car. This gives me ample time to pester Tam.

"You need to stop this clandestine affair with this married man."

"I am not sleeping with him. We are just friends," she promises.

"We use the words *friends* too loosely these days. You need to stop doing that. You are going out with him after dark. You are taking him on weekend excursions. You eat with him, laugh with him, and flirt with him. You are having an affair!" I whisper loudly.

"It's only an affair if you sleep with him," she says.

"Well, call his wife and see if she concurs. I don't feel good about this, Tam. It's leading to trouble. I can feel it in my bones."

"Do not start that West Indian prophecy crap. We are only *friends*," she insists, raising her voice.

This is so unlike her. I have never known her to date a married man. She has dated older men, white men, and she even dated a deaf man once. But married men are not her style. She must be going through something, and over the next few weeks we are going to get to the root of her problem, because she has got to stop dating Stan. Our conversation settles as Stan and Dick walk into the lobby. We are seated in the fourth row of the theater. The Alliance is an excellent house for opera, intimate enough to see each character's facial expression, yet large enough not to be blown away by their powerful voices. Dick doesn't know the story of *Carmen*, so I find myself explaining it to him during the performance. It's good that no one is sitting directly behind us, because his constant questions are very annoying. I want him to be interested;

However, he is ruining the experience, and he needs to wait until the performance is over. This is the first time one of Dick's nuances has gotten on my nerves. I guess we are becoming a real couple.

Once the show ends, Dick and I nix the idea of dessert and head back to the house. Over the last four days, Dick has been at my place. Tonight he decides to go home and I couldn't be happier. I enjoy having him around, but tonight I want to sleep alone. As soon as we kiss good night, I hurry to the bathroom and wash the makeup off my face. Immediately following, I crawl into the bed. Mentally, I plan tomorrow's workday. This has been a long week. It is difficult to go to work when your man is an entrepreneur. I don't mind, because real estate yields him great returns. In fact, I am a little jealous that he has time to dedicate to his music career. I wish I had more time to write. My marketing job burns out most of my creative juices. However, I have promised myself that I am not going to complain. At least I have a career. I could be unemployed and broke. We all have our own blessings and I am very thankful for mine.

Good night.

Chapter 10

We Meet Again

Today, Tam calls me during lunch to inform me she is ending it with Stan. Coming to the realization that she cares for this married man leads her to this ultimate decision.

"I don't want things to get out of control," she admits.

"Well, do it before it's too late," I add.

Tam mentions writing a letter to end things, but I quickly remind her of my fiasco. As a result, she chooses to break up over dinner. Knowing the difficulty, I wish her the best. By the end of the day, I am surprised to find myself missing Dick. I thought about him several times today, but no more than usual. Although we have no plans tonight, I hope he comes over. Since it has been such a heavy week, I am starting my weekend today at 4:00 PM. I stop by the store for a pint of Häagen-Dazs butter pecan ice cream, my favorite. I have to monitor my intake or I would buy it every day. I walk into the house, hoping that Dick has called, but he hasn't. Since I just saw him last night, I choose not to call. I'll just relax, write a little, and go to bed. I fade off to sleep. However, the ring of my phone startles me. Looking at the clock, I wonder who in the hell is calling me at two in the morning.

"What?" I answer irritably.

"Hey, it's Evelyn."

This chick better have a fantastic reason for calling me this time of the morning, or she is going to get cursed out.

"I need you to come to Northside Hospital," she continues.

"Why, Evelyn, is it another surprise party?"

"No. Tam has been hit and she is in critical condition."

I drop the phone. Jumping from the bed so fast, I become light-headed. Hastening around the room, I attempt to put on my pants, my top, and my shoes at the same time. I've left Evelyn, yelling on the phone receiver.

"Are you okay? Where's Dick?" she asks.

"I'll be there in a minute."

I hang up the phone. Having no time to think about Evelyn asking about Dick, I will give her the benefit of the doubt. I am sure she is worried about Tam, her only friend. If something happens to her, she will have no one, including me. Leaving the house, I call Dick to ask him to meet me at the hospital. Three rings and he finally picks up.

"Dick, I am sorry to wake you. It's Tam, she is at Northside Hospital. She was hit or something, I don't know. Evelyn was vague."

"Do you need me to come and pick you up?"

"No, just meet me there."

"Okay, be careful." He hangs up.

I jump in the car, say a prayer, and dash out the driveway.

The information desk says Tam is in the west wing on the fourth floor. Praying Tam is okay, I continuously mash the elevator button until it finally opens. When I get to the floor I run into the waiting area to speak with Evelyn. She is not there, but I see Dick standing by the door. Running into his arms, I hold on tight. However, as I look over his shoulder I freeze. Romance is sitting in the waiting room temperately posed, watching me in the arms of another man. It is a good thing I am in the hospital, because my heart nearly stops.

"What's wrong, baby?" Dick asks.

I grab hold of his arm and pull him away from the waiting room.

"That guy sitting in the waiting room, did you talk to him?" I whisper.

"No, why?"

"That is Romance, my ex. What is he doing here?"

"I don't know, go ask him," says Dick.

I slowly walk back into the waiting room to see Ro sitting in the same position. Standing by the outside of the door, Dick leans to the left of the frame just to make his presence known, yet not to intrude. I sit down in the chair next to Ro.

"What are you doing here?" I ask.

"I came to see if Tam was all right," he says calmly.

"Tam? You came here to see Tam?"

"She is your best friend. I thought you might be upset. I want to let you know that I am here for you."

I put my head in the palms of my hands and sigh.

"I see I'm not the only one here for you," Ro proceeds curiously.

I don't want to look at him. He knows every one of my expressions and he can read my like a book. I turn away and begin to speak. "How did you find out about Tam?"

Just then, Evelyn dashes into the waiting room. "There you two are. I have been down the hall looking for you. They moved Tam to another floor. Let's go."

Standing at the same time, we speak simultaneously.

"She called me," Ro states.

"She called you?" I ask.

"Come on, let's go," rushes Evelyn.

Looking at her, we stand in silence.

"What?" questions Evelyn.

She looks at us, turns, looks to the left, and sees Dick

standing at the door. "Oh. Well, I didn't know. I called the first emergency number for you, and it was Ro. We can talk about this later. Let's go!"

She takes Ro by the hand and escorts him down the hall. Dick and I follow behind. We get to Tam's floor and the nurses will allow only one family member in the room. I want to go, but I don't want to leave Dick and Ro in the room together. On the other hand, I don't want to stand in the hall with Dick and Ro, either; therefore, I ask Dick to wait for me by the door.

"I'm her sister, may I go in now?" I say to the nurse.

"You can only stay a minute," she responds.

I slowly open the huge wooden door and my heart suddenly feels pressure. Tam is wearing a neck brace and her face in badly bruised. She has tubes and needles coming out of her stomach, arms, and mouth. I walk over to her bedside and gently stroke her hand. As her eyes widen, I know she knows I am here. Although she cannot talk, I softly speak to her.

"We are all here for you. And when I say all, I mean all. Dick, Ro, and I are *here* for you."

I wasn't going to mention that Ro was here, but I know it will do her heart good to know I am in such a predicament. Tam lets out a small grunt that would have been a huge laugh if she were able to open her mouth. I lay my head by her arm and hold her hand until the nurse comes in and whispers, "She needs her rest."

I kiss Tam's hand and rise from her side.

"I love you," I whisper.

She winks her eye.

"I'll be right outside in the lobby."

I walk out of the room and close the door. When I get to the lobby, I see that Evelyn has switched partners. Ro is moved aside and she is speaking with Dick. I don't know whom to address first. I could kick Evelyn's ass for calling Ro. She knew exactly what she was doing. If I sit with Ro first, it will look like I want to be with him. If I go over to Dick first, Ro will think I couldn't care less that he is here. So after reviewing the situation, I decide to stay here by the door. Whoever makes the first move will be the one I speak with. I stand here for about thirty seconds; then Dick excuses himself from Evelyn and comes over.

"Are you okay?" he asks.

"I'm fine. Tam looks horrible. What was Evelyn saying?"

"She said that Tam was leaving dinner with Stan and as she was going to her car in the deck, a car came speeding down the ramp and hit her."

As we are speaking, Ro comes over to join the conversation. My stomach begins to flutter, as he introduces himself to Dick.

"How are you doing, man? I'm Romance."

I quickly interject, "I'm sorry, guys. Romance, this is . . . Will Dickson. Will, this is Romance."

Romance gives Dick a firm handshake.

"Well, I see that you are okay and it looks like I am not going to be able to see Tam so I am going to go," says Ro.

"Okay," I say, relieved.

"Call me and let me know how she is doing," says Ro, turning away.

I know he is very upset, because his speech is monotone, his jaw is taut, and his body movements are uptight and formal. He nods to Dick, waves good-bye to Evelyn, and walks away.

"So, that is the infamous Ro?" says Dick with a smile.

"Why are you smiling?"

"Because you are sweating bullets. I have never seen you so roiled. And you introduced me by my full name. What's up? Do you honestly think he wouldn't know?"

"I am upset about Tam, and that is the only thing wrong with me."

"Okay, Miss Lady. Whatever you say. But you know he still cares or he wouldn't have been here."

Leaning my head against the door trim, I stand against the

wall in silence. Walking over to the chairs, Dick turns to me and speaks. "The question is, do you still care about him?"

Dazed, I stand in complete disbelief of the entire evening. I cannot believe a car hit Tam. I was surprised to see Ro and more surprised at how Dick is handling things.

The remainder of the night passes as Dick and I try to find comfort on the waiting room sofa. We stay at the hospital until noon, when the nurse comes out and tells us that Tam's condition is stable. Although her neck and jawbone are fractured, she has no internal bleeding. Since all we can do is wait, Dick and I go home to take showers. He has a performance this evening, which he must prepare for, and I decide to take a nap before returning to the hospital. As I'm continuously worrying about Tam, my nap only lasts for an hour. I prepare a sandwich and head back to see her. As I am leaving the house, I see Ro pulling into my driveway.

What is he doing here? I say to myself.

"Are you alone?" he calls from the car.

I nod my head and stay positioned on the doorstep.

He gets out of the car, holding a beautiful bouquet of flowers. "The flowers are for Tam. How is she doing?"

"Stable, yet about the same," I say.

Without me looking into his eyes, we stand in awkward silence.

"Have I been replaced?" he sternly asks.

"You can't be replaced. You are not a piece of china. I have moved on. Just like you."

"What do you mean? I haven't moved on."

"Who was the girl you were with in the Blue Room?"

"Just a girl. It's nothing serious. I had a feeling you would be there with him and I didn't want to be there alone. Maybe we should go in the house and talk."

"I have to go see Tam," I nervously insist.

He takes my keys from my hand, opens the door, and extends his hand for me to follow. I stand in the doorway watching him walk into my home; a sight I thought I would never see again. Walking in behind him, I immediately start to purge.

"I am so sorry. I have not been cheating on you the entire two years. I started seeing Dick after our argument. I was angry and he was convenient. I was trying to convince myself that I didn't need you. I never meant to hurt you and that is why I was breaking it off with him—"

Ro interrupts. "Then why are you still seeing him?"

"Because . . ."

"Because what?" he asks.

"Because when you left, I didn't want to be alone."

"So there is nothing special about Dick. He is just keeping you company?"

Now, I would be lying if I sat here and said Dick is not special. I really care about Dick, but I also care about Ro. Therefore, I ignore the question and ask, "Why are you here, Ro?"

"Why do you think I am here?"

I hate when he answers a question with a question. If I knew why he was here, why would I ask? Then again, I know why he is here. I just want to hear him say it.

"If I were to forgive you, what would happen?" he says.

Torn, I have no idea what to say. I want him to forgive me, but things will be so much simpler if he does not.

"I don't know," I mumble.

"Well, you think about it," he says before leaving

Immediately, I fall onto the futon. What is this about? Is he trying to get back with me? If so, why doesn't he come out and say it? I cannot start dating him; I am dating Dick.

"I don't know what to do!" I scream in the center of the floor.

Picking up the flowers, I head toward the hospital. I know Tam is going through her own crisis, but I have got to tell her about this. It may sound selfish to most people, but Tam would want me to keep her informed. She will be angry if I make a drastic decision without consulting her first. I get to the room and Evelyn is sitting by her bedside.

"Get out, I need to talk with Tam."

"You cannot usher me out like that."

I am starting to detest her. I did not ask her why she called Ro, because I don't care to hear her excuse. Her voice annoys me, her face makes me sick, and I wish she would go away.

"I said it's my turn to see Tam. You know we both can't be in here at the same time."

"Then wait your turn," she snaps.

I look at her and look at Tam. I know Tam wishes she could speak, but she can't, so I speak for her. Quietly, I stand here for a second, and then I rush out of the room and down to the nurses' station. I grab a nurse and run back into the room.

"I don't know what she was doing, but she was standing over the bed with a pillow. It looked suspicious. They were arguing before the accident and I don't know what she might do. Please, please ask her to leave," I beg with a small tear in the corner of my eye.

"Miss, could we see you in the hall?" the nurse says.

"But I . . ." stutters Evelyn.

Well now, I fixed that little problem. I wish Tam could laugh, because I know she would be bubbling over by now. True, this is a lot of drama for someone in such a serious condition, but Tam loves drama. She does not want everyone tipping around on eggshells or having pity parties for her. I reach into my purse and pull out a piece of paper.

"I wrote something for you."

She squeezes my hand as I read.

U & I
Undoubtedly, U . . . Inspire me
Ultimately, U . . . Impact my soul
United with U . . . I become utopian
Divided from U . . . I become unsound
U feel my uproar even if I say nothing

U feel my unhappiness even if I smile
U uncover the truth, with the blink of my eye
Unparalleled, U & I
Unclad, I come to U
When they say unusual . . . U say I am eclectic
When they say uncouth . . . U say I am honest
When they say uncertain . . . U say I am free
U come unbiased . . . I can be me
I thank U
I love U
For our undivided, unearthly, unconditional union
U & I

I become teary-eyed by the last line. Although I wrote the poem, I sometimes don't realize what I have I written until I read it aloud.

"I am going to frame it for you. But enough of the mushy stuff. Girl, I cannot wait to tell you what is going on. You are going to die . . . I'm sorry, I didn't mean to say that."

Words are so powerful. We really need to be careful what we say, especially during delicate moments like this. I begin to tell her about Romance coming over and our conversation. Her eyes widen, then shrink. I know she is just as surprised as I am. Although she can't speak, her expressions tell a story of their own. At the end of my account, I once again remind her how this chaos is all her fault.

"If you hadn't been messing around with that married man, we wouldn't be at the hospital and none of this would ever have happened. You know this is all your fault."

Tam cuts her eye at me, lifts her arm, and strokes my hand. Smiling from one corner of her lips, she lifts her hand and slowly raises her middle finger. And with that single gesture, I know my girl is going to be all right.

* * *

Tam remains in the hospital for two weeks and the doctors insist her neck brace stay on for an extra month. No matter the time of day, she always has an array of company. Although she told me she was ending things with Stan, he comes to visit her nearly every day. I am in no position to give out advice on love. However, I wish that she would stop seeing him. Of course, I keep Tam up to date on my love triangle. Romance calls daily. Yet I have been avoiding his invitation to dinner for fear that he will ask me about Dick. Tam says that I will eventually have to face him and that sooner is usually better than later. Therefore, I agree to go out to dinner with Romance on Wednesday. I don't know what I am going to say since we left things so open. Nonetheless, I know we need closure on this chapter before we can begin again. This is the problem with on-and-off relationships. When things end abruptly and couples reunite in a few months, we carry that first-chapter, breakup baggage with us into the second chapter. Then the ambiguous second chapter ends in hostility. I must be sure that Romance truly forgives me for my actions. Moreover, I must make him understand why I was unhappy with our relationship in the first place. If we can bring closure to these issues, we may be able to salvage a little of what we had. Then again, with Dick in the picture, I feel split. I don't know whom I want or what I want. Ro is the sensible choice but Dick is so much fun. In fact, he is due over here momentarily. Our open and honest communication is what I like most about our relationship. I am going to tell him about dinner with Romance on Wednesday. He knows that I still care for Ro and he knows that there is a possibility we may get back together. And although this puts him in an awkward position, Dick handles it well. He says it's important that I be happy and if I am happiest with Ro, he will settle for a platonic relationship. At one time I didn't think that was possible. However, I feel Dick and I can have a great friendship, if only we can stop having sex.

His truck is pulling into the driveway, so I rush to open the door as he walks in. Watching him move, I know why women stop him on the street just to tell him he is beautiful. He is absolutely amazing. If only these women would get to know him, they would be even more mesmerized. He is so peaceful, fun-loving, and intelligent. Funny, if I weigh the pros and cons between him and Ro, Dick would win, hands down. Unfortunately, Ro still has a hold on my heart and I am not willing to let go of him. History with a person does count for something . . . right?

"Hi, baby," I say as I jump into Dick's arms.

"I brought you something." He hands me a little red box, wrapped with pink velvet ribbon.

I take the box and scuttle to open it. It is a sexy, red lace teddy.

"Ooooh, thank you." I hold it up to my body and prance around. "Would you like me to try it on?"

"No, wait until you come over on Friday. I have a special evening planned," he says.

I lean over into his lap and kiss his soft lips. As we kiss, he palms the back of my head and lays me down on the floor while whispering, "You know what I like about you?"

"What?" I say as I kiss his earlobe

"You are uninhibited and passionate. You go with the flow. A lot of women would have said 'don't put me on the floor, let's go get in the bed.' Why does sex always have to be in the bed?"

"It doesn't. I never want sex to be boring, I think experimenting keeps the relationship fresh," I add.

"I am so glad you said that." Dick smiles as he sits on my stomach.

"Your are heavy. Get up!"

He moves to the side, pulls me up, and sits me atop his stomach. Dick looks at me curiously, "What if Ro asks you to stop seeing me, what would you **say**?"

"I would tell him no," I declare, attempting to assure Dick.

"He is never going to trust you around me. I am a man and I know this. I also know it is going to come down to him or me, and when that moment comes, don't just go with your heart, go with your soul."

Maybe he does care whether or not Ro and I get back together. He sits up and wraps his legs around the base of my hips. Pulling my hair away from my face, Dick clasps his hands loosely around my neck.

"I want to be with you," he says with a dauntless stare. And as I am about to speak, he interrupts. "Don't say anything. I just want you to know."

He rises, pulls me off the floor, and smiles. "Let's go to the movies."

I awake Wednesday morning after a restless night. Nervous as I am about my dinner tonight with Romance, my stomach is so upset I cannot eat lunch. I wish he would call and cancel, but he does not. I come home, change into a nice dress, and meet him at the restaurant. Comparing Ro's entrance to Dick's, the feelings do not match up. I feel rejuvenated and excited when I see Dick. It is nice to see Ro, but not quite as stimulating. Walking to the table, Ro attempts to kiss me on the lips, but I slightly turn to the right so that his lips land on my cheek.

"You look nice tonight," he compliments.

"So do you."

"I hope I haven't kept you waiting too long."

"I haven't been here long at all," I comment politely.

This conversation is such a facade. I want to know if he wants to take me back, and he wants to know if I am still sleeping with Dick. It is so absurd how drastically a situation can change in a matter of months. Ro and I have spent years together, laughing until we fart and crying until we snort. I have seen him pick his nose and he has heard me snore like a hog. This man has even purchased my tampons when my period made surprise appearances. But now we sit at a table across from each other like strangers, daring to go outside the barriers of "politeville." This is foolish.

"Do you want to get back with me?" I state candidly.

"That depends."

"Come on, Ro, cut the bullshit. Either you forgive me or you don't. I don't want to be punished over and over again for this mistake. What do you want? I have repeatedly apologized. If we can get over this hump and talk about why things went wrong. There may still be a future for us, if you are willing."

"When are you going to stop fucking Dick, or do you have plans to date us both?" he states firmly with a matter-of-fact expression.

Well, how about that for candid statements? It seems that I can dish it, but I don't swallow it well. Speechless, I sit at the table openmouthed.

"Did you understand my question?" he continues.

Still, unable to speak, I slowly nod my head up and down.

"You are still sleeping with Dick, aren't you?" he asks.

"Well, not right this second," I respond with a bit of juvenile humor; however, Ro is not amused.

"Look, I have slept with him. However, we have decided to be friends and I will continue to be his friend, even if you and I get back together."

"That is not good enough," Ro says with sound resentment.

Silently, I think to myself. I know I am asking a lot. Hell, I don't know if I would agree if he were asking me to do the same. Scared to admit, maybe, I don't want this relationship to work. I watched a talk show once about women who were scared to confront their love and relationship issues. There-fore they made life so unbearable for their mates that eventually their partners simply walked out. I criticized those ladies for not having the courage to speak their feelings and here I sit, doing the exact same thing. I should have learned something from that show instead of taking the information and using it as my own scapegoat. Television will program the mind if we are not careful.

Our appetizers arrive and we eat in silence—and I know this conversation is near its end, so I decide not to order dinner. Ro pushes his plate aside.

"Call me when you get it together," he vexes.

Excusing himself, he leaves the table. I cannot believe he is walking away. It is like he has dumped me twice. I don't know how I expected this conversation to turn out, but it wasn't like this. He didn't even look back. More importantly, he didn't pay for the appetizers.

The next day is a blur. I keep thinking that I should have said something different. Yet I have to be honest with Ro as well as myself. I am not sure if I want to get back with him. But for my satisfaction, I wanted him to ask. I want him to forgive me so that the ball will be in my court. Human nature is surely a piece of work, isn't it? Before I go to sleep tonight, I pray for some clarity on this situation. This is way beyond my control. I need some help and I need it fast.

Good night.

Chapter 11

Three's a Crowd

To assist Stan with getting Tam home, I take off work on Friday. Since she has always had to do things by herself, independent Tam thinks she can do it alone. Tam's father died when she was eight and her mom has been living with cancer for the last eight years. As a result, she is a very strong, proud woman, not accustomed to asking for help. I meet Stan in the lobby while Tam is getting checked out. He is usually quiet, but today he is more loquacious than ever.

"I am so glad you are here. I know you don't think I am good for her, but I want you to get to know me better."

Surly, I reply, "Why?"

"Your opinion of me is important to Tam and that makes it important to me."

"Are you planning on getting divorced?" I ask Stan.

"My divorce just became final."

"I didn't know you were separated."

"You didn't ask," he states.

I guess he told me. In the hall, we wait together while the

nurse wheels Tam from the room. Her bruises have healed, but she is still sporting a big white neck brace.

Once we get into Tam's house, Stan helps her onto the couch. While Tam was in the hospital, Stan cleaned her refrigerator, purchased new groceries, and washed her linens. When she said she had everything covered, I didn't realize Stan was taking care of everything. I'm a little jealous. These are things her best friend should be doing.

"Do you need me to stay? I can break my date with Dick."

"No, go enjoy your Dick," she laughs.

"Don't say it like that. He is my friend."

Her speech is slurred because of her jaw fracture, but her sense of humor is just fine.

"Call me if you need anything," I say, walking toward the door.

"We will," says Stan.

"I was not talking to you," I mumble underneath my breath.

Approaching the house, I stop by the mailbox and grab the mail. I only go to my mailbox every three days, because I hate receiving bills every day. Even if they come consistently, at least I don't have to look at them. The phone is ringing as I walk into the house. However, I choose to ignore it. Instead, I sit on my counter and open the mail.

"What is this?"

Opening a piece of mail from the Hallmark Corporation in Kansas City, Missouri, I read the letter aloud.

"Thank you for your interest in the Hallmark Corporation. We received a sample of your writing style."

Though I didn't send anything to Hallmark I continue reading.

"We were impressed with the works you sent us. We would like for you to call our offices and speak with Ms. Susan Wright to set up an interview."

What is this? How did they get my work? Maybe Ro, the only one who would have access to my poetry, sent them some samples. I never thought about writing card greetings. I swear that Ro is something else. I magnetize the letter to the refrigerator door and prepare for my date tonight. I am wearing my red teddy with a pair of nice-fitting jeans and strappy heels. Not too dainty, but very sexy, in a Victoria's Secret/Levi's kind of way.

I arrive at Dick's house, open the door, and immediately smell the lavender-scented candles. Light jazz is playing in the background. I prefer old-school artists such as Nina, Miles, and Donny, but Diana Krall sounds wonderful. Dick greets me at the door wearing a pair of loose-fitting jeans that fall right below his pelvis, the sexiest part of a man's body. That indention below the waist where the femur joins the pelvic bone floors me every time.

"I love your Levi's/lingerie look," says Dick, kissing me on the cheek.

Yeah! He gets my statement.

"I am digging the candles," I say, smelling the aroma lingering about the room.

Dick covers my eyes as he leads me to his dining room. As he removes his hands, I see that the room is set up like a spa.

"What is this?" I ask.

"This is for you."

Removing my jeans, Dick helps me onto the massage table and gives me a towel. As the doorbell rings, my imagination pictures an angry Ro punching Dick in the face just as the door opens. Carefully, I lie still, listening while Dick stands at the door. However, to my surprise, he ushers in three nicely built men and gives a pleasing introduction.

"This is Mick. He will be your masseuse. This is Donovan. He will be giving you a facial. And this is Mark. He will be giving you your manicure and pedicure."

"Fellas, this is my girl. Excuse me, my lady."

He walks over and kisses me on the forehead. "Enjoy!"

This is the life. It's like a magnificent TV episode. However, Cliff never did anything like this for Claire Huxtable. This is on a *Dynasty*, Joan Collins level. It is definitely a step up from what I am accustomed to, but I can get used to this. As I lie here enjoying my massage and pedicure, Dick asks to play his new song.

"I would love it." I beam.

He turns downs the music and begins to sing. As I listen more, the words sound familiar. Soon, I realize that he is singing my sand poem.

"That's my sand poem! How did you get my poem?"

Laughing, he responds, "I went down to the beach the next morning and took a picture of it. I liked it so much, I made a song. I hope you don't mind."

If this is a plot to get ahead in the race, Dick has just crossed the finish line and I am prepared to give him his award. Enthralled, I sit and listen to my song as I get rubbed and buffed by three caretakers. Did I already say that this is the life? If not, *This is the life!*

Finishing his song, Dick walks into the kitchen to complete dinner. Donovan starts on my facial once Mick asks me to flip over to massage the front of my thighs. Mark starts on my hands, while Dick is setting the table. After the men finish my body, hands, feet, and face, Dick takes them to the front room and escorts them out. Still lying on the massage table, I watch Dick's slightly bowed legs amble slowly into the dining room. My eyes gradually move up his body and focus on his large strong hands as he helps me off the table. Weak, I fall to the floor, for these masseuses have kneaded my muscles to dough. Smiling from ear to ear, Dick carries me like a damsel in distress and places me in my chair at the dinner table. Tuna steak and pasta are tonight's main courses.

"Everything looks scrumptious. This evening has been so incredible."

"Just wait," Dick teases.

We eat our dinner with light conversation and everything is delectable. After dinner, Dick takes the dishes to the kitchen while I go to the sofa, pick up his guitar, and begin strumming.

"Do you mind?" I ask Dick.

"Do you know what you are doing?" he yells from the kitchen.

He comes into the room and straddles behind me. Strategically placing his hands on top of mine, Dick positions my fingers correctly. Creating a sensual, musical moment, we strum the guitar together. I begin to confess how I feel. I lean my head against his shoulder. As he kisses my neck, the doorbell rings.

"Dessert has arrived."

"There's more?" I ask with excitement.

Running to the back, I slide on my jeans while thinking to myself, What can he do to top my massage and dinner? As I walk into the dining room, Dick comes over and asks me to go back to the bedroom.

"Who was at the door?"

"Come on, let's go." He ushers me into the bedroom and sits on the bed.

"I want us to have a memorable, exciting night," he says.

"I do too."

"And I want us to have it with another woman," continues Dick.

My skin begins to tingle from shock as I rise and walk toward the door. Placing my hand against the edge of the door, I push it closed and lean against the frame.

"Have you lost your damn mind?" I shriek.

"Calm down and think about it. It is completely safe, she is a friend of mine."

"You want me to sleep with you and your girlfriend? Are you crazy?"

"I thought you might enjoy it. I wish you would consider it."

Sliding down the door and onto the floor, I close my eyes, praying for this nightmare to end. I put my head in between my knees to catch my breath.

"Are you thinking about it?"

"Yeah, I'm thinking about how I want to fight you! I can't believe you would do this."

Dick walks over, sits beside me, and attempts to kiss me.

"No, no, no. Stop it! Why would you invite some girl over here without first talking to me? I have never slept with a woman and I don't have any intention to. Why did you think I would be cool with something like this?"

"You seem like such a free spirit. You said you like trying new things to keep a relationship fresh."

"First of all, you and I are not in a relationship. Second of all, it has only been a couple of months. It is still fresh!"

"I'm sorry, Lily. I'll ask her to leave and once we have talked about it in more detail, maybe you will change your mind."

Rising, I move away from Dick as he opens the door to tell his friend that tonight is not going to happen. Peering into the living room, I see our supposed date for the evening is the girl who jumped into his arms at the Blue Room. I am stunned that Dick thought I was going to share my body with someone I don't know. Just then it hits me. I shared my body with Dick when we were still strangers and I guess to him, it's all the same. This is why first impressions are so important. Thoughts of this evening's events have me queasy. Feeling sick to my stomach, I decide to go home. I walk into the dining room to look for my shoes.

"Where are you going?" Dick calls out.

"Home."

"Hold up, please," he persists.

He escorts his girlfriend out the door and rushes to deter me from putting on my shoes.

"I don't feel well, I want to go home."

"You can rest here. I am sorry I upset you, please stay."

I sit down as Dick places a pillow behind my head. I don't know what to think about tonight. Was he buttering me up with the massage so that I would agree to the ménage à trois? Or were his actions sincere? He looks genuine, but I realize we are very different people. I'm not sure what kind of sexual energy I exude, but it needs to change.

"This will never work," I state peacefully.

"I disagree. We simply are not on the same page."

"No, baby, we are not in the same book. Your lifestyle is different. If I become your girlfriend, you will want to experience things that I will never agree with."

"Don't knock it till you've tried it."

"See, I don't live by that motto. There are several things. I have no desire to try and I am okay with that."

"I didn't mean to insult you by asking Karen to come over. She asked about you at the club. She thinks you are cute. Not knowing if you had ever had a threesome, I thought you would like it. You should be open to try new things."

"Not me. If I am sleeping with you, then I am sleeping with you only."

"It's no different from you sleeping with me one night and sleeping with another man the next. Either you are monogamous or you are not. Would it have been different had I asked the masseuse?" Dick questions.

"I am not into any type of threesome activity. I don't want to see you in bed with another man and I am not getting in bed with another woman. Period. But you are correct in saying that either you practice monogamy or you don't. My current track record shows I don't. But I do want to be in a serious, monogamous relationship where I am loved, spoiled, and respected. And this is . . . this is not it. I have to wipe the slate clean and start over."

"I see," Dick whispers.

I lie down on the couch, in attempt to cease my pounding headache. Covering me with a blanket, he retires to the bedroom. I quickly fall asleep and wake up the next morning and let myself out. I want to rush over to Tam's to tell her about my evening, but I don't want to interrupt her morning with Stan. As soon as I walk into the house, I feel a heaviness come over my heart. Falling onto the futon, I sleep the rest of the day. Waking around one in the morning, I finally crawl into bed.

Good night.

Chapter 12

Should I Stay or Should I Go?

I call Ms. Wright with Hallmark on Monday and she schedules an interview for me the following Friday. I should receive my airline ticket this week. I have never been to Kansas City. This may be the new start I desire.

I finally speak with Tam on Thursday, when I receive my ticket.

"Where have you been?" I question.

"I have been staying at Stan's house," she admits.

"What?"

"His house is five minutes from the school. Therefore, he can check on me during the day."

"You and Stan are becoming close, aren't you?"

"He's a good man. He is nurturing, protective, and sincere."

"Lucky you."

"It's not luck. I knew what I was looking for, so I asked God to deliver it when I was ready to receive it."

"It's sound so simple when you say it."

"It's not simple it's just . . . well, it's like going to the grocery store having no idea what we want to eat. We will walk up and down every aisle and pick up random objects until our buggy is full. When we do that, we end up taking home things that we would never have purchased had we taken the time to make out a list. I know what I want. Therefore, I make my list, purchase my items, and go home."

"That is so strict and rigid. Don't you ever venture to the cookie aisle?" I ask.

"Only if it's on the list. I stick to the list, I rarely deviate."

"But I'm more spontaneous, an impulse buyer. I like to grab an item or two off the list."

"And that is why you end up with drama and men you don't want. I have to go. Call me later."

I hate when Tam is right. I always have some sort of drama going on in my life. Maybe I am addicted to drama. I loathe boring relationships and I like adventure. It gives me something to write about.

"Do I crave drama to feed my creativity? Could this be an addiction worse than alcohol?"

Ro calls me on Friday and asks to come over. Part of me wishes he hadn't called, but since he did I tell him yes. He brings a couple of movies and we sit and watch them just like old times. Yet the energy is different. There is certain unease about the evening. He doesn't mention Dick and neither do I. I do, however, ask him about my interview, but he insists he didn't send my poetry to Hallmark. Not that he would ever admit it.

One week passes and I have not heard from Dick. I wouldn't know what to say if he called. Should I apologize for reacting so abrupt or were my actions justified? Tam says I should not feel embarrassed. She says if he didn't know, he could only assume. I said he should have known. However, she replies, saying that's what I get for sleeping with a man I hardly know, and I could only agree. Once again, she is right. If only I would start taking her advice before I mess up.

Ro and I end up going out a few times during the week. Between the movies, miniature golf, and dinner, Ro and I discuss many of our unresolved issues. He asks me about Dick a few times. Yet when I tell him that I am not seeing him anymore, I don't think he believes me. I am not sure where all of this is going; however, I am taking it day by day. Kissing my cheek while saying good-bye, Ro drops me off at the airport this morning. My plane arrives in Kansas City an hour and fifteen minutes later. Riding up the escalators, I get to the top and I see a man holding a card with my name on it. This may sound crazy, but I have always wanted this to happen. It seems as though people with their names on those cards are so important. I walk up to the man and pointing at the card, I speak. "That is my name."

"Are you here for a meeting with Hallmark?"

"Yes."

"I am your driver. Follow me."

I hold my head high and follow the short, clean-shaven man in the black suit. Passing through the corridor, we step into a shiny Lincoln and drive off. Wow, I am one of the important people—a person with a driver. Not to sound vain, but I wonder if the other passengers standing around were curious about my identity. Silly as it may sound, I always make speculations concerning the identity of the name-card people. If I have time during a layover, I give them identities and stories. I have a very vivid imagination. What can I say? I am an only child.

We arrive at the office and immediately I am called in to speak with Ms. Wright.

"Nice to meet you," I say.

"Pleasure to meet you as well. Have a seat."

She begins asking a series of questions from my writing experience to my relationships with my friends. It is a very personal interview. Interestingly enough, she asks, "What inspires you?"

Pondering a moment, I confidently tell her, "Love. I am inspired by love."

"Do you have to be in love to write?" she asks with concern.

"No. The thought of love makes me write. The passion, the heartache, the drama, all of the ups and downs."

After a few more questions, she asks me to wait in the hall. Soon a very distinguished gentleman comes out and shows me around the office. He introduces me to his assistant and she and I go to lunch. After lunch, I head back to the airport to go home. They said I would hear something from them in a couple of weeks.

My driver gets to the airport and as scheduled my plane takes off at 6:30 PM. Looking out the window, I think to myself. Maybe it is not the drama that I crave. Maybe I yearn for the passion of love, the consistency of love's inconsistency. One minute, love can have us swimming in joy; the next we can be drowning in misery. Some people like stability and for that reason, they would rather be alone than to go through the paradox of love. However, I thrive on love's fickle nature. I scramble through my purse to find a pen. On the back of a pamphlet, I begin to write.

Bitter Honey
The taste of it
The sour can make you cry, the sweet can make you
    weep
The taste of it arouses mixed emotions.
Sorrow, joy, pain, bliss on each point of the square
Or rather, the circumference, for this circle is a never-
    ending cycle

Going round and round the cipher
Yet the constant nucleus looks different from each angle.
How could something so beautiful be so ugly?
How could something so sweet be so sour?
How could something so infinite be so finite?
Maybe we all look from different angles.
Maybe we taste different things.
Yet no matter how sour, how ugly, how finite,
some pallets interpret the sweet, the beauty, and the
    infinite vision.
And opposite of the same.
Some float in the flame.
Some swim in the flame
The flame of bitter honey
Not knowing the next taste of love.

When I return home I immediately call Tam to tell her about everything. However, her news is ten times as exciting. She and Stan are getting married and the wedding will be next month. She wants a small ceremony with a few friends and family. I am thrilled, yet shocked. Stan just got divorced and now he wants to marry Tam. I think she is moving too fast and of course I tell her so. However, she assures me that she is happy.

"We don't have forever to get it right. Life is too short. Once we find happiness, we should relish it," she says during our conversation.

"As long as you are happy, I am happy," I say.

I think Tam's accident changed her view on many things. When we see our life flash before our eyes, it makes us realize the preciousness of life. Tam has always been the settling-down type. I only hope Stan is the one.

"Does he give you everything on your grocery list?" I ask.

"Everything, with coupons," she laughs.

* * *

Dick asked that I call him after my interview, so I call him this evening. Although he isn't in, he calls back as soon as he gets the message. I tell him about Tam and Stan and he is just as shocked as I am.

"I don't know if I will ever get married," he confesses.

"Why?" I ask.

"I don't think I will find anyone who can appreciate and understand my needs."

"You are a lot to swallow," I agree.

"I don't care if she swallows as long as she doesn't spit it out on my stomach," he jokes.

"You are so nasty."

"And you love it."

"I do," I admit.

I miss talking to Dick; he is one of a kind. Not my kind, but he's definitely an original.

"Once you get the job, you promise to keep in touch?" Dick says.

If I were to leave, I would like to keep in touch with Dick. But I also had intentions of keeping in touch with my friends from high school and college. It just doesn't happen. We probably keep in touch with one or two people from our teenage and young adult years. It is not done purposely; people grow apart. We find others to fill our needs. I cannot imagine keeping in touch with everyone I said I would keep in touch with over the years. I would never get off my e-mail or telephone.

"Of course I will keep in touch. But I don't have the job yet."

"Did you ever find out how they got your work?" asks Dick.

"No, but I am pretty sure Ro sent them my poetry."

"How are you guys doing?"

"Okay. It's not the same, but he's trying," I admit.

"Well, maybe I can see you in the next week or so."

"Maybe. We'll talk. Peace."

I rush to get off the phone, because I hear Ro pulling up in the driveway. As he walks into the house, I see attitude written all over his face.

"How was your day?"

"How did you get home from the airport yesterday?" Ro inquires.

"I took the train."

"Why didn't you call me? I told you I would pick you up."

"It wasn't a big deal, so I took the train," I repeat.

"Did Dick pick you up?" Ro questions.

"What? No!"

He walks over to the phone and checks the caller ID. Seeing Dick's phone number, Ro starts yelling. I ignore him, go into the bedroom, and close the door. I can still hear him arguing from the other room, so I finally I open the door and yell back.

"I am not still sleeping with Dick!" I slam the door shut.

Minutes later, Ro knocks on the bedroom door.

"What?" I scream through the door.

"Open the door."

"Are you done?" I ask.

"Yes."

I unlock the door and return to the edge of the bed. Standing, he attempts to justify the sudden explosion. Although I pretend to listen, I don't want to hear what he has to say. "Please stop. I'm tired and I want to go to bed."

"Fine. I'll talk to you tomorrow." He walks out, slamming the door behind.

Naturally, the next day at work I receive a dozen flowers with an apology note saying he wants to take me to dinner. He even said I could pick the place, which is a step in the right direction. But it's only a tiny, baby step. Therefore, I decline dinner.

* * *

Next week I receive a letter stating that Hallmark wants me to come out for a second interview. I fly out the following week and stay in Kansas City overnight. It is a nice town. It's not Atlanta, but it offers some nightlife mixed with town and country living. I feel that the interview went well and I am right because the following week Susan calls and offers me the job. Yeah! Unfortunately, it pays five thousand a year less than what I make now. Booo! That's over four hundred less a month. I don't want to lose that much money. However, if I want a career in writing this would be a great move.

Over the next few weeks, Ro and I have a few more dates and a few more arguments. Continuing to bump my head against the wall, I cannot convince Ro that I stopped sleeping with Dick. This is ridiculous. Although I go to lunch with Dick one day this week, there is no way I can tell Ro; he would flip out. Honesty isn't working and lying isn't working. Right now I don't think anything will make our relationship work. As an attempt to clear my mind, Tam and I go to the Blue Room one night. My plans are to go out and enjoy myself with my friend before she becomes a wife and release some energy onto the microphone. The host calls my name around midnight and I get up and read. By the applause, it seems my poem goes over well. Yet as I am walking off the stage, I look over to the left corner and see Ro standing there. Though he refuses to admit it, he is here to ensure that I am not here with Dick. As soon as we get outside, the arguing begins. However, the argument this night is not about Dick, but about my poetry. Failing to realize that my writing is a release for me, Ro insists that I am telling the world our business.

"No one knows what my words are about. Hell, I don't always know," I yell.

Not caring about his temper tantrum, I walk away from the argument. He shouldn't have been sneaking around trying to catch me in a lie. This reunion is going nowhere and I am slowly realizing that although I love Romance, sometimes love just ain't enough.

Stan and Tam's wedding is this weekend and the bachelorette party is tonight. After hours of dancing and wiping the sweat from our glistening, naked entertainment, the girls retreat to Tam's house. We spend the night in order to prepare for the wedding tomorrow. I awake around 8:00 AM and my cell phone starts ringing at eight thirty.

"Where are you?" Ro asks over the receiver.

"I am at Tam's house."

"I thought you were coming home after the party."

"We changed our mind. My clothes for the wedding are here. I will see you at the church."

Just then Tam's doorbell rings. It's Dick. I asked him to come over to bring Tam's wedding gift. In the something old, something new, something borrowed, something blue adage, I am responsible for the new. Hence, I took a picture of her and Stan at the beach and I had it made into a locket. The jeweler didn't have it finished until a day ago. Fortunately, Dick volunteered to pick it up because the place is next to his music studio. Evidently, Ro hears the girls scream Dick's name as Tam opens the door.

"Is Dick over there?" he asks with rage.

Tired of covering up my friendship with Dick, I decide not to lie. After all, I told him that we would remain friends and I am not ashamed of it. I'm not saying I have earned his trust. But if Ro wants to be with me, he must have more conviction in our relationship.

"Yes, he is," I respond.

Suddenly, he slams down the phone down and I am left with nothing but dial tone. He is acting so childish and I am so sick of this back-and-forth relationship. I have said all I can say and I've done all that I am willing to do. It is Ro's turn to decide whether he wants to be with me. Out of frustration, I grab the nearest paper and scribble. While I am writing, Tam hands me the box given to her by Dick. Smiling, I give the box back to her.

"This is for you," I say.

Opening it, Tam begins to cry. In the seven years I have known Tam, I have never seen her cry.

Wiping her tears, she gives me a hug. "I am so happy."

"I see," I say with a soft smile.

It's not I am not happy for Tam. But part of me wishes that I too could be as happy. How could she seize happiness in a matter of months that I haven't been able to capture in two years? I thought I was happy with Ro once, but looking at Tam's expression, I begin to rethink my passing moment of joy. Maybe I was never really happy at all. During this moment of recollection, Tam's doorbell rings. Evelyn goes to the door, then rushes back and whispers, "It's Ro. Should I let him in?"

"No, I'll go outside and talk with him," I say, balling up the poem.

I step into the front yard in an attempt to speak with him in a quiet, adult, manner. However, he is steaming and accuses me of staying the night with Dick.

"I cannot trust you as long as he is still in the picture," he yells.

Although I start quiet, my voice builds by midsentence, and before long I am screaming at the top of my lungs. "I don't even think you could trust me if he were not in the picture. I keep telling you that it is over!"

"I don't believe you!" he yells louder.

"Then why are you here? Leave! I don't care anymore!" I shrill.

"Fuck it!" he says with his teeth clenched together.

I fling the crumpled piece of paper at his feet and storm off. Ro paces back and forth while huffing and puffing as if three pigs were behind the door. Crashing his beer bottle on the concrete, he hops in the car and drives away.

Why is he drinking beer at nine o'clock in the morning? I remember when he didn't drink beer. Has this madness driven him to drink? Whether it has or not, this relationship has become volatile and unhealthy. As I reenter, I hear the girls scurry away from the window. At once, Tam pulls me to the side.

"We need to talk," she says, pulling me into the guest room and closing the door. "What are you doing with your life?" she asks.

"Living day to day," I say sadly, shrugging my shoulders.

"Remember when you asked me what I meant when I said I love you?"

"Yeah, why?"

"Because I love you. I love you. I thought of all the qualities you have and how happy you make me. I looked for those same qualities in my man and I found Stan. You have so much to offer. True, you slip up every now and then, but those mistakes are not always accidents. Please, don't get so caught up focusing on the scenery down the road that you fall in the manhole. My friend, you are a beautiful person and you deserve a beautiful love. I want you to go home tonight, look in the mirror, and find it."

Tam kisses me on the nose, leaves the room, and prepares for her wedding. Teary-eyed, I sit contemplating Tam's words of wisdom. Her company brings me such peace in my world of chaos. Even when I don't, she believes in me and knows that I am a beautiful person. As I sit longer, I realize that she is the one who sent my poetry to Hallmark. Never did I consider Tam, but now I have no doubts. We have a great relationship and I love her so much. Wiping my face, I walk into the bedroom and assist Tam's mom with helping dress her daughter.

* * *

The wedding is beautiful. Tam and Stan are married in a courtyard underneath a peach and white gazebo. Her yellow, peach, and white tulips surround the couple as they say their own vows. Tam's off-white, vintage wedding gown is both elegant and stunning. Made from Victorian lace, it has a fitted strapless body and a tiny bolero jacket made of raw silk. The soft silk below the waist is cut on the bias; consequently it glides slightly against her body as she floats down the aisle. She looks like a queen, which is perfect, because she is.

The reception is inside a 1950s-era scenic ballroom. I didn't notice Ro once during the wedding. Nonetheless, at the reception, he quickly discerns me through the crowd and politely asks me to join him at his table. Hand in hand we walk, then sit alone at a table for six. As I eat a piece of cake, we make no eye contact. Thus, we have become one of those couples I remember seeing in the restaurant. We do things together because it is what is expected, but we no longer enjoy it. He knows it and I know it. Yet we won't admit it to each other.

"Why can't we promise to grow old together like Stan and Tam did today?" he says.

Slowly removing the fork from my mouth, I look him straight in the eye and speak. "Because we stopped growing a long time ago."

Ro pauses and looks to the ceiling as if he is recalling an old memory. Although his head stays lifted, he focuses his eyes on me.

"I was once told that anything that is not growing is dead," he murmurs.

I glance over at Tam and Stan as they make their way to dance floor. My heart putties as they dance for the first time as husband and wife. Turning my attention back to Ro, I whisper, despondently, "Exactly."

I slide my chair away from the table, slowly rise, and begin to walk away. Ro grabs my hand in an attempt to make me turn around. I stand still, but I know not to look back.

"If you leave now, that's it. It is over. We can't be friends, we can't be anything. You and I will be no more," he says as I tightly wrap my pinky around his.

I long to stay, and simultaneously I know I must leave. My esophagus blackened from the large lump of coal in my throat, I can't swallow. I know Ro is a man of his word and he has said many things. Never has he said it was over and I am positive his words are very earnest. Inhaling a deep breath, I slowly unwrap my finger from within his and walk away. Saying good-bye to Stan, I lean over and kiss Tam on the cheek.

"Are you okay?" she whispers as I nod yes.

When I get home, I hurry inside to gel with my comfort zone, the futon. Lifting up my skirt, I sit Indian style while propping up my head with my elbows resting on both knees. Feeling a drop of wetness hit my ankle, I weep an involuntary cry. I stretch out onto the cushion, as my legs start to tingle from the numbness. Like a contortionist, I move throughout twenty positions attempting to be comfortable. Yet I find no comfort, because my heart aches, and no matter the position I succumb to, the knife wound deepens. This stabbing pain increases with every breath and I cannot sleep. This night, my futon and I mourn the death of my relationship with Romance and the night seems to never end. Finally, I see the sun peering in through my curtains as I sluggishly rise and make my way to the bathroom. Still in my attire from the night before, I look at my fatigued body in the oval mirror."

Thank God, I don't feel as bad as I look," I say to my reflection.

Then, out of the blue, a smile appears and I know I am going to be just fine. I blow myself a kiss, run my fingers through my hair, and trot away from that broken-down image. More than ever, my body could use an apple, peach smoothie.

As I blend, I flip through my letters on the bar and once again read my letter from Hallmark. Without hesitation, I pick up the phone and leave a message for Ms. Susan Wright. Guess what? I am moving to Kansas City.

Although I have several projects to finish, the final two weeks at my job breeze by. However, it's moving weekend and I have packed only one room. I sell most of my furniture. Actually, I sell all of the furniture except for the futon. I need a new start and with it come new things. But the futon and I are one. Parting with it is like—well, it's too painful to think about. Therefore, along with the futon, I decide to keep my books, my grandmother's dishes, my favorite teddy bear, my Bose stereo, and of course my 345 CDs. Everything else can go and quickly it does. My friends come over to pick through my unwanted belongings, and the rest can go to charity. Tam, Stan, and a few of his friends come over to help me pack the truck and I am ready to move. Sitting centrally in the floor of my empty apartment, I gaze at the space. It is amazing how much larger a place feels when all of the clutter is gone. Much like life, clutter makes you feel crowded and heavy. Every now and then, we need an emotional spring-cleaning. My purification is happening this summer. Placing my blanket in the center of my floor, I lie down. As I am about to close my eyes, there is a knock on my door.

"Who is it?" I yell.

"Open it up and see," says the voice.

It sounds like Dick. I press my ear to the door, but I stay silent.

"It's Dick, open up," he continues.

"Prove it," I yell through the door.

"Okay, stick your coochie out the window."

Flinging open the door, I gasp at his crudeness. "You are such a pervert!" I roar.

"You know I am not going to let you leave town without saying good-bye."

"So you just stopped by. What if Ro was over here?" I ask with my hands defensively placed on both hips.

"It wouldn't stop me from saying good-bye. But it would change how I would like to say good-bye . . . if you know what I mean." He flirts, trying to lift my oversized T-shirt.

Yielding to temptation, I turn and invite him in. "Come on in."

He grabs a large basket from beside the door and hands it to me. "This is for you."

Setting the basket on my blanket, I unwrap the purple tissue paper only to find all of my favorite things—lavender, oatmeal almond soap, herbal teas, and rain-scented candles. It even contains Mac lipstick in Photo, my favorite shade.

"I know you pay attention to detail, but I am impressed," I say with a smirk.

At the bottom of the basket I see a small pink box.

"What's this?" I ask, shaking the box.

"Stop shaking it and open it."

I open the box, filled with panties; four pairs of tiny, colorful, cotton panties. Sure, satin panties may seem sexier to some, but Dick knows I am a cotton girl. Satin underwear never stays in place. I give a quirky smile as I speak. "What possessed you to buy me panties?"

Grinning like a sneaky Cheshire cat, Dick gets up and walks back to my cracked, open door. Reaching outside the door, he comes back in with a larger box. Displaying a hearty laugh, he hands me the box. Like a child on Christmas morning, I instantaneously begin unwrapping.

"Well, you must have something to wear with your new dresses," says Dick.

Inside the box are the four, previously admired, designer dresses, and of course, the panties perfectly match each dress.

"I cannot stand you!" I say, hitting him on the shoulder.

"I want you to go to your new job in style."

Smelling of scented oils, I soak in every drop of his manhood as I hold him close. Neither of us wants to let go. Thus, we grip tighter as minutes pass.

"I swear if you were not a big, sex pervert, you would be Mr. Right," I jest.

"We are who we are. I am going to miss you, Lily," he whispers.

Squeezing my shoulders in his hands, Dick leans over and gives me a quick peck on the forehead, a longer peck on the nose, and a full passionate smack on the lips.

Woozy from his fervent affection, I speak softly. "I will miss you too."

"Yeah, yeah. You will forget all about me in a few months," he jokes.

"Never. Mr. Will Dickson, I want you to know that you will always be remembered as my favorite Dick."

Laughing together, we embrace one last time. The next morning I get in my truck, fondly, wave bye to my old life, and welcome my new one. Hello, Kansas City.

Good morning.

Chapter 13

A New Beginning

Thankfully, I do not have to report to work until next week. Although I am staying in the corporate apartment, I hope to find my own place within a couple of weeks. A few of the girls from my new job come by on my third night in town and ask me out to a jazz club. I despise going out with people I don't know, but I accept their invitation because I don't want to be rude. It's funny how people usually put on the nice face when you first meet them, especially in corporate America. For example these women come to the apartment, like the three wise men, bearing welcoming gifts, smiling and laughing as if they want to be my best friend. If they saw me out in the club, or in the grocery store or even in church, they probably wouldn't speak. Instead, they would look me up and down, secretly comment about my wardrobe, and wonder where I bought my fabulous shoes. They would not ask where, for that would be too gratifying; they would just wonder. It's so stupid. Why are women afraid to compliment each other? I compliment women all the time and they stare in question, as if to say, What does she want? or What is she

up to? I am not up to anything. If you look nice, I like to compliment you. Women get so many crass remarks from men
that they should enjoy a pleasing remark from someone who
wants nothing in return. But that's just how I see it.

Anyway, I meet my new "coworker friends" at the hottest
jazz spot in town. Packed with affluent society who love to
flaunt their wealth and middle-class workers who love to pretend, this has to be the most bourgeois place I have ever set
foot in. As I unintentionally make horrendous faces to display
my discontentment, it is apparent I despise flaunting. Along
with name-dropping, it is one of my greatest pet peeves. Continuing to look around the room, I notice that everyone is
adorned with designer clothing, designer jewelry, and/or designer accessories. This jazz club could double as a big trunk
show. I waltz to the table, have a seat with the girls, and attempt to mingle. The first topic of conversation is the new
collection from Manolo Blahnik. I don't believe it, I am at a
table full of Evelyns and we all know how I feel about her.
Boy, do I miss Tam! However, if this is my new life, I should
try to fit in. I'll make a stab to change the conversation.

"Do you ladies go to poetry readings?"

"We used to a couple of years ago. It was a fad," says
Reisa, my coworker.

"We come here 'cause things like jazz never go out of
style," says Coral, who works in my department.

"Are you saying poetry is a fad?" I ask.

"No, but listening to people perform poetry onstage is very
passé. They still have a poetry night at a spot in the city, but
only hippies, gypsies, and struggling artists hang out there.
Most of them don't work, but love to complain about the
system," Coral continues while giggling with her girls.

I see that I am going to get along real well with these girls,
I say underneath my sarcastic grunt.

Coral sounds like an imbecile. Unaware of her ignorant remarks, she gives Reisa a high five as if she has just spoken

brilliance. An uncontrollable force, within the bowels of my stomach propels me to debate.

"So what constitutes a fad?" I question.

"You know. Things that are hot for the meantime, but lose their thunder after a few months," she says with a gaze that questions my intellect.

"But what makes fads hot? Who determines 'the hot thing' for the moment?" I continue.

She pauses and looks at her girls, who look confusingly back at her. Then Coral speaks. "We do," she says with confidence.

Now, I could leave it alone, but again, my gut will not allow me to let it go. She doesn't determine a damn thing. She is a commercial ho. Her pimps are Fashion Television, Hollywood, and MTV. If she sees it on the runway, she buys it. If the stars are doing it, she does it. If MTV plays it, she listens. They are the powers that be. They determine "the hot thing" in her world. There is nothing wrong with a trend-follower, but it differs from a trendsetter and I will continue to debate until she admits that she is not the latter. Therefore, I persist.

"I heard that lavender is the new color for the summer," I say.

Making a horrid face, Reisa replies, "Where did you hear that?"

"I believe it was on the fashion channel," I continue.

"Well, whites and off-whites are the colors for the summer. I just went to Neiman's and got several outfits in ecru and white. No one is wearing lavender. Plums were two years ago," Coral vaunts with concurring remarks from her peanut gallery.

"Why did you buy whites?" I ask curiously.

"Because it is what everyone is wearing this summer."

"So it's the 'hot thing' for the moment?" I ask.

"Right," she says.

"And you decided that, right?" I ask with sarcasm.

"What do you mean?"

She knows what I mean; she just wants to play dumb.

"I mean, you and your friends had a council and decided that whites and off-whites were the perfect colors for this summer."

Coral says nothing, but her facial expression says it all. I giggle quietly to myself as the girls swiftly change the subject of conversation. My point has been made. Now I guess I can see what the rest of this club has to offer. I mingle away from the table the remainder of the evening. Thank God I decided to drive, because I am leaving as soon as I finish overhearing stock tips from table number five.

I call Tam immediately when I arrive home. I know it's late, but she must hear about my entertaining evening. She laughs as I tell her about my new pseudo girlfriends, Coral, Megan, and Reisa. It's only been a few days, but it is so comforting to hear her voice.

"I saw Dick today," she tells me.

"Where?"

"I ran into him at the bank. He asked if I had heard from you. He said he is coming to see you once you get settled."

"No, he can't come here. This is my new life. I cannot drag my old baggage into my new life."

"Oh well, you better tell him that. I have to go to bed. My husband is calling me. Call me next week once you start work. Love you."

"Love you too."

It's so funny how she drags out the word *husband*. It must be a newlywed thing. Her voice revels in bliss. Sitting on my blanket, I look through my pictures. I stare for minutes at a picture of Dick and me at the beach. Finally I rouse from my daze, kiss the picture, and lay it on top of the pile. Stretching out on my blanket, I go to sleep.

* * *

Monday morning comes and wouldn't you know it: I oversleep. I have to rush to get to work so that I won't arrive late. I jump in the shower and quickly jump out. Having no time to think about breakfast, I throw on my dress and head to work. The corporate apartment is only a few miles from the job, so I can still make it on time. Huffing and puffing, I come to a burdensome four-way stop. Although this concept is simple—people sit at the stop sign for minutes, looking at the car opposite them waiting to see who will go first—it's asinine. Finally, it's my turn and I have ten more minutes before I am officially late. I drive another mile and get stuck behind a tourist going seven miles an hour.

"What is he doing?" I yell.

I have to go around him. Just then the car behind me attempts to go around both of us and clips the tail end of my truck.

"*Damnit!*" I yell.

We pull over to the side of the road. Steaming mad, I hop from my truck and start cursing. "What in the hell were you doing?"

A stocky gentleman gets out of his car, rushes over to my door, and asks, "Are you okay?"

I begin rolling out words so fast, I sound as if I'm fluently speaking a foreign language. "No, because of you I am going to be late for work on my first day. You saw me trying to go around the slow car. Were you not paying attention?"

His cell phone rings. Accordingly, he turns his back to me and places his right hand in the air, motioning me to silence.

He has some nerve, I say under my breath.

While on the phone, he walks around the back of my truck and looks at the damage. I jump back into the truck and call the office to inform them of what has happened. My boss's

assistant, Sarah, comes to the accident to make sure everything is okay. We sit in her car until the police arrive.

"Thanks for coming."

"No problem, anything to get away from the office," she
comments with laughter.

Sarah is adorable. She is five-two, 115 pounds with
strawberry-blond hair. She is from Louisville, Kentucky,
but she has the attitude of a New York City girl. She doesn't
wear much makeup, but her eyebrows are perfectly arched
and her hair is short and sassy. The few times I have seen
her, she has been in a sharp business pantsuit, but today she
is in a red linen dress.

"Is that the guy who hit you?" she says, pointing.

"That's him. He has been on that stupid phone since the accident."

"He's cute." Sarah beams.

I glance over at his profile. "He's all right."

Once the police arrive, we get out of the car and exchange
information. The officer advises us to go the hospital for insurance purposes, but we both decline. As he hands us our
papers, the driver hands me his card. Taking it, I read it aloud.
"Mr. Wealth Fulmore. Real Estate Investor with Hampshire
and Fulmore Realtors."

"I'm sorry I hit you. My insurance will cover everything,"
he says.

"It sure will," I add.

We both laugh. As he leans back against his car, I notice
that he has a beautiful smile.

"Well, aren't you sorry you yelled at me?"

"No. You still made me late for work."

"Where do you work?" inquires Mr. Fulmore.

"Hallmark. Today is my first day."

"Are you in marketing?"

"No, creative development. I'm a writer," I say with enthusiasm.

Again, his cell phone rings and he excuses himself to answer it. While he is on the phone, I check out his attire. Wearing a beautiful, tailor-made, slate-gray suit, he stands close to six feet with very broad shoulders. I'm positive his suit is tailor-made because with his athletic build, that sort of garment could not have come off the rack. Quickly, he hangs up as I pretend to look the other way.

"So, you are from Georgia?" he says, looking at my tag.

"Not originally, but yes."

"Well, I take it you are new in town. If you are looking for a place to live, call me."

I look at his card once again and place it within the police report. Winking at me, he adds, "Even if you are not looking for a place to live, call me."

"I have to go to work," I respond curtly.

While walking away, I look back over my shoulder to discover he is watching me stroll while leaning against the hood of his car. I knew I shouldn't have looked back. Men tend to think women are interested when they look back. I don't want him to think I am at all interested, because I'm certainly not. I lean into Sarah's window, tell her everything is cool and that I will follow her down the street to work. Walking back to my truck, I wave bye to Mr. Fulmore and drive off.

Although the day starts disastrously, my workday goes well. I meet the other team members in my department. Surprisingly, seven of them are men, only two are women. Most of the day, I fill out paperwork, and the next thing I know, it is time to go home. I stop to buy fast food on the way in. This once a month habit has become daily since I moved here. I can't get used to this corporate apartment. I'm not comfortable cooking in the kitchen or sleeping in the bed. I must find a place to live this week. As I am browsing through the classifieds, my phone rings. It must be Tam; only she and my mother have this number and I spoke with my mom earlier.

"Hello."

"Hi, beautiful."

"Dick!" I say with zeal.

"Well, well, you sound happy," he says.

"It is so good to hear from you. I miss you."

I didn't mean to blurt that out. I do miss him, but I don't want to give him any ideas.

"You have been on my mind as well and it's good to hear your voice," he says.

"So, how have you been?" I ask.

"Lonely."

"Not you. All of the women chase after Dick."

"Maybe. But the one I want runs away from me. What should I do?"

"Give her a little time, perhaps she'll come around," I say, playing along.

"What if in time she forgets about me?"

"I am sure that won't happen."

"I hope not. What are you wearing?" asks Dick.

"A tank top and the blue pair of the panties you bought me."

"Do me a favor. Take off the panties and tell me how it feels when you touch yourself."

"Dick!" I scream.

"What? Okay, I'll talk first."

He begins telling me in great detail how wonderful it would feel if I were gently putting his very erect manhood inside me. He continues with vivid imagination as he moves me about the bed, the bathroom, and the kitchen, changing positions a dozen times, but culminating between numbers sixty-eight and seventy.

"Are you coming?" I ask innocently.

"All over your body," he moans.

"No, no. Stop it! I mean for real, not for play-play."

"Of course I am. That is the purpose of phone sex."

"Well, I am a phone sex virgin. I like in-person sex."

"I can be there this weekend," Dick hurriedly comments.

"No, Dick. I can't keep seeing you. We are just friends, re-member?"

"I remember. But promise me this. Take a bubble bath tonight and while you are in the tub, touch your body in some way that you have never touched your body before and think of me while you're doing this."

"Okay, Dick," I say with a sheepish giggle.

"Are you going to do it?"

"Perhaps. Good-bye, Dick." I hurry to hang up.

I fall back onto the futon, sighing. That Dick is crazy. I cannot believe he called me to have phone sex. He didn't even ask; he just did it. You're not supposed to sneak in an orgasm in phone conversation. He is—I begin to laugh—hilarious. I really miss him. Sexually, we are on different levels, but he is such a great person. As I scribble his name over and over on my notepad, I think about what life would be like with him. Next thing I know, my pad is covered in his name and it looks like something a teenager in love would do during science class. Placing my book on my dresser, I go into the bathroom and look through my box of toiletries to retrieve the bubble bath. Maybe I will take Dick up on his request. I draw my bathwater and sit in the bath filled with scented bubbles. Leaning my head back against a rolled towel, I close my eyes. Picturing Dick, I replay our moments at the beach. I can't quite recall all of my thoughts, so we'll just say I have an ex-tremely pleasant bath. As I stretch out for the evening, I can't get rid of the stupid grin on my face. Miles away, Dick still has a fascinating effect on my temperament. I anticipate his laughter as I tell him about my bath. I am sure to sleep well tonight.

Good night.

Chapter 14

Healing Takes Time

My boss teams me up with Dale, a laid-back Californian. He has been very resourceful so far and I think we will work well together. Although it's only been a week, Sarah seems to be the only person I bond with. Therefore, before the day is over, she and I make plans to go to the movies. Since she lives close to the job, she offers to pick me up. Although our arrival is fifteen minutes before the movie starts, it's Friday night and the lines are extremely long.

"If we wait in this long line, we will miss the beginning of the movie," I tell Sarah.

She stands there for a minute, looking at the people in the line. Suddenly, her eyes light up, she tugs on my ponytail, and whispers with excitement, "I have a plan. Stay right here." She bolts out of line.

"What is she up to?" I whisper.

Watching her walk to the front, I see her speak with a few guys at the front of the ticket line. She talks with them for a minute when one of the guys turns around and I see that it is

Mr. Wealth Fulmore. I wonder what she is saying to him. Briefly hugging him, she comes back to join me in line.

"Come on, let's go," she says while pulling my arm.

"Are we leaving?"

"No, we are going to the movie. The guys got our tickets with theirs. That's the guy from your accident."

"I know. What did you say to him?"

"I told him we were going to miss the movie unless he was kind enough to purchase our tickets and I handed him the money. Of course he didn't take it. He said it would be his pleasure on one condition."

"Which is?" I ask with great hesitation.

"If we would sit with them in the movie."

With a frown on my face, Sarah pulls me from the line and pushes me toward the men. As we approach, I see them nod and comment quietly to themselves with small chuckles. Robert and Omar, Wealth's friends, walk in with Sarah. Wealth and I follow.

"Thanks for getting the tickets," I say.

"No problem. I am glad that I get to see you again. Would you like anything to eat or drink?" Wealth offers.

"No, thanks . . . I take that back. I want some chocolate."

We catch up with our party and take a seat in the movie theater. Wealth sits to my right, Sarah sits to my left, and Robert and Omar sit the left of Sarah, with one seat in between them due to high levels of machismo. I keep my eyes straight ahead, flicking Sarah on the ear as we sit.

"Sit down, enjoy the movie. You know you like him," she whispers.

I lean and speak into her ear. "I do not like him."

The movie begins and we sit in silence for the next hour. As I become uncomfortable in my seat, I place my hands on the armrest to move around. However, my hand graces the top of Wealth's arm.

"I'm sorry," I whisper.

He nods and moves his hand. Unfortunately, he moves it to my leg. Therefore, I easily slide my leg from underneath his hand and cross it over my other leg. Looking at me, he smiles as he licks his bottom lip. I give a brisk smile in return, keeping my lips taut. Sarah is right. He is cute. Then again, it's probably the dim lights.

After the movie, the three guys walk us to the car where we stand for a few minutes saying good-bye. Wealth pauses in silence. Then, with his well-manicured hands, he lifts my face to his. "Allow me to take you to dinner."

Lowering my face, I sigh. Wealth seems nice, but I don't want to go out with him. Frankly, I don't want to go out with anyone. I came to Kansas City to work, write, and relax. "It's really bad timing."

"Well, if dinner is too much of a commitment, at least let me take you to lunch. You have to eat lunch."

"She sure does and she gets a whole hour," interrupts Sarah.

"Well, aren't you in my business?" I say to her.

Snarling at her remark, I glimpse over at Wealth, who is waiting on my answer. The pressure is on and I suppose lunch will not hurt.

"Okay, lunch. I'll call you," I say to Wealth.

Thanking him again for the evening, I enfold my arms around his body before we leave. As soon as I get in the car, Sarah starts teasing. "I knew it! I knew you liked him."

"I am only going to lunch because I didn't know what to say. I do not like him. I don't want to be involved with any men right now. I am just getting over my last relationship."

"Please, life is too short to turn down dates. Go to lunch and have fun. It's not like he asked you to Cancún and you better call him," demands Sarah.

"I will. Now take me home."

* * *

I get into my stuffy apartment and sit on my futon. Leaning my head against the armrest, I wonder what Ro is doing. I wonder if he is turning down dates due to the pain of his last relationship. He's probably not. Honestly, I hope he is dating. He definitely deserves happiness, the kind of bliss I was unable to give him. He's a good man; it's too bad he's not the man for me. Finding myself in awe of my sincerity, I think to myself, *Does this mean I am over him?* Amazing, there was a time I thought I couldn't live without him. Isn't growth a remarkable concept?

"I am over Romance. I am over him!" I shout throughout the room.

Suddenly, I halt in my steps.

"I may never see him again," I say with devastation.

Glum, I collapse within the same spot I just celebrated my triumph. Overflowing with simultaneous joy and sorrow, I roll over onto my fleece blanket, take the neatly stacked pictures, and haphazardly spread them on the floor. Moving aside the pictures with Ro, I place them in order by month and year. Changing my mind, I put them in order according to emotions. The first picture of us is at Tam's wedding, when I finally realized it was over. The middle pictures are when we were head over heels in love. Whatever that phrase means. And the final pictures are when we were just friends. I speak aloud as I attempt to puzzle the pieces of my last four years with him.

I sit motionless, truly not knowing whether to laugh or cry. Therefore, I'll just close my eyes and go to sleep.

Good night.

Chapter 15

It's Only Lunch

I guess I am into the swing of things because, as in Atlanta, Friday and Monday seem to run concurrently. The weekends seem nonexistent. Arriving at work early Monday, I get to my desk and read the neon Post-it left by Sarah. "I enjoyed the movie, let's do it again. Sarah."

While putting my things away, I call her. "I got your sweet message. But you could have shortened it down to 'Call Wealth.' Because that's all you wanted to say."

She giggles in her girly high-pitched octave. "No, I really did have fun. I don't click with many people in the office. I'm glad you're here."

"That's sweet, now go ahead and say what you really want to say," I tease.

"Girl, what time are you going to call him?"

"Around noon tomorrow."

"Tomorrow!"

"I have things to do. I am not calling him today."

"Whatever. I'll talk to you later."

I place the receiver down just as my project partner, Dale, walks up.

"You ready to get to work?" asks Dale with great enthusiasm.

"I sure am."

We walk into a small, beige and red conference room and start creating. The rest of my day is spent with Dale working on our presentation. Although we have until Friday, we both agree to have it completed by Wednesday. We are working on a new line of children's greeting cards. Although neither of us has children, we both have a very juvenile spirit. Dale is a joy to work with and I hope the rest of my projects happen this effortlessly. We part at the end of the workday with a solid foundation. Two more days and we should have a presentation well worth a pay increase. I know it's a little soon, but there is nothing wrong with a little wishful thinking. By Wednesday, Dale and I are bonding about anything and everything. He agrees to take Sarah and me to the poetry spot downtown. I guess Dale is one of the hippies Coral mentioned earlier. Come to think of it, he does wear sandals and khakis every day, but that's okay with me. At least he is not shallow, like some of my coworkers. For example, I get nothing but a closed-mouth fake smile from Coral and Megan whenever we pass in the hall. Hell, they don't even speak to Sarah unless they need some sort of administrative duty.

Social class structure is apparent everywhere we look. The executives do not hang with the administrators. The blue collars don't eat with the white collars. This is just like high school, when the cool kids couldn't be seen with the not-so-cool kids. From birth until death, we jump from one group to another, attempting to fit in. I presume we can't help it. The desire to be accepted is a glitch in our DNA. But everything must be done in moderation. Once we change who we are and what we stand for in exchange for approval, there needs to be some serious self-reflection.

As I sit in deep meditation at my desk, Sarah walks up

behind me and spins my chair around. "What are you doing for lunch?"

"I don't know."

"Well, I know. You are going to lunch with Wealth. He's on line one."

"What? Did you call him?"

"No, Omar called and asked me on a date. He mentioned that you had not called Wealth and so I told him to tell Wealth to call you. Hurry, pick up."

Anticipating my conversation, Sarah takes a seat on the corner of my desk as I pick up and speak with Wealth. Our conversation is short and sweet.

"I see I had to track you down," he says.

"I've been busy."

"Busy playing hard to get," Wealth continues.

"Ha, ha. Are we on for lunch today?" I ask.

"Meet me at Friday's, down the street."

"See you at one."

I look up at Sarah, after I place down the receiver.

"Finally! He's cute, he's rich, and he's persistent. What more do you want?" she asks.

Sarah pats my back as I sigh, slumping over onto my desk. As my mind replays her question, I shrug my shoulders. Who knows what I want? I need time to rebuild my energy. I left so much of it in Atlanta that I came here on empty.

"Hold up, did you say he is rich? How do you know?" I ask.

"Omar told me. Well, he didn't say those exact words. He actually said Wealth is an ex–professional football player. He started a real estate company and he only closes on homes starting at a half million or more."

"Well, he should have a nice nest egg," I say with surprise.

"And you, little birdie, are about to miss out on it."

Sarah gets up and walks away. She gets a couple of feet

from my desk, whips around, and winks as she comments, "And he has a big dick."

Gasping with surprise, I give her a puzzled look.

Sarah continues. "Did you see him in those jeans the other night? Trust me. I am never wrong about these things."

She whips back around and walks down the hall. I laugh, watching her twist down the corridor in a floral printed skirt. To be a country girl from Kentucky, she sure has a lot of sass. The funny thing is, she's probably correct. Wealth looks like he has a big dick. But if only Sarah knew, I have had enough dick to last me a lifetime. I am going to lunch with this man and that is it.

I walk into the restaurant where the hostess immediately greets me and shows me to the table where Wealth is waiting. Standing and giving me a cordial hug, he extends his hand for me to sit.

"You look very pleasant today," he initiates.

"Thanks, you don't look too bad yourself."

The server comes to the table and takes my drink order. Wealth taps my hand and comments, "I already put in an order of appetizers."

"But you don't know what I want."

"That is why I ordered the combo. It's a little of everything."

He arrogantly winks and smiles. I can tell he is used to women following behind him and answering to his every call, and I am not about to be one of them. He is a charmer and his personality is cute, but not enough to win me over. Despite the occasional caressing of my arm, our conversation during lunch is very professional. We talk about career goals, dream jobs, and corporate America. Wealth varies the conversation, however, with an interesting question.

"If you could remove one of your character flaws, which would it be?"

I sit perplexed, suddenly feeling as though I am in an interview. I'd like to liberate a couple of my flaws. Silently, I think to myself. Which one should I start with?

"Go through the list and pick one," Wealth adds, laughing. Is he reading my mind?

"I am trying to go through the list as fast as I can. I don't have *that* many. Let's see, I find it difficult to focus on one thing for long periods of time, because I bore easily. That is the flaw I would remove first."

"Interesting. Does that boredom cross into your personal world or is it strictly professional?"

"Both," I say. "What about you? Which flaw would you remove?"

"Oh, I have no flaws," he says, grinning as he sips on his lemonade.

Sure he laughs, but I can tell by his placid expression that he truly believes he is flawless.

"Besides, you can't ask me the same question. You have to ask me a different question."

"Fine. What is one personality trait you lack, that you would like to attain?"

Closing his eyes, Wealth thinks for close to thirty seconds. He opens his eyes and speaks. "I don't know if you consider this a personality trait. However, I am never satisfied with myself. I always either want more or feel as though I could do a better job. Therefore, I am never content, hence I am never at peace."

"Professional or personal?" I ask.

"Both."

I look at Wealth with a small grin and he smiles. He has beautiful teeth and I like a man with pretty teeth. We gaze at each other in silence for the last minute of lunch. Finally glancing at my watch, I realize it is time to go back to work. Wealth stands and escorts me out to my rental car, for my truck is still in the body shop.

"I thank you for a wonderful lunch."

"Thanks for joining me," Wealth says as he opens his arms for a hug.

Giving him a brief hug, I turn and get into the car. Wealth leans into the window and hands me a paper.

"What is this?"

"I know you are still looking for a place to live. I circled some things you may be interested in. Some of the properties are for sale and some are for rent. Let me know what you want. I would love to help."

"I'll call you," I say, facing forward while placing my shades on.

"We'll see."

As Wealth steps away from the car, he leans his head to the left and blows me a slow-motion kiss with his index and middle fingers. He remains in that pose until his hand is down by his side. It reminds me of something from *Casablanca*— classic and nostalgic yet at the same time very tacky and out of place. I don't know about Mr. Wealth Fulmore. There is something attractive about him. Still, he is not my type. However, I am going to call him about finding a town house, because I cannot stand the corporate apartment too much longer.

I stop to see Sarah on my way to my desk. Her eyes light up with excitement as I lean on the corner of her chair to give her the details of my lunch.

"Did you have fun?" she bursts with energy.

"Oh yeah! We skipped lunch and went to my place for a quickie. You are right, he does have a big thing," I say with a serious tone.

Sarah's eyes widen as her mouth flings open. "You are joking!"

"No, I'm serious. I wanted to do him, so I did and it was good. We may even do it again tomorrow."

Sarah doesn't know what to say. I can tell that she

doesn't completely believe me, but she is wondering what really happened.

"I'll give you more details after work," I say, leaving her puzzled.

Before I can get to my desk, my phone is ringing.

"Did you really do it with him?" she whispers eagerly.

"Girl, *no*! We had lunch and I came back to work. He's a nice guy, but not my type."

"You scared me. I was starting to believe you. I'll talk to you later."

She is hilarious and I love her energy. Sarah is the type of girlfriend that doesn't pass judgment; one with whom I can have candid conversations. If I had slept with Wealth, she would have accepted it and asked for details, a girl after my own heart. I finally get back into work and before I realize it, it's time to go.

After work, I stop by the market to pick up the classifieds and a rental magazine. I go home and spread all of the papers on the floor. Grabbing my highlighter, I begin circling the ads. There are so many properties to rent, but I may want to buy. This weekend, I want to visit several townhome communities in the area. I glance over at the papers given to me by Wealth. At the top of the paper, he scribbled his cell phone number in red ink and so I decide to give him a call. He picks up his phone on the first ring.

"Wealth Fulmore, may I help you?"

"Greetings, Mr. Fulmore. I am looking over these papers you gave me and I want to see some of these properties."

"Excuse me, who is this?"

"You wreck my truck, fondle my leg at the theater, harass me at work, then attempt to woo me at lunch. If you do this to all women, you must never have time for work."

Wealth bursts into laughter. "Well, well, I am surprised to hear from you. What properties do you want to see?"

We go over the properties and come up with a list of five.

He agrees to pick me up early Saturday morning to view each one. I don't bother with small talk. Thus, after I give him directions to the apartment, we hang up minutes later. I start to gather the papers and walk into the kitchen to pour a glass of tea when the phone rings.

"Yes, hello," I answer.

"Hi, lady, it's Wealth. I have a question to ask you."

"What's up?"

"I have an occasion I must attend Saturday evening—"

"You want to reschedule?" I interrupt.

"No. I want you to be my date."

"I don't know," I hesitate.

"Look, we can spend the day looking at townhomes and spend the evening dancing under the stars."

"The event is outside?" I ask.

"It's at the home of one of my associates. He has a big party this time every year. Most of the activities and dancing take place in the back by the pool. You will enjoy yourself and you will meet some new folks. Important people, the kind of people you need to meet."

Biting my bottom lip, I think about it for a moment and then I agree it won't hurt to get out and meet new people. "Okay, I'll go."

"Good, so I will see you Saturday morning."

After we disconnect, I think about Wealth's comment. He said the party would be filled with important people, the kind I need to meet. What does he mean by important people? Are these the type of people with drivers waiting for them at the airport? I guess I will have to wait and see. Sarah is going to flip tomorrow when I tell her. I pour a glass of tea and walk back into the living area. Turning on the television, I quickly flip through the channels as I sit on the blanket. I am not a big TV watcher, but I am glad this apartment has cable. There is an old Bette Davis movie on channel 32, cooking on 33, and a commercial on 34. After the station break, perhaps there is something on worth watching. I walk to the bathroom to retrieve my nail file. As I am walking back to my blanket, I hear the voice of Billy Dee Williams.

"Could this be?" I say aloud. "It is, it is *Mahogany*!" I squeal. "I adore this movie."

Diana Ross radiates elegance and Billy Dee is the essence of debonair in this film. I plop down in front of the tube to watch the picture and sing along while filing my nails. After the movie, I lie down on the blanket and begin dreaming about Billy Dee. I know it's a movie, but where is my Billy Dee? Are they only on television?

I know, I know, it's silly. Besides, he's probably looking for Diana Ross. Good luck and . . .

Good night.

Chapter 16

We All Deserve a Little Color in Our Wardrobe

I see Sarah first thing in the morning, but before I can tell her about the date, she blurts out, "What are you going to wear?"

"Damn, news travels at the speed of light around here."

It seems Wealth informed Omar and he informed Sarah. She has gotten over the excitement of me saying yes and has moved into the arena of my attire for the evening.

"We have to go shopping."

"Shopping for what?" interrupts Reisa as she walks up to Sarah's desk.

"Aren't you nosy?" I say, turning around.

"No, just curious."

Sarah leans across her desk to tell Reisa about my date. She loves to brag. She doesn't care if it is not about her as long as it is someone she likes. "She is going to a big gala on Saturday night with one of the top Realtors in the city."

"You are going to the Whitney party?" Reisa asks with a hint of surprise.

Reisa turns to Sarah to explain the Whitney gala. I really despise the smug of arrogance when she talks.

"John Whitney throws a big party every year, the last weekend of June for the Realtors' association." She turns back to me and says, "I'll be there. Maybe I'll see you?"

Taking the stack of papers from Sarah's desk, she walks away. Sarah and I look at each other. Nothing has to be said; we hear each other's thoughts.

"I'll see you later today. Maybe we can shop tomorrow after work."

Hastily, my day progresses; therefore I fail to see Sarah the remainder of the day. I go home after work and give myself a pedicure. I have never been one to go to the salon and let others pick and file at my feet. Women seem to enjoy it, but I don't. It is personal and more relaxing to do it myself. I polish my toes in a neutral color, because I don't know what color dress I'll find tomorrow. I wish I could call off work and shop all day. It has been so long since I have dressed up and gone to a semiformal event that I am actually keyed up.

The next morning at work, Sarah and I make plans to leave around 3:00 PM and go shopping. However, I get a call around noon to meet her at her desk. As I approach, I see Sarah flirting with a cute delivery guy. She signs for the package and hands it to me.

"What is this?" I ask.

"It's a package for you," she says, shrugging her shoulders.

I set the box on her desk and open it up. It is a sexy, burnt-orange dress with spaghetti straps and extra fabric that criss-crosses at the bustline. I remove the dress and hold it up to my body. Sarah grabs the card out of the box and reads it aloud.

"I look forward to Saturday. With your complexion and your body, you are going to look fabulous in this dress. See you soon, Wealth."

"Do you like the dress?" I ask Sarah.

"I think it's nice," she states.

"I don't know. I want to wear a dark color. I don't do orange."

"Orange will look good on you. Everyone is going to be in a dark color. This will make you stand out."

"Exactly, I don't want to stand out. I want to fit in."

Startling us and interrupting our conversation, Sarah's phone rings. She leans over her desk to answer, says, "Hold," and hands the phone to me.

"Who is it?" I whisper.

She points to the card, indicating Wealth.

"Tell him I am at lunch. I don't want him to ask me about the dress."

She picks up the phone and speaks. "Wealth, I think she went to lunch. I'll have her to call you when she returns. Yes, it's here. Okay, I'll tell her. Bye." She ends the conversation.

"What did he say?" I ask.

"He wants you to call him. He says he hopes you like the gift."

"I do, but I wanted to go shopping myself."

"We can still go. We have to get shoes and a purse. I know you don't own anything to go with orange," says Sarah.

I put the dress back into the box and we go to lunch. After work, we go to the mall and get a great pair of tan strappy sandals. I also purchase a dark brown strapless dress, lest I chicken out of the orange.

When I get home, I call Wealth and thank him for the dress. Of course, he acts as if it is no big deal.

"I know the color is a little daring, but I didn't want you to wear black or brown. Most women at these affairs wear the typical black dress," Wealth comments.

"You can't go wrong with black," I quickly add.

"But you are going to wear the dress?" he asks.

"I am. I bought shoes to go with the dress after work."

"Good and you should wear your hair up. You have such a long neck. Show it off more."

"Okay, Wealth. I'll see you Saturday morning?" I ask to confirm.

"Yes, I'll pick you up at eight AM."

"Bye."

First the dress and now my hair; he is really concerned about my appearance. I don't like this. If I don't wear the dress, I'm sure he'll be upset. Therefore, I feel obligated to wear it. Thus, moving in front of the full-length mirror, I get a better view. Amazing, it's a perfect fit.

"Oh well, I guess a little color won't hurt."

I remove the dress and call Tam. She and Stan are doing great. She says she plans to visit the latter part of summer. I tell her about Wealth and the party. She thinks it is nice that he bought me a dress. She says the average women would appreciate a kind gesture. She also remarks that Wealth has no idea that I am not the average woman.

"If he wants to purchase me a dress, that's fine, but let me pick it out," I tell her. "I don't know him that well and he doesn't know me, so finding something in my taste is going to be difficult."

Tam says it's the thought that counts and I agree. However, should I suffer in orange because he wants to be thoughtful?

Eight o'clock sharp, Saturday morning, Wealth pulls up in front of my apartment. He is wearing a pale yellow golf shirt and a pair of slacks. I watch, laughing, as he walks to the front door. His strut is erect and expedient. He is the complete opposite of Dick and Ro. Ro is tall, lean, and conservative. He only owns a few slacks, because he mostly wears jeans and oversized khakis. Furthermore, he wouldn't be caught dead in a pale yellow golf shirt. Ro's wardrobe only consists of black, blue, brown, and gray. Dick, on the other hand, would wear a bright yellow golf shirt, but only if it fit tight and the sleeves were ripped off. Wealth is of a different sort. I never imagined going out with a guy like him. I wonder what he sees in me.

After an exhausting day of house hunting, we retire to my place around three to rest and prepare for the evening. I have an interest in two of the places we saw today. Not to be hasty, but I want to make a decision this week. Agreeing to be back at my place around eight tonight, Wealth casually mentions his anticipation of seeing me in the orange dress. After waving bye to him on the doorstep, I hastily check my phone messages. Elated to hear Dick's voice, I immediately sit and return his call.

"Hi, Dick," I say as he answers.

"What's up, beautiful? What are you doing?"

"I have been house hunting all day. I am tired," I admit.

"Well, rest."

"I can only rest for a while, because I am going to an affair tonight."

"Who are you going with, Sarah?" Dick asks curiously.

"No. I'm going with my Realtor. It's some big function the Realtor association throws every year."

"Who is your Realtor?" Dick questions.

"A guy named Wealth Fulmore."

"Of Hampshire and Fulmore Realtors?" he asks, then continues. "I have heard of him. You're going to the party with him?"

"He asked me," I say with a bit of guilt.

"Well, haven't we climbed up the social totem pole?"

"It's a business event. It's not a date. I am going for the connections," I respond.

"Whatever you say. What are you wearing?"

"A burnt-orange dress with spaghetti straps."

"What? You're wearing orange, but you don't wear bright colors."

"I know that and you know that, but Mr. Fulmore does not. He sent the dress over to my job as a gift. I have to wear it."

"Do you want to wear the dress?" Dick asks.

"Kind of," I say with doubt.

"Look, don't wear it if it is going to make you uncomfortable. You won't feel your best, and your personality is so forthright you won't be able to hide it. On the other hand, you will look gorgeous in burnt orange. So I say go for it—with the dress, not with Wealth Fulmore."

"I know what you mean. I have to go. I just wanted to say hi. I'll call you back tomorrow."

"Okay. But listen, I am coming to see you this summer. I am not taking no for an answer. Uh-uh, don't argue. I'll talk to you later. Bye." Dick hangs up.

Still laughing at Dick, I prepare myself for the evening. By 7:15, I am dressed and ready. I am determined not to make him wait. Careful not to wrinkle my dress, I sit on the edge of the futon and await his arrival. At 7:50 Wealth knocks on the door. When I open the door, Wealth is stunned.

"You clean up well," he comments.

That's really not the compliment I wanted to hear, but oh well. He kisses the top of my hand and we leave.

We pull up to the oval driveway in front of the home, or shall I say mansion? The valet driver greets us after we enter the gate. Stepping from the car, we walk toward the entrance. An amazing floral landscape surrounds the driveway of this stone home. The foyer floor is marble, the walls are white, and at the end of the foyer there are double stairs leading to the balcony. There are people mingling throughout the dining area. Waiters are serving appetizers on tiny black trays. Men and women are drinking wine and serving up their fake, cocktail party laughs. We continue through the home and into the back by the split-level pool with a disappearing edge.

Wealth takes my hand and introduces me to the host, Mr. John Whitney. Mr. Whitney is a short, distinguished-looking gray-haired gentleman; well tanned as if he just flew in from Waikiki. He kisses my hand, compliments my dress, and offers us food and drinks. Wealth asks me to excuse myself, for he needs to speak privately with John for a moment. I walk over to the fruit and place some pineapples and strawberries on a saucer. Standing by the pool, I watch the socialites giggle and chatter. Besides the host's wife and two other women, I am the only one wearing color. Here, there are at least fifty renditions of the little black dress and I had no problem being number fifty-one, but here I stand, the only one in orange. I move away from the pool and journey back into the gorgeous mansion. As I am looking at the paintings on the wall, Wealth comes up behind me and kisses my neck.

"You look so pretty with your hair pulled up."

"Thank you," I respond with a slight nod of my head.

We walk through the home as he introduces me to more of his friends. I have small talk with their dates as he and his associates talk business. Although the band is playing great music, no one is dancing; everyone is still standing around talking. After hours of greeting and smiling, Wealth is ready to go. I, for one, am glad because I am exhausted. The valet brings the car around and Wealth hands me the keys, saying he has had too much to drink.

"So how are you going to get home?" I ask.

"I was thinking I could stay at your home."

"Wrong. Maybe you will have sobered up by the time we get to my house."

After driving for five minutes, Wealth tells me to change direction and go to his home.

"If I take you home, how will I get home?"

"You will take the car home. I can come and get it tomorrow."

I really do not want to see Wealth tomorrow, but it sounds like the best plan because he is not staying at my house.

Wealth's home is half the size of Mr. Whitney's place, yet I still consider it a mansion. I drop him off at the front door, get directions back to my house, and after thanking him for a lovely evening, I drive off. I drive for fifteen minutes, before I realize that I am lost. The scenery looks nothing like my side of town. Consequently, I start to panic. I call Wealth, but he doesn't answer. I try Sarah and she doesn't answer either. I ride around for another ten minutes, but I seem to be going in circles. It's 1:00 AM. Everything is closed and I don't see a gas station in sight. Maybe I can backtrack to Wealth's house. Hence, I turn around and make my way back down the street. At 1:20 I pull into Wealth's circular driveway. Frazzled, I jump out of the car and vigorously ring his doorbell. After a couple of minutes, Wealth comes to the door in his boxers.

"What's wrong?"

"I got lost," I whine.

"Come on in."

I walk into Wealth's spacious home and take a seat at the bar centered across his silver and black kitchen. He hands me a cup of tea.

"Why don't you stay here?" Wealth offers.

I really want to go home, but I dare not tackle the roads again. Knowing Wealth put away several drinks tonight, I don't trust his driving skills. Hence, it looks like I have no other options.

"Okay, I'll stay, but I am not sleeping in the same room as you."

"Do you see how large this house is? We can sleep in different wings if you like," he boasts. "I'll get you a T-shirt and shorts and show you to your room."

I stroll into a burgundy room and put on the clothing. As I sit on the corner of the king-size sleigh bed, I hear music coming from the room downstairs. Walking to the end of the hall, I call Wealth.

"Come on down," he yells.

I walk down to the open living room. He is sitting on a red leather couch listening to The Eagles.

"You like The Eagles?" I ask with doubt as he nods his head yes and sips on a beer.

"Are you surprised?" Wealth asks.

"No. Well, a little. I figured you would listen to Earth, Wind, & Fire or Boney James to wind down.

"I listen to them also. Would you prefer I change the music?"

"No, I like The Eagles," I say, humming to the tune "The New Kid in Town."

"Would you like something to eat or drink?"

Responding no, I sit across from him on the love seat. Over the next three hours, we openly talk about everything. He is very political; I am not. He wants a big family; I do not. He doesn't like to travel and I do. We don't have much in common. Yet he is quite interesting. His eyes intrigue me. When he says one thing with his mouth, his eyes often say something else. I can't help but think that he gave me wrong directions on purpose, knowing I would end up back at his place and eventually agree to stay over. He turns the music down, walks over to the love seat, puts my leg across his lap, and begins massaging my feet.

"At the restaurant you said that you bore easily. Is that why you are single?"

"No, I am single because I just moved here and I don't like long-distance relationships," I tell him without making eye contact.

"So you left your man in Atlanta and moved here."

"Not really."

"So what happened with your last relationship?"

I look at him as he rubs my feet. I could be vague and say we broke up, but he is going to keep prying until I tell him why, so I am going to be honest.

"I cheated on my last boyfriend. Our relationship was already in trouble and once I did that, we could not recover."

"So you broke his heart and moved here to avoid seeing him?"

"No, I moved here to start over. Our relationship was over long before I cheated."

"Interesting," he says. "I cheated on my ex-girlfriend. Not because the relationship was over, I was just greedy. I broke her heart and she tried to kill herself."

"Damn, are you that good?" I jeer with a surprising face.

"Indeed I am," he says with poise while I look away and pretend not to smile.

"I'm going to bed," I tell Wealth.

I retire to the bedroom and lie comfortably amidst the thick down covers. When I awake, it's almost noon. I go to the restroom to wash my face and when I return to the bedroom, I notice a new pair of sweatpants, a jockey tank top, and some flip-flops. Running downstairs to the kitchen, I see Wealth in the weight room working out.

"Are those clothes for me?"

"Yes, unless you want to wear your dress home," he says as he benches his weights.

"Thank you. Have you eaten?"

"We can eat when I drop you off at home. Let me jump in the shower."

He places the weights on the bar and takes a deep breath. I lean over, gently kiss his rippling abs, and then sit downstairs and flip through his CDs. Minutes later, he comes down, grabs his wallet, and we head to the garage. His three-car garage houses a silver Jaguar, a black Range Rover, and a red BMW 525. Wealth tells me to grab the keys off the wall.

"Which pair?" I ask.

"I don't care, you're driving. This way, you can learn your way around town."

I grab the keys to the Range Rover and we head out of the

garage and drive toward town. We eat Mexican at a quaint restaurant down the street from my place. Due to our fatigue, there is little conversation over lunch. I pull up into my driveway, leave the SUV running, and hop out. Wealth steps out, gives me a hug, and says good-bye. I walk into the house and prepare myself for work tomorrow.

Over the next few weeks, Wealth and I go on a few dates. The Saturday before I move into my new place, we go out to dinner with Sarah and Omar. I always enjoy my evenings with Sarah, but when she is with Omar she acts different. Unlike her normal character, around him she seems quiet and demure. After we eat, Sarah suggests we check the poetry spot downtown. Wealth, wanting to go to the jazz spot uptown, is reluctant but finally agrees. This poetry place, nowhere near as cozy as the Blue Room, is moderately dim with a lazy, laid-back atmosphere. We find a table near the band and order drinks. Sarah immediately starts harassing me to read. Although I still write, I haven't read anything since I moved here. Wealth and Omar join in her harassment. Still, I deny their request.

"I'm not in the mood. Let's just listen to the others."

We sit and listen to the other poets. Some are really good and others are boring. While Sarah discusses the poets, Omar and Wealth loudly confer on all of the beautiful women. They are commenting on everything from hair to body parts. As an attempt to get Sarah's attention, I step on her foot and nod toward the men with my eyebrows frowning toward the center of my face. She pretends not to hear them. Therefore, I decide to ignore their remarks until Omar takes the conversation to another insulting level.

"Man, look at the lips on her, I bet she can . . . You know what I'm saying." Wealth gives an agreeing laughter just before I hit him on the shoulder.

"Excuse me, do you see us sitting here? Your conversation is rude and insulting. You don't talk that way around your dates. Right, Sarah?"

Sarah shrugs her shoulders as if she doesn't care, but I reiterate, "Well, I find it offensive and you need to stop."

Omar smiles and speaks to Wealth. "You got you an opinionated one this time, didn't you?"

Wealth grunts and gives a concurring nod.

"You can speak to me, Omar, I am right here," I say, forcefully tapping him on his hand.

Omar says nothing and I am surprised that Wealth is not sticking up for me. Furthermore, I don't know what is wrong with Sarah.

"You know what, guys, I think I will read."

I rise from the table and sign up with the host. Silently, I come back to the table and impatiently wait my turn. Although I am ready to leave, I want to have my moment to speak before we exit. I anxiously tap my nail against my teeth, as I sit and listen to the guys have small talk. Sarah still remains quiet. Finally, the host calls my name. I am the final reader. Hence, I am bound to make a lasting impression. Grabbing my book from my purse, I walk to the tiny stage, stand at the microphone, and begin my piece. The piece I read is entitled "Beauty: What's Hot and What's Not." The poem speaks about how guys constantly look at the shell of a woman instead of the true beauty she has to offer. I mention how sometimes men end up with the wrong women just because she has nice legs or nice eyes or great lips. Basically, the poem talks about how shallow men can sometimes be. As I finish, the crowd graciously approves with a round of applause. I look over at our table and Sarah, awake from her trance, is also applauding. However, as Omar looks curiously at Sarah, Wealth is looking angrily at me. But I don't care if he is vexed; minutes ago he was begging for me to perform. I only gave in to the request. Subsequently, when I return to the table, Wealth clutches my arm, stands, and says he needs to speak with me.

"Well, I'm ready to go," I tell him.

"I think that's a good idea," he says.

I am so glad each couple drove separate cars, because I would rather walk home than ride in the same car with Omar. He is as irritating as a yeast infection. Sure, he is cute but he has the personality of an asshole. And speaking of assholes, once we get to the car, I have to deal with Wealth.

"What in the hell is wrong with you?" he shouts.

"Nothing. What's wrong with you?"

"Why were you bitching the entire time? Omar and I were only joking."

"I don't think you're funny."

"And I didn't think your poem was funny. It was juvenile and ignorant. If you are going to read about something, make it a social issue or at least something important," Wealth continues.

"It wasn't meant to be funny. If it offended you, then maybe you are guilty. Take me home."

"Gladly," he says.

There is an icy chill to the silence shared on the ride home. As we pull into my driveway, he gives me a frigid look and without saying a word, I get out of the car and walk into the house. Wealth peels off before I can get in the door. Tossing my keys on the counter, I begin vehemently pacing the floor. Up until now, Wealth has been a perfect gentleman. But when he gets around Omar he acts like a fool. However, I am not blaming Omar, for Wealth is a grown man, in control of his behavior.

I run to the phone to call Sarah. I know this is her last date with Mr. Omar.

"Sarah, call me when you get in. I have to talk to you about tonight."

I pace to the bathroom and start the shower. Although my

evening has been a disaster I am still excited about moving in the morning. My new place, a two-level town house, is ten minutes south of here. It has a large, modern kitchen, two huge bedrooms with walk-in closets, and a study with built-in cherry-wood bookshelves. Accented with hardwood floors and a bay window by the door, this home has everything I desire. I have never been one for extensive decorating, but with a little paint and some nice accents, it will be very chic. This being my first real estate purchase, I pray it's not a mistake.

After my shower, I check the voice mail to see if Sarah has called, but she has not and neither has Wealth. Not that I am expecting him to call, but an apology for his rude behavior would be nice. Having the desire to read, I peruse my box marked "Lily's books." Tonight, within the callous realm of reality, I need to escape into a world of fantastical fiction. I fumble through the box to find Sidney Sheldon. I read a few chapters, then drift off to sleep.

Good night.

Chapter 17

Beware of the Glitter, It May Be Gold-Plated

I check my voice mail first thing in the morning and still no message from Sarah. This is not like her; I am starting to worry. As soon as I get dressed, I hear a car horn blaring in the driveway. Peeping from my window, I see Dale approaching my door. I swing open the door and without delay Dale grabs the first box and places it in his truck. I am so glad that I asked him to help. I asked Wealth to help, but he said moving furniture was for professionals and that he would pay for moving men, but that he wasn't moving a thing. I tried to tell him it's only a futon and a couple of boxes and that didn't require moving men, but it is no use. Thankfully, Dale agreed to help. Within the hour everything is moved and we are at my new town house. After moving the few items in, I sit in the center of my living room floor. Taking in a deep breath, I officially embrace my new start here in Kansas City.

"My place looks empty. I think I need more than a futon and a lamp. What do you think?"

"I think you're right. I love your place, though. Don't clutter it with too much furniture," Dale continues while sitting next to me.

"I won't, I don't like a lot of furniture. All I need is a bed, a dinette table, an armoire, and a few pillows. Oh, and a ceiling fan, gotta have a ceiling fan."

Just then the doorbell rings. Surprised, we both look at each other, waiting to hear the second bell before going to the door.

"Maybe that's Sarah!" Excited, I run to the door.

I open the door and a scruffy, brawny man in a faded blue jumpsuit confirms my address. After I concur with the address on the clipboard he asks me to sign on the dotted line.

"What is this?" I say, pushing the forms away.

"Your furniture."

"I didn't order any furniture," I assure him.

"This is your name and this is your address. The furniture has been paid for and we are delivering it."

"Hold up. Look on the invoice and see who paid for this furniture."

He flips through the pages and finds a name. "It says Mr. Wealth Fulmore."

"I knew it. Take it back," I yell as Dale opens the door wider.

"Is everything okay?"

"No. Wealth purchased me a truckload of furniture."

"Great, now you don't have to go shopping!"

"What? I should take the furniture?" I ask.

"Why not? If you don't like it, exchange it or send it back."

I am not sure about it, but he's right, I can always send it back. "Fine, move it in."

When Accent Movers finish their jobs, I have a fully furnished home. I hate to say it, but Wealth has great taste in home decor. Still, I feel funny about accepting such an expensive gift. My heart races as I walk from room to room in awe of my new home. This furniture, worth over fourteen thousand dollars, ornaments my two bedrooms, the dining room, and the study. I shake my head as I gaze upon my beautiful wrought-iron and glass dining room table. Then I rush upstairs to see how my new canopy bed looks in my bedroom. Feeling like a princess, I fall onto the bed and grab my cell phone from my purse. I must call Wealth to thank him for the furniture.

"This is Wealth," he answers.

"I love my furniture. Thank you, thank you, thank you!" I chant gleefully.

"It's no problem, I couldn't have you sitting in that lovely home with only a futon and a lamp."

"But you didn't have to buy me a houseful of things. I must pay you back."

"Good. Have dinner with my parents and me tomorrow night," he suggests.

Meeting his parents is serious. I am not ready to meet his parents. Sure, I am excited about the furniture, but I haven't forgotten about his moronic episode last night.

"I don't know about meeting your parents."

"They will love you. Please come to their anniversary dinner tomorrow night."

"Okay, I'll go. But we still have to talk about last night," I respond sternly.

"I am sorry. I was wrong. I should have put Omar in his place. He gets carried away. But your poem embarrassed me. I am not used to my women speaking their mind."

"And I am not used to men making me their woman without asking."

"Okay. Well, I want you to be my girl. What do you say?" Wealth asks casually.

Pausing, I remark with laughter, "If I say no, are you going to ask for the furniture back?"

"Of course I will," he responds with a pleasing outburst.

"Well, I guess I have to be your girl. What time are you picking me up tomorrow?"

"Dinner is at my house at seven. Can you come over?"

"I'll see you then. Thanks again for the furniture."

"I'll see you tomorrow. Come early. Bye."

My face bears a cheesy grin as I hang up the phone and recline on my queen-size bed.

"Shoot! I still haven't heard from Sarah." I dial the phone and on the third ring, she picks up.

"Where have you been?" I question maternally.

"I have been here. What do you mean?"

"No, you haven't. You have got to come see my new place."

"Oh, I am so sorry, I forgot you were moving today. I don't feel well, maybe I can come tomorrow."

"I'm busy tomorrow, come over Tuesday after work."

"It's a date. I'll see you tomorrow at work. I have to go." She hurries off the phone.

Something is wrong with her. We are going to have a long talk at lunch tomorrow. But for now, I am going to Target for linens, towels, and cute stuff. I grab my keys, my credit card, and head to the store.

When I return, I sit in the driveway of my new home and stare in amazement. I know it's just a town house, but again, this is my first purchase. My transition here to Kansas City is still hard to believe. Interrupting my moment of ecstasy is Beethoven's Fifth ringing through my cell phone.

"Hello."

"Hi, sweetie."

"Hi, Mommy. I moved into my house. You have to come and visit."

"Okay, I'm going to come this summer. But listen, I had a crazy dream about fish last night. Are you pregnant?"

"No!" I scream.

"Are you sure? I had the dream," she continues.

"I am positive. I'll call you back once I get into the house." Giggling, I hang up the phone, grab my bags, and walk into the house.

My mom is so funny. In my early twenties she would have killed me if I became pregnant out of wedlock. These days she wants grandchildren so bad, she prays I'm pregnant with every fish dream. I place my bags on the bed and pull out the towels. Although they are new, I wash them anyway to make sure all of the dye is removed. I spend the rest of the evening jovially, folding towels and decorating my room. Afterward, I reach in my purse for my favorite black ballpoint pen and pause for a moment of sentiment as I write in the cards I purchased at the store. Altogether, I have a thank-you card for Wealth, missing-you cards for Tam and Dick, and an anniversary card for Wealth's parents. Stretching out across the bed, I begin writing. I miss Dick a lot more than I thought. I love his smile, his sense of humor, his charm, and his intellect. I hate to admit it, but I think I love him, everything about him. I never told him, but maybe it's time. Therefore, I'll send him a blank card and fill it with things I . . .

Never Told Him
When I need love, I think thoughts of you and I know
*   there is love*
A love so many times has been taken for granted
Not knowing what it truly is
*   A gift, a blessing, a chance*
Maybe a glance across the room, when eyes meet and
*   souls connect,*
The crescendo of heartbeats and the silent thoughts
In the beginning
The loads of fun, followed by aches of laughter

I like you . . . a lot
Day after day, time together is spent, meals together are
    eaten, nights together are created.
I like you . . . no, I really, really like you
Somewhere in the middle
My dreams consist of you, my thoughts consist of you,
    my scent consists of you
My reason . . . you
I like you . . . I love you
In the end
I never told you
I like you . . . I miss you
            My gift
My blessing
            My chance
My glance across the room
Our eyes met
May our souls always connect

He may not be the one, but he means a lot to me and he
should know it. I place stamps on the envelopes, place the
cards in my purse and rest comfortably in my new, cherry-
wood canopy bed.
    Good night.

Chapter 18

Guess Who's Coming
to Dinner

Excited to tell Sarah about my new furniture, I rush by her desk before starting work; however, Sarah is late for work this morning. This is so unlike her. I don't hear from her until around noon, when she buzzes my phone.

"Where have you been?"

"I had to go to the doctor this morning."

"Are you pregnant?" I hastily question.

"No, I needed him to look at my wrists."

"Come to my desk," I tell her.

Five minutes later, Sarah walks up to my desk.

I take her arm and look at the big purple bruise on her right wrist. "What in the hell happened to you?"

"I don't want to talk about it."

"You better tell me."

"Omar and I had a little fight," she whispers.

"There is no such thing as a little fight. If he hit you, tell me."

"He didn't hit me. We were arguing. I got angry and

knocked his glass out of his hand. When I tried to leave, he grabbed my arm. I bruise easily."

"Stop seeing him right now. You cannot keep going out with him."

"Look, he is nice. He gets angry sometimes, we all do. I can handle it. Guys like him usually don't like country girls like me. He's showing me new things. Please, let it go," she begs.

"I don't like it and I don't want to hear it. We'll talk about this later."

Huffing, I grab my folders and walk into the conference room to meet Dale. After work, I rush home to take a shower and get dressed for dinner tonight. I am nervous about my appearance. All of my clothing is dark and I know Wealth likes color. Maybe I'll wear my off-white dress Dick purchased for me. When I put it on with a pair of tan Mary Janes and a tan hip belt, it's perfect. I curl my hair, place part of it up in a French roll, and leave some hair hanging loose in the back. When I arrive at Wealth's home, he greets me at the door, with a semiwarm hug and an anomalous expression.

"Are you not happy to see me?"

He says nothing but steps onto the porch.

"We have a problem," he says in low voice.

"What?"

"Angela stopped by."

"Who is Angela?" I say curiously.

"My ex-girlfriend."

"The one who attempted suicide?" I ask.

"The one and only. She came by to drop off a gift for my parents. When I told her they were coming over, she decided to stay."

"So there is one more for dinner. What's the problem?"

"She doesn't know that I am seeing someone else."

"So we'll tell her together," I say, walking into the house.

When we walk into the foyer, I hear her yell from the kitchen. "Honey, is that your parents?"

"No, it's . . . um."

I cannot believe he is stuttering. Either he is still seeing this woman or she is completely nuts and he is afraid of her. The first thing I see as she rounds the corner is her flowing, cascading blond hair. She is about five seven, 135 pounds. Besides her long blond hair, her other outstanding feature is her size 38-DD bustline. She looks like a tall version of Pamela Lee Anderson. I must confess; she is striking. I walk up to her and introduce myself. Cordially, she asks, "Will you be staying for dinner?"

"Of course, I wouldn't miss it," I respond quaintly.

The top of Wealth's head is starting to sweat. He doesn't know what to say. I suppose that is how I looked when Dick met Romance at the hospital. It's funny to see someone else in a sticky situation.

His parents arrive at seven and the games begin promptly at 7:05. Although Angela originally has no plans to stay for dinner, they immediately changed upon my arrival. His parents aren't going to know what to think. Wealth greets his mom and dad at the door while Angela and I stay behind him at the end of the foyer. With his parents are his two brothers. I quickly notice that one of them is identical to Wealth. Once everyone walks into the house, Angela greets his parents and his brothers. During this greeting, Wealth introduces them to me. We all progress to the living room by the piano and that is when I discover Wealth is a twin. He mentioned that he had two brothers but never said that he's a twin. We settle in the living room and Angela sits beside his mom and swiftly starts conversation. I can tell by the dreary look on his mom's face that she doesn't care too much for Angela. Sitting next to his twin, Winston, I strike up conversation while Wealth's dad joins him in the kitchen.

"So you're the new lady in my brother's life?" questions Winston.

"It seems I am one of them."

"Don't worry about Angela, she's crazy. My brother is not still seeing her. She just wants to make a scene. Since the suicide thing, Wealth has been scared to upset her, so he lets her have her way."

"Funny, he told me everything about her except for the fact that she is white."

"All of his girlfriends since high school have been white. When we walked in the door, we were surprised to see that you were not."

Winston and I start laughing as we look over at Angela kissing up to his mom.

"I can only imagine what my dad is saying to Wealth. This evening should be quite interesting."

Wealth calls everyone to the table. Winston steps in front of Angela, to ensure that she doesn't make it to the table next to Wealth. I sit to Wealth's right and his brother Reed sits to his left. His parents sit at each end and Angela sits across from Wealth and next to Winston, who starts dinner conversation.

"So, Wealth, how did you two meet?" Winston winks at me as he puts Wealth under pressure.

"I told you already."

"Tell him again, sweetie, it's such a great story," I say, brushing the top of his hand.

Angela's eyes widen as she listens to Wealth tell the story about the accident. Of course, I add my little details of romance.

"How long have you two been dating?" asks Angela.

Speechless, Wealth looks at me. "About two years," I say with jest just as Angela nearly chokes on her salad.

"I'm only joking, it's only been a few months."

Wealth's dad smirks, while his mom sits silently at the table as if no conversation is taking place. The rest of dinner is fairly quiet except for a few comments about business and career. As we listen to low classical music while eating, a cell phone starts to ring. Everyone looks around the table, but no one claims the phone. I know that it's my ring; however, embarrassed, I decide not to answer it. A minute later, it rings again. Having no choice, I apologize, smile politely, and go to my purse to retrieve my phone. It's Tam. It must be important, because she called back to back. I look back at the table as they all gawk at me. I apologize again, excuse myself from the table and I answer the phone.

"Hello," I whisper.

"I'm pregnant!" screeches Tam.

I begin to scream with excitement. "What! You're pregnant? I can't believe it. You are the fish dream."

"I just found out. You have to be the godmother," she says.

My voice is still elevated as I continue my conversation. Wealth walks over to me.

"Is everything okay?" he asks, pulling me farther away from the table.

"Yes, Tam is pregnant, I am so excited," I say to Wealth.

"Well, do you have to be so ghetto about it?"

I pretend he did not make that ignorant statement. I calm my voice and continue talking with Tam.

"I am at a dinner party. I will have to call you back. I love you and I am so happy for you and Stan." I hang up the phone and return to the table with Wealth.

"I apologize for the screams, that was my best friend. She just found out she is pregnant," I say with a big smile.

"Well, I hope she is married. There are so many young girls raising children alone," Mrs. Fulmore comments.

She has some nerve to make such a crass comment. However, I remain respectful and assure her that Tam is married.

"Yes, Tam is married to Stan. This is their first child," I say with a bogus smile.

The remainder of dessert is quiet. Afterward, the family retires to the living room as I assist Wealth in the kitchen with the dishes.

"I think my parents like you," he says.

"I didn't appreciate the ghetto comment and why are you so nervous?"

"We'll talk later. Let's go back in with my family."

Once we get into the living room, Wealth's brother Reed is playing the piano. Thus, his mom begins to sing a sweet melody to his dad. This family is straight out of Hollywood. They are rich, beautiful, talented, and funny. They should be an NBC sitcom, titled *The Fulmores*. The brothers stand after Mrs. Fulmore finishes her song and present the anniversary gift. They give a small box to each parent and in each box is a set of keys.

"What are the keys for?" asks Mr. Fulmore as Wealth hands them a picture of their new boat. "My sons purchased me a boat?"

"No, dear, they purchased *us* a boat," says his mom as she stands and gives them a long hug.

This is unreal, I think to myself. I remember buying my mom a pair of diamond earrings once and I thought I was really doing something. Impressed, I gaze upon the picture of the boat. After the hugs, Wealth pulls me into the foyer and whispers, "Did you bring a gift for my parents?"

"No, but I did get them a card," I say proudly, handing him the envelope.

Telling me to wait, he runs upstairs, and then comes down in a couple of minutes with a gift.

"Here, you can give them this," he whispers.

"What is this?"

"It's a plaque that will go in the main room of the boat," he answers.

"Why do I have to give them a gift? I just met your parents."

"It will look bad if you don't have a gift. Angela has a gift."

"So I have to compete with Angela?" I say with slight anger.

"Please don't start, just give them the gift and shut up."

I know this man did not just tell me to shut up. Has he lost his mind? He must have me confused with Angela, the crazy girl. I would make a scene but this is his parents' night, so I will give them the gift and leave. I snatch the plaque from his hand, walk into the room, and give his mom and dad the card along with the plaque. She unwraps the gift and reads the plaque. It is made of mahogany wood with a gold faceplate and it has an inscription about family and love. I give them both a hug, tell them it was a pleasure to meet them, and excuse myself after saying good-bye to Angela and the brothers. I cut my eyes at Wealth, pick up my purse, and forcefully walk out the front door. Roiled, I stand outside huffing for a few minutes, thinking Wealth is going to come out and apologize, but he does not. As I get in my truck, I hear his door open. At first, I think it is Wealth, but as I look, I see it's Winston. He runs over to get my attention.

"I am not sure what happened, but I'm sure it's my brother's fault. Please excuse his behavior and don't let it be a representation of our family."

"It was really nice to meet you, Winston. I have to go," I say with a smile.

"This may be very inappropriate, but here is my card. Call me . . . if you need anything."

He hands me the card and steps away from my door. I wave good-bye to him as I drive away. When I get down the street at the stoplight, I take his card from the passenger's seat and read it.

"Dr. Winston Fulmore, gynecologist. Obstetrician specialist. He's a doctor?" I say aloud.

This family is truly unreal. I'm dating a millionaire Realtor and his twin brother is a doctor—a specialist. What does his older brother do? Run a small country? This may seem normal

for some people, but I don't mingle with that many successful, wealthy, African-American families. I have really been
hanging out with the wrong crowd. I should have moved to
Kansas City a few years ago.

I toddle into my house of Wealth and start to rethink this
furniture deal. Wealth can be a jerk and I don't want this gift
to be the reason I stick around. I call Tam for advice. However, she is so excited I soon forget my problems and talk
about the baby for an hour. Everything is happening so fast.
Tam is married and now she is pregnant. A few months ago,
we were single, having a great time at the Blue Room. Well,
she was single. I was in limbo. I guess not much has changed
in my life. I'm still in limbo, only now dating an obsessive,
controlling fool. Removing my shoes, I sit at the foot of my
bed and glance over at my beautiful wooden armoire.

"A rich fool, but a fool nevertheless."

Before I take a bath, I decide to check on Sarah. She answers the phone in haste.

"You okay?" I ask.

"I'm okay, I'm about to leave the house."

"It's late. Where are you going?" I question, praying she
doesn't mention Omar.

"I'm going out."

Although she doesn't say his name, her brevity tells all.

"Please be careful," I beg.

"I will. See you at work tomorrow."

I don't know what is going to happen with the two of them,
but I know it is trouble. I iron my clothing for work tomorrow
and run my bathwater. I haven't had one of Dick's sexy late-
night phone calls in a while. At first, they stunned me, but
now I miss them. Dick is one in a million. Sitting in the tub,
I imagine the personality of our offspring. That would be one
very artistic kid. Either he would be extremely smart or his

brain would go into overload and he would be insane. I laugh aloud, imagining Dick as a father. What a trip. After I rinse off, I crawl into my bed and pray. I pray for clarity, happiness, and peace of mind. I also thank God for my friends and family and I say a special prayer for Sarah.

Good night.

Chapter 19

Double Trouble

My next few days are routine. I go to work, come home, write a little, and watch television and sleep, exactly in that order. I haven't heard from Wealth and it has not bothered me one bit. His company is pleasing, but I am not goo-goo-ga-ga over him. Frankly, if I never hear from him again, it would be just all right. But there is the problem of the furniture, and though most women would say there is no problem, I feel guilty. We have only been dating a month, we have not slept together and I have a problem with taking such a pricey gift. I don't care what anyone says, expensive gifts bear attachments, and I don't want to owe Wealth a thing. He won't agree, but I need to work out a payment plan.

Bright and early Wednesday morning I receive a call from Wealth. He says, in a stern tone, that he wants to have lunch to discuss our future. The way he emphasizes *future* sounds like we have been married for five years with three kids and bountiful mutual funds. Humoring his seriousness, I agree to meet him for lunch. At exactly noon, I walk into the restaurant and spot his shiny bald head as soon as I walk in. As I waltz to the table, I am beginning to dread our anticipated conversation.

Before I can sit down in the booth, he speaks anxiously. "How come you haven't called?"

"Because I was waiting on you to call," I answer.

"You are the one who walked out. I thought you would at least call and apologize," he continues.

"Look! I don't appreciate the ghetto remark or you telling me to shut up. I will not tolerate it and if you feel the need to speak to your *woman* in that manner, then you need to find another one."

He peers at me with squinted eyes as he rolls his tongue around the inside of his cheek. "No girl has ever talked to me like that."

"That's because you are used to dating girls, not women. They may run around chasing your rich ass, but I am not. Now, what are we eating for lunch?"

Wealth picks up his menu and orders the chicken sandwich for both of us. Other than the occasional "you should have called first," not much is said during lunch. Afterward, we agree to start over as if the evening never happened and he invites me over to his place tonight to watch a couple of movies with his friends.

"Is Omar going to be there?" I ask.

"No, he's busy. He and Sarah have been seeing a lot of each other," he confesses.

"I don't like it. They got into a fight and Omar bruised her arm."

"Yeah, Omar can get out of control at times. I'll talk to him."

Wealth walks me to my truck, kisses my cheek, and I go back to work to finish my day. I haven't said much to Sarah. I think she is avoiding me. My mom always says that if you have to hide a relationship, there is something wrong. Indeed, there is something very wrong about Sarah and Omar. I need to take her to lunch this week and speak to her. I hope she is not too defensive.

I rush home after work, shower, and arrive at Wealth's place around eight. Winston greets me at the door. Unfortunately, thinking he is Wealth, I give him a soft, sensual kiss. Naturally, Winston does not immediately stop the kiss and it is not until I place my hand around the back of his head that he pulls away.

"You know I'm Winston," he says with a smirk.

"Damn it! Why did you let me kiss you?"

"All I did was open the door and you starting kissing me. I didn't have time to say anything," he says innocently.

"Whatever. Don't do that again."

Dating an identical twin is spooky. Of course, I didn't mention the smooch to Wealth. But Winston is a superb kisser. I walk into the house and call for Wealth, but he is not here.

"Where's your brother?"

"Gone to the store, he'll be back."

I sit on the floor and lean my head against the love seat, while watching television. From the corner of my eye, I notice Winston staring at me.

"Why are you staring at me?"

"Is it obvious?"

"Apparently," I say.

"Would you like something to drink?" he asks, deliberately ignoring my question.

"Some juice would be nice."

Winston returns with my juice and his beer. Sitting across from me, he strikes up conversation. "You don't look like someone who would date my brother."

"And you don't look like a coochie doctor, but you are. Looks can be deceiving."

Winston turns up his beer and chuckles. "Yeah, but you don't act like someone who would date my brother."

"Well, why don't you tell me about the women your brother dates?"

"They are usually insecure, money hungry, and very unstable. He likes them helpless so that he can be their savior. The only thing you have in common with his ex-girlfriends is their beauty."

"Is that so?" I say curiously.

If I didn't know better, I would say that Winston is flirting with me. A fidelity test game, I am sure, he and his brother have played since high school.

"Maybe he's growing up," Winston suggests.

I nonchalantly shrug my shoulders and continue drinking my juice until I hear Wealth opening the door. As he comes around the corner into the living room, I stand and we kiss each other on the forehead and cheek. Following behind him are three of his friends, Nan, Tracy, and Ellis. Tracy and Ellis are married. Nan is here as a blind date for Winston. Wealth ushers in five pizzas and sets them on the coffee table along with two movies. He pops in one of the movies. However, the conversation takes precedence over movie watching. I ignore the chitchat until Tracy starts her conversation off by asking Winston if he knows a good cosmetic surgeon.

Winston eagerly replies, "Yes, my office partner's brother practices cosmetic surgery. I'll call you tomorrow and give you his number."

"Great. I've finally decided to get this wide nose of mine contoured."

I glance over at Tracy, yet I see nothing wrong with her nose. It looks like a regular nose to me. It doesn't have a European cut, because her descedents are not from Europe. But, I think to myself, different strokes for different folks. I can't imagine someone cutting slices from my nose to give it a more narrow appearance. Then again, I could never afford it, so it wasn't an option.

Just then, Wealth turns to me and asks, "Have you ever thought of having any work done?"

"Nope," I say, focusing my attention toward the movie.

Tracy jumps in. "Girl, after I get my nose done, I am definitely going for a larger cup size."

"Be careful, bust enhancement can be addictive," Winston comments.

"Yeah, Angela enhanced her breasts three times before she was satisfied," admits Wealth.

I knew her chest was too big to be true. Women with her tiny bone structure don't grow breasts that huge. It's unnatural.

"There is no way I would pay thousands of dollars to inject plastic substances into my body," I comment.

"It is so worth it. I got an enhancement and it gave me so much more confidence," interjects Nan.

Wealth confidently speaks up as my ears start to ring from the shock of this conversation. "Don't worry, baby, I will pay for any surgery you want to have done."

"Girl, he is a good one. Ellis told me that he would only pay for one thing—my breasts or my nose. Anything else, and I will have to pay for it myself."

"Well, nothing is too much for my sweetie pie," Wealth adds while rubbing the back of his hands against my cheek.

I have heard of women like Tracy and Nan, but I have never met one in person. Tracy doesn't need plastic surgery. She's a pretty girl. She has a round face, almond-shaped eyes and an oval mouth. She probably wears a 36-B, which is fine for a size 6. I could possibly understand if her chest was completely flat, but it's not. It's hard to believe she is going to alter what the Creator has given her. I glance over at Winston, who peeps my expression from his peripheral view. He lifts his eyebrows and quickly shrugs his shoulders as to say that he doesn't get it either. At least there is a connection with someone in this room. Soon the conversation dies down and everyone joins in on the movie.

Three hours later, Nan, Tracy, and Ellis prepare to leave. Nan and Winston exchange phone numbers, but as soon as she leaves, Winston, surprisingly, tosses it in the trash. While Wealth is in the restroom, I ask Winston about Nan.

"Why did you agree to take her number, then throw it away?" I ask.

"She said she wants to call me, so I gave her my card. She voluntarily gave me her number. I did not ask for it. I am not going to call her. Therefore, it is wasted paper in my pocket."

"Well, Dr. Fulmore, I am glad I'm not chasing you. She seems nice. You should call her."

"She's not my type," he quickly confesses.

"Well, you should be honest."

"Okay, I will. You are my type. I hate that my brother saw you before I did, 'cause I know you would be better off with me instead of him," he brags, moving a step in my direction.

"You don't know anything," I say with an attitude.

While rolling my eyes, I take a step away from him. With a small hint of laughter Winston whispers, "You are so cute."

He walks to the front door and yells to Wealth, "I'm out! Talk to you guys later."

Seconds later, Wealth comes out of the restroom and sits down beside me. He motions for me to sit in his lap and I feel the pressure building. We have not had sex yet and I know that it's only a matter of days before he tries something. When I sit on his lap, I feel him stiffening. I am not ready to have sex. Therefore, I have to deter his sexual thoughts with intellectual conversation. Most men can't answer serious questions while thinking about getting laid.

"What attributes are you looking for in a woman?" I question.

He pauses for a moment, while playing with my hair. "I want a wife with attributes like my mother. Faithful, sincere, and proper. She needs to know the salad fork from the dinner fork. Little things like that are important. I want her strong, but she must know her place as the woman of the house."

Ordinarily a comment like that would make me upset, but I have to respect his sincerity. To some degree, I concur with his statement. However, I would choose the word *role* instead of *place*. In a relationship, each person has to play a role. They both can't play the same role or else they will be fighting for control the entire time; hence, the problem with Ro and me. There are times to lead and there are times to follow. Just like there are times to rebel and times to submit. In my past relationships, I always wanted to lead. I was so afraid that if I didn't lead, I would be taken advantage of. However, I have learned that the supporting role is just as important as the main character's. In a relationship, the most difficult concept to grasp is also the most important thing to achieve: balance.

"I also want a woman who would be a great mother for my kids. She has to be intelligent and giving," Wealth continues.

I feel his rise going down. Thankfully, without failure, it works every time. I move off his lap and sit beside him. "May I ask why you choose to date women outside your race?"

"Those are the women who come on to me. I only have to smile and they approach me. I hate chasing women. I have dated women within my own race, but it usually doesn't work out. They find out I have money and they start asking me to buy them things or they assume I am out of their league and they stop calling."

"I'm sure that there are some sisters out there who will chase after you," I respond.

"Where? You didn't. I had to beg you for a date."

"You didn't beg me, you asked me out and I said yes."

"And if you had said no, I would never have called again."

"Well, lucky for you, I didn't say no," I sass.

Wealth smirks. "Yeah, lucky for me."

Leaning over my body, he kisses me on the lips and gently lays me down on the chair. I assume the deterrent is only temporary, because when he lies close to me he is hard as a rock. I need to tell him that I don't want to have sex and that I want

to take my time. Therefore, I slowly pull myself off the couch
and slide onto the floor.

"I can't do this," I admit.

"What's wrong? Are you not attracted to me?"

"No. I mean yes, I am. I just need to wait. Sex can change
a relationship and I think we are going at a really good pace.
Maybe I should go home," I say hesitantly.

Wealth looks at me, looks down at little Wealth, and looks
at me again. "I think that's a good idea."

Standing, Wealth gives me a hug, walks me to the car, and
continues to speak. "My family and I are going out on the
boat Sunday. I want you to come."

"I'll let you know," I say, getting in my car.

Blowing him a kiss through the window, I drive off. It's a
silent ride home tonight. No music, no traffic, just thoughts.
Sometimes I get the feeling that Wealth is going to try to
change me. Surely, no one is perfect, but you have to accept
and respect your mate for perks and their flaws. Wealth
doesn't feel as if he has any flaws. Ironically, that misconcep-
tion is his biggest flaw.

Without hitting the lights, I walk in the door and lie down
on the futon while listening to my messages. The first one is
from Dick. I instantly perk up, listening to him sing over the
machine. He says he loved the card I sent and he also says
he's coming to visit the first week of next month. As exciting as that sounds, I don't know about his visit. Is it right to
see your ex while you are dating someone else? Even if Dick
and I are not intimate, I think it violates the dating rules.
Lying back on the bed, I think. Who am I fooling? I haven't
seen Dick in so long, he'll probably have my panties off
before his one-syllable name can leave my mouth. I should
call and talk to him. I roll over and dial his number, and after

three rings I hang up and try his cell phone. He answers on the first ring.

"What's up, Dick?"

"What's up, beautiful?"

"Are you really coming to see me?" I ask.

"I will be there in two weeks.

"What if I don't want you to come?"

"You don't want to see me?" Dick asks.

"I do, but I'm dating this guy and it could be messy."

"Look, baby, if you don't want to see me, I won't come. But I want to see you. So I have made plans to come visit you, my friend. I know you miss me. I can tell by the excitement in your voice and by your poem. So . . . let me know."

He is so damn cocky. I never know what to say when he flips the script. I wasn't sure about seeing him until I spoke to him. Now I can't say no.

"I'll see you in two weeks," I say with a complete change of tone.

"Can't wait."

I get butterflies in my stomach when I think about Dick. I forgot to ask him how long he plans to stay. I guess it doesn't matter because I'm already excited. Stripping on the way to the shower, I leave a trail of clothing from the bedroom to the bathroom. As soon as the water steams my chest, I hear the phone ringing. Thinking it may be Dick calling back, I jump from the shower and tiptoeing on my trail of clothing, I make my way back to the phone. Disappointed to see it's a local number, I answer with frustration.

"Yes."

"What are you doing?"

"Who is this?" I ask.

"It's Sarah."

"Hey, baby, what are you doing? Where are you?"

"I'm south of the city. Can you come get me?"

"Can you give me the directions?" I ask.

"I'm at the Star Drive-In." I don't know how to get here from your house."

"How did you get there?"

"It's a long story, just please come and get me," she begs as she begins to cry.

"Okay, don't cry, I'm coming. The Star Drive-In, I'll be there."

Naked, I run to the closet, grab my sweats and a T-shirt, and place them on my wet body. "I knew something was going to happen. I have to call Wealth."

The phone rings and rings, but he doesn't pick up. I call a second time, but he still doesn't pick up.

"Who can I call? Who can I call? I don't know anyone's phone number!" I yell.

I could call Dale, but he may spread Sarah's personal life all over the job, and that wouldn't be good. I can't believe I have been here close to two months and I have only three phone numbers. I sit on the corner of the bed and try to call Wealth again. Of course, no answer. Vigorously running my nails against my teeth, I suddenly remember.

"Winston! I forgot he gave me his card. I'll call him."

I run into the garage and remove his card from my glove compartment. Luckily, his cell phone number is on the card.

"Please answer, please!" I beg while the phone is ringing.

"Hello."

I speak hurriedly. "Winston, I need a favor. Do you know where the Star Drive-In is? My friend Sarah is stranded there. Can you give me directions?"

"Who is this?

"I'm so sorry. It's Lily. I need you, please," I implore.

"Okay, I live near there, I'll pick her up and bring her to your house. Where do you live?"

I give him the address and a few landmarks. Minutes later, Sarah and Winston are knocking on my door. Obviously, Sarah is distraught. I give her a long hug as Winston walks in.

"Winston, thank you so much," I state during our hug.

"Why did you call him Winston?" asks Sarah.

"You didn't tell her?"

"No, she looked distressed enough," he says.

"Remember when I mentioned that Wealth has a twin? Well, here he is. Winston, meet Sarah. Sarah, this is Winston Fulmore."

Sarah couldn't care less. Nodding to Winston, she walks over to the futon and falls out.

"You have a nice place. I love your furniture. We have similar taste," Winston says, admiring the decor.

"No, you and your brother have similar taste. He bought everything except the futon."

To prevent Winston from entering any farther, I slide my body in front of his. "Look, I don't mean to kick you out, but I need to talk with Sarah. Thanks again. I really owe you."

Using my shoulder, I politely push Winston out the door. Then, rushing over to Sarah, I question, "What happened to you?"

She looks up at me with a disappointing look. "I don't want to tell you," she whines like a toddler.

"What did that fool do? Did he leave you?"

"We had an argument over an ex-boyfriend. I got very upset and started yelling. He said that if I wouldn't stop yelling he was going to leave me, so I dared him. And, and . . . he left," she cries.

I walk into the bathroom to get Sarah some tissue. When I return she is stretched out on the futon. Lifting her head, I place it in my lap. Gently, I rub my hands through her hair while she finishes her story. "I really like him. I don't know why we keep arguing."

"You cannot keep seeing him, Sarah. He treats you like crap. I don't care how much I adored a man, I would not allow him to leave me in a dark drive-in at twelve in the morning. He is a jerk."

"But at times he can be so sweet and he is so fine. Don't you think he is fine? He is educated, he introduces me to new things, and he is in a different class of people. I like that. He is like Wealth. Don't you like experiencing new things?"

"Wealth does not act like Omar and if he did, I would leave him."

"Can I stay here?" Sarah asks.

"You better, 'cause I am not taking you home tonight. You can borrow some clothes for work tomorrow," I say.

Sarah wipes her face while removing her shoes. "Thank you."

"Yeah, yeah, I'll give you your bill when you check out in the morning."

I go upstairs and gather her towels and sheets. Following me upstairs, she slumps to the guest bedroom.

The morning comes as soon as my first dream phase begins. I hit the snooze button twice. Finally, I get up and I knock on Sarah's door. Talking on her cell phone, she ignores my knock.

"Who are you talking to? I ask, praying she doesn't say Omar.

"He just called to make sure I was all right," she rushes to admit.

"What about last night!" I yell, opening the door. "We have to go to work. Don't get left. That will make twice in twenty-four hours," I say unsympathetically.

I close the door, go into my bedroom, and prepare for work. Ten minutes later, I hear Sarah sounding sick in the bathroom. I wrap the towel around my body and knock on her door.

"Are you okay?" I yell through the door.

"Yeah, I'll be ready in a minute," she says faintly.

I get dressed and go downstairs to the kitchen. Fifteen minutes later Sarah joins me in the kitchen.

"Are you pregnant?" I snap.

"Why are you asking me that?"

Giving her a firm look, I say nothing.

"I don't know," she continues.

"Well, we are going to find out during lunch today. I'm sure there is a clinic around town. We'll call when we get to work. Let's go."

The phone rings as we are walking out the door. I ignore it and rush out. When we arrive at work, I listen to Wealth's two messages on my voice mail. His tone sounds concerned about the emergency last night; therefore, I decide to call him before my meeting. Yet when I tell him that I called his brother, his disturbance turns away from Sarah and toward his brother. Nonetheless, he does agree to talk with Omar. After our debate, he gets to the original purpose of the call. Again, he invites me to go with him on Sunday. After thinking about his ornery temperament around his parents, I decline his invitation. Naturally, after I say no, he wants to get off the phone. Like a big pouting baby, he gets upset whenever he doesn't get his way.

Soon as I hang up the phone, I get out a piece of paper and begin to write another part to my beauty poem. This one is for women. Specifically Sarah. I hope she realizes that it doesn't matter how nice a man looks if he treats her like crap. She has got to end this terrible relationship. We as women sometimes are so caught up in the material things that a man has to offer that we lose our self-respect in the process. I'm calling it the "He-Got Blues." He's got this and he's got that, but he doesn't have the decency to treat his woman with respect. We need to let these men go. I am going to take some of my own advice and back away from Wealth; maybe Sarah will follow my lead.

I fold up the paper and place it in an envelope. Slipping it in Sarah's purse, I make my way to the conference room and take my seat next to Dale. Like riding the bus to school, Dale always saves me a seat next to him. He would take offense if I didn't sit here and I would take offense if he didn't want me here. After we get the gist of the project, we pass limericks to each other the remainder of the meeting. Our redundant project leader explains the project within the first ten minutes, then spends the remaining hour reiterating what he said in the beginning. We get our assignment. An hour passes, and Dale and I leave the meeting and walk up front to leave for lunch. Sarah is waiting for me at the door.

"Can I go with you guys?" she asks.

"Yeah, come on," Dale and I say in unison.

During lunch I tell Sarah about Wealth and me. We haven't talked in so long I had to catch her up. She thinks I should go with Wealth to the lake on Sunday, but I dare not listen to her love advice. Dale simply laughs as we yap about our boyfriends. He never talks about his love life. I don't think he has one. I don't know why, though, he is a handsome man. Therefore, I think it's time to pry.

"Dale, do you have a girlfriend?"

Dale smiles and taps his fork against his plate. "Not exactly, but I do have someone special in California."

"How do you keep a long-distance relationship going?" Sarah asks.

"Terry works for the airline so we see each other twice a month."

"Oh, is she a flight attendant?" I ask.

"No, a pilot," he brags.

"Damn," Sarah and I say in harmony.

"Next year, we plan to move in together. I am going to move back to California and work from there. I would like to start writing my book. If we have kids, maybe I'll become one of those stay-at-home dads."

Dale continues eating with a big smile on his face. I would

smile too, if my future spouse were a pilot. I guess he doesn't have to talk about his love life, because it is smooth sailing. It seems that the relationships getting the most airtime at lunch are those in the most trouble. Alas, my relationships get their fair share of talk time.

We return to work and I finish my day at my desk. Staying an hour over, I decide to get a head start on an idea I have for our new line of birth greeting cards. Sarah stops by my desk before she leaves, but she says nothing about the poem. I assume she hasn't seen it yet. Becoming fatigued around six fifteen, I head home, However, I do manage to stop by Home Depot to pick up paint chips. I am not sure about the exact hues but I want my bedroom to be a shade of mauve and my guest room a shade of gray with a maroon wall. I have always wanted a white kitchen to contrast my silver and black appliances, which I now have. The living room area is still undecided. However, I want the downstairs bathroom to be olive and the master bathroom to be red. I don't normally like bright-colored walls, but a red bathroom is sure to wake me up in the morning and since I am not a morning person, a red bathroom is perfect. As I walk into my home and place my things on the kitchen counter, I realize that we forgot to go to the doctor for Sarah. She thinks she is slick. I know she failed to remind me on purpose.

Calling her, I ask, "Sarah, why didn't you remind me about going to the clinic?"

"Because I am not pregnant."

"Well, I am bringing a pregnancy test with me to work tomorrow."

"You don't have to. I have one, I'll take it right now," she fusses.

"Call me back and let me know?" I insist.

"All right. I am going to rest. I'm sleepy."

"Okay, babe, I'll see you tomorrow."

I have a feeling that she is pregnant, yet I pray she is not. To raise a child as a single mother is not a task I would wish on anyone. Especially when the possible father is an idiot. After washing my hands, I grab Oreos from the pantry, milk from the fridge, and walk from room to room imagining my colored walls. I really should have painted before this furniture was moved in. It is going to be a pain to move these things around the room in order to paint. Perhaps I'll have a painting party.

"Yes, that's a great idea," I say aloud.

I'll invite everyone over for chips and dip and while they are here we can paint. It will be a painting housewarming and I will do it the weekend Dick comes so that we can put his strong muscles to use.

Before I forget, I need to write his visit on my calendar so that I can clear my schedule. I need to confirm his flight time. Therefore, I try calling his cell. As usual he picks up on the first ring.

"Dick."

"What?" he says with irritation.

"I'm sorry, is it a bad time? What happened to hi, beautiful?"

"Hi, beautiful. It's bad timing. What do you want?"

I have never heard him in a bad mood. Curiously, I wonder what's wrong. However, I don't have the courage to ask, at least not right now. "When are you coming here?"

"July eleventh. My flight gets there around three. I'll call you back with the flight number. Is that all?"

"I'm going to have a painting party that weekend. I hope that is okay."

"Yeah, whatever."

"Call me back when you feel better."

"Bye," he whispers and hangs up.

Well, his behavior is very strange. I have never known him to be so crabby. Something must really be bothering him. I hope everything is okay. After writing down my decorating ideas, I decide to turn in early. I can't help but think of Wealth every night as I go to sleep in this luxurious bed. If we don't end up together I am going to have a hard time bringing another man into this room and I bet he knows that. I lie here picturing us in bed together and I begin to get a headache. I really don't want to sleep with him. It's not that he is not attractive, because he is. But it's a different type of attraction. I like his personality, most of the times. He's funny, he's cute, and he is cultured. However, sexually he doesn't do it for me. Now, Winston on the other hand is very sexy. Which is odd, because that is his identical twin. How is one twin sexy and the other is not? As I lie in bed, pondering the question more, I realize sexiness is not a look, but an aura. It is how that person carries himself or herself. It's a confidence that emanates from within. I wish Wealth had it but he doesn't. Maybe it is because he's insecure. He comes off confident and sure, but inside he is a self-doubting little boy who pouts when he can't have his way, and there is nothing sexy about that.

Just before I drift off to sleep, a distant memory pops into my head. One morning I was at the gas station pumping my gas before work and this older gentleman at the pump across the way kept smiling at me. As he finished, he began walking toward me. I tried to hurry and finish pumping, because I didn't want to be bothered, but he reached me before I could get back into my car. He cleared his throat, politely said, "Excuse me," and in a distinguished voice began to speak.

"I don't want to bother you, but I would be remiss if I didn't stop and tell you how beautiful you are."

I smiled and said thank you. Tipping his hat, he told me to have a great day and walked back to his car. It is amazing how powerful words can be. That simple gesture happened four years ago and I remember it like it was yesterday. It didn't matter how bad I may have looked on that day, for no one would have been able to convince me that I was not beautiful. On the other hand, had he said, "I would be remiss if I didn't stop and tell you how ugly you are," I could have looked great, but I would have gone back home mortified.

Although we have our own minds, words have such a powerful affect on our hearts and spirits that they can overpower what we think about ourselves. We must learn to let others' words and actions work to our advantage even if the intention is meant otherwise.

When Evelyn, Tam, and I go out together, we always get different compliments. Men constantly walk up to Evelyn and tell her she is pretty. Tam, because of her voluptuous body, hears the "girl, you are so fine" compliment. However, my compliments revolve around sexy and sex appeal, and up until recently I hated it. I always related the sexy comment to men desiring to have sex with me. It is okay now and then, but every once in a while I want to hear the pretty comment or the fine remark. I used to constantly ask Tam, "Why is it that men like to look at Evelyn's face and admire your body, yet all they want to do is sleep with me?"

Never realizing that it truly bothered me, Tam would laugh and tell me I was crazy. I would change my dress or cover up more to diffuse the compliment, but it didn't work. Now I realize why. Confidence and self-assurance mixed with a hint of smugness can't be concealed, and there is nothing wrong with being perceived as sexy. It is not in the clothing or the makeup or the accessories. It is the person. I think deep down everyone wants to be desirable and sexy and everyone has that potential. But it is something you can't buy, and Wealth is living proof of that. Yet I have it and I am so proud that others think of me as a sexy individual. Sex appeal is something that will last. After Evelyn's face starts to wrinkle and Tam's body grows weak, I will still be sexy. We see sexy elders all the time. Lena Horne is sexy, Sophia Loren is sexy, and at sixty I too will be sexy. I sink under the covers while chuckling at my thoughts.

"I cannot wait until Dick gets here so that we can be sexy together," I say aloud as my final thought before I fall asleep.

Good night.

Chapter 20

Man Overboard

I am so glad that today is Friday. This has been a long week. I find it difficult to go out more than one night during the week because by Friday, my body is dog-tired. Sluggishly dragging my feet, I plop down into my chair and read a big thank-you note on my desk from Sarah. Folded in half, on typing paper, it looks like something a second grader would create for his or her parents. At the end of my homemade greeting card was a note:

PS. I'm pregnant.

"*What*!" I scream. "My mama and those damn fish."
I immediately grab the phone and call her desk. "I knew it!"
"We'll talk at lunch," she whispers and hangs up.
I don't know what she is going to do. Omar has knocked her up, which makes me dislike him even more. Now she is going to have to make a life-changing decision. Today, lunch will be moved up an hour, because I am not going to be able to be creative until I talk with Sarah. Around 11:00 AM, I

grab my purse and walk to Sarah's desk, but she is not there. Minutes later she returns from the restroom.

"Let's go to lunch," I say, grabbing her purse and holding it in the air.

Heavily sighing, Sarah reroutes her calls and walks with me toward the front door. As soon as we step outside the office, I start babbling. "I told you. What are you going to do?"

"Have a baby. Women do it every day," she says casually.

"What about Omar? You can't stay with him."

"I don't plan to. The child may not be his."

"*What! Who? When?*" I scramble to complete a sentence.

"I have protected sex with Omar, but I ran into my college boyfriend when I went to a reunion months ago and we had a one-night stand. It was so passionate but unfortunately unprotected. I am going to make an appointment with the doctor when I find out how far along I am. I will know whose child it is."

"You are taking this very well."

"No need crying now. Besides, my tear ducts are empty from last night's big bawl," she says with a slight smile.

I give her a hug and we walk into the café. We eat a nice quiet lunch with no baby discussion. Sarah doesn't need chastising. What she needs is my support. Calm, silent behavior will encourage her more than my impatient jibbering. On the way back from lunch, Sarah asks me about Wealth. "Have you spoken with him?"

"No, why?"

"I think you should go with him on Sunday. It is this Sunday, correct?"

"Yes, and why should I go?"

"Because it says something when a man wants you to meet his parents. I have been in two serious relationships and only one of the men wanted me to meet his parents and that was because he was trying to convince them that he was not gay."

"But I have already met his parents," I tell her.

"But he wants them to get to know you. He wants their approval. That means he likes you. I wish I had men inviting me on their parents' yacht for Sunday tea. Go and have a good time."

I lag behind, contemplating her remark. Maybe I should go. I'll give him one more chance and if he shows out this time, then that is it. When I get home tonight, I'll call him. I follow behind Sarah and go straight to my desk. Grabbing my notepad, I head to conference room D. The remainder of my day must be spent in silence. This is the only way I am going to be ready for my presentation on Monday.

I am feeling hunger pains by six. Therefore, I immediately prepare dinner as soon as I get home. While cooking, I attempt to call Wealth, but he is not there. I decide against leaving my message to join him on Sunday, for I might change my mind. I simply tell him to call me. Hoping to hear from Wealth before retiring, I stay up a little later than normal. To pass the time, I speak with Tam before going to bed. Unfortunately, she is having a terrible week. Between morning sickness and severe mood swings, she says she is surprised Stan has not walked out. As bad as I feel for her, I cannot control my laughter when she says her breasts feel like ten-pound weights dangling by a thin cord. Amidst her crankiness, I do manage to ask her about Wealth's invitation. Oddly, she agrees with Sarah, saying I should go on the boat and enjoy myself. Not commenting on her concurring remark, I hastily end the conversation. After dinner, I lie on the futon and finish my bag of Oreos. Thank God for my high metabolism. Holding the empty bag, I doze off to sleep before making it to the bedroom. However, I awake in the middle of the night, crawl upstairs, slide into my bed, and finish my peaceful sleep.

* * *

Saturday morning I rise early to go purchase my paint. There is a big one-day sale on designer paints and I have my eye on a Ralph Loren Ruby Red for the master bath. After filling my basket with brushes, paint, decorating books, and painting accessories, I have a grand total of $303.89. What happened to the sale? I had plans to go shopping for a new outfit for the lake tomorrow, but I decide against that plan once I leave the Home Store. If I am wearing a new outfit tomorrow, it will be painted on. Speaking of tomorrow, I haven't heard from Wealth. He must be still pouting over my decision to forgo the boating trip. I guess I will try him again when I get home. I rush into the house as the phone is ringing.

Grabbing the phone, I answer partially out of breath, "Hello."

"Are you okay?"

"Yes, who is this?"

"It's Winston. I am calling to see how you and Sarah are doing."

"We are fine. How are you?" I ask joyfully.

"I'm fine."

Gauche silence fills the next few minutes on the phone.

"Listen, are you going on the boat tomorrow with your parents?"

"It's my last weekend off for a while. I may not have an opportunity to see the boat until late summer, so I'm sure I will go. Why?"

"Because I want to go. Wealth asked me earlier and I haven't been able to get in touch with him to tell him yes. I think he is upset that I declined, but I have changed my mind."

"Well, he is out of town and not coming back home until Monday. He is going straight to the lake from his trip. But you can ride with me. I'm sure he will be happy to see you."

"Good, what time shall I be ready?"

"It takes about forty minutes to get there, so I'll see you around six."

"*Six* in the morning?" I ask loudly.

"Oh yeah, if we plan to catch any fish, we have to start early," Winston says.

"I'll see you at six," I sigh.

We hang up the phone. I go back to the truck, grab my paints, and put them against the garage wall. After retrieving juice from the fridge, I walk upstairs to my bedroom. Pulling out seven outfits, I lay them on the bed. Studying each of them as if they were notes for a big exam, I cram my brain to come up with the perfect combination. I have to wear something cool, but sophisticated—casual with a touch of class. I don't want to pretend I came from money. However, I want to look as if I can handle money if it were somehow thrust upon me. I need an outfit that says I have class and I can be arrogant if necessary, but I don't have to, because my personality says enough. Can an outfit say all of that? If so, none of my clothes do. After hours of experimenting in the mirror, I think I have cracked the case. I decide to wear my gray ankle-length pants and a white linen blouse. With my hair in a ponytail, a thin black belt, and black mules, it's a very '50s look. One can never go wrong with the '50s. That is when women were undeniably the embodiment of femininity. It's an Audrey Hepburn meets Dorothy Dandridge mood. Wealth is going to be pleasantly surprised.

After ironing my clothes, I run to the store to get some wine and fruit to bring on the boat tomorrow. Returning home, I make a few phone calls, then prepare myself for bed. I attempt to call Sarah, but as usual, she is not home. She's probably with Omar. I don't know what it is with her and that dreadful boy. But he has got to go. To relax, I pop in a few jazz CDs, put them in rotation, and crawl into bed with my pint of Häagen-Dazs butter pecan. I swear God put Haagen-Dazs on this planet for women, because sometimes there is no substitute for a bowl of ice cream. And ice cream wouldn't be ice cream without

Haagen Dazs. As I finish my treat, I start to think about Dick. Lately, every time I close my eyes, he comes to mind. I hope to hear from him before I fall asleep, because I really want to know what is bothering him. Running downstairs, I place my half-eaten pint in the fridge. On the way up, I grab a sheet of paper from the printer and rush upstairs to snuggle in bed. Usually when I write, I know exactly what I want to say. But tonight, I write aimlessly.

> **At what point does like become love?**
> *At what point does love fall into love?*
> *I ask when and what differences do they all have?*
> *If I desire to see someone, if it makes me happy to be in*
> *   their presence—*
> *I like them?*
> *If their presence moves me to ecstasy—*
> *I love them?*
> *If their presence creates an emotional imbalance above*
> *   and beyond,*
> *Am I in love?*
> *Or am I emotionally dependent upon someone else's*
> *   feelings instead of my own?*
> *Or are they one in the same? The same in one?*
> *Are they stepping-stones or separate buildings?*
> *'Cause you can love someone and not like them,*
> *And you can like and never love.*
> *But if you happen to visit all three, at what point do you*
> *   reach the next level?*
> *When do you graduate?*

This is going absolutely nowhere, so I fold the paper, place it on the nightstand, and lie down. After tossing and turning for about twenty minutes, I drift off to sleep.

* * *

I awake in the morning to the sound of a continuous doorbell. I look over at the clock and it is 6:05 AM.

"Shoot, I overslept."

Running downstairs, I hear Winston at my door calling my
name. Apologizing profusely as I fling open the door, he
walks in. He says nothing, yet looks me up and down as I
stand there in an oversized T-shirt.

"What's under your shirt?"

"If I have to explain . . ." I say with a hint a flirtation.

"Hurry and get dressed or we are going to be in trouble,"
he suggestively responds.

I dash upstairs while yelling, "Make yourself at home. I'll
be fifteen minutes."

Thankfully, I prepared last night. I jump in the shower and
five minutes later, I am dressing. Seemingly at the same time,
I lotion my body, style my hair, and put on my earrings. Dart-
ing downstairs, I tell Winston to grab the wine and fruit. Then
scurrying back upstairs, I brush my teeth, place the sunblock
in my purse, slide on my mules, and carefully walk back
down the stairs.

"How do I look?" I say with a big smile.

"Very youthful, yet very sexy. I like it," Winston admits.

"Let's go."

He has the basket on one arm and me on the other. We get
in the car and we are off to the lake. Car conversation is minimal as I stare out the window enjoying the scenic route.
Upon arrival, we have problems finding the boat. Finally,
after thirty minutes of searching, we walk to the correct pier
and find his father fishing from the edge. Winston and I walk
up and greet his dad. At first glance, Mr. Fulmore thinks that
Winston is Wealth, but as we get closer he realizes the truth.
However, looking peculiar, he does not hold his tongue when
addressing me.

"Did you switch brothers? 'Cause I could have sworn you
were with Wealth."

"No, sir, I only rode up here with Winston. I am still dating Wealth," I say, slightly embarrassed.

"Good. Good!" he says without looking away from the lake.

Winston hands me the basket and sits down with his father. I take the basket back to the boat. Assuming this is bonding time with Mrs. Fulmore, I prepare myself for the agony. The butterflies in my stomach begin to flutter as I approach the stairs. Wearing a huge, floppy pale pink sun hat, Mrs. Fulmore is lying out on a dock chair soaking up the sun. I place the basket on the table by her seat as she peers underneath the brim to acknowledge my presence.

"I'm glad to see you and Wealth made it."

"Well, actually, I came with Winston," I dither.

She flips back the brim of the hat and gives me a bitter look.

"I mean I rode with Winston. I am waiting for Wealth to get here."

She flips down the brim, looks at the basket, and replies, "What did you bring?"

"Some wine and some fruit."

"Well, dear, that is very sweet of you. The fridge is just inside the door. Have a look around the boat."

She points behind her. I am not sure why she makes me nervous, but I shyly rise and take the basket inside.

It's a beautiful boat. The wood is dark oak and the trimming is brass. There are no fingerprints anywhere; it looks as if it is still on the showroom floor. Careful not to touch a thing, I keep my hands close to my side. Walking back onto the deck, I sit next to Mrs. Fulmore. We sit for ten minutes, before any words are spoken.

Finally, she speaks. "Dear, what is your name again?"

Here I am worrying about impressing her and she can't recall my name. "Lily. I am named after my grandmother."

She says nothing. Seconds later she looks over at my hair. "Your hair is interesting. How do you make it do that thing?"

Her tone would make you think my hair is doing circus tricks. I have natural or nonpermed hair. Today I wear it in small twists which to some people is a phenomenon. I infer that she is one of those people. Usually, I make some cunning remark about me being born like this, but since this is Wealth's mom, I will appease her, this time.

"I take two strands and twist them together. Since I don't have a perm, it curls."

"Oh," she says in a condescending manner.

I will give her the benefit of the doubt, because I am sure she has wanted to ask that question since she first met me. But her next comment is not as easy to swallow.

"My hair is too straight and fine for such a style. I guess you have to have nappy hair for that sort of thing."

Now, if I were not so proud of my nappy roots, this woman would be going overboard. Lucky for her, I love my hairstyle and my appearance. So she and her fine, straight hair can go directly to hell.

Yet I smile and politely retort, "Kinky hair works best."

She doesn't comment, but continues to look out onto the water. Sitting here in silence for an additional ten minutes is torturous.

Suddenly, she sits up and looks down the pier. "Did you say you were waiting for Wealth?"

"Yes," I reply.

"Did he know you were coming?"

"He asked me earlier and I wasn't sure I would be able to come. But I thought I would surprise him."

She replies with a simple "Hmmm." Then she flips up her hat, looks at me, and says, "Well, maybe you should have talked to him first."

Just then I glance down the pier and see Wealth walking hand in hand with Angela. My eyes widen and my mouth flies open. Mrs. Fulmore gives me one final look up and down, rises from her seat, and goes to greet her son. I sit embarrassed in the chair not knowing whether to ditch into the boat or dive into the water. By the time Wealth gets to the deck, I have ducked into the cabin to call Winston on his cell phone. I walk into the boat's restroom and whisper to him, "Winston, I need you to stop fishing and come to the boat immediately."

"What's wrong? What did Mom say?"

"Nothing, but Wealth is here with Angela. Come now!"

We hang up the line. Tightly shutting my eyes, I sit on the closed toilet lid with my head in my lap.

"What should I do?" I whisper.

I cannot let Wealth know that I came here to be with him. But how can he not know? After several deep breaths, I stand. Staring into the mirror, I fix my hair and walk out, prepared to face Wealth.

Before stepping onto the deck, I stand behind the curtain peering in between the cracks attempting to hear the conversation between him and his mom, but I hear nothing. I do, however, see Angela holding Wealth's hand while smiling and tossing her hair back over her shoulder. I take one more deep breath, put on my happy face, and step onto the deck. I can tell by Wealth's astonished expression that Mrs. Fulmore has yet to warn her son of my presence.

"What are you doing here?" he asks, startled.

I smile pleasantly, put my hands on my hips, and answer, "You invited me, remember?"

Wealth looks puzzled. I can tell by his jittery body language that he is just as embarrassed as I am. He begins stuttering. "But . . . you told me no."

Just then Winston walks up from behind Wealth. Strolling around the couple, he stands beside me and places his arm around mine. Smiling at his brother, he comments, "But I am so glad she told me yes."

Wealth's lips tighten as he stares, like a hawk, at his brother. I take focus on my shoes, for I don't know what to say and to whom to say it. Although his comment saved me from immediate embarrassment, I look like the floozy, flip-flopping between twin brothers. Winston and Wealth stand on the deck in a staring contest for minutes until Mrs. Fulmore interrupts.

"You boys should go help your dad with the fishing."

"Good idea, Mom," says Wealth.

Without addressing me, he excuses himself from Angela and walks down the pier. Winston pulls me to the other side of the deck and whispers, "I am so sorry. I didn't know he was bringing Angela. Do you want to go home?"

Part of me does want to go home. However, I will feel defeated if I retreat home. The other part of me wants to stay and have a great time on the boat with Winston. I can show Wealth that I am just dandy, even if he can replace me with Angela at the drop of a hat. So, with that notion, I decide to stay.

"Let's have some fun," I respond, winking at Winston.

He gives me a hug, tussles my hair, and says, "I love it!"

The thought of me sitting on the deck conversing with Angela and Mrs. Fulmore makes my stomach cramp. Winston knows this; thus, he clutches my hand and we head down the pier to grab some fishing rods. The key to making the remainder of this day successful is to stay close to Winston. Sadly, pride rules over common sense, damn near all the time. Winston and I walk arm in arm down the pier, find a quiet spot, and begin to fish. After a couple of hours the two of us catch a grand total of five fish. With shame, we take our fish, our poles, and stroll back to the boat. Wealth and Mr. Fulmore are standing on the dock cleaning their catch. Mrs. Fulmore is inside relaxing and Angela is sunbathing on the top deck. Mr. Fulmore is bragging about his catch for the day and how his sons have disgraced him with their terrible fishing skills. He and I laugh as I kneel and look into his bucket filled with bream and trout.

"Would you like me to fillet a few of these for you?" I ask Mr. Fulmore.

"Do you know how to fillet a fish?" he asks.

"Very well."

My father would take me fishing on Saturday mornings. He believed that every child of a fisherman should know how to fillet a fish. Although I can act girlie and squeamish about touching slimy fish, today is a day for showing off my skills. I think it will impress Mr. Fulmore as well as Winston. Wealth is probably not going to care for it, but I did not come with Wealth; therefore, he can't tell me how to act. Putting on the gloves, as any proper lady would, I take the knife and open the fish from head to tail. Carefully, I pull out the bone without tearing up the fish, and as suspected, Mr. Fulmore is impressed.

"She's a special little lady. I like her," he boasts.

In unison both Fulmore brothers reply, "Thanks."

They look at one another as I simultaneously look away into the ocean. Winston then grabs a few of the fish and heads to the beach area to fire the grill. Since the first meeting I can tell that there is some hostility between these twins. I am not sure what it is, but there is an absolute sign of tension.

The rest of the evening is surprisingly peaceful. Angela comes down from the top deck once the fish is done; however, she remains on the boat with Wealth. Winston and I eat on a blanket with Mr. Fulmore. Mrs. Fulmore gets a headache, takes some medication, and spends the evening sleeping inside the boat. Some family getaway this has been.

As dusk appears, Winston and I head home. Arm in arm, we saunter back onto the boat to grab our things and say good-bye to Angela and Wealth. Of course, Wealth says nothing, but Angela gives me a cordial hug and invites me to go shopping with her sometime. As I respond with a simple nod, she knows and I know we will never go shopping together. Yet I give her credit for trying to make the best out of a situation as thwarting as this. Picking up my basket, I walk back to the car with Winston, and soon as the car starts, Winston and I immediately start to giggle. The giggling spills over into irrepressible laughter. Who knows what will happen tomorrow? But today's adventure is over. Winston turns up the music volume and we sing to Stevie Wonder, The Doobie Brothers, and Prince on the way back home.

We pull up to my house around 9:30 PM and sit in the driveway for a second when he leans in the backseat to hand me my basket. As we watch the drizzle hit the windshield, Winston suggests that I open the garage and he pull in. His tone suggests he wants to come in, and honestly, I wouldn't mind, but I am not going to offer. I take the basket, lean over, and kiss him on the cheek. I thank him for rescuing me today and I get out of the car. After opening the kitchen door, I turn, wave bye, and walk into the house. I put my things down and crash onto the futon.

Seconds later, there is a knock on my kitchen door leading to the garage. Knowing it is Winston, I mosey to the door. With a boyish smile, he stands at the door, arms folded, with his head leaning against the door frame.

"Yes, dear Winston, what can I do for you?"

"I need to use your restroom," he says with a small chuckle.

With one arm folded against my chest and the other hand underneath my chin, I look at him in disbelief.

"Really," he says with a glowing smile.

I slowly place my arms down by my side and usher him to the restroom. Pretending to read a book, I go back and sit on the futon until he is done. When he walks out of the restroom he heads back to the kitchen door yelling, "I'm leaving now."

"Okay, close the door behind you," I yell without looking up.

"Okay, I'm really going to go," he continues.

"Bye!" I yell as if I don't care.

Winston is quiet. Finally, I hear the door open and close. I get up from the futon and walk down the hall. Winston is standing on the inside of the door.

When I come around the corner, he smiles. "You are determined to make me ask to stay awhile."

I nod my head yes.

"Fine. May I keep you company for a little while?"

I nod my head yes again and motion for him to follow me. Winston closes the garage door and walks into the living room. Remaining in the kitchen, I get us some drinks and join him on the futon.

"Television or music?" I ask.

"Neither. Let's do something different. Come up with something."

I lean my head back against the chair and close my eyes until an idea surfaces. I go upstairs and pull a puzzle out of my closet. Tam bought me a 3-D puzzle a year ago. At the time I was fighting with Romance and this was supposed to be a distraction from calling to make up with him. I never opened it. However, it is perfect for this occasion. Returning downstairs, I open the box and scatter the pieces on the floor.

Winston removes his shoes and sits on the floor across from me. "Now, this is what I am talking about. I haven't put a puzzle together since I was a teenager."

We sit there flipping over the pieces so that they all face upward. I talk to him about his career and he asks me about mine. After the conversation is in full swing I ask him about his brother.

"What is the deal with you and Wealth? I sense some tension between you two."

Winston hesitates at first, then slowly begins to open up.

"I don't like a lot of the choices he has made and he knows it. My brother can be very immature at times and we find ourselves getting into arguments over who has the better life, the

biggest house, and the best-looking girl. Don't say a thing. I
know it's silly."

"Oh . . . okay," I say nonchalantly.

We continue to find puzzle pieces that clearly do not fit together. Scrambling around on the floor searching for inter-
locking pieces, we finally we get a match. This puzzle is
much more difficult than I thought. Instead of fun, it's evolv-
ing into a chore. I give a big sigh and fall out onto the scattered pieces. Laughing, Winston picks up the remaining
pieces, dumps them on top of my face. Closing my eyes, I
leave them there.

"Get up. Come on, you started this project," Winston says,
tapping my shoulder.

I pretend not to hear him as he leans over and brushes the
pieces off my cheek. His presence grows closer and my heartbeat races. Winston's nose brushes against my cheek and I
can feel his breath against my skin. He softly places his lips
on my cheek, then slides them onto my lips. Upside down, we
lie on the floor kissing with his nose in the groove of my chin
and my nose in the groove of his. Somehow he manages to
pull my body around and on top of his and we continue to
kiss. Suddenly, my mind catches up to my lips and I realize
that I am kissing the twin brother of the guy I am supposed to
be dating. Overwhelmed, I push him away.

"I'm sorry. This is wrong," I say to Winston.

"It is," he agrees but with hesitation.

Brushing the puzzle pieces away, I move my body off the
floor and onto the futon. Winston continues to lie on the floor
with his hands clasped on top of his face. "I don't mean to put
you in a compromising situation. I just . . . I just wish that you
were not dating Wealth."

"But I am . . . I think. Honestly, I don't know what I am
doing with Wealth, but no matter what happens with our relationship, I feel awkward being with you."

"Just so you know, I have never kissed or dated any of Wealth's women."

"Yeah, right."

"No, really, I have never been attracted to any of them," Winston admits.

I pull my legs up onto the futon and stare at the ceiling.

"Until you," he continues.

Moving closer, he sits on the floor in front of the chair and leans his head back against my feet. His head gently rests on my thigh and that is all I can remember, before falling asleep.

Good night.

Chapter 21

Too Close for Comfort

I awake in the morning to a persistent knock on the door. Slowly, I open my eyes to see Winston asleep in the sitting position on the other end of the futon. My legs are stretched across his lap. The knocking continues, so I rise and walk to the front door. As I peer through the curtains to the right of the door, I rub my eyes and do a double take. I just saw Winston in the room asleep and now I see him standing on my doorstep. I rub my eyes again to verify that Wealth is standing on the porch. The shock awakens me like a pot of black coffee. I run back into the room and forcefully shake Winston to awaken him.

"You have to go upstairs. Wealth is at the door."

His sluggish body is not moving fast enough. Therefore, I grab his arm, pull him off the futon, push him up the stairs into the guest bedroom, and close the door. Running down the stairs, I open the door to greet Wealth. Appearing angry, he silently struts into the house and sits on the chair across from the futon. I take a seat directly across from him and Wealth sighs heavily as he stares into my eyes.

"What are you sighing about?" I ask as if I don't know.

"Why did you come to the boat with my brother?"

I pause to think about this question. I could tell him the truth and be embarrassed or I could keep him wondering about my relationship with his brother. Yet I somehow find sincerity deep within his expression. However, is he upset over the fact that I would choose his brother over him, or more so, that his brother would once again come out on top? I can't let him think that his brother won me over. Hence, I choose to be honest.

"I came to the boat to be with you. You should have known that. I would not date your brother behind your back."

"No, you did it in my face!" he says with a tone of anger.

"Look, I came to the boat to see you! I wanted to surprise you, but instead, you had a surprise for me. I was too ashamed to tell you that I was there to see you, so your brother stepped in and pretended we were there together. Now I want to know, if we are dating, why are you still seeing Angela?"

"So you are not seeing my brother?" he asks.

"No! And do not try to change the subject."

"I did not want to go to the lake alone. You said no, twice, so I asked Angela, but I am not still dating her."

"Whatever, Wealth," I say in disbelief.

"Don't whatever me. If I believe you, you need to believe me. Do not go on any pretend dates with my brother and I will not use Angela as a backup. Can we start over, from this point right here?"

He rises and walks over to me. "Do you want to still go out with me?"

I hold my head down and take a deep breath. Wealth kneels and lifts my chin with a hand.

"Do you?" he asks again.

"I guess," I say softly.

"It's either yes or no."

I am tired of starting over with Wealth. I want to start anew with Winston. But I met Wealth first, and I cannot disregard that fact. So either I date Wealth or leave them both alone.

"Yes."

Wealth places his hands on my face and kisses me and attempts to lay me down on the futon, but I tighten my back so that I cannot be moved. Remembering that Winston is still upstairs in the bedroom, I try to rush Wealth out the door.

"I need to start my day, I have a lot to do," I mention to Wealth.

"Okay, but I need to ask you something. Will you go with me to the NAACP black-tie affair on Sunday?"

"Do you have events going on every weekend?" I gripe.

"I am a member of many organizations. They expect me to be at these functions, so I have to go."

"Fine. I'll go," I say, pushing him toward the foyer.

He shakes my hand to secure the deal, then gives me an embrace sealed with a kiss. As he walks to the door, Wealth turns around and smiles. "Your furniture looks good in here. Do you mind if I take a quick tour?"

He can't take a tour. His brother is upstairs asleep. He will never believe that there is nothing going on, if he sees Winston.

"The place is a mess. You can see it later," I quickly respond.

Swiftly, I ease my way to the front door.

"I see you have paint. When are we painting?" he asks.

"This weekend, now go."

Stepping onto the porch, I watch him get in his car and drive away. I then rush back inside, go upstairs, and awaken Winston. Tugging at his arm, I eventually roll his two-hundred-pound frame from the bed.

"You have to leave," I say to him repeatedly.

Finally, he stumbles from his slumber, shakes his head a number of times, rubs his eyes, and walks down the stairs. Searching for his shoes, which I have tucked way under the futon, he begins to put them on slowly. As soon as he gets both shoes on and heads for the kitchen door, the doorbell rings. I freeze looking at him. He looks at me and both our eyes widen in bewilderment. I scurry to the front door, look out the curtain, and panic when I see that it is Wealth. I smile and hold up my finger for Wealth to wait. Behind the door, I vigorously point for Winston to go away. He shrugs his shoulders, not knowing which way to go, and this Abbott and Costello routine continues until Wealth knocks on the door again. I quietly tell Winston to go into the garage and wait. Thank God, his car is still in there or we would have been discovered. Once he is secure, I innocently open the door to greet Wealth.

"Yes, Wealth?"

"What took you so long?" he asks in concern.

"I had to hide my other man," I say, chuckling.

He laughs and walks into the foyer.

"I left my shades on your chair," Wealth says while walking into the living room.

I walk closely behind him to ensure that he doesn't veer off the path from the front door to the chair and then back to the front door.

"What time are we painting on Saturday?"

"Be here at eight AM," I say, ushering him to the door.

He gives me another kiss and leaves. After Wealth drives off, I wait a few minutes before retrieving Winston from the garage. There is no way that I could keep this up if I wanted to. Dating both of these men would be thoroughly exhausting. By the time Winston walks back into the house, he is wide-awake and bombarding me with questions.

"What did he say? Did he know I was here? What did he say about Angela?"

"He apologized. He doesn't know you are here and he said Angela was his backup date. He assures me that they are not still dating."

"Do you believe him?"

I shrug my shoulders and curl up my lips. "I have no reason not to. I'm not completely innocent, I did show up with you. So we decided to start over. We're going to some NAACP thing on Sunday."

"So you two are still going to date?" Winston asks.

"Yes . . . Now it is time for you to go because I have to go to work."

I force Winston out of the door, go upstairs to jump in the shower and prepare for work. Although my workday has yet to begin, I am already worn out.

I stop by Sarah's desk before going into my department. She looks worn down and washed out, as if she hasn't slept all weekend. Sitting on the edge of her desk, I place my hand over her paperwork. "Are you okay?"

"I have had morning sickness for the last forty-eight hours. They should call it all-day sickness. I feel like crap," Sarah says as her head falls to the desk.

I gently stroke her hair and comment, "Everything will work out. When is your doctor's appointment?"

"Thursday. Are you going with me?"

"Of course."

Just then Reisa walks by and places a stack of paper on Sarah's desk. Sarah does not look up.

"What's wrong with her?" asks Reisa.

"I don't know," I say to her.

"Well, when she wakes up, tell her I need these done by today."

"Yeah, yeah," Sarah says from her slumped position.

Reisa frowns at Sarah and walks away.

"Are you going to be okay today?" I ask Sarah.

"Yeah, go to work, I'll see you around lunch."

I kiss the top of her head and walk to my desk. The day is unusually quiet. However, it works in my favor, because I create best in quiet and I have some writing due by Wednesday. My presentation goes well and I work through

lunch in order to leave work thirty minutes early. Sarah
leaves around one. I hope the sickness passes soon, because
if she feels half as bad as she looks, I don't know how she
is going to take it.

On my way to the car, I run into Dale. As I catch up to him,
I invite him to the painting party. He says that Terry will be in
town this weekend, but that they will come over and help for
a few hours on Saturday. Hopefully, the painting will not take
two days, especially with everyone's help. I should get the
entire job accomplished by Sunday. It will be exciting to see
some color on the walls and it will be twice as exciting to see
Dick. He gets in on Friday and I cannot wait. Sure, I invited
Wealth to the party, but he stays clear of manual labor. He'll
probably come up with some lame excuse by Friday and I will
not hear from him until sometime Monday morning.

Immediately after work on Thursday, Sarah and I go see the
doctor. I despise a doctor's office atmosphere. I don't care if I
am the patient or the person who came with the patient, it's
miserable. I hate the music, the old magazines, and the sickly
people sitting to my left and right. There is nothing to do but
wait and the entire experience is repulsive. The doctor called
Sarah in an hour ago and she should be coming out soon. So
I grab the *People* magazine and pretend to read the cover story.
However, instead of reading, I study the other pregnant women
in the office. Everyone looks so young. I may be the oldest
one in the office. Have I missed my time? I thought I read that
today's women wait until they are older to have children. If so,
the women in this office failed to read that article. I look at the
nervous woman across from me and I can tell that this is her
first pregnancy. She is probably in her early twenties, she
comes from a nice background, and she married into money.
It's obvious from the poise, the designer shoes, and the colos-
sal diamond on her wedding finger. Her baby will be the first

grandchild in the family so all of the pressure is on her, and that child is going to be spoiled rotten. The woman sitting to my left has an entirely different story. This is her third or fourth child. She is so comfortable in the office that she has removed her shoes and is lying in the chair as if this office is her living room. This well-seasoned mom is the type who will wait until the last minute to go to the hospital, spit the baby out, and go back to work the following week. She doesn't bother reading the boring magazines; she has her own book. However, she sleeps with her book covering her eyes because the kids at home have worn her out. Finally the young girl to my right is no more than fifteen years old. She is sitting here doing her algebra homework with her mother, who looks to be my age. I cannot fathom being a grandmother before the age of thirty-five, but I can tell by this woman's body language that my unwanted fantasy is her unwanted reality.

"I'm ready," Sarah says as she taps me on the shoulder, interrupting my daydream.

I grab my purse and we leave. In the elevator, I glance over, detecting the expression on Sarah's face. It's apparent her doctor's visit was not what she expected. As her watery eyes take focus on me, the tears begin to roll down her cheek.

"I'm only a few weeks pregnant."

I say nothing, because I am not sure what this means. A few weeks could be five or ten.

"It's Omar's baby," she wails.

Staggered, I lean against the other side of the elevator. Suddenly, my eyes tear up as if I were carrying Omar's child. As the doors open, I extend my palm and the two of us, teary-eyed, walk hand in hand to the truck. To the nosy outsider, we look like a loving, homosexual couple overwrought with joy due to the success of our artificial insemination. If only it were that simple.

* * *

That evening, Sarah stays at my home. We don't talk about plans; we just eat pizza and work on that laborious 3-D puzzle. Around 8:00 PM, Wealth calls to reassure himself that I am going with him on Sunday. Soon after, Winston calls to see if I have changed my mind about Wealth. Thirty minutes later, Dick calls to inform me his plane lands at two. Due to the relentless phone calls, I have a feeling this weekend is not going to go as smoothly as I first imagined. Poor Sarah spends the evening paving the trail from the living room to the restroom. She is really having a rough time. I am not sure what she is going to do, now that she knows the father is Omar. But I am going to pray that he gets some professional help. After getting to the second tier of the 3-D Eiffel Tower, Sarah and I decide to call it quits. To ease her sickness, I make Sarah a cup of chamomile tea with ginger and honey. After laying out a set of towels for her, I prepare for bed. As I place my head on my pillow, the phone rings. Unfortunately, I have to run downstairs to find the cordless one. Sliding into the kitchen, I grab the phone and answer in haste.

"I just called to say good night," says Winston.

"What are you doing?"

"I know that we have already talked tonight, but I just wanted to—"

"You cannot keep calling me like this," I interrupt.

"May I come see you this week?"

"For what? You have no reason to come see me."

"I just . . . I . . . we have to finish the puzzle," he says with a hint of laughter.

Walking back to bed, I giggle, but I don't want him to think that it is acceptable for him to call me every night. However, it is so hard to be strict when my feelings are evident.

"I'll call you tomorrow from work. Good night," I quickly retort.

"Good night."

After we hang up, I lay in the bed staring at the ceiling. I do not know how I get myself into these crazy situations. I wanted to take things slow with Wealth so I made the decision to get to know him before I sleep with him. Surely, this is a step in the right direction. How was I supposed to know he had a twin brother that would catch my attention? I have got to practice self-discipline. Just because I see things that I want doesn't mean that I can have them. This is a concept I have struggled with since childhood. I hate to admit it, but I am spoiled. I always brushed it off as determination, because when I go after things, I don't stop until I am successful. Nevertheless, I need to learn how to be satisfied and grateful for the wonderful things I have. This is a very important lesson and if it is not learned and put into practice it will cause a disturbance in achieving peace. And what good is success without peace? Therefore, tonight after praying for my friends and family, I add this to my list of prayers.

"I want to learn how to be happy with what I have. I have been blessed with wonderful friends, relationships, and career options and I am grateful for all of these things. I want to appreciate all of the goodness that has been placed in my life so that when the turbulence comes, I can find peace in the goodness until it passes. Selah."

Good night.

Chapter 22

Surprise, Surprise!

It's Friday afternoon and I nearly walk out of my shoes trying to hastily leave work. I am on my way to the airport to pick up Dick. At the same time, I am filled with guilt and excitement. Waving good-bye to Sarah, I skip to the car and drive to the airport. I get to the terminal and eagerly check the monitors. It says his plane is on time, so he should be here in fifteen minutes. The anticipation is exhilarated as I wait in the coffee shop on the main lobby. Once the monitor changes from ON TIME to AT THE GATE, I quickly discard the latte and rush to the lobby where I can see him come up the escalator. Within minutes, I see Dick. With his tussled hair and green shades, his look never disappoints. As he steps off the escalator, I run and jump into his arms. We hug as if he has been off to war. A childlike innocence is plastered on my face, yet a womanly temptation is burning inside. Amidst the tickles and giggles, we finally make it to the truck and drive home.

We exit the truck and as soon as my front door flings open, the temptation spontaneously combusts. Firmly gripping the

back of my neck, Dick sucks my bottom lip, while using his
foot to close the door behind. In one swift move, he pulls off
my dress, lifts my bra, and grazes my nipples with his teeth.
I wrap my frail limbs around his shoulders as our bodies hit
the floor. Pinning my hands to the rug, Dick takes a feverish
bite into my neck as his shorts dangle around his ankles. My
blood vessels rise to the surface as I gasp for air. Tossing me
like a puppet, my master effortlessly flips me over and forces
my hips in the air. I have a moment to catch my breath while
his actions subside. Blowing cool air onto my back, he teases,
as his erect extension slowly circles my lips. Knowing I'm
within the calm before the storm, I hold my breath. Suddenly,
as intense as lightning, he enters me from behind and my
back uncontrollably arches with every forward thrust. My
nails embed into the floor as his wide body envelops mine.
Twisted in this passionate hurricane, our bodies land in the
bedroom. Woozy, I think the storm is over, yet a thunderous
roar clashes as his hips tightly press my body against the wall.
Wrapping my legs around his waist, he drives his body into
mine. His strong hands cling to the wall as his dark, muscular legs slightly bend and part for support. From the waist
down he is all force, yet he holds me in his arms with such
fragility. As if I would break if he were to let go. The whirl-
wind subsides, leaving our legs still intertwined, as we lie
here gazing into each other's eyes. He smiles while gently
running his index finger down the center of my face and the
outline of my lips. The king of the jungle has devoured his
prey and now he wants to cuddle with his lioness. This is the
essence of Dick, a perfect combination of submission and
prowess; a quiet storm that makes me quiver as if the world
is crumbling. When I am with him, I forget about everything
and everyone.

Gazing over at the clock, I see it's 10:00 PM and I have
missed five phone calls, dinner, and the play for which I
prepurchased tickets. Euphorically, I rest here in his arms,

exhausted, hungry, and out of sixty-five dollars and it's all right. I don't care; know why? Because I have Dick and Dick is GRRREAAAT!

Around 11:00 PM after a quick power nap, we awake, take a shower, and decide to go eat. I call Sarah to invite her out; plus, I'm excited for her to meet Dick. We end up at an interesting café, filled with a mix of people from all walks of life. It's one of the few places open past midnight. Sitting at the table, we catch up while waiting for Sarah. I love to hear the zeal in his voice as he speaks about his music. They are working on an album and he asks me to come to the studio to put one of my spoken word pieces on one of the songs. Of course, I oblige. Showing me his appreciation, he reaches under the small table and runs his hands down the inside of my thigh. I continuously titter as we play footsies under the table and hold hands.

"I have really missed you," I say with gleaming eyes.

"I love you," he answers.

I freeze and moisture forms in my mouth as I attempt to say the words in return. However, before any more words are spoken he leans over and kisses me. Interrupting our smooching, my muted cell phone buzzes.

"Hello."

"Hi, baby, I am outside," answers Sarah.

"Okay, come in."

"I am, but Omar is with me. He is parking. He doesn't know about the baby, so don't tell him."

"Fine. Whatever," I grunt.

"And I need you to be nice," she adds.

"You're pushing it."

She hangs up and I go greet her at the door. Once we walk in, Omar stops at the bar, and Sarah takes a look around and immediately heads to the restroom. Thinking she is sick, I quickly follow behind her. When we get into the restroom, she begins panting.

"Are you okay?"

"I just saw my ex," she says with angst.

"Your ex what?"

"My ex from college. Remember? I told you we dated in college and I ran into him and we had the one-night stand. I thought this was his child," she says quickly, vigorously pointing to her stomach.

Sarah begins pacing back and forth, fanning her face with her hands.

"It's okay. We will sit where he can't see us. Where is he?"

We peep out the door; however, she can't see him. Therefore, like Batman and Robin, we stand close to the wall by the bathroom door and peer around the corner.

"There he is." She points.

"Where? What does he have on?" I ask.

"Jeans and a white shirt."

I look around the restaurant and see five men wearing jeans and a white shirt.

"Which one is he? Be specific."

She takes my head and points it in the direction of her ex-boyfriend.

"He is right there! The fine one with the curly Afro," she claims.

Now, ordinarily this would be specific enough; however, the only man with an Afro and a white shirt is Dick. My Dick. And so she needs to be a little more exact.

"What? Right there? The dark-skinned one?" I ask, short of breath.

"Yes," she exclaims.

"What's . . . what's his name?" I say, stuttering.

Yanking me back into the bathroom, Sarah speaks the most dreadful words. "William Dickson. I call him Will, but I think his friends call him . . ."

My right eye immediately begins to twitch and my knees get weak and at the same time we say . . . "Dick."

My heart plummets to the pit of my large intestine and I feel moisture in my panties. I think the jolt to my stomach made me pee on myself. Therefore, I run into the stall.

"Are you okay?"

From the stall I make an attempt to reply. "Um . . . I . . . um."

"Where are we going to sit?" she continues to ask.

Silently, I come out of the stall, wash my hands, and grab Sarah by the shoulders. Looking her straight in the eye, I slowly give her the disturbing news. "It doesn't matter where we sit because your Will is my Dick."

Pausing for a second with a blank stare, Sarah bursts out laughing, while holding her stomach.

"Stop playing," she roars.

As I stare at her with a daunting expression, she realizes the truth.

"He can't be," she panics.

Taking short deep breaths, we pace the floor in opposite directions. Suddenly, we are startled by a forceful knock on the restroom door.

"Sarah, are you okay?" asks Omar from the other side.

She freezes and looks at me. I motion for her to answer.

"I'm a little sick. I'll be out in a minute."

She props her hips on the sink with her head in her hands and whispers at the speed of light. "Dick knows about the baby. I called and told him that it might be his. He was very upset and I haven't spoken to him since. I know he will say something. What are we going to do?"

Sighing, I shrug my shoulders and place my forehead against hers. Peering up from underneath my eyebrows, I respond slowly and confidently, "I have no idea."

I take her by the hand and lead her out of the restroom. Omar is waiting by the corner and the three of us walk to the table. As we approach, Dick's mouth opens and his eyes bulge from their sockets.

I lean over and whisper into his ear, "Close your mouth, sweetie. I know."

I stand and introduce Sarah, Dick, and Omar as if they have never met, and believe it or not we quickly make it through dinner without Omar ever knowing the truth. After dinner, we each walk to our respective cars and I ask to speak to Omar alone to allow Sarah a moment with Dick. Furthermore, I must assure Omar that Dick is only a friend, to thwart him from running back to Wealth telling him otherwise. After minutes of separate conversation, I walk toward the truck.

Bemused, Sarah waves and calls across the parking lot, "I'll call you."

Nodding my head, I throw up my hand and sprint to the truck to speak with Dick. Before I can sit down in the car, Dick is scrambling to form a sentence. "What in the hell . . . how did you two . . . I can't believe you know her!"

"Yeah, that six degrees of separation is a bitch," I say, swallowing the lump in my throat.

We pull off and go to the house. Dick doesn't know what to say or how to say it. Still shocked over the idea that she knows my precious Dick and his precious dick, I too am thunderstruck. I know he's been with other women, but it seems so tainted now that I am aware of his relationship with my friend. We pull into the garage, yet, staring at the windshield, both of us remain in the car.

Finally, the silence is broken when Dick speaks. "She says the child is not mine."

He gets out of the car and walks into the house. I grab my doggy bag and follow him up to the bedroom. He takes a minute to gather himself, and then we sit in the bed and converse about him and Sarah. He tells me about their brief college love affair at Ohio State and the one-night stand a few months back. Dick never knew where Sarah worked or he says he would have put the connection together. He confesses that he once cared for her. But he also mentions that she is very unstable and insecure—two things I already know. Yet he smiles when admitting her sweet, lackadaisical character and her naive spirit. Plus, it was his first interracial love interest and he says he was curious. Throughout our conversation, I realize that horrible tone in his voice a few nights ago was due to Sarah on the other line telling him about the child. Ain't that some mess?

What a difference a day makes. Yesterday, I wanted it to be the other man's child. Now that the other man is Dick, I am so glad that Omar is the father of this baby. Selfish this may be, but the thought of Sarah carrying Dick's baby makes me violently ill. In fact, this entire evening has me feeling nauseated. Yet I am sure a little of Dick's dessert can make it all better, so I cuddle up to him and kiss his neck. And for the first time, he is not is the mood. This is so unfair. Just because Sarah's Dick is now my Dick, I can't get any dick. As a last attempt, I kiss his chest and gently stroke my hand over his limp lower body. Still, I get no response. Finally, I turn over, pull the covers over my shoulders, and eventually make it to sleep.

Good night.

Chapter 23

Here a Dick, There a Dick, Everywhere a Dick, Dick

I awake around 7:30 AM to the smell of chicken and waffles. Running downstairs to the kitchen, I see Dick standing in front of the oven, wearing nothing but a towel. I walk up behind him and run my nails down his dark broad back. Placing both plates into the oven, he whips around and gives me an impulsive kiss. While he is lifting me up onto the kitchen counter, his towel drops to the floor, so naturally he slides himself inside me.

"Sorry about last night. I'll make it up to you before we start painting," he says in between kisses.

I agree with a soft whimper and I finally get my dessert just before breakfast. Temporarily forgetting about the painting party, I swim in Dick's splendor until I hear a knock on the door. Lifting me up, he walks with me wrapped around his waist into the living room. The clock says 8:00 AM and I instantly remember telling Wealth I wanted to start painting around eight.

"It's Wealth," I murmur to Dick.

Carefully removing me from his waist, Dick goes upstairs as I rush to the front door to tell him to hold on. I peep through the curtain and, relieved to see that it is Sarah, I answer the door in my T-shirt.

"What took you so long?" she asks with a peculiar frown.

She leans over and sniffs my T-shirt and begins smiling. "I know what you been doing," she calls out like a young girl.

"Shut up."

We walk into the living room and Sarah sits down on the futon, but immediately jumps up. "You haven't been doing it on this futon, have you?"

"No, Sarah."

She sits back down.

"Not this morning," I continue.

Sarah makes a disgusting noise, then goes into the kitchen for juice.

"I'll be back. I have to get dressed."

I run upstairs and hear Dick taking a shower. This is going to be an awkward day. I hop into the other shower, quickly wash, and grab my towel to dry. When I walk out, I hear conversation going on downstairs. I assume Dick is downstairs talking with Sarah; however, when I walk into the bedroom, I see Dick sitting on the bed.

"Look, you know I've been seeing Wealth. He thinks you are only a friend."

"I am only a friend, right?" he asks with uncertainty.

The vagueness is starting over again. I knew I shouldn't have slept with Dick, but I couldn't help it. At least I'm not sleeping with Wealth.

"I'm not sleeping with Wealth," I confide.

"You don't owe me any explanations," he says while kissing my forehead.

Dick gets up and grabs his white T-shirt.

"But thanks for telling me," he adds. "Let's go paint."

"Okay . . . Sarah is downstairs."

Dick says nothing. He continues walking down to the living room. Minutes later when I walk downstairs, I am surprised to see Sarah and Dick talking to Winston.

"What are you doing here?" I ask.

"You said it was a painting party, I figured you needed help."

"I knew Wealth wasn't coming," I comment.

"Oh, he's coming. He's going to be late. I didn't realize you had several helpers."

"Yeah, I assume everyone has met," I say.

Dick walks into the garage and gets the paint. We decide to split up the rooms. Sarah and I take the living room. Winston gets the downstairs bathroom and Dick gets the kitchen. He has the most painting experience and with the corners and cabinets, the kitchen will be the most difficult. We each pick five CDs and place them into the disc player. Sarah turns up the volume and hits PLAY. We pull up the blinds, open the windows, tape the corners, lay down the plastic, and begin painting. Fifteen minutes into painting the living room, I realize that this is going to take all day, all night, and tomorrow. Painting is a lot of work. She is starting on the left and I am on the right. Our plans are to meet in the middle, but even with large rollers this could take hours. As time passes, I hear a knock on the door.

"Winston, could you get that?"

Winston opens the door, then walks back into the restroom. In walks Dale and his friend. I step off the stool and walk into the foyer to greet them.

"Hi, guys. I hope you are ready to work. Dale, where's Terry?"

"This is Terry," he responds with a veritable smile.

To my surprise, the love of his life, Terry, is a man. I try to conceal my shock that Dale is gay, place a huge smile on my face, and hug Terry as if he is my long-lost friend. I bring the guys into the living room to meet the others. I cannot wait to see Sarah's look. She has no poker face and it is going to be hilarious. I take the remote and turn down the stereo. Dick comes out of the kitchen and Winston peers from the restroom.

"Everyone, this is Dale and Terry. They are here to help."

Sarah's eyes pop out of her head.

"Oh my God, you're gay?" she asks in the highest pitch her soprano voice can reach.

Not only does she have no poker face, but she also has no couth. Dick extends his hands, greets them both, and walks back into the kitchen.

Winston speaks from the restroom while Sarah still stands with shock written all over her face. "Sarah, close your mouth."

Dale laughs and walks over to her. "I thought you knew," he says.

"I had no idea." She looks Terry up and down. "But he's cute . . . good taste," she says, giving him a thumbs-up.

Dale and Terry pour some of our paint into a tray and head to the foyer. I turn the music up and we all get back to work. Amongst the silly conversations, loud singing and spontaneous dance routines, the painting is actually coming along. I am surprised at the progress and the difference it is making.

The pizza and wings arrive and after three hours of painting, it is time to take a break. Winston has completed the bathroom and he's doing the edging in the kitchen with Dick. Dale and Terry are almost done with the foyer. However, Sarah and I have only completed two walls of the living area. I grab the plates and cups, and then we all gather in the dining area. Sitting on the floor, we devour the food. While eating, I hear a car pull up. I go to the door and see Wealth walking up the driveway. I greet him with a hug.

"You can do better than that. Bring those lips here," he says, pulling on my shirt. Keeping my mouth closed, I give Wealth a short peck on the lips. I am uncomfortable kissing him around Winston and twice as much around Dick. I introduce him to everyone and he sits down and eats beside me.

Dick watches us from the corner of his eye as Wealth tries to feed me his pizza. Normally, Wealth is not the gushing romantic. However, I sense he is making a point. The point being, I am his girl. Therefore, I appease him for the moment, before running upstairs to use the restroom. As I leave the bathroom, Wealth's looming presence by the door scares me. He takes my hand and pulls me into the bedroom.

"You look so sexy in that tank. I want you, right now," he says, attempting to lay me down on the bed.

"Are you crazy! Everyone is downstairs. I have to finish painting."

"Who cares? We'll make it quick," he whispers.

"I care. What are you trying to prove?"

"What are you talking about?" he says, seemingly innocent.

"Why do this here, right now? This is not like you. We have to go downstairs and paint."

I get up and walk toward the door. Following, Wealth sighs; however, on the way to the door, he trips over Dick's bags. He looks at me in question.

"What?" I say, trying to conceal my guilt.

"Are these your friend's bags?"

I look at the bags as if I have never seen them and reply, "Yeah, I guess they are."

"Why are they in your room?"

I am quick to retort, "Wealth, I sleep in the other bedroom."

"But this is the master bedroom."

"But I like the other room better. Now let's go."

I grab him by the hand and lead him downstairs. Thank God, I have so many clothes that both bedroom closets are filled. He doesn't know where I sleep and if he ever spends the night, I'll have to remember to make the guest bedroom a little more lived in.

Once we get downstairs, the gang has continued painting. However, Dick and Sarah are having a tickle-fest on the living room floor. Unfortunately, I can't say anything about it, or I will look jealous. Hence, I stand watching until they stop. Wealth grabs a bucket and pushes me into the dining area while Dick and Sarah finish the living room. Three more hours pass and the entire downstairs and guest bathroom upstairs are complete. Everyone is fatigued. Dale has his head in Terry's lap, Sarah is outside breathing fresh air, and Wealth and Dick are in the kitchen talking. Grabbing my camera, I take random snapshots of everyone to capture the moment. I stop in the living room and take a picture of Winston, who is stretched out on the floor. As I lie down beside him, he begins massaging my shoulders and for a brief second, I start to enjoy the attention. At that moment, I remember Wealth and Dick in the very next room. The paint fumes must be affecting us all.

"Stop it . . . your brother."

"It's just a massage, relax."

"You and I will talk about this later, but for now you must stop."

Winston rises and walks outside to join Sarah just as Dick and Wealth come into the room.

"Why didn't you tell me Dick was into real estate?" says Wealth "We have so much in common."

"More than you know," I say under my breath.

Dick looks at the walls and makes the executive decision to call it quits and we all agree. Dale and Terry immediately leave while everyone else gathers in the living room. After saying good-bye to them, I walk back into the room and see the others sitting on the plastic-covered furniture. Again, I get myself into the strangest situations. I am in a room with a man I am sleeping with but not dating, a man I am dating but not sleeping with, his twin that I secretly desire, and a friend who has had a past sexual relationship with the first man. All we need is a corpse and this could be a perfect cast for Clue.

"Well, thanks for everyone's help," I say, hinting for someone to leave.

Winston is the first to make a move. I walk him to the door, give him a hug, and he leaves. One down; two to go. However, the last two are not going to be so easy. For some reason, Sarah doesn't want to leave and Wealth is not going anywhere as long as Dick is here. So the four of us finish the pizza and watch a movie. Wealth sticks to me like glue, assuring everyone of our relationship. I feel like a piece of Fulmore property.

Finally, around ten, Sarah decides to go home. Unfortunately, her leaving makes the situation even more awkward. With Dick on one side and Wealth on the other, the minutes tick-tock at a snail's pace. Although Dick is cool, he doesn't appreciate Wealth's aggressive behavior. Therefore, soon after Sarah leaves, Dick goes upstairs to bed. I excuse myself seconds later and run upstairs.

"Let me get you some towels," I yell to Dick.

I want to make sure he stays in my bedroom if Wealth decides to come upstairs. I guess I'll have to sleep in the guest bed tonight. When I come back down Wealth is stretched out on the futon.

"What are you doing?" I ask.

"Maybe I should stay here tonight."

"Why? You have never stayed here before. Do you not trust me here with Dick?"

"Nope," he says very clearly.

"Look, if you are going to be with me, you are going to have to trust me. If I say he's a friend, then he is a friend. I will see you tomorrow when you pick me up."

Wealth lies there for a moment, then gets up and stands by the chair. He looks up toward the ceiling as he runs his hands across the futon cushion. "Why don't you get rid of this old thing?"

"Are you crazy! This is the futon! Do you know how many stories and memories this futon holds? Between breakups, deaths, and births, this chair is a piece of history. My history. This futon is not going anywhere."

"Okay, okay. I just thought—"

"Case closed," I interrupt, ushering him away from the futon and toward the door.

Walking down the foyer, Wealth stops and points toward the ceiling. "I trust you. I don't trust him and I will see you tomorrow at six. Wear something sexy but conservative. Oh, and wear your hair down. The head chairman loves women with natural hair," he adds.

He kisses me tenderly on the lips and walks to the car. As he walks, I wave good-bye and mock, "Wear your hair up, wear your hair down, wear something sexy, wear something bright."

I abhor his little comments and I will not be his arm piece. Flopping down on the futon, I hear Dick walking down the stairs. He must have been waiting for Wealth to leave.

"You are so obvious," I say as he rounds the corner.

"I can't believe you are dating such a geek," he says with laughter.

"He is not a geek. He's sweet."

"He's uptight. No wonder you can't sleep with him."

"I didn't say I couldn't, I said I wasn't. There is a difference."

"He's not your type. I know you. If anything, Winston is more your type."

Wow, maybe he does know me. But it doesn't matter, I am going to continue dating Wealth and that is that.

"You're jealous," I brazenly state.

"Maybe I am," he says, walking into the kitchen and repeating the phrase.

I go upstairs, into my room, and get my book from within the nightstand. In the guest bedroom, I sit Indian style in the center of the bed and write my thoughts into my journal. As I look up, I see Dick standing in the doorway.

"I miss watching you write."

I smile and continue writing.

"Did your boyfriend scare you into sleeping in here?" he says, laughing and pointing into the guest room.

I say nothing and simply continue writing. Dick cannot stand to be ignored. It infuriates him and I enjoy it.

"Do you hear me talking to you, young lady?"

I keep ignoring him.

"If you don't say something, I am going to throw this glass of water on you," he teases. "Then lick it off drop by drop."

I can't help but laugh even though I try to hold it back. I stop writing, place my journal down and walk into the bathroom. As soon as I close the door, I hear him reading my poem aloud.

Admiration

Could I be your Mona Lisa?
Not to be placed aside and gazed upon
But so that the history of my beauty will always be a
  mystery to you . . .
Priceless, forever lasting, becoming more valuable in
  time.
A beauty sublime for your pleasure,
I promise to always be your treasure
If I could be your Mona Lisa.
Could I be your garden of purple roses?
Not to decorate your environment for others to be
  jealous.
But so that the rareness of my beauty
Can complement and heighten your love
For beautiful things.
My scent reminds you that there is a God.
So odd . . . I captivate your attention every time.
I promise to keep you as mine
If I could be your garden of purple roses.
Could I be your collection of black diamonds and
  pearls?

Not so that you can show me off to your family and
    friends.
But so that the value of my beauty withstands
generations upon generations.
So natural—So Strong,
Time will never separate the bond
And all who know you know how fond you are of your
    gem.
My love feeds off one and you are him.
My protection.
If I could only be your collection of black diamonds and
    pearls.

Dick finishes the poem while I stand in the bathroom doorway. Placing the book on the bed, he sits on the corner and stares.

"I don't know what you are looking for, but he's definitely not the one for you," says Dick.

He gets up, kisses me on my forehead, and walks into my bedroom. Minutes later, I crawl in bed next to Dick. We spoon and go to sleep.

Good night.

Chapter 24

I Thought Tokens Were for the Train

It's Sunday evening and I am preparing for my date with Wealth. It feels awkward getting ready for a date while Dick is walking around watching. He keeps attempting to kiss my body while I get dressed, and as tempted as I am, I can't fool around with him hours before my date; it's just not right. I am finally dressed, my hair is up, and my nails are done.

"How do I look?" I ask Dick.

"I can show you better than I can tell you," he says, grinning.

"I'm serious. I want to look really nice. Does my hair look all right? I look classier with it up, right?"

"Why are you so nervous? As always, you look gorgeous. I don't like this guy, he has you doubting yourself."

"He does not. I just want to look nice for him," I contest.

Licking his lips, Dick walks up, pulls my body into his, and softly rubs his lips against mine. We stand in the living room kissing until the doorbell rings.

"Get the door, I have to reapply my lipstick. Wipe your lips," I say swiftly while running upstairs.

Five minutes later I make my entrance. As I walk downstairs and around the corner, I lock eyes with Wealth. He smiles his infamous fake corporate grin and looks at his watch. I glance over at Dick, who is staring in awe. He is gazing as if he hadn't seen me a few minutes ago. Ironically, I get the perfect reaction, but from the wrong guy.

"Are you ready? I don't want to be late," Wealth says.

I nod my head, grab my purse, and follow Wealth to the door.

"You two have fun," says Dick as he walks up behind me and whispers in my ear, "You look beautiful."

I turn and mouth a silent thank-you, then walk away with Wealth.

Upon our arrival, three very zealous women immediately greet us. They rush up to Wealth as if he were giving away one-hundred-dollar bills. Each of them stares me in the face until Wealth introduces me as his lady; then they each give a fake smile identical to Wealth's facade of a grin. They must have learned that stupid expression in high-society school, first semester in "We Are Better Than Everyone Else 101." Wealth and I continue to walk around as he introduces me to more people. Every time I try to mingle alone amongst the crowd, he asks me to stay close and for the next hour I am stuck to his side, pretending to laugh at his stale real estate jokes. This event is neither fun nor exciting; it is boring with a capital B. Hours later, we sit at table 19 with three other society couples and eat dinner. Banquet food is rarely good, and this is no exception. The look is more appetizing than the taste. The bread is hard, the chicken is dry, and the potatoes have no seasoning. However, on a positive note, the salad and vinaigrette dressing are delicious. After dinner there is a silent auction with proceeds to benefit a local kids' foundation. I have never been to a silent auction before. There are several items donated from professional athletes, team owners, and the NFL. Wealth bids on a classic Warren Sapp jersey, a Bulls cap signed by Michael Jordan, and a Lakers jersey signed by the 2001 championship team. The best part of this evening is when he lets me hold the bidding paddle. We get Warren's jersey for five hundred dollars and the Bulls cap for twelve hundred. However, there are several folks bidding on the Lakers jersey and the bidding grows to twenty-five hundred. Currently, the gentleman sitting to our right is our only standing competition, and as long as I am holding this paddle he is not going home with that jersey. Wealth tells me to stop, but I am drunk with power and I keep going. I raise the paddle at twenty-seven hundred and peer to my right. He gives a slight raise to twenty-eight hundred. I quickly motion the paddle as the auctioneer says twenty-nine hundred. Wealth leans over and squeezes my hand.

"That's okay, I don't want the jersey that bad," he whispers.

But he doesn't understand, I cannot let this man win. I have the power. I have the paddle and I must have the jersey. I look at Wealth and speak in my baby soft voice. "But, sweetie, I want the jersey. I love the Lakers."

I lean forward and bat my eyes. Wealth sighs and peeps at the other gentlemen. Turning toward me, he says, "Go ahead, get the jersey."

I give him a big smile, look at my opposing bidder, and nod my head, foreseeing the victory. Needless to say, the Lakers jersey now sits at table 19 for the cool price of thirty-seven hundred. I love spending someone else's money. It is exhilarating, almost orgasmic. I kiss Wealth on the cheek, excuse myself from the table, and go to the restroom. As I'm walking down the hall, reality strikes me in the head. I just bought a piece of fabric with scribbling all over it for close to the closing cost on my town house. That is insane! Even though it is not my money, I am overextending my credit line with Wealth. Eventually, he is going to want a payment and I hope it's not tonight. I walk into the stall and close the door. Seconds later, two other women walk in and immediately start talking about Wealth.

"Did you see Wealth Fulmore tonight?" asks one girl.

"He is looking good as usual."

Blah, blah, blah, he always looks good. I want to hear some juice, I ridicule behind the stall.

"Did you see his date?" says the other girl.

"Yeah, she's cute."

"I'm surprised. I thought he would bring the white girl again," she continues.

The other girl asks for lipstick and responds to the comment. "Truth be told, I heard the guys bet him that he couldn't find a real sister to bring and he told them not only would he have a sister, but she would be a true, pro-black, natural sister. I guess he showed them."

The two girls laugh and walk out.

Well, well, I asked for juice and got sour lemonade and it is bitter going down. I refuse to believe I am his date because of a bet. I could go in there and show out, but this is a distinguished affair and I am a sophisticated woman. However, when we get in the car, I am going to let him have it. I check my hair in the mirror and walk back into the reception hall. Sitting down beside Wealth, I graciously smile. It kills me to keep quiet, but I am holding my tongue. Thankfully, the evening is ending.

As soon as the event is over, we walk out to the car and I am ready to explode. However, I decide to handle it differently. I am going to ask him questions until he confesses.

"Thanks for bringing me, I had fun," I start.

"Yeah, everyone loved you."

"Really? Well, what if they didn't? Would you not bring me to any more events?"

"Of course not. I don't care what other people think."

I look out the window at the beautiful city lights. This

questioning is going to take too long. I have to expose him right now.

"I know about the bet," I say, still looking at the view.

"What are you talking about?"

I turn to Wealth and tighten my lips. "You know what I am talking about. The white girl, black girl bet."

He gives me a tiny hint of laughter. "It wasn't a bet, it was conversation. I brought you to this dinner because I wanted to. There are lots of beautiful brown women that I could have brought, but I wanted you to come. The one I find attractive, delightful, and intelligent. So tonight isn't about my conversation with the guys, it is about you."

He is so full of himself as he dances around conflict so effortlessly. Maybe I need to take some of those high-society classes. Arrogantly, he answers the problem and manages to slip in a compliment. I don't know whether to slap his face or kiss his lips.

"You're right. I am attractive, delightful, and intelligent and I am glad you recognize that. Although I am not fully convinced with your answer, it will do for now."

Wealth smiles and nods his head. The rest of the ride home is silent except for the Best of Luther Vandross crooning through the CD player. Sadly, Wealth attempts to sing along, but he is no Luther. He is not even a Milli Vanilli. Poor baby, he can't sing. I want to ask him to stop, but I just grin and bear it. Thank God, all the lights are green on the way home.

We pull into the driveway and I get out expecting Wealth to attempt to come in, but he does not. He says he has an early showing in the morning. I say good night with a kiss, grab my jersey, and watch him pull off. I hear giggling as I open the front door. Curiously, I walk down the foyer into the living room and get a nice surprise. Dick is lying on the floor with Sarah. They are working on my puzzle.

Dick looks up at me and speaks. "Hi, baby, how was your night?"

He doesn't even rise to greet me, perhaps because Sarah is stretched across his right leg.

"It was great. Look what I got," I say, holding up the Lakers jersey.

"That's nice," he retorts and continues to help Sarah find a piece of the puzzle.

All I get is "that's nice." This nice jersey cost thirty-seven hundred. Of course, he doesn't know that, but I could at least get a better response.

Sarah looks up and comments, "I hope you don't mind me being here. When I called, Dick told me you went out with Wealth and he asked me to come over."

"*Mi casa es su casa.*" I smile.

"*Gracias*," says Sarah.

I say good night and walk upstairs to get ready for bed. I hope she understands that *casa* is Spanish for *home*, not *man*. Because if she makes her moves on Dick . . . well, she just better not. I light my candles and take a bath. Leaning my head against the tub, I close my eyes. However, the cackling from downstairs is ruining my meditation. I try to maintain my peaceful state but it is no use. Between thoughts of Dick and Sarah, Wealth, and my presentation at work tomorrow, there is no serenity. Therefore, I rise and go into the bedroom. I set my alarm, close my door, and fall asleep.

Good night.

Chapter 25

Opportunity Knocks

My presentation goes very well. My boss, Susan, calls me in after the meeting to tell me how impressed she is with my work. I have never worked for a woman before, but I am enjoying my experience thus far. Everyone tells me how difficult it is for a woman to work for another woman, but I, gratefully, don't share that same theory. Women in corporate America have enough challenges without ganging up on each other. Unfortunately, I think Susan and Sarah are the only two women in this office who understand this premise. Speaking of Sarah, I haven't seen her all day. I am not sure if she is here. Dick came upstairs last night around 3:00 AM, so I am assuming she didn't get home until three thirty; consequently, she may have called out sick. Normally, I don't see her until lunch. But today, I am skipping lunch so that I can leave an hour early to go home to Dick. I only have one more day with him. He leaves Wednesday morning and already I know that I am going to miss him. I stop by the store on the way home to pick up some flowers for Dick. Most men may not admit it, but I think they enjoy receiving flowers. I walk in my front door and Dick greets me in the foyer. He beams as I hand him his bouquet of white roses and lilies. As he places his arms around my waist, he hands me an invitation. I open the card and read my cordial invite to dinner. As Dick escorts me into the living room, I see he has set the room to resemble a restaurant, complete with linen tablecloths and candles. Not only is my place stunning, but also Dick is immaculately dressed. Wearing a crisp off-white linen shirt, brown slacks, and a pair of dark brown Gucci loafers, he is a fashion photographer's dream.

"This is a nice surprise," I say, kissing his soft lips.

He gives me a hug, takes my things, and motions for me to go upstairs.

"Go get changed, while I set the table," he says.

I walk into the bedroom where Dick has laid out my dress and my shoes. I jump into the shower, get dressed, dash on perfume, and rush downstairs.

"I didn't know any good restaurants so I created one," he says while pulling out my chair.

I smooch his cheek and sit down. I smile thinking to myself about Dick's romantic side. Abruptly, I remember my last romantic interlude with him.

"Hold up. This isn't a setup or anything. Sarah isn't going to come out of the closet wanting a threesome," I joke.

"Damn, you found me out. Come on out, Sarah, she is on to us!" he says with laughter.

I look at him as I also look around the room. Although part of me is sure he is joking, I put nothing past this man. For dinner, we have salad, Hawaiian chicken breast atop spicy saffron rice, and fresh steamed broccoli. For dessert, I have chocolate-covered strawberries, my favorite. And they are even better when they are hand-fed by Dick.

"Remember our first night in the studio?" Dick asks.

"How can I forget it?" I beam.

Hand in hand, we retire to the futon. With his head leaning against the back of the chair, Dick shows off his gorgeous smile. "You know, I have done a lot of wild things, but that night is one of the most memorable, beautiful nights I have ever had with anyone."

"I would have to agree with you," I say, eating my last strawberry.

Our background music for the evening is a rotation of Sting, Michael Franks, Barry White, and Marvin Gaye. It is such a strange combination, but oddly enough, it works. Dick positions me on the futon and begins massaging my calf muscles.

"Would you consider moving back to Atlanta?" Dick asks.

"Maybe, if the circumstances are right. Not any time soon, though. I love my job."

"But if you are with me, you don't have to work. You could help me scout properties and write. Wouldn't you like that? I am saying that maybe we could live together and see where things go," he says, softly kissing my calves.

I am silent. My stomach flutters and my heart races. I would love to be impulsive, pack my things, and move in with Dick. However, I have a good job, one that I love, and I am not so sure about shacking up with Dick.

"Dick, I really care about you, but I can't move right now. Things are going extremely well for me. I want to see what this town has to offer."

"Well, I can't move here. My business and my contacts are in Atlanta. Plus, the band is there."

"I am not asking you to move here. A permanent commitment or marriage is not what I want right now."

"I only mentioned moving in. I told you how I feel about marriage. It's not for me. But I enjoy your company, and I want you around every day, and who knows what that may lead to?"

As nice as that sounds, I can imagine living with Dick three years from now and he's still saying marriage is not for him. Furthermore, what if I move in with him and we start not to get along? I can't risk that right now.

"Just think about it," he says, kissing my back.

Then he turns me over and starts nuzzling my breasts. Lifting me into his arms, he walks upstairs and lies down in the bed. As he holds his body over me, I watch his hips slowly grind into mine. As we become one, I am mesmerized by his silhouette against the wall as his back casts shadows of slow rolling, arches, and contractions like that of a snake. Concurrently, his stiff python pleases me to tears. All I can do is think about having this treatment every day if only I would move back. I tell you, dick is amazing. Oh, and Dick . . . he's not half bad either.

Good night.

Chapter 26

Distinction vs. Dysfunction

Reluctantly, I take Dick to the airport Wednesday morning before work. I wish he could stay for a few more days, but we both have to get back to our regular lives. He kisses me goodbye and tells me that he will come back to visit, but I don't think he will. His mouth says one thing, but his eyes say something else. He is upset that I turned down his invitation to move back to Atlanta. His live-in offer is a big step for him. However, I cannot alter my life to shack up with a man in hopes that one day it will become something more. I am financially independent, I am dating and meeting new people, and this is what I need. Things may change in the future, but currently it is unquestionably the right decision.

I slowly walk back to the deck while watching the planes fly overhead. For minutes, I sit in the truck, thinking about Dick, before driving off. If only this were a movie. I would leave the car in the deck, rush to the ticket counter, purchase a ticket, and dart through the airport to join him on the plane. Moving recklessly throughout the airplane, our eyes would connect. Then rushing to each other, we'd kiss passionately in the aisle. Everyone on the plane would clap and cheer; if only life were like the movies, with perfect endings. How come we never see the outcome once the couples return home? What happens when one of them is out of a job and the reality of making spontaneous, life-changing decisions sets in? All we ever see are the credits rolling after the last passionate kiss. However, there are no credits to roll in real life. Time just keeps moving, and as this thought settles in, my eyes fill up with tears. However, I close my lids to keep them from rolling down onto my cheek.

"Good-bye, Dick," I say to myself in the car. "I'll miss you."

I give the deck attendant a crumpled dollar and drive to work.

The next couple of weeks breeze by. Work, as usual, is great. Dale and I have been working together on several new accounts. I am going to miss him when he moves back to California with Terry. Sarah is steadily gaining weight. She hasn't started to show; however, her breasts are busting out of her tiny little blouses. I think pregnancy is such a beautiful thing. I pray Omar doesn't ruin this special time in her life. She can't afford to be stressed during her pregnancy.

Wealth and I are still dating. It is going on three months and we still have not had sex. What is important is that I said I wasn't going to sleep with Wealth until I am sure about our future or until I felt I could trust him with my body. I haven't always made good decisions when it comes to sexual relationships, but I made a promise to myself that I am going to change and I am making progress. Wealth seems to be okay with it, which surprises me. He is used to groupies and women who worship the ground he walks on. These women drop their panties on the drop of a dime and I hear how he talks disrespectfully about them. I am finally applying the morals my mom taught me, and for that I think he respects me. We go out two or three times a week. He has an event to attend every weekend and I am there on his arm with a polished smile. But to be honest, I am sick of these functions. Even he admits that he doesn't enjoy going to them and that he goes out of obligation. I don't know how he keeps up the facade. But being his lady does have its perks. We occasionally have dinner at the mayor's mansion. I have been introduced to the chief of police, who told me to call him, personally, if I ever need his assistance. Furthermore, Wealth holds positions on several boards of directors, which entitle him to free promotional items. Last week he acquired a treadmill from some company that received major funding from one of the boards. Fortunately, Wealth didn't need another treadmill, so he gave it to me. He gets passes to movie premiers, sporting events, and concerts. I tell you when you have money it's easy to keep it because people give you everything. In a couple of months we are flying to Vegas for a boxing event. Like I said, the benefits are incredible. But, as usual, perks come with responsibilities, and today is my day to pay up. I am invited to have tea with Wealth's mother and her southern ladies' social club. I dread spending the evening sipping tea with women who still wear under slips and white gloves. However, I have to go because if I'm Wealth's lady, this is one of my social obligations. Therefore, I call Sarah to invite her; that way I will have someone to talk with. She tries to turn me down, but I will not take no for an answer.

Sunday afternoon, promptly at 3:00 PM, we arrive at the Fulmore residence and their housekeeper greets us at the door. She walks us through the home and onto the back patio where the ladies are gathering. There are ladies in flower-print dresses, white shoes, and sun hats. Between the front door and the patio we have managed to step back in time. I have never seen such a sight.

"Would you ladies like some tea?" offers the housekeeper.

"I know I was invited over for Sunday tea, but I didn't realize that we would actually be drinking tea," I whisper to Sarah.

"I would like to have a cup," she says.

"I'll pass," I say.

We walk over to a table and have a seat.

"This is like a movie," whispers Sarah.

"We are only staying for an hour, and then I will say you have a previous commitment."

"Why me? I don't want Mrs. Fulmore to be upset with me," Sarah whispers.

"Well, I don't want her upset with me either."

"Fine, we'll stay until we feel it is okay to leave."

Sarah politely smiles as she receives her tea. In walks Mrs. Fulmore, wearing a white linen dress printed with enormous pink and yellow roses. She is accessorized with white flat mules, several tennis bracelets, and rose-colored Jackie O shades. She is definitely a lady of distinction. She greets the ladies by the patio door, looks up, and waves at us. We put on our smiles and wave back. Since I have been dating Wealth, I swear I smile more than a beauty contestant during pageant week.

Mrs. Fulmore finally graces our table with her presence. Leaning over, she kisses both my right and left cheeks as if we are in Italy.

"I am so glad that you came," she states.

"Thanks for the invitation. Sarah, this is Mrs. Fulmore. This is Sarah Tether."

"Please call me Nancy," she states. "Nice to meet you, Sarah. I am so glad you came. You ladies mingle and enjoy yourself."

Then she glides away in the same manner she arrived and continues to greet her guests. Sarah and I sit at our table alone until two other young ladies enter onto the patio. I assume they decide to sit at our table because we are the only women here under the age of forty.

One of the women looks like Winston and Wealth. The other is a very attractive Asian-American woman. Sarah and I make introductions as the ladies sit.

"Hi, I'm Bobbi, Nancy's niece, and this is Tao," says the Fulmore look-alike.

"Nice to meet you," Sarah and I say in unison.

We sit and chatter about the latest fashion, *Sex and the City*, and women's roles in America today. While we are talking I can't help but notice the rock on Bobbi's hand. I am surprised Sarah hasn't said anything.

"Are you engaged?" I ask Bobbi.

"I am," she squeals.

"Oh my God, your ring is gorgeous," says Sarah.

"Thanks, can you believe he picked it out himself? We are getting married in Hawaii, but we are having a reception here in September."

"Congratulations."

Minutes later, Mrs. Fulmore rings a tiny bell and stands at the front of the patio. She thanks everyone for coming and makes a few announcements. Apparently this social club has several charitable events every year and they decide which charity is most deserving at these meetings. After her remarks, she unveils the menu and encourages us to eat.

The menu is fabulous. The long buffet table is covered in a peach tablecloth, and all of the appetizers and entrees are embellished atop silver platters. In front of each platter is a menu card describing the dish. As the line forms at the left end of the table, I glance at the first item. We have a choice of Spinach with romaine or vegetable delight with balsamic vinaigrette or creamy ranch. There are three choices of appetizers: shrimp shish kebabs with onions, blue caviar, or fried green tomatoes. There are four entrees:

salmon steak with garlic noodles, vegetable lasagna, Hawaiian chicken with yellow rice, or prime rib with new potatoes. Desserts are at the other end of the patio. I hope they are half as delectable as these entrees, because I am a big dessert eater.

Sarah, Tao, and I return to the table while Bobbi walks around with her aunt Nancy showing off her rock of an engagement ring. As expected, the food is scrumptious. The presentation is beautiful, the smell is savory, and the taste is palatable. Mrs. Fulmore must hire out Wolfgang to cater these events. This food is so delicious that I am discovering new taste buds. Looking over at Sarah, who has her face buried in the Hawaiian chicken, we agree that this luncheon was a good idea. Although the salmon entree leaves me very satisfied, it would be a sin not to try the desserts. I place my napkin in my dish and before I can rise, servers are removing my plate and offering me a dessert saucer. I rise and go to the dessert table. On my way to the table, Mrs. Fulmore, or Nancy as she now prefers, stops me. She asks me to sit with her for a while so that we can talk. Although I abhor having conversation with her, I cannot decline. I walk over and look at the choice of desserts. There are at least fifteen different pies and cakes. All of them are decorated and adorned with fruits, peppermint leaves, and whipped toppings. I study them carefully, for I am not one to try new foods, especially outside the home. However, as everything has been so wonderful thus far, I opt for the coconut lemon cake. I am usually a chocolate lover, but I loved coconut cake as a child, so I think, *Why not.*

I take my cake back to the table and sit with Nancy and her friends. She introduces me as Wealth's new interest and I hate it. I sound like a hobby. As if Wealth went shopping one day, picked me up, and decided to play me every weekend; however, I graciously grin and keep quiet. She instantly starts interrogating me about my job and career choices. She asks everything except for my paycheck amount, yet I can tell she is very curious to know. Continuing to speak, she asks about my mother, father, and the history of my family. I should give her my Social Security number and have her do a background check, because that would be much quicker and I could eat my dessert in peace. Finally, after twenty minutes, she quiets down and takes a bite of her cobbler. Quickly, I raise my fork and take a bite of my cake. Eating a tiny piece from the corner, I slide it off the fork with my mouth closed, mimicking her exactly. I wait to experience the culinary delight and . . .

"Oh my, this shit is horrible," I say mistakenly.

"Excuse me," says Mrs. Fulmore.

Did I say that aloud? I was so overwhelmed by the repulsive flavor that my taste buds must have opened my mouth and let out those awful words. Oh my God, oh my God, oh my God! What am I going to do? She is looking at me. I must make up something. I can't think. What rhymes with "this shit is horrible"? Sitting here with a dumb smile on my face, I watch Nancy give me a puzzling look.

"I said . . . the pit . . . is durable."

She looks even more perplexed than before. Very curious, she asks, "Honey, what does that mean?"

Of course it means nothing, I made it up. Yet I must quickly come up with a meaning.

"It means . . . that . . . my stomach, the pit . . . is durable . . . meaning full. Yet this cake is so good . . . that . . . I can't stop eating it," I say with a huge smile while praying that she buys it.

She pauses for a second, then nods her head with the other ladies. I am not sure what the nods mean. It might be a setup.

"I am so glad that you like it, because that is my dessert," says the lady to my right, who happens to be Wealth's aunt, Mrs. Fulmore's sister.

"Well, I do. I have never tasted anything like it. And . . . you made this?" I ask.

"Yes, the food is catered, but we all bring our favorite dessert recipes." She smiles and squeezes my arm. "Maybe there will be some left for you to take home," she adds.

Thank God, I made it through that crisis. However, the worst is yet to come, because now I am forced to sit here and partake of the heinous dessert. I knew I should have picked the chocolate.

Sarah walks up to the table and asks to speak with me. I excuse myself and walk away with her, while she is whispering in my ear, "Don't mention that I am pregnant. I don't want them to think bad about me."

"I'm not."

"These are not the type of people who have children out of wedlock."

"These people have issues like everyone else. The only difference is that they have enough money to buy a big ol' broom to sweep their problems under the table. But don't worry, I am not saying a word."

"Good. Now, where's the restroom?" asks Sarah.

I point inside the patio door and she walks in. Right now I could walk away from the table and that nasty coconut cake, but I left my purse by the dessert, so I must go back. As I sit down, I push my dessert to the side and join in on the laughter as if I know the context of the conversation. I have a feeling that Mrs. Fulmore is going to ask me about Sarah, so I try not to make eye contact.

"Dear, what did your friend want? Is everything all right?"

I know this woman is Creole, but is she psychic as well. Maybe I can use this opportunity to make my exit from the party.

"She wanted to remind me of another engagement we have to attend this evening."

"Oh, really, where are you going?"

Well, isn't she inquisitive? Mrs. Fulmore, the nosy Creole psychic from New Orleans. She should have her own talk show. She probably knows voodoo, also. I knew there was something odd about her and Mr. Fulmore. He is so sweet and kind. Why would he marry her? Under normal circumstances he wouldn't. She probably took a piece of his hair and concocted a love potion or buried his underwear in the backyard.

As I tear myself away from my vivid imagination, I look at her and politely say, "A friend of ours is performing at a poetry house this evening. It starts at seven."

"I used to attend those back in the sixties. I thought I was so cool and chic."

"I'm sure you were then and you still are now," I compliment her.

Leaning over, I give her a hug and a kiss her on both cheeks—hell, when in Rome . . .

"You better get going," Mrs. Fulmore says.

Great! I killed three turkeys with one blow. I didn't tell her about Sarah, I am leaving this boring tea party, and I didn't have to eat that crappy cake.

"Oh dear!" calls Mrs. Fulmore. "You forgot your cake. Want me to wrap it up for you?"

"Thanks. I'll eat this tonight before I go to sleep."

Mumbling underneath my breath, I comment, "Man, if I eat this tonight I may go to sleep . . . *forever*."

Catching Sarah's arm on her way back to the table, I walk with her to grab her purse. We say good-bye to Tao and Bobbi, walk through the house, and get into the truck. I sit down and immediately bow my head.

"What are you doing?" asks Sarah.

I hold up one finger until I finish praying. "I'm asking forgiveness for all of the lies I have told this afternoon. I can't spend too much time with that woman. I have enough sins to account for. Hanging with her is sure to guarantee me a front row seat in hell."

We drive home. As I pull into the garage, I hear the phone ringing from inside. I calmly sit in the truck and listen to it ring. I hate rushing inside to try to catch the phone, because most of the time it's too late. My new theory in life is to never rush. For when we rush, small details are often neglected. Furthermore, I am too hyper. I am going to slow my pace with everything so that I can take in more of my surroundings.

I leisurely walk into the house, throw my keys on the counter and my coconut cake in the trash. I walk upstairs and run my bathwater, and as soon as I look under the counter for the bubbles, my cell phone starts ringing. I get my purse off the bed and answer the phone. It's Stan. Tam started having pains and she had to go to the hospital. She wanted Stan to get in touch with me. The doctors say it is normal for a first pregnancy and they will keep her overnight to monitor the baby's heartbeat, but that she should be fine. I am unable to speak with her, but he assures me that all is well and that I don't need to fly there. Stan says he'll call when she wakes up in the morning.

I hang up, take off my clothing, and sit in the tub. I am so glad Stan is there for Tam. I only wish that I could be there during her pregnancy. I guess God knew that she would have Stan, therefore, he moved me here to Missouri, knowing Sarah would need someone. I sink lower in the tub and continue bathing. As I attempt to clear my thoughts and relax, I think more about Sarah. Stepping from the cool water, I rinse and dry off. Then I slide on my panties and one of Dick's tank tops, before slipping into bed. I lay contemplating Sarah's situation. She is going to need someone in her life. Someone who treats her with the kindness and respect she deserves. She hasn't told Omar about the baby because she's afraid that he will deny the child; plus, she finally confessed that her father would vehemently disagree to an interracial relationship. She doesn't have anyone to confide in or rely on. I hope she knows that I am here for her. It's so strange how things work out. She was occupied trying to get me a date with Wealth and she ends up pregnant by his friend. Deep down, I know that all things happen for a reason and I would like to think that those reasons are associated with blessings, and Sarah is definitely in need of a few blessings. I pray they come soon.

Good night.

Chapter 27

Spontaneity Makes Us Fun; Practicality Makes Us Adults

At last, Sarah decides to tell Omar about the baby and he does exactly what she expects. He says she is trying to set him up and that the baby is not his, and although Sarah anticipated this reaction, it still sends her into a tizzy. He does agree to a blood test, but until then, he says he is not going to help her with this child. This week she has to tell the job about her pregnancy, because she is starting to show. There is already office gossip about who the father is. Some say it's Dale and others think she was artificially inseminated for her and her female lover. I guess office gossip is the same no matter the city. Our company has a maternity leave policy and Sarah has been here long enough to receive those benefits, so she decides to work up until the time of pregnancy and take off four months after. I am not sure what she is going to do about a babysitter. I guess we will figure that out when the time comes. Finally, noon arrives and I call Wealth to check his lunch plans.

"Hi, Wealth."

"Can I call you back? I'm in a meeting," he quickly suggests.

"Yeah."

I hang up the phone and go back to work. Minutes later my phone rings. It's Wealth.

"Hello," I answer.

"Why is your girl trying to trap Omar?" he asks without saying hello.

"Excuse me. Sarah is pregnant with Omar's child. She did not trap him, they are in this mess together."

"Well, he says it's not his, so I have to believe him."

"Fine. We'll see once they take the test," I say to Wealth.

"So, how has your day been?" he says.

"That's something you should have asked me four sentences ago. I really don't feel like talking now and I have to go back to work. I'll call you later," I say, hanging up.

He has some nerve accusing Sarah of trapping Omar. Why would anyone try to trap a lowlife? That's like fishing for fish bones. If I were to get pregnant by Wealth, I would strangle him if he accused me of trapping him. I know some women do things like that, but I am not that type of woman and neither is Sarah. Omar is not even rich . . . I don't think.

I pick up the phone and call Tam to check on her, and after two transfers, I finally get her on the line.

"Hi, baby, how are you feeling?" I say to her.

"Tired. This baby is wearing me out. I'm almost four months. What am I going to do at nine?"

"I wish I could be there. I miss you. You have to send me pictures. I want to see each month of your pregnancy."

"Yeah, okay. But you still need to visit. You know I can't fly after my third trimester and I can't drive, because I will have to stop and pee too many times."

"You are silly. I will come visit," I promise.

"Oh, how was your visit from what's his name?" asks Tam.

"Ha, ha. You know his name."

"Oh yeah. It's Dick, right?"

"It was nice. I'll give you details later. Hopefully, I will get to see him. When I come visit."

"You're in love with that boy. I don't know why you can't admit it. What is wrong with you?"

"I don't know," I say, discouraged.

Looking up, I see my boss, Susan, walking down the corridor. "Look, I'll call you back either tonight or tomorrow."

"Okay, I love you."

"Love you too. Bye."

Susan walks to my desk and asks me to meet her in her office after lunch, around one. Without question, I agree, yet I wonder what she wants to talk about. I watch her in a sharp blue pantsuit forcefully walk back toward her office. She wears a different suit every day. The only articles I have seen her repeat are shoes and blouses and I have been here four months. I am glad we are not required to wear suits. They let the creative development department wear whatever we want, within reason, of course. We are the artists, often misunderstood, yet appreciated. We can't be constricted with suits and ties, for they stifle our creativity. Our superiors probably think we are nuts. However, as long as they keep paying us, they can think whatever they like.

I repeat Tam's message to myself. "You are in love with that boy. I don't know why you can't admit it."

I wonder what made her say that. I love Dick, but in love? I don't think I am in love. I pull out my notepad and begin to write a few lines. Dale walks up to my desk as I write my last line and snatches the pad from my hand. He walks around to the front and begins to read it. Seconds later, he responds.

"I like this. What are you writing this for?" he asks.

"For me. It's not for work. Give it here!" I reach for the pad, but he moves it away.

"It's a little explicit, but I am liking it. Is there a title?"

"They are just thoughts I wrote down. It doesn't have a title," I say.

"Well, give it one."

"Fine. What's His Name? That's the title."

He nods in agreement and places the pad in my hand.

"Let's go do some work," says Dale.

I grab my notebook and Dale and I head to the meeting room.

After lunch, I stop by my boss's office.

"Is now a good time?" I ask.

"Come on in, close the door," she says.

As I walk in, I suddenly become nervous. No one likes to be called to the principal's office. My heart starts beating fast. However, for the first time, I know I haven't done anything wrong. I haven't been late, I haven't taken too many days off, and I have been receiving great comments on my work. Therefore, I should have nothing to worry about.

"I want to talk to you about Sarah," she says.

"Okay."

"Is everything all right with her? She has not been herself lately. She has been late to work and she looks fatigued. I know about the pregnancy, but this is not like her. I only ask you because I know that you two are friends."

I'm relieved that the meeting is not about me, but I wish it weren't about Sarah either. I was never a tattletale friend. I know Susan means well, but she should be talking with Sarah.

"She is dealing with a lot of things. But, she is okay. You should talk with her."

"Okay, I will. Thanks for coming in," she says.

I nod and walk out of the office. I walk by Sarah's desk to speak to her, but she isn't here and this has become common lately. I go into the ladies' restroom and call her name. However, she is not in here either. Maybe she took a late lunch. I go back to my desk, finish my day, and drive straight home. Although it is only Wednesday, I feel as though it is Friday and I am tired. I am going to go to sleep when I get home. As my house comes into view, I see Sarah's car sitting in my driveway. I moan because I know that this means Omar has done something stupid, but right now I am too drained to hear about it. As I pull up to the house, she pulls out of the driveway so that I can get into the garage. Leaving the door open, Sarah walks in. The moment I look into her eyes I see that she has been crying.

"Omar says I should have an abortion and that he will never support my decision to have the baby."

"So he's admitting that this child is his?" I ask.

"No. But he says even if it is his, he doesn't want to be with this child or me!" she bawls.

Sarah stretches across the futon as I go get her some tissue. This scene is becoming a little too familiar. I go into the kitchen and heat her up some food.

"Are you okay, do you need me to stay down here with you?" I ask.

She shakes her head no.

"Okay, the food is on the stove, you know where the towels are, I believe you still have clothing over here, and the linen on the bed is clean. If you need me, call me. I am so tired, I have to go lie down."

I don't want to be insincere, because I am here for her. Nevertheless, I can't do a thing about Omar not wanting her or this child. She is probably better off without him, but that is not what she wants to hear right now. More than anything, she doesn't want to be alone, so as long as she knows that I am in the room across the hall, she will be fine. I go upstairs, close my door, and lie perpendicular across the bed. I sleep for hours, but the ringing phone awakens me. I look at the clock. It's ten and I can't believe I have been asleep for four hours. Rolling over, I grab the phone. It's Dick. I haven't spoken to him since he left.

"Are you asleep?" he asks.

"I was, but it's okay. How are you doing?"

"I have been busy writing. We have more gigs coming up in September. We are doing a college tour."

"Congratulations. Are you coming here?" I ask.

"Not sure."

"I thought about you today, I even wrote something inspired by you," I say.

"Really?" he responds with doubt.

"Yes. I miss you," I blurt out.

He is silent. All I hear in the background is music.

"Did you hear me?"

"Have you given any thought to moving back here?" he asks.

"I have thought about it but nothing has changed."

"Okay, well, I miss you too."

"What is wrong with you? Why are you getting all serious on me? What happened to the fun, spontaneous Dick that never wanted to settle down?"

"I never said I didn't want to settle down. I said I have issues with marriage, but I want to find a woman I can be with," he says in a staid tone.

"I don't know what to say."

"It's cool. I didn't call to upset you. I just wanted to hear your voice. I'll let you go back to sleep. Call me later."

"Okay . . . Hey, I love you," I add, but it's too late, he hangs up the phone.

He sounds strange. This is a different side to Dick. He is usually very friendly and jovial. I can tell things are changing in our friendship. Intimacy does that. Usually, it affects the woman more than the man, but I have learned to master the game. I never want to be the helpless woman running after a man who only wants to be her friend. Look at Sarah. She is a mess and that will never be me. There is nothing wrong with love as long as it is a mutual understanding between both parties. I hate to sound technical, but love is complicated. It should come with instructions and diagrams. I don't want to become so vulnerable that my emotions govern my decisions.

"I cannot allow myself to be put in that situation," I say to my twin self.

"So, will I ever be able to completely fall in love?" my twin says back.

Hold up! I think my mom once said it's okay to talk to yourself as long as you don't answer back. However, I just answered back. What does that mean? Am I going crazy? I sit in the center of my bed looking from side to side, yet keeping my head straight ahead. One twin wants to love and the other is afraid to love. Maybe if I talk to my scared twin and let her answer back in writing, it won't be considered talking to myself. I jump up and grab my journal. As my scared twin throws out thoughts of love, my strong twin answers on paper. This is truly unusual. It is the first time I've written anything to myself. I read it again and at first it reads like gibberish. Yet as I read it a second and third time, it makes perfect sense. I fall back onto my pillows and place my journal on my nightstand.

"I have to see him," I whisper.

I will take a couple of days next month and go back to Atlanta. I need to share some laughs with Tam and I need to share some thoughts with Dick.

Good night.

Chapter 28

The Fabric of Our Loves

Two weeks pass and I have been extremely busy at work. I haven't had much time to spend with Wealth; however, we still see each other at least once a week. We had a beautiful evening the other night. He came over and we made pizza from scratch. Then we fed it to each other while watching reruns of *The Cosby Show* on Nickelodeon. He confessed his crush on Denise Huxtable as I confessed that I wanted to be Denise Huxtable. It was a wonderful night. Sleeping together, we curled up on the futon and for once he didn't attempt to remove my clothing. It was a sweet, innocent evening. A nonsexual dating relationship definitely cuts down on the stress. Yet I know the anxiety is building and I don't know how long Wealth is going to be patient. Furthermore, I have to admit, I am becoming curious. I want to wait a few more months, just to be sure, but a few more nights like this last one and our relationship may move to the next level.

I look at the calendar on my desk and circle August 12 with a red Sharpie pen. I am going home to Atlanta for a few days.

Although I was not raised in Atlanta, I consider it the home of my roaring twenties and I will be there in two weeks. I spend my morning at work planning my trip back home. I know it's two weeks away but I anxiously anticipate the visit. Tam, Evelyn, and I are going out Friday night; Saturday, Tam and I are shopping for the baby; and I want to spend Saturday evening with Dick. I would like to surprise him, but because we have such separate lives, I don't think surprising him will be a good idea. Therefore, I will call him the week of my visit. I am excited to see Tam waddling around in maternity clothing and although she is only four months, she says she has gained almost fifteen pounds. Certainly, I am just as excited about seeing Dick. His visit was three weeks ago and we have only spoken twice in those weeks. I used to talk with him every other day and I miss his conversation and laughter. If he lived here, without question I know we would be together. But he is not moving here and I can't move back there and I guess there is no compromising. However, when I see him I am going to tell him how I feel and who knows, it may change his mind about moving. Surely, this would mean I would have to do something about my boyfriend. However, if I had to draw straws, in no way does Wealth compare to Dick. I miss Dick tremendously, and if he made the effort to begin a relationship with me, Wealth would have to go. I am so engrossed with drawing doodles around the twelfth on my calendar that I don't see Sarah standing in front of my desk. Finally, she leans forward and grabs my pen. I look up at her strange expression.

"Omar's mom wants to meet me."

"What?" I ask.

"She called up here and she wants to meet me this weekend. What should I say?"

"Go meet her. She is going to be the child's grandmother. Maybe she wants to be involved."

Sarah walks around, picks up my phone, and clicks on line

three. She agrees to meet with Mrs. Richard on Saturday. Once she hangs up, she leans on the corner of the desk.

"I wonder if she knows I am white," she says with a puzzling look.

I gasp at her statement as if I didn't know. "You're white? Why didn't you tell me?"

"Maybe if I lie out over the next few days, I can pass for nonwhite. Look at Mrs. Fulmore, she's as light as I am."

I look at her and grin. Sarah grabs my purse and hands it to me, which is our cue for lunchtime. As we start to walk down the hall, I reach over and pat her on the bottom.

"You can get as dark as you want to. But your ass is going to give you away every time," I say, showing off my ethnically structured rear end.

She hollers and pushes me away. We stroll to the car and go to lunch. I call Wealth before leaving work to invite him out for dinner. My refrigerator is bare and I don't want to stop by the store. As much as I love home cooking, eating out is a more simple solution. Unfortunately, he is not home and not answering his cell. Sarah has a hair appointment, so she can't go. Yet I don't want to go alone; it seems so desperate and lonely. Who eats at a restaurant alone? Half the pleasure is the company. Therefore, I call Winston. I haven't seen him in a while and I definitely enjoy his company. His office puts me on hold for ten minutes. Finally, he comes to the phone and answers with agitation.

"Hi, Winston, it's Lily."

"Hi, love, what's going on? Is everything okay?" he asks as his agitated voice starts to soothe.

"Yes. I am seeing if you have plans for dinner this evening. If you are available, would you like to attend dinner with me?"

He pauses. I can hear someone speaking to him in the background. I don't know if he is listening to them, or pausing to think of a way to turn me down. I quickly speak, to ease the tension. "If you can't go, I will understand."

"No. I am not busy, I just don't know what time I will get out of here. If you're hungry, you better go without me. But if you can wait, I'll call you back in an hour or so."

"I can't promise I will wait, but please call me back."

"Will do. I have to go."

So much for dinner plans. I really need to get out and meet more people. However, meeting people is not the problem; liking those people enough to hang out with them is. The only people I like at work are Dale and Sarah. My boss, Susan, is cool. I could socialize with her if she weren't my boss. That is an awkward situation. Hanging out after hours with the boss can lead to tension is the work environment. I did enjoy Tao's company at Mrs. Fulmore's tea. However, I met Tao through Wealth's cousin, Bobbi. Therefore, according to social rules, I would have to invite Bobbi and Tao out for an evening. I can't bypass Bobbi to hang out with Tao, especially since Bobbi is related to Wealth. It wouldn't be proper and the Fulmores are a very proper family.

After failing to find a dinner partner, I drive by the Farmer's Market to get a fresh spinach salad. Tonight's dinner is going to be very light. Walking back to the car from the store, I pass through a spiderweb and it completely freaks me out. I can tolerate many things but walking though a spider's web is not one of them. What if the spider lands on me as I am destroying his home? What if he decides to spin a web on my head or lay eggs in my hair? The hypotheses drive me crazy. As a result, I walk in my door, begin stripping and heading toward the restroom. I immediately have to shower and wash my hair. As extreme as it may sound, it is one of my quirks. I step out of the shower, wrap my hair in a towel, and throw on a silk nightgown, which is rare evening attire for me. I am a cotton tank, boxers, and sweats girl. Yet, occasionally when I feel feminine, I like the feeling of silk against my skin. It is nice loungewear, yet it is too slippery for sleeping attire. Sometime during the night, either your breast hangs out, the gown is twisted right when your body is lying left, the hem of the gown has worked its way up around your waist, or the straps have fallen to your elbows. It looks great on the body, but is not practical and comfortable like cotton.

Grabbing my salad, I turn on the TV, sit Indian style on the futon, and enjoy the feeling of silk against my skin. With each bite I take, I begin to think of Wealth, for he reminds me of silk; and the more I think, the more I realize I can compare all of the men I know to fabrics. Wealth is like silk. He looks great on the body because he gives off a certain image. But just like silk he is high maintenance. He knows he has a lot to offer, mentally and financially, and because of this his trust is not easily gained. Therefore, I have to be patient and handle him with care. Furthermore, because of his elite statue, he expects only the best. These characteristics translate to stains easily and dry-clean only. Just like silk, he feels good and looks good, but he is not always practical.

Romance, on the other hand, is polyester. A man-made fiber that can take on many textures. Polyester can fool you. These days polyester can look and feel like silk, cotton, or linen. It's a tricky one. Yet, like my old friend Ro, it means well. Polyester doesn't deceive on purpose, it just wants to give you a finer look on a realistic budget. It never goes out of style and will continue to improve with time. Everyone has a little polyester in his or her closet because it is practical. Unfortunately, it doesn't allow us to breathe. This is an awful trait of polyester and no matter the fancy texture, it remains the same. I need my fabric to breathe.

This brings me to cotton. I love cotton. Cotton moves with the body. Sometimes we have to be delicate, but most of the time it's machine washable and tumble dry. Dick is definitely cotton. He feels good and he is practical. Sure, it wrinkles and shrinks, but it wears so well. Besides, we can iron the wrinkles and buy according to shrinkage and it may take a little time to get the perfect fit, but once we have that fit, it lasts forever. There is nothing like a pair of perfect-fitting jeans. They may shrink a little in the dryer, but when you wear them for a couple of hours, they conform to your shape. This is how I feel about Dick. It may take some work and strategy, but I know I can get that perfect fit, and once I do, it is going to be well worth the effort.

I lean over and grab the remote as my right breast falls out of my silk gown. This would not have happened in a cotton tank, which only confirms my theory. I go upstairs and change clothing. On my way downstairs, the phone rings. It's Winston.

"Are you still up for dinner?" he asks with eagerness.

"I think I'm in for the night."

"Well, how about I grab something to eat for us and come over for a few minutes?"

I look over at the clock. It's only 7:20 PM. "That will be fine. I'll see you in a few."

I hang up, run back upstairs, and pull on my jeans. I wonder what fabric is Winston. I go into the restroom, divide my hair down the center, and place it into two pigtails. It's still wet and although cotton absorbs moisture, another great property, I don't like the water dripping down my shirt.

Thirty minutes later, I hear Winston pulling into my driveway. I thoroughly enjoy his company; however, I must enjoy it in moderation. When he is around I have to constantly remind myself that I am dating his twin brother. Opening the door, I greet Winston with a cordial hug. He is wearing dark gray slacks and a faint gray shirt. Surprisingly, he is wearing glasses. I have never seen him in glasses before. It's a sexy look. He comes in with two large bags and places them on the kitchen counter.

"I brought Chinese, little girl," he says with a smile, while tugging on my pigtails.

"I can't eat Chinese. It makes me sick," I say with a frown.

"I didn't know. I'm sorry."

"It's okay, I had a salad. Come in here with me and eat."

We walk into the living room and sit on the futon. Grabbing a pillow, I place it to my left as I lean on the right arm of the chair. The pillow is my fort. It will ensure that Winston stays a safe distance away from me. He sits at the other end of the futon, placing a pillow to his right. We both know the tension is there and we know we can't cross that line. It would be best if we didn't hang out at all, yet we are thrill seekers. Desiring the excitement of temptation, we live on the edge.

Over the next hour, we talk about his career, his parents, and my friends in Atlanta. I tell him about Romance, Dick, and Tam and he shares stories about his ex-fiancée. He was engaged to his high school sweetheart. They took a break during the first years of college, but started dating again before graduation. They dated while he was in medical school and he proposed right after graduating. However, during his first year of residency, she lost interest and confessed that she could not deal with the stress of being a doctor's wife. She didn't want to become second behind his patients.

"The truth is she had fallen for another man and wanted to be with him," he says with vexing temperament.

"Well, maybe she couldn't deal with the title 'doctor's wife.'"

"The other man is a doctor. They have been married for two years. They just had a beautiful little girl."

"How did you know that?"

"I delivered her," he says calmly.

"You really like awkward situations, huh?" I ask, laughing.

"It wasn't my idea. She went into early labor. Her doctor was away at a conference and I was taking his patients. I could have passed her on to another doctor, but when I went in to talk with her, she was so scared. She asked me to stay and I couldn't turn her away. She trusted me and that meant a lot."

I listen to his sincerity as I watch him finish his Chinese noodles. Looking into his eyes, I see that Winston is a good man. Nevertheless, I can tell that this woman hurt him and it only makes it more difficult for the next.

"I better get ready to go. I have an early morning," he says, walking into the kitchen.

I rise and stand in the foyer waiting for him to come around the corner. He gives me a hug, grabs my pigtails, and pulling me close to him, kisses my forehead. Winston places his hands on my shoulders after the kiss and looks me in the eye.

"What is my brother? Your boyfriend?" he asks curiously.

"He didn't pass the note and ask me to check the box, but if I have to give it a title, I would say yes."

Winston slides his hands down my arms and grabs my hands. He kisses the right hand first and then the left.

"It's good to see you," he says with a wink of his eye.

He turns and walks out the door. Slowly, I walk down the foyer. Cutting off the lights and the television, I make my way upstairs, remove my jeans, and slide into the bed.

Going back to my fabric analysis, I come to the conclusion that Winston is like linen. He is similar to cotton, just as practical and comfortable, but a little more troublesome. Linen wrinkles like old skin. No matter how many times it gets ironed, one sit creates more wrinkles. It looks best when you are standing around or walking. It's machine washable, if laid flat to dry, but best results are when dry-cleaned. I like Winston, but I have to be careful or else I may create wrinkles that will never be ironed out.

Closing my eyes, I begin comparing myself. What fabric am I? Wool, perhaps? It has great texture and is practical. Wool is a little more maintenance than polyester, but less than silk. Unfortunately, if it gets too close to the skin, it will itch. I'm a great friend, but once you delve deep into my psyche, there could be problems. Wool pants wear very well if taken care of, but for your protection you best get them lined.

Good night.

Chapter 29

Ulterior Motives of a Man

I awake to Tam's 6:30 AM phone call. She is excited about me arriving in Atlanta tomorrow. She is picking me up from the airport and wants to check the flight and time. I would normally be upset about my phone ringing at that time of the morning, but this is Tam and I love her so much. I laugh as she tells me about how crazy it feels to have sex while she is pregnant and how she never thought she could love a man the way she loves Stan. As I hear the happiness in her voice, immediately Dick comes to mind. As Tam rambles on about how she loves her life, I unintentionally tune her out while my imagination fills with thoughts of Dick.

"Girl, are you listening?" yells Tam.

"Oh yeah, I'm sorry, I zoned out."

"Well, I will see you tomorrow morning. I love you, bye."

"Love you too."

I click the phone and toss it on the pillow. I have never been one to covet another's lifestyle, but I can't help but long for the same happiness as my friend Tam. It's beautiful and I want it. Staring at myself in the mirror, I poke out my bottom lip and begin to pout. The pout turns into an overexaggerated frown, which turns into a cross-eyed, snarled-lip, psychotic facial expression. I continue making faces in the mirror until I break out laughing. I can remember doing this as a child as my mother would say, "Stop doing that. Your face is going to freeze that way."

I wonder why parents say things like that. They know your face will never freeze that way, so what's wrong with making faces? For a child it's fun and for an adult, it relieves stress. If I ever become a parent, I hope I don't overuse those exaggerated parental expressions such as that. Yet I am sure I will, because every day I become more and more like my mother. It's amazing. I pull myself out of bed, walk into the bedroom, and start the shower. While I let the water run down the center of my back, the words *beauty* and *love* ring over and over in my mind. I hurry and finish showering, grab a towel, and run back into the bedroom. Sitting on the edge of the bed, I begin to write the beauty of love.

I toss my book onto the center of the bed and finish preparing for work. The day creeps by at a slug's pace. I anticipate my trip home as if I were ten years old headed to Disney World. I spend every hour asking Sarah if it's time to go home. Finally when 4:45 arrives, I grab my things and start making my way to the front door. I stop by Sarah's desk to ask her plans for the weekend. She is going shopping with Mrs. Richard. It seems that Omar's mom is a very nice woman. She believes that this child belongs to her son and she says that she will support Sarah, even if her no-good son decides not to. Mrs. Richard divorced Omar's father several years ago because of his abusive behavior. However, he is a wealthy man and she received more than half during the settlement. She knows her son is very much like his father and she encourages Sarah to be strong and independent. She agrees that a child should have a father figure in his or her life. However, Mrs. Claire Richard tells

Sarah, and I quote: "The only asshole we have to deal with is the one God gave us."

I look forward to meeting her. Sarah says she's a chain-smoking ex-model of the '60s. She had Omar at twenty-three and started doing print work after he was born. She and Mr. Richard moved here from California when Omar was eleven. Sarah says that Claire never mentioned how Mr. Richard became wealthy, but she is surely reaping the benefits. She lives in a five-bedroom home with a live-in housekeeper, drives a 700 series Mercedes, and travels abroad at least twice a year. Claire promises Sarah that her grandchild will never go without a thing he or she needs, and Sarah couldn't be happier. Giving Sarah a hug, I tell her to have fun and shop for me.

"I'll return to work on Wednesday," I add.

"Are you bringing Dick back with you?"

As I wink my eye and smile, I turn away and walk out the door. It would be nice to bring Dick back with me, but we have so much to work out. Not to mention, I am still dating Wealth. I would feel guilty about suddenly dumping him. So first things first, I want to simply tell Dick how I feel and then we will see what happens. As soon as I get home, my phone is ringing. I look on the caller ID and see that it is Dick. I quickly grab the phone.

"Hello!"

"Is everything okay?"

"Yes, I just walked in. How are you? Did you get my message?" I say anxiously.

"Slow down. Yes, I got it. When will you be here?"

"Tomorrow morning. Can I see you tomorrow night?" I ask.

Dick is silent.

"What's wrong?"

"I have a show at the Blue Room tomorrow night."

"Good! Tam, Evelyn, and I can come."

"Well, okay," he says with hesitation.

"You don't want me to come?"

"Yes, please come. I need to see you."

"Good. You can see as much of me as you like," I flirt.

"We'll talk. Call me tomorrow," he says before he hangs up.

I don't understand. He didn't flirt back. He always has some sexy response whenever I flirt with him. Oh well. I am sure he wants to know where he stands with me and we do have a lot to talk about, so I am not going to jump to conclusions. Instead, I am going to pack my sexiest dresses, wash my hair, and try to get some rest.

The packing process, which normally takes twenty minutes, takes an additional thirty due to unremitting phone calls. First it's Sarah, then it's my mom, then it's Tam, and finally it's Wealth. He wants to come over and stay the night. He knows that I am going to Atlanta tomorrow and he wants to make sure my last thoughts are of him before I leave. I hesitate at first, but then give in, so he will be here in an hour. I finish packing my bag and jump in the shower. As I am drying off, I hear the doorbell ringing. I run downstairs and open the door. As Wealth steps in he grabs the corner of my towel and wraps it around his neck. Stripped, I stand before him. Wealth has never seen my naked body. I turn to rush upstairs, but he grabs my hips and pulls me close to his chest. I can feel his erection pulsating against my lower back. As much as I want to wait before having sex with Wealth, the size of his erection is turning me on. I make a poor attempt to move away from his body, but I end up turned around staring him in the eye. He picks me up as I wrap my legs around his hips. Kissing me, he slowly walks down the foyer and into the living room. He lays me down on the futon and sluggishly takes off his shoes, his tie, and his shirt. He is so slow, my flame is quickly dying down. He kisses my lips and runs upstairs.

"Where are you going?" I yell.

"I have to take a shower. I've been out showing houses all day," he yells from the stairs.

"What is this strange behavior?" I mutter.

If that were Dick, we would be rolling around on the floor right now. He wouldn't care about a little sweat, he would want to capture the moment. But I must keep reminding myself that this is Wealth, not Dick. They are two different men with two different personalities. If I want the spontaneous, uninhibited man, I have to take him with all of his issues. If I want the more settled, distinguished man, I have to wait until he is fresh before we can have sex. This is crazy. I don't even want to do it anymore. I walk upstairs to get dressed before he gets out of the shower. I'll convince him that I am too hungry to have sex and then once we eat I'll have to convince him that I am too full to have sex. I hope he buys it, because the moment has been ruined and he is definitely not getting any tonight. It's been five months; a few more weeks is not going to kill him. Wealth steps out of the bathroom, butt-naked, and strolls by the bedroom on his way down to the living room. I clear my throat as he passes by.

Stopping in the doorway, he gives me a puzzled look. "Why are you dressed? I thought we were . . . you know."

"Baby, I really want to wait. Besides, I'm hungry."

He wraps his towel around his waist and sits on the bed.

"I have been waiting. I wanted you on our first date. It's been almost a year," he says.

I roll my eyes towards him and correct his statement. "It's been five months."

"Five months, twelve months, whatever. It's been a long time and I don't want to wait any longer. If we are in a relationship, why can't we have sex?"

"We can. Just not right now. I want to make sure it's right before we take it to the next level."

"Are you sleeping with someone else?"

"No," I say without pause.

He leans over, kisses me, while stroking my hair. "I want you and I want to be with you. I guess I can wait alittle longer."

He puts on his pants and walks to the car. Seconds later he returns with a pair of jeans and a shirt. He changes into clean clothes and we go eat.

After a quick bite, we return to the house around ten and turn in for bed around eleven. Remembering my tall tale, I walk into the guest bedroom and pull back the sheets.

Wealth stands at the door laughing. "How long are you going to keep this up?"

"What?" I ask as I bat my innocent eyes.

"I know you sleep in the other bedroom. I don't know what happened that weekend, but if you say you aren't sleeping with him, I have to believe you. Go get in your bed."

What a relief. I am so glad he knows. I didn't want to have to sleep in the guest bed just to hold on to a lie. Stripping down to his boxers, Wealth slides into the bed beside me. This is the first time he has been in my bed and it feels weird. Before I get settled in, he immediately starts kissing my neck and back. I know that I am not going to get any sleep tonight. I close my eyes and try not to be persuaded by his advances and then he stops. Certainly, I am relieved he stops, yet I want to know why. I turn around and face him. I can see his facial expression due to the faint streetlight peering through the window. He looks confounded as he sighs.

"I'm still hungry," he comments while getting out of the bed.

Wealth walks toward the bedroom door and asks, "What's in the fridge? Anything sweet?"

"I don't know. Check and see," I say.

He walks downstairs as I turn back over and close my eyes. I keep thinking that his behavior is strange, but then again,

Wealth is strange. Therefore, I don't ponder on it for long.
Minutes later, I hear him walking up the stairs. He stands at
the foot of the bed and I can feel him staring at me. I open my
eyes, turn over, and ogle back.

"Did you find something to eat?" I say, becoming perturbed.

He nods his head yes, but still stands there with his arms
folded. I look at him for a second and he stares back. Finally,
I shrug my shoulders and ask, "What?"

He smiles, pulls back the sheets from the foot of the bed,
and jumps in, landing his chin in between my legs. He pulls
my panties to the side and begins . . . you know . . . eating. I
am so taken aback that I can't gasp for air. I stop breathing
and for almost thirty seconds, I take in no air at all. But then
my mouth flies open and as I wheeze for oxygen, the shrillest
sound leaves my lungs. Echoing like a soprano howling for
help, I involuntarily express this sound repeatedly. To keep
from further embarrassing myself, I take my left hand and
grab the bedpost and cover my mouth with my right. Close to
forty minutes and several convulsions later, Wealth slides
down by the foot of the bed, rises, and walks into the bathroom. I am frozen with my left hand still stuck to the bedpost.
I am not sure what just happened. Why did he please me and
didn't make an attempt to please himself? Maybe that's what
he is doing in the bathroom. He has been in there a few minutes. I finally pry my fingers away from the post and try to sit
up. Wealth comes into the bedroom with a warm towel and
begins to clean me. He comments while laughing, "I'm a
messy eater."

I burst into laughter as he takes the washcloth back into the
bathroom.

What a sweet gesture, I say to myself.

It's almost as kind as offering to sleep in the wet spot—ten
points for Wealth. Walking into the other restroom, I jump
into the shower. It is sweet for him to wash the private areas,
but his little trip to the dessert bar has me sweating from

head to toe and I need to shower. I am praying that when I walk back into the bedroom, he is not naked, sprawled out on the bed, thinking that it is now my turn to orally stimulate. I tiptoe to the door and peek inside. Surprisingly, Wealth is changing the sheets. Here I am thinking one thing and all he is doing is making sure that no one has to sleep in the wet spot. I walk up behind him and pinch his behind. He kisses me on the cheek and whispers in my ear, "Sleep well."

We both get into bed and go to sleep. He tries to cuddle for a moment, but it doesn't work. Eventually, he ends up on his back and I on my side. Before I fall asleep I think about the behavior of men. They can be as bad as women. He knows that I will see Dick this weekend and he knows how close I am to Dick. Although I am sure he wanted to have sex tonight, once he realized that intercourse was not taking place, he moved to plan B. Wealth wants to make sure that when I board that plane tomorrow morning my mind is on the night before instead of the night to come. He definitely has ulterior motives and for that I deduct one point. However, he did make my body tremor and shriek and as I turn to watch him quietly sleep, I decide to bump him back up to ten.

Minutes later I begin to drift off when I hear this appalling noise. What is that? I look over at Wealth and his mouth is wide open. He snores like a Harley Davidson in need of a tune-up. Just when I think I have a ten, I have to settle for an eight. Snoring is an automatic two-point deduction. I pull the sheets over my head, move closer to the edge of the bed, and start counting sheep.

Good night.

Chapter 30

The Dick Is Mine

I safely arrive in Atlanta at 10:40 AM. Tam says she will be waiting for me at Seattle's Best Coffee Shop. As soon as I round the corner and the coffee shop comes into view, I see her sitting at a round table sipping on bottled water. She has cut her hair into a cute Hollywood pixie style and it looks wonderful. She doesn't see me walk up to the window, so I stand there for a few seconds until I get her attention. As soon as she notices, Tam jumps up and runs out of the shop and gives me the warmest hug. She looks incredible. She has on a denim skirt and a white gauze peasant shirt. I grab her arm and we leave the airport. From the time we meet until we pull into her driveway, we are yapping like schoolgirls at camp. Her little tummy is starting to bulge and her chest has filled out to a full C cup. I have been in Kansas City for close to six months and I cannot believe how many things have changed.

We go into the house, throw the bags down, and head back out to go shopping. We are supposed to shop for the baby; however, once we stop by our favorite boutiques, Olive and Bill Hallman, and head for Shoemakers in Midtown, I know this is going to be a day of shopping for us. While shopping she tells me all about Evelyn and how she has joined the church and become supersanctified.

"Everything that comes out of her mouth has something to do with the Lord, and that is great. But she wants to pass judgment on everyone else and that's not right," continues Tam.

I tell Tam about Dick playing at the Blue Room tonight and how I can't wait for our Blue Room reunion. Evelyn and I aren't always in sync with each other, but it would be nice to hang out with her tonight, so we call and invite her. She is not home; however, after listening to her long spiritually encouraging greeting, I leave a message.

"What's up, Evelyn? I'm in town for the weekend. Tam and I are going to the Blue Room tonight to hear Dick's band and it wouldn't be the same if you were not there. I hope you can make it. Call Tam when you get this message. Hope all is well. Peace."

Tam grabs the phone before I can hang up and adds her two cents. "We are not taking no for an answer, so have your tail home by seven."

We get out at the mall and shop for the next four hours.

On our finally arriving back at the house, Stan greets us with a culinary feast. We have pasta salad, chicken with rice, asparagus with carrots, and chocolate mousse for dessert. It seems Tam has taught him a few things about cooking. I tell Tam that if she eats like this every day, she is going to be two hundred pounds before she delivers this child. Stan assures me that he doesn't cook like this every day and this is a special meal on the occasion of my visit. Of course I don't believe him. He spoils Tam rotten, waiting on her hand and foot. The way they make silly eyes at each other during dinner can make a person sick. Don't get me wrong, I am so happy for her, yet it is funny to see my "I don't need a man to make me happy" girlfriend so gooey-eyed and in love.

We both retire after dinner to take a nap before we go out.

Evelyn calls while we are sleeping and tells Stan that she will be ready by eight. I am so nervous about seeing Dick that I can't sleep well. I pray he is happy to see me. Around seven thirty, we are dressed and ready to leave the house. I am wearing a white BeBe rayon tank dress with a braided rawhide belt hanging just off the waist. I have slide-in heels the same color as my belt and a very tiny vintage leather clutch. Tam is wearing a black knit low-cut V-neck top with '60s-print capri pants. Her little black sandals are Gucci and so is her purse. We arrive at Evelyn's close to eight and she is not ready. She wants to see what we are wearing before she can get dressed. I don't know why she waits, because she still decides to wear what is laid out on the bed, a pair of low-waist jeans and a strapless pink shirt with side slits. We get to the club at eight thirty just before the band is about to start. There is one table left so we rush to it and sit down. Just as we sit, I see Dick standing by the stage. Grabbing Tam's arm, I speak. "There he is. Would you just look at him?"

"He is fine," she comments.

Evelyn looks at him and frowns. "I don't know. The displaced Afro is so dated."

We fall out laughing at this moment of déjà vu. I want to say hello to Dick before he walks onstage, so I rise and walk toward the stage. He spots me a few feet away, halts his conversation and comes to greet me with a compassionate hug.

"I am so glad you could make it. Where are the girls?"

I point to the back table. He throws up his hand as they wave to him.

"What are you doing after the show?" he asks.

"I was hoping to see you."

"Okay. We can go somewhere and talk. Right now I have to go."

He kisses my cheek and runs back to the stage. Minutes later, we are drinking virgin daiquiris and grooving to the sounds of SoulTyme. While we are catching up, the evening speeds by. When I look at the time again it is after midnight. The band has finished its set and Dick is mingling with the crowd. Finally, he and two of the band members join us at our table. We sit and laugh for another hour, reminiscing on the first night we all met. Dick and I have our own conversation going on through eye contact. He places his hand atop mine and asks if I am ready to leave. Tam removes his hand from mine and cuts her eyes at me.

"You are not going anywhere with this man. We came together. We are leaving together," she says in a very stern voice.

I look up at her as if she is crazy, and she gives me the biggest smile.

"We are going somewhere to talk. I'll bring her back to the house tonight," Dick promises.

Bring me back to the house? I hope he is kidding.

We all rise and are about to leave when this Native-American beauty walks over to our table and taps Dick on the shoulder. As he slowly turns around, all of us fall silent.

His eyes widen. As he looks her in the face, she says, "I'm so glad I caught you. I think I left my keys in the house. I need yours."

I should know by the stunned look on Dick's face and the "Oh, shit" expression on the face of each of the guys that something is awry. Everyone freezes. Dick reaches in his pocket and hands the girl his keys. She takes them from his hand and kisses his cheek. Glancing over his shoulder, she speaks to everyone. Dick, slowly coming from his stupor, decides to introduce her.

"Guys, you know Celeste," he slurs.

She speaks, and then turns her attention to us.

"These are my friends Lily, Tam, and Evelyn. This is Celeste."

She extends her hand to greet each of us, then turns toward me and speaks. "You're the writer?"

Slowly, I nod my head. Who is she and why does she

know that I am a writer? Maybe this is his sister or his temporary roommate.

"Dick has told me so much about you. How long will you be here?"

"A few days," I say with garbled speech.

"Honey, we should have her over for dinner."

This doesn't sound like a sister, brother relationship.

"Yeah, okay," he murmurs.

Well, that tone sounds familiar. That is the same response I get whenever I begin to flirt with Dick. I look over at Tam, who is gazing at Dick with her face frowned up. Evelyn, also staring, has one eyebrow up and the other down. I glance back at Dick, who is looking at the floor, and from my peripheral I see his two bandmates staring off into the club. Celeste reaches around to shake our hands once again before she leaves. And as she shakes my hand I notice the unique diamond ring on her ring finger. It's a band with inset diamonds. The band wraps around her finger like a snake. I want to comment on the ring, but my gut will not allow my mouth to speak for fear she will mention the ring and Dick in the same sentence. And if she does, I will faint, 'cause my legs are getting weak from the sight of her standing here with her toned arms propped on his broad shoulders. However, as she shakes Tam's hand and comments on her pregnancy, Evelyn can't contain herself.

"That is a beautiful ring," she compliments.

"Thank you," she says with a huge smile.

Thank God it's only a ring. It means nothing, says my mind as my heart races a mile a minute.

"Dick has great taste, doesn't he?" she says as she lays her head on his shoulder.

If Tam doesn't get behind me, I am going to hit the floor.

"It is nice to meet you ladies. Baby, I'll see you tonight," she says before walking away.

All of this conversation takes place in a matter of minutes, yet it seems like hours. As if we just witnessed a murder, we all stand in silent shock. Finally, Dick's friend breaks the silence.

"Well, Dick, we'll see you at rehearsal tomorrow." They swiftly say good-bye to us and leave.

Dick and I stand there staring at one another. I see no one else. As far as I am concerned, we are the only two people in the room. I know this man is not about to tell me that this woman is his girlfriend. I swear that better be a friendship ring. But what if it's not? Could Celeste be his fiancée?

Dick sighs, slowly blinks his eyes, and speaks. "Yes."

"Yes? What do you mean, yes?"

"I know what you are thinking and the answer is yes," he says in a raspy voice.

"Just say it. Don't assume I am thinking anything."

Dick pauses and looks away. Tam moves from beside Evelyn to my right. Dick sighs once more and faces me. "Celeste is my fiancée."

I am going to vomit. I am going to vomit right now. I can't describe this feeling. I suddenly become light-headed, my stomach becomes upset, and I know that everything I have eaten in the last twenty-four hours is going to come up.

"I was going to talk to you tonight. I didn't want this to happen," he says, attempting to grab my hand.

"Excuse me, Dick."

I rush into the restroom. Tam and Evelyn swiftly follow. I get to the sink and lean my head on the cold porcelain.

"It's okay. It will be okay," says Tam.

"What do you want us to do?" says Evelyn, as if we are going out there to beat him up.

I can't speak, I can't walk, and thank God I can't cry. My faculties have shut down. All I can do is keep myself balanced by holding on to the sink. Tam and Evelyn stand over me, rubbing my shoulders. I don't know how to tell them this but I wish they would go away. They want to be here for me, but there is nothing that they can do. Suddenly, my breathing becomes heavier and heavier and I start to hyperventilate. Tam pushes my head down below the sink so that I am staring at my knees and my breathing starts to subside. After several minutes, I decide to leave the restroom and go face Dick.

"We are going home," says Tam.

"I'll make sure he says nothing to you," Evelyn says as she opens the bathroom door.

I look at the two of them and smile. "It's okay. Dick and I were going to go somewhere and talk and we still are. I'll be home later."

I see Dick sitting at a table with head in his hands. I walk up to him and run my hands through his hair. He looks up at me with sad eyes.

"I'm sorry," he says sincerely.

Silencing him, I cover his mouth with my finger. "Are you ready to go talk?" I say softly.

Tam and Evelyn walk up beside me and try to pull me to the side. I grin and nod as an attempt to convince them that I am okay. Cautiously, they let me go. Dick rises and we leave the Blue Room.

Dick and I go to the studio. He walks into the dark room and turns on the lights. As I stand behind him, my mind fills with memories of the time he and I were making love in the sound booth. Now I have to sit and talk to him about his fiancée, and my heart, which he now holds in his hand, is breaking. We walk into the sound booth. He grabs a pillow and sits against the wall. I face him taking a seat against the opposite wall. He sits Indian style and I sit with my elbows propped on my knees as we begin to talk.

"I met Celeste last year. We didn't start dating frequently until six months ago." I look at him in silence as he continues. "She's a good woman. She's cool as hell and she's beautiful."

As he compliments her, I close my eyes and imagine picking up a microphone, hurling it across the room, and striking him in the face.

"I was going to stop seeing her as things developed with you, but I didn't know what you were going to do about Romance and then you moved," he continues.

"Why didn't you say something?" I ask.

"When I am with you, there is nothing to say. I don't want to think about anyone else."

"That's bullshit," I loudly retort.

He sighs and looks away. "I didn't want you to stop seeing me."

"We have never been an exclusive couple, but at least I told you about the others. You are my friend and I was always honest with you," I say with a blank face.

"True. I should have said something."

I feel myself getting angry. Therefore, I stand and begin walking around.

"What about the ring, Dick? What the hell? Your fiancée?" I shout.

"After I realized that you and I were never going to be, I figured, why not? She wants to be with me and she is good to me. You have Wealth and you are not moving back here, so why should I hold up my life waiting on you? I didn't ask her to move in until two weeks ago and I gave her the ring the day she moved in. We haven't set a date. The ring is just a promise that I am committed. I had no idea you would be coming to visit."

I begin laughing aloud. I can't believe this situation.

"Why are you laughing?" he says, rising.

"To keep from crying."

I lean against the wall with the right side of my face stuck against the paneling. "I came back to tell you I love you. I wanted you to know how I felt. I didn't know how we were going to be together, but I was willing to try to work something out. Here I am worrying about whether or not my panties matched my dresses. Never did I think you'd be into someone else's underwear. How vain of me."

Dick walks over and I am praying he doesn't touch me, because if I feel his hands on my skin, I am going to break down. As long as he keeps his distance, I will be okay. Yet he pulls me from against the wall and holds me in his arms. I bury my head in his chest and the water immediately fills my eyes. What starts out as a simple tear turns into overwhelmed bawling. Here we stand, clutched in each other's arms, and the same room where it all started is the same room where it all ends. For an hour, we hold each other until our arms grow numb. Lastly, Dick runs his lips down the center of my face and kisses my nose.

"I don't know what to say," he mumbles.

Leaning over with his lips against mine, I whisper, "Maybe next lifetime."

And with that line, we leave the studio and he takes me to Tam's house. I quietly sneak in and crawl into bed. Balling into the fetal position, I try to ignore the stabbing pain in my chest. I lie still in the bed for hours before finally falling asleep.

Good night.

Chapter 31

Claiming What's Mine

The next morning, Tam softly rubs my shoulders, awakening me. I try to assure her that everything is all right. I tell her about my conversation with Dick and luckily, I make it through the heart-to-heart without crying. She says that if I want him, I should go after him. But I don't have the energy. He seems happy and I have to respect that. I had my chance. Besides, I cannot be upset with him for falling for another. I am with Wealth and he had to witness our escapades firsthand.

"I should have told him how I felt earlier. But I didn't know how I felt until recently. I thought he would be there whenever I got ready to love him and that is messed up."

"But it's not too late. They haven't set a date. He may be wanting you to come after him."

"Stop it, Tam! It's too late! He is happy, she is happy, and I need to pack my tears and go back to Kansas City."

Pausing, she sits down. Finally feeling defeated, Tam starts a new conversation. "Well, what do you want to do today?"

I shrug my shoulders nonchalantly.

"You are not going to sit here and sulk. Get dressed. We are going to the movies."

When she leaves, I rise and listlessly walk into the bathroom. Then rushing back into the bedroom, I get my journal and return to the restroom. Sitting on the edge of the bathtub, I write about this day, this reality, and this pain.

It takes me a couple of hours to get motivated and dressed. Eventually, Tam and I go to an early afternoon flick. And wouldn't you know it, she picks a sappy love story. I sit through the entire movie, yet I can't tell you a single character's name, because I think about Dick the whole time. How could he fall in love so quick as to give her a ring? Maybe Tam is right. I should go after him. If he rejects me, I can't feel any more pain than I feel right now. Furthermore, I don't want to have the what-if disease. What if I had told him earlier? What if I had fought for him? What if I begged him to move to Kansas City? What if I offered to move back here?

We walk next door to the restaurant after the movie and I call Dick on his cell phone while we are eating to ask him to meet me in the park. He promptly agrees. We plan to meet in an hour. I pull a page from my journal and begin scribbling down questions.

"What are you doing?" Tam says, grabbing the paper.

I snatch it out of her hand while answering, "There are several things I must ask him before I make my plea. I have to write them down so that I stay focused.

1. Is Celeste pregnant?
2. Are you in love with her?
3. Are you in love with me?
4. Why did you ask me to move back to Atlanta?
5. If I had said I would move back, were you going to stop seeing Celeste?
6. Is there any chance that we can ever be more than friends?

I am not sure about that last one. If he says no, it could really hurt. I'll put a star by number 6 and wait and see how the conversation is going.

"Enough with the twenty questions. Tell the boy you love him and that you will do anything to get back with him," says Tam.

I agree with the love part, but I am not sure that I will do *anything* to get back with him. I look at Tam and lean my head to the side.

"Anything to get back with him?" I question.

"You need to make up your mind. If you are the one who messed up, you are going to have to be the one to compromise. Do you want him back because you love him or because someone else does?"

I bite my bottom lip pondering upon her last statement. I am sure that I love him. Yet the sudden burst to have him to myself probably has something to do with Ms. Celeste. All I know is that the thought of not having him around drives me crazy.

"Look, girl. I am your friend so I am saying this out of love. You cannot keep playing with people's emotions. Do not, I repeat, do not tell Dick that you want him back unless you are a hundred percent sure that you can commit to him."

"I will commit."

"What about Wealth?"

I shrug my shoulders and let out a whimper.

Tam looks at me with grave concern. "You are not sixteen and we are not bidding on dates for the prom. These are people's lives. You already have one strike with Romance and you're working on two and three. I don't want to see you get out."

She pulls out her credit card. "Lunch is on me."

After she signs the slip of paper we get in the car and go home. I immediately jump into the driver's seat to go meet Dick. I give Tam a hug and assure her that I will do the right thing. Unfortunately, I have no idea what the right thing is anymore. When I didn't want to fight for him, she tells me to. Now that I want to fight for him, she tells me not to. I toggle back and forth with right and wrong, until I pull into the park's lot. I place my hands on the steering wheel and pray for my words to represent my sincere heart. I know that I have made lots of mistakes, but I am not a mean person; a little self-absorbed, maybe, but surely not spiteful. However, if I need to let Dick go, I need the strength to be able to walk away.

I get out of the car and head for the swings. Although we never said where to meet, I know he will first go to the playground. As I approach the sand area, I see Dick sitting peacefully on one of the blue swings. I walk up behind him and give him a push. However, my 125-pound frame does not compare to his 195-pound muscular body, and the swing doesn't move. He leans back and brushes his hair against my face. Jumping out of the swing, Dick takes my hand and we go sit atop a grassy knoll by a large oak tree. Trying not to get flustered, I pull out my piece of paper. Curiously, Dick leans over and attempts to read the paper as I am speaking.

"I have some questions. Please just answer them and then we can talk."

He nods yes and my hands start to shake as I speak. "Is Celeste pregnant?"

He shakes his head no without hesitation.

"Are you in love with her?"

He nods yes with some hesitation.

"Are you in love with me?"

He nods yes with more hesitation.

"Okay, you have to talk for this one. Why did you ask me to move back to Atlanta?"

"Because I wanted you here with me," he answers without delay.

"If I had moved back, were you going to stop seeing Celeste?"

He smiles, then smirks. "You wouldn't have had it any other way."

Well, this is going good. I am going to ask the last question. "Is there any chance that we can ever be more than friends?"

Dick pauses and begins to speak. "We are more than friends now and we will always have that. You mean a lot to me and you always will."

What in the hell does that mean? This question does not require a deep answer.

"You were supposed to nod yes or no, not give me some philosophical answer."

Dick burst out laughing and lays his head in my lap. He looks into the sky and asks for permission to talk.

"What is this all about? I didn't think you ever wanted to see me again," he says.

Sighing, I tell him, "I want you. Why did you have to go fall in love with some other woman? I was going to get it together soon, if only you had waited."

"You see, Lily, the world revolves whether you give it permission to or not," he laughs.

"It's not funny. I love you, Dick. It's killing me that I can't be with you."

"And you don't think I know how that feels?" he says in a more serious tone.

I can only assume he is talking about Wealth. Then again, he could be talking about Romance. Until now I didn't realize how many chances I have had to be with him. I am the only one to blame for my hurt feelings and I can't even be upset with him.

"Where's your journal?" he asks, lifting his hands to my side.

I reach in my bag and pull out my book.

"What are you doing?" I ask.

He holds up his hand as he flips through the pages. I rarely allow others to flip the sacred pages of my book, but this is Dick.

"I want to read you something. I remember you wrote this when we first started dating. I'm not sure who it was to, but I remember you sharing it with me and now I want to share it with you."

Butterfly

My love for you is like that of a butterfly
It should be appreciated in its caterpillar stages
Not placed aside or stepped on,
Taken for granted like that tiny yellow and black insect
    that appears mysteriously every year,
Around springtime . . . I think.
Sure they come in abundance, those tiny creatures are
    everywhere.
But not all caterpillars are the same,
such as those who pretend to love you.
Some of them, too, are moths in disguise.
But like the habits of a caterpillar, I feel my way around,
checking out my surroundings.
Taking step by step, Oh, I hurry not.
For I know if survival is meant to be, the outcome will be
    such a glorious beauty, well worth each and every
    tiny step.
And just before that beautiful metamorphosis,
I may seem in a dormant stage, as that of a cocoon.
Be patient, my love, for I am not sleeping
Yet giving you a little time to prepare yourself
for the beauty you are about to witness.
And once emerged from my cocoon you will see a
    vibrant prism of colors, colors Mr. Crayola himself
    could not imagine.
My colors come from Mother Nature, Mother Earth.

*I flit and flutter, dancing right before you but always out
    of reach.*
*I want to be admired, I want to bring beauty into your
    life.*
But please don't try to capture me or hold me down.
If I am unable to fly, I am unable to breathe.
*I don't have to be in your possession to be faithfully
    yours.*
And now as a butterfly you appreciate me.
You gaze upon my beauty and confidence.
You want to take notice, now that others are noticing me.
But what about earlier?
*Don't you understand that I had to go through every
    stage in order to give you the beautiful love you see
    before you today?*
*You must learn to appreciate my love, no matter what
    phase it is in.*
Love is Love is Love is Love.
*It should not be placed aside or stepped on. Taken for
    granted like that tiny yellow and black insect that
    appears mysteriously every year,*
Around springtime . . . I think.

Before he finishes I get chills. My life has come full circle.
I can identify with that moment like it was yesterday. How
about that? My own words come back to bite me in the butt. I
wrote that for Romance. He took me for granted, as if I were
always going to be there, no matter what. Ironically, I have
become Romance and Dick stands where I stood eight months
ago and all I can do is apologize.

"I am so sorry," I say softly.

"No need to apologize. Everything happens for a reason,
even pain. And if I had to go through a little pain to have an
experience with you, I can't think of a better reason."

I cover my face and chuckle. We both rise and begin to walk back toward the cars.

"So, tell me about Celeste. I need the 411 on the girl who took my precious Dick away," I say while holding his hand.

He smiles as he tells me about her background and personality. He mentions that she is originally from the Midwest, but moved to Atlanta to pursue the arts. She is a ballerina with the Atlanta Ballet, he boasts. She seems to be an outstanding woman, not to point out she is drop-dead gorgeous.

Once we get to my car, Dick quiets down and leans on the hood. Extending his arms, he surrounds me with a passionate embrace. As I gaze into his eyes, I want so badly to kiss him, but it will only bring up old memories. Then I think to myself, why not? Memories never hurt anyone. He can always pull away if he doesn't want a kiss. I lean in slowly, waiting for him to stop me, but he doesn't. Our lips melt as one when I feel moisture from his tongue. For a few seconds, we stand locked together as Dick runs his hands through my hair, pulling me closer. As rapid memories race through my mind, I see Dick hovering over my body, as we are about to make love. Then the sudden jolt of knowing it's only my imagination, and the harsh reality that I will never see this image again strikes me down. I break the connection by pulling my lips inward. Dick turns away while pushing me toward the car door.

"You better get out of here, before . . . you just better go," he says in haste.

I open the door and get in. He stands there with his hand on the hood. I crank up the car and roll down the window.

"One more thing," I say. "I know she's a dancer and all, but when we did our thing . . . it was . . . you know. And I hope it will always be . . . well, you know."

Dick leans into the car and whispers, "You will always have the most stars in my little black book."

He kisses my cheek and taps the top of the car as I pull off.

I am so glad I kissed him, because his kiss said more than he would ever allow himself to say. And as for his last comment, it may or may not be true, but it is exactly what I needed to hear. Smiling, I watch him waving good-bye through the rearview mirror.

"You're right, Dick. Everything happens for a reason, even pain. And if I had to go through a little pain to have an experience with you, hell, I can't think of a better reason."

Good night.

Chapter 32

I Never Cared Much for Baseball

I spend the next day hanging out with Tam and Stan. Moving up my flight, I leave that night instead of the next morning. I arrive in Kansas City around 10:30 PM. I try to call Wealth, but he is not answering his cell phone. Sarah is asleep and I hate to take a taxicab home, but it may be my only option. I could call Winston, but it seems I only call him whenever I am in an urgent situation. Amazingly, he comes through more times than Wealth. Oh well, I'll give him a call anyway, and as usual he picks up on the first ring.

"Hey, Winston, what are you doing?"

"I'm on my way home, I've been at the hospital since nine this morning. Where are you?"

"I'm at the airport. I was calling for a ride, but I will take a cab home. I know you are tired."

"I can come and get you, but I will have to crash at your place," he says with a little spunk.

"Ha, ha! I'll take the cab."

"Call me tomorrow," Winston says.

"Sure. Bye."

I hang up, follow the street transportation signs, and stand in line. By the time the cab makes its way out of the airport and onto the highway, Wealth returns my call.

"Hey, baby, I see you called."

"Where are you?" I ask.

"I'm at home resting."

"Oh, well, I didn't want anything. Just wanted to say hello," I say to Wealth.

"All right. Well, I'll see you tomorrow, right?"

"Yeah," I say with little or no zeal.

"Good. I can't wait." He ends the conversation.

I hang up and give the driver new directions to Wealth's house. I want to surprise him. We pull up to the circular driveway and I ask the cab to wait. After knocking on the door several times I hear the lock turn and, shockingly, Angela greets me with a twenty-dollar bill. Eyeballing her, I take the twenty from her hand and tap the bill on the door frame.

Screeching as if I were a ghost, she yelps. "I am so sorry, I thought you were the delivery guy."

She runs back into the house as my temper starts to flare. When I see Wealth, I could easily punch him in the face, turn, and walk away. Seconds later, he struts to the door in a pair of jeans.

"Why didn't you tell me you were back?" he says calmly.

"Why didn't you tell me you were fucking Angela?" I say just as serene.

"You didn't ask."

Still composed, I respond, "My fault. It slipped my mind."

My nostrils flare. Like a bull attempting to steer into the matador, I am seeing red.

"So, where do we go from here?"

I am so angry, yet mentally exhausted, I can't even argue, nor do I want to, so I simply respond, "I'm not sure about you, but I'm going home."

I walk away and get back into the cab.

"Where to, ma'am?" asks the cabdriver.

"North Estates. The original address."

I should have known he was sleeping with someone else. His little empathetic act was entirely too calm. He is not the type of guy who waits. Winston is the type of guy who waits. Wealth is the type of guy who gets what he wants or finds it elsewhere. I am such an idiot. I grab the phone and call Winston.

As soon as he picks up, I start questioning. "Did you know your brother is sleeping with Angela? Why didn't you tell me? How could you let me look like a fool? I thought we were friends."

"Where are you?" he says with concern.

"Going home."

"I'll come over," continues Winston.

"No! You cannot pacify this situation, you can only make matters worse. I only called you out of frustration. I'll talk to you later."

I hang up and as I lean my head back on the nasty cab seat, my eyes close. Once we pull into my driveway, I look and see that the meter reads $19.90. I give him the twenty I took from Angela and four more dollars from my pocket. The driver walks my bag to the door and I go in. Leaving my bag in the foyer, I crawl upstairs and into my bedroom. Stretched across the center of my bed with my legs dangling off the edge, I replay everything that has happened. Two men have dumped me in two days. One I love and the other I like. One leaves me for a Native American and the other for a Caucasian. Grabbing my teddy bear, I frown.

"I guess it has not been a good weekend for the sistas, huh, Teddy?"

He nods his head to agree with me. At times like these, his button eyes look so sincere as if he feels my pain.

"Beware, delusion is prone to make us find comfort in the strangest of places."

What am I thinking? It has nothing to do with race and has everything to do with me. I allowed Dick to get away and had it not been for Celeste, I was going to dump Wealth anyway. I can't be upset that he beat me to the punch.

"Oh, what a tangled web we weave . . . when yada, yada, blah, blah, blah!

"Well, Tam, I have received strike two and strike three. I am officially out. I am hanging up my jersey."

Game over!

Chapter 33

Life Without Dick

"Am I hearing things, or is someone knocking on my door?" I say to my teddy bear still sitting by my side.

Leaning over, I look at the clock and see it's 8:30 AM. I'm still in the same position as last night, my clothes are stuck to my body, and my feet still dangle off the bed. As the knocking continues, I grab teddy and make my way downstairs while rubbing my eyes. Stumbling, I eventually make it to the front door. Peeping through the side curtain, I slowly open the door.

"Who are you?" I say with my deep morning voice.

"What? It's me, Wealth," he says.

I slam the door in his face and turn around. Again, he starts knocking and yelling through the door.

"I'm joking. It's Winston. Please answer, it's Winston. You called me last night. I was worried," he persists.

Huffing, I return to the door and open it. "Whoever you are, what do you want?"

"I want to make sure that you are okay."

I extend my arms and give a big Miss America smile. "Look at me. Don't I look grand?"

He pauses and shakes his head. "For a crackhead, yeah," he laughs.

At that moment, I know it is Winston, but I did look into the driveway to double-check the vehicle. Winston walks into the foyer.

"I really thought you were Wealth."

"Do you really think that my brother would come to your house at eight thirty in the morning to make sure that you are okay? It's not his style. But I'm sure you will receive a dozen roses by noon." Pausing, he continues. "I'm sorry I didn't say something."

I walk into the kitchen to pour some juice as he carries on.

"If it makes any difference, I did talk to him. I told him that you were special and that he needed to take a chance on a real woman for once."

I glance around the kitchen corner to get a view of his face. "Really? What did he say?"

"He said you were special . . . but that you wouldn't have sex with him."

I gasp as Winston continues. "And I am so glad that you wouldn't. It really crushed his ego. I don't think any woman has turned him down, at least not in his adulthood. He deserves someone like Angela. They are both conniving and crazy."

Rounding the kitchen corner, I concur with his statement. "That's right, to hell with both of them," I say, staggering and raising my orange juice glass.

"Have you been drinking?" Winston says.

"Not yet."

Winston looks in disbelief, rises, and rubs my arm as I walk by.

"I have to go into the office. I only stopped by to see how you were doing," he says before heading toward the door.

I grab on to his arm and in my best distressed, soap opera

voice I call out, "Please don't go! I need you here! If you leave me now, I don't know what I will do."

I continue clinging on to his pant leg as I work my way to the floor.

"And the award goes to . . ." he says, clapping his hands.

I let go of his leg and fall out onto the floor as if I have fainted. He steps over my legs and walks to the door. I call out from the floor, "Bye, Winston, thanks for stopping by."

"Anytime, babe. Talk to you later," he says before closing the door.

I lie in the middle of my floor staring at the ceiling. I never noticed the interesting pattern in the textured paint. They look like tiny starbursts. I wonder how they did that. Funny, when we are trying to clear our mind of chaos, it's amazing how trivialities such as paint texture calm the spirit. Still lying on the floor, I look around for the remote. I see it on the table across the room.

"If only I had mastered my telekinetic senses as a child, it sure would come in handy right now," I giggle to myself.

I muster up enough energy to slide my fatigued body across the floor and lift myself up to get the remote. Then like a slug, I slide back to the center of the floor, grab a pillow off the futon, sit my teddy bear by my side, and flick on the TV. I turn it to the Cartoon Network and for the next four hours I bond with Daffy, Bugs, Porky, and Pepe Le Pew. Then out of the blue, during the third Pepe cartoon, strange feelings of emotion begin to consume me. I can't understand why Pepe keeps getting turned down. So what he's a skunk, they need love, too. Every single episode, he gets rejected and every single episode he keeps trying. Where does he get the energy?

"Why won't they draw him somebody to love?" I wail.

A downpour of tears rains from nowhere. I can't believe I'm crying over a stupid animation. Am I losing my mind? I lie on the floor crying into the pillow. I want to call Dick, but I can't, and I want to see Wealth to make me feel better about losing Dick, but I refuse. I can't swim for sinking. I am drowning in this stinking sea of love. As I take a deep breath, I realize that not only am I drowning but I am also stinking. I need a bath. I look over at my teddy for comfort. However, if I am not mistaken, he is saying, "Get me out of here, this chick is crazy."

Okay, it is definitely time to get up; my own team has turned against me. I make it to my feet and walk upstairs to the restroom. After drawing my bathwater, I cut my phone off ring. I don't want to be bothered the rest of the day. I will spend the next twelve hours recouping, twisting my hair, manicuring my nails, and giving myself a pedicure. Tomorrow, I will return to work polished and professional. Soaking in the bath for an hour, I get out and begin my pedicure. A day of pampering is always good for the soul. I turn on my stereo and sing along with my soul mate, Nina Simone. I am slowly coming out of my stupor when I hear the doorbell ring. I really don't want to answer, but something in my heart makes me walk to the door.

"Who is it?" I yell.

"You have a delivery."

I look out of the curtains and see a Flowers Are Us royal-blue hat. I open the door with a crabby expression.

"You're late. You were supposed to be here by noon," I say to the flower man.

"Are you—" he starts.

"Yeah, yeah, they are for me. Give 'em here," I interrupt, removing the two dozen red and white roses from his hand. I sign the slip and close the door. I guess the extra dozen is to make up for the late delivery. I don't bother reading the card; I place the vase on the table by the futon and return to my pampering. With Nina Simone and Billie Holiday crooning in the background, I paint my toes, paint my nails, twist my hair, and clean my house. There is nothing like depressing music to make you appreciate life.

As dusk arrives, I slip into a nightgown and crawl into bed. While lying here, I think about Wealth's flower apology. Roses? I don't even like roses. I should have known it wasn't going to work out; we're too different. I am a Häagen-Dazs girl and he's a Ben & Jerry's guy. The two should never mix. Häagen-Dazs people have simple, classic taste buds. Ben & Jerry's people don't know whether they want ice cream or an appetizer. I swear their ice cream is filled with all four major food groups; there's just too much stuff. What is that about? As my thoughts continue to ramble, a bomb hits, making me sit straight up in my bed.

"What if he wants me to return the furniture?" I whisper.

This is exactly why we shouldn't take expensive gifts from men we date. I don't want to buy new things. I like my nice, expensive furniture. I don't think Wealth is the spiteful type, but then again, who knows? My karma has been on a rampage lately.

"If he tries to take the furniture, it's war. I'll be delivering those same two dozen roses to his bedside . . . in the hospital."

Good night.

Chapter 34

Getting Ready for Mr. Stork

Sarah and I leave work early today to go to her doctor's appointment. Normally, I don't go with her to the office; however, she plans to find out the sex of the baby today and she wants me with her. We walk into the lobby and lucky for us, there is no one waiting, so Sarah signs in, sits down, and within minutes, the male nurse comes to the door and calls her name. She goes in alone for her physical and the nurse ushers me back into her room for the sonogram. This past month has flown by and it's hard to believe that Sarah is twenty-three weeks, or for those mathematically challenged, close to six months. I stand beside the nurse looking at the little black and gray screen. Her doctor points out the baby's head, stomach, and feet and then she asks, "Would you like to know the sex of your baby?"

With the expression of a young girl, Sarah exclaims three consecutive yes responses.

"You are having a baby girl," says Dr. Watts.

Sarah looks up at me with a tear in the corner of her eye.

"We're having a girl. A little girl, oh my God, I can't believe I am having a little girl."

The doctor smiles and turns to me. "Are you her partner?"

"Who, me?" I ask, looking around.

"I am not her partner as in her lover. I am her girlfriend as in confidante, buddy, homegirl," I continue.

Confused by my response, the doctor pauses, then tells us that everything checks out great and that she should prepare to deliver around January 10. Sarah gets dressed, makes her next appointment, and we leave. We stop by Mrs. Richard's house on the way home. Sarah can't wait to tell her about her granddaughter's arrival. I too am excited about the announcement of a little girl. Although the sonograms aren't a hundred percent accurate, the baby was facing forward and we all could see the missing link in between her legs. It's definitely a girl. We pull up to the house and before I can stop the truck completely, Sarah jumps out and rushes toward the door. Seconds later, a fair-skinned, green-eyed beauty comes to the door. Sarah asks for Mrs. Richard and the young girl yells out to her mom. Sarah's expression lightens once she discovers that this is Omar's sister.

We walk in and Mrs. Richard makes her entrance from the right spiral staircase. She is so graceful and elegant, it seems as though she is floating instead of walking. She is wearing an Asian silk robe and tiny slippers adorned with sequins. Her salt-and-pepper hair is pinned up into a swirl atop of her head and her gold earrings dangle almost to her shoulders. I can tell she is an eccentric woman.

"Sarah, darling, what did the doctor say?" she asks from halfway down the stairs.

"We're having a girl," Sarah says as she rushes to meet Mrs. Richard.

The two of them squeeze as Sarah leads her to meet me. After we meet in the foyer, Mrs. Richard invites us into the parlor area for drinks. I am not sure if she is an alcoholic, but the bar is stocked as if it were Saturday night at the hottest club in town.

"Would you care for a drink?" she asks me.

"Some juice would be great," I reply.

She pours Sarah and me a glass of juice. Just then Omar's sister walks in and introduces herself. "I'm Cailah, Omar's baby sis."

"I'm Sarah and this is my friend Lily," Sarah answers.

Cailah sits and listens to our conversation.

"You have a lovely home, Mrs. Richard," I compliment.

"Thanks and please call me Claire.

Claire is just as eager as Sarah about the news. She proposes that Sarah move in with her at least for the first year of the child's life, and without hesitation Sarah agrees. When Claire excuses herself from the room, I whisper to Sarah my doubts about her moving into the home. However, Sarah says that she doesn't see anything wrong with the idea and that this gives her an in-house sitter and a mansion to live in.

"This is a sweet deal. This place is so big that I don't even have to see Claire if I choose," she whispers.

Although it may have its perks, I have a feeling that Claire is going to be a bigger handful than Sarah thinks. "What if she tries to tell you how to raise this child?"

"Good! I need some advice. Trust me, this will be good for us," Sarah says, patting her stomach.

Claire returns with several pieces of paper in her hand.

"We are going to need an excellent nanny. Therefore, I took the liberty of asking around and I have received several resumes. By the way, I spoke to Omar today," she casually mentions.

"Well, I haven't spoken to him in a few weeks."

Claire lays out several resumes and begins talking about the future of her first granddaughter. Pointing to one of the resumes, she continues to speak.

"This one speaks three languages and is CPR certified.

Omar is going to come around," she says. "He wants to make sure that he is the father. I told him that I had no doubts in my mind, but he's stubborn like is father. When I became pregnant with Omar, he questioned me as well and we were married. Oooh, look at this one, she is a trained dancer. This means our little Coral could be the next Martha Graham."

Sarah can't get a word in; however, when she hears the name Coral, she raises her hand and speaks up. "Who is Coral?"

"Oh, I just threw that name out there, we can decide on her name later. But so you know, it must start with a C. All the women since my great-grandmother have had names starting with the letter C and I wouldn't want to be the first to break that tradition."

Sarah looks at Cailah, who is staring off into space. Cailah looks back at Claire and then turns and gives me a blank stare. I can tell by her face that she is a little concerned. I warned her. Claire is very sweet; however, she is very lonely and if Sarah thinks she will be able to hide out from Claire in this five-bedroom home, she is sadly mistaken. Claire gets up and invites us to the backyard, as she waters her plants. However, we have to get going.

On the way out, she continues on about the baby plans. "Omar said that you agreed to take a paternity test. Is that correct?"

Sarah nods her head

"Well, once the test results are back, we will set up the trust fund for little Cypress." She gives us both a hug and closes the gigantic wooden doors.

Sarah sighs as she leans on the outside of the door. "Cypress?" she says to me. "She never seemed that weird before today."

"Really? Her clothing is a dead giveaway. What black woman you know walks around her house in a kimono and belly dancing shoes?" I ask, leaning over to rub Sarah's belly.

"Well, little Corinthia, I hope you take from your mother's side of the family."

Sarah laughs and pulls me to the truck.

We spend the next month helping Claire prepare for the baby. We turn one of her many guest bedrooms into a baby room. Mrs. Richard, being the queen of estate sales, finds an antique mahogany baby bed with complementing dresser. We stencil tiny teddy bears in silver on the bottom frame of the bed, then replace the brass dresser knobs with matte silver ones. With the coercing of Claire, Sarah decides to go against pink or blue baby accessories, because natural wood has a more classic look. Sarah gives her apartment a sixty-day notice and in two months she will be moving into the Richard manor.

I become so engrossed with helping Sarah, I have failed to realize that I haven't gone on a date in a month. Wealth called a few times; however, two minutes into each conversation I get the feeling he's lying and I am no longer interested. On the other hand Winston and I talk on the phone two to three times a week. Although his brother and I are over, we agree to remain friends. Anything more would seem weird, and I can only imagine how much the family would have to say about it. We both concur it's not worth it. Yet he says that our friendship is worth working on and if it ever leads to anything else, he may encourage it.

Tomorrow is Tam's birthday. I arrive to work early today to call 1-800-FLOWERS. I want to order her a large bouquet of tulips, her favorite flower. Until I spoke with the representative, I never realized that tulips come in at least fifteen different colors in the U.S. alone. If they fly tulips from overseas, the variety jumps up to twenty-five. That is amazing, there are even black tulips. Now, how sexy is that? I decide upon a bouquet of peach and yellow. The woman assures me that they will arrive before noon tomorrow. These days anything and everything is available at the touch of a phone call or the connection of the Internet. If funds are available, I can purchase a twenty-five-carat blue diamond in a matter of days, or an island in a matter of weeks. The world is accessible for some, yet there are still people down the street who can't get a decent job or a decent meal. Amazing.

Our art department has been finishing the latest assignment, Waterfront Collection. Each card has beautiful sceneries of water, oceans, lakes, and waterfalls. However, the messages on the cards are about love and relationships and these cards are detailed. There is a card to explain just about anything you are feeling, and this day my thoughts are consumed with Dick. I wish I could see him . . . without Celeste by his side. We haven't spoken since my visit to Atlanta and that has been a month and two weeks. I decide to call him tonight, praying he doesn't blow me off, for I will be crushed. We agreed to maintain a friendship, but what does that mean? Is it possible to be friends once the intimacy is over? Or is that just a title we create to keep from saying that is my ex-lover? Part of our friendship is the flirting and teasing, but with him in a relationship that part is over. So how do we grow to the next level of being friends? Feeling helpless, I will take Dick in whatever capacity I can, because I do not want to lose him.

I get home around seven, after leaving dance aerobics. Yes, I have a new interest. I used to dance as a youth and I have decided that I need to work out more often, hence dance aerobics. I go twice a week and man, is it a workout! If aerobics teachers are adrenaline-pumped, then dance aerobics teachers must be on speed. My teacher talks a mile a minute and dances ten times as fast. I immediately run my bathwater and soak in the tub. When I add peppermint bath soak, my muscles relax and my pores open. It is so refreshing. As I lean my head back against the porcelain I think about Dick even more. Grabbing an extra pen and pad, which I keep in my bathroom, I start to write. However, I only write a few lines, and then I draw a blank, which is when I realize that I haven't written anything personal in a month. I run phrases and lines through my head, but nothing flows out. It's as though I have no emotions to draw from. Sure, I write at work, but that is professional, not personal. When I am writing for work, I am concerned about pentameters and structuring. When I write for my journal, it is straight emotion, no chaser, and with no love chaos, my emotions dwindle. This is tragic. I should be able to write about something other than love. I can write on injustice, hatred, peace, or family. But those things don't move me like love. Love is my muse and without it I am going to have problems writing. It's only personal right now, but what if it leaks into my professional life? This is exactly what my boss asked me about during my interview. It seemed like a dumb question at the time, but now it is has hit home. I get out of the tub, dripping wet, and rush to the phone to call Dick.

"Please be there. Please be there. Please be there," I whisper all the way to the phone, and just as I am about to pick it up it rings.

With my hand on the receiver, the ring freezes my actions. After a second, I slowly pick up the phone and answer, "Hello."

"Hi, beautiful," says the man.

It sounds like Dick, but my mind is surely playing tricks.

"Is this—" I start to ask.

"You know who it is," he interrupts.

"*Dick!*" I squeal.

"Calm down. I don't have good news," he says in a sorrowful tone.

"What? Celeste is pregnant?" I am quick to ask.

"No. Tam is in the hospital. I hate to say this, but she lost the baby."

A boulder plows into my stomach and I cave.

"Hey! Are you still there? Answer me!"

"Yeah," I mumble.

"I was at the hospital visiting a friend when I ran into Stan. He wanted me to call you."

"I'll be there tomorrow. Can you pick me up from the airport?" I manage to murmur.

"Call me and let me know what time."

"I'll call you back," I say, hanging up the phone.

Falling onto the bed, I begin sobbing. I have to go home. I have to be with Tam. I don't know what could have happened. A month ago, the doctor said everything was fine. I pull myself up, wrap my towel around my body, and run downstairs to grab my purse. Rambling through my wallet, I find my credit card, call the airlines, and book a flight that leaves at ten in the morning. Finally, I put on a T-shirt while grabbing some clothing and tossing it in a bag. Once I get several items into my luggage, I come to a crashing halt, sliding to the floor, and begin to cry.

"Why, Tam?" I sob.

Here I am worrying about a stupid emotional writing block and my closest friend is lying in the hospital going through pains I can't imagine. I swear life deals us blows too hard to handle and I know that is why there is prayer. During moments like this, that is all we can do. I fall to my knees and pray for Tam and Stan.

"God, please give them the peace of mind to make it through this. I hope they stay strong enough to get through this together and I pray that Tam is strong enough mentally, spiritually, and physically to try bringing another life into this world again. Because she deserves it and you know this better than anyone. Please let her be all right. All of these things I ask in your name. Amen."

Good night.

Chapter 35

Sometimes the Only Answer Is Prayer

I walk out to the Delta curb and I see Dick waiting a few cars down. However, I am so upset about Tam that my feelings for Dick have become null and void; thus I am silent the entire ride. He inquires about my stillness several times, but I only have enough energy to say, "I'm fine."

Once we arrive at Tam's floor, I feel a knot in the pit of my stomach. I want to see her, but I don't know what to say. Dick and I slowly open the door and walk in. Tam is asleep and Stan is by her side watching television. I walk over and embrace Stan.

He rises and lets me sit by Tam. "The painkillers make her sleep a lot."

"What happened?" I whisper to Stan.

"She went into early labor. Her body couldn't handle it. I don't know," he mumbles. "I really can't explain it right now."

He and Dick leave the room for a minute. I sit there and rub the hair away from Tam's face. She awakens and looks over at me.

"Hey, pretty lady. How are you feeling?" I ask.

She shrugs her shoulders and turns away. I can't help but look at her stomach. I still can't believe that she lost the baby. I am trying to conceal my feelings, for I will start crying and I know this will only make her cry. Therefore, I am placid.

"There is nothing to say, you know, but I'm so glad you're here," she whispers.

She leans over and grabs my hand and fades back off to sleep.

Dick and I stay at the hospital until visiting hours are over. Afterward, we grab some fast food and he takes me to Tam's house. As I walk up to the front door I see the vase of tulips I had delivered. In all the chaos, I failed to remember that today is Tam's birthday. I grab the vase, open the door, and walk into the house. Dick follows behind me and places my bag inside the door.

"Are you going to be okay?" he asks.

"If I say no, are you going to stay?" I ask with a serious facial expression.

Dick blurts out a short laugh and rubs his hand over his mustache. "You know I will."

Any other time, I would take advantage of the moment, but tonight I couldn't care less.

"I'll be okay," I say, patting his shoulder.

I walk into a semidark home and sit down on the couch. Seconds later, Dick sits down on the couch beside me.

"She's coming home tomorrow. She is going to be fine," he assures me.

"I know," I say without looking at him.

He taps my leg, then whispers, "Maybe we could put the baby's things in a box and place them in the garage. It may hurt too much to see them right now."

"I don't know. She may want to do that herself. I don't know what to do."

Dick rises and walks to the door. Standing at the door, he yells back into the room, "When are you leaving?"

"The day after tomorrow. I wish I could stay, but I have to go back to work," I respond.

"I'll see you tomorrow," he says before closing the door.

After he leaves I walk into the baby's room and look around. Tam has put so much work into decorating. It is going to crush her to walk by this room every day. Maybe I should put some of the baby's stuff in a box. I would like to ask Stan what he thinks. I pick up the phone and call him at the hospital. Surprisingly, Tam answers.

"I'm in the house . . . um . . . Happy birthday."

She is quiet for about three seconds. "It is my birthday, isn't it? Some birthday present," she says.

"Is Stan around? I need to ask him something. I'll see you in the morning."

She doesn't say good-bye or hold on, she simply passes the phone to Stan. I ask him about the baby's things and he doesn't know what to do. Finally, we agree to put all of the things into the baby's room and close the door. If Tam wants us to get rid of them, we will do it tomorrow. I tell Stan that I will see him in the morning and we hang up.

As I sit down on the couch, my mind starts to imagine a little kid running around their house. This is so unfair. I know we shouldn't question the decisions of the Most High, but how can we not? As humans, we need to know why. I am Tam's best friend and she would be a great mother. She did the right thing. She committed to a man and together they created life. Isn't that the plan? There are unsure mothers bearing kids into bad situations every day.

"Why would you take a child that would be received into a loving home with loving parents? It makes no sense," I say aloud.

Walking to the linen closet, I grab a blanket and lie down on the couch. With my mind still pondering on why bad things happen to good people, I can't sleep. After a couple of hours of tossing and turning, I go into the kitchen to make chamomile tea. I sit in the dark, drinking my tea, until my eyes begin to feel heavy. Eventually, my mind clears and I fall asleep.

Hours later, at the crack of dawn, I refresh myself with a hot shower. As soon as I put my shoes on, I hear the cabbie outside honking his obnoxious horn, so I grab my purse and rush out of the house.

As I step onto Tam's floor, I see Evelyn. She gives me the warmest hug, as if she and I are the best of friends. This episode has put so many things into perspective. We walk in and see Tam sitting up with her legs hanging off the side of the bed.

"I'm ready to go home," she says as we walk in the door.

"That is what we are here for," says Evelyn.

Stan and the doctor walk into the room and once we all speak, the doc asks Evelyn and me to leave. We stand outside the door, pacing the hallway. From my peripheral I see a man who looks identical to Romance walking down the hall with flowers. I slowly turn my head and realize that this is not a look-alike, but that this is Romance. I am stunned. I haven't seen him since Tam's wedding. He walks right up to us and just as I am about to speak, Romance talks to Evelyn. Other than a slight nod, he doesn't acknowledge me. He asks Evelyn about Tam's health and hands her the flowers. He makes a conscience effort not to look at me and I am so shocked by his behavior, my greeting never leaves my mouth. Romance knocks on the door, rushes in to comfort Tam and Stan. He exits the room, tells Evelyn to give Stan the card, and leaves. He did not say one word to me. What in the hell is wrong with him? After he gets on the elevator, I quickly interrogate Evelyn.

"Why is he here? And did you notice that he didn't even speak? Wasn't that rude? I am not asking for pleasant conversation, but he could have at least spoken. How did he know she was here?" I quickly ramble off.

"Romance is doing some contract work for Stan. They have become buddies. And I guess he didn't speak because he didn't want to hear your voice," she adds quaintly. I hate I even asked her.

"Like the sound of my voice is going to burst his eardrums!" I banter.

"So what, he didn't speak. You were content with never speaking to him again."

"I would speak if I saw him," I retort.

"He is not you, so you can't expect the same behavior. When you left, you didn't care if you ever saw him again. Now he doesn't care if he ever hears from you again. Deal with it and move on. Oh, and you better not bother Tam with this mess, because she has enough to deal with," Evelyn says in a matronly manner.

I lean my head against the wall and tighten my lips. She sounds like Tam. I guess they have become closer since I left. Every time I come here I get a poison dose of realism. It is vain to think that life is somehow halted once we leave the scene, and we as humans have our vain moments. However, once again, the reality bat strikes. Old boyfriends move on, they heal and eventually find new girlfriends. Unfortunately, there is nothing we can do about it. Except hope that we look better than the new girlfriend and pray she has no style. Stan opens the door and tells us that the doctor has officially released Tam and that he is going to get the car. We walk into the room and help Tam into the wheelchair. She resists, but it is hospital policy. Therefore, we push her behind back into the chair and wheel her downstairs. Riding back with Evelyn, I ask her about the baby's things and what she thinks we should do. She says Tam will, personally, want to put the things away.

"Tam is so strong that this may be a healing process for her," she comments.

I, on the other hand, would be a wreck. I wouldn't be able to go back into the house until someone had cleaned out the room. Knowing Tam and Stan need some time in the house alone, we decide to stop and get some food before we come over.

During lunch, Evelyn grills me about Dick. "Is he going to marry that girl?"

"I don't know."

"She's really pretty. What does she do?"

With an attitude, I give a short response. "She's a ballet dancer."

"Well, what's up with you two?"

"Nothing. We decided to be friends. Stop asking me about Dick. Let's talk about you. Who are you screwing these days?"

"Watch your mouth. The only man I am dating is the Lord."

I laugh so hard at her answer that my drink spews from my mouth and onto Evelyn's blouse. As I am apologizing, she is rising and walking to the restroom. While she is in there, I reflect upon my reaction. I should not have laughed at Evelyn; I am glad she is nurturing her spiritual side. But her response was so unexpected. I will apologize when she returns.

However, as soon as she gets to the table she speaks. "Let's go!"

"I'm sorry, I shouldn't have laughed."

"That's okay. They ridiculed Jesus too and I am not ashamed to admit what he has done for me. We'll see who'll be laughing on Judgment Day."

I feel as though my Sunday school teacher is reprimanding me for playing in class and I stand here accused. Evelyn's tone has changed and I now see that she is serious. I never meant to mock. I attend church and I am serious when it comes to spirituality. However, I would never say I am dating the Lord. Her comment threw me off.

"Again, I apologize."

She grabs her purse and we walk to the car.

Stan greets us at the door when we arrive. Within the quiet, dark house, he pulls us into the kitchen, whispering, "She's been upstairs in the baby's room since we walked in the door."

"What is she doing?" we whisper back as he shrugs his shoulders.

"I asked if I could come in and she said not now, so I have been down here since we got home," he says, walking back into the living room.

Evelyn and I follow close behind Stan and sit downstairs with him. We put on the television and turn the volume down low. After an hour, Evelyn and I agree that someone should go check on her. We nominate Stan. He walks down the hall and knocks on the bedroom door. From the living room, we hear her say come in. Stan walks in and we sit impatiently waiting for his return. A minute later, he walks back into the living room and says that Tam wants us to come into the room. Slowly Evelyn and I approach the baby's room. We see Tam resting in the center of the floor covered with a baby blanket as she holds the teddy bear we purchased on my last visit. I glance at Evelyn, who is fighting, just as I am, to hold back the tears.

"Come lie with me," Tam says in a faint voice.

We each get a blanket and lie on the right and left side of our friend. Tam lies on her side in the fetal position. Evelyn is on her stomach with her legs stretched out and I am on my back with my right leg crossed over my left. Yellow and peach baby blankets cover our bodies, yet everything below our knees is exposed. We look like triplets as we lie there is silence for hours.

Finally, Tam speaks. "I love you guys."

We each turn our heads toward her and smile.

"We love you too," Evelyn and I say simultaneously.

On this night, nothing else is said. Tam puts her arm on my

shoulder and we lie on the floor of the baby's room until each of us falls asleep. I am sure we are no substitute for the newborn child that is supposed to fill this space. Nevertheless, on this night our friendships reach new levels of trust, respect, and honesty and for this we all are grateful.

Good night.

Chapter 36

Sugar and Spice
and Everything Nice

Evelyn takes me to the airport early the next morning. I kiss Tam good-bye and promise to come visit on my next days off. She even says that she will come see me in a few months. After giving Stan a hug, Evelyn and I leave. Five minutes into the car ride my cell phone begins to ring. I look at the caller ID and see that the call is from Dick.

"Well, well," I answer.

"Where are you?" he asks.

"On my way to the airport. I have to be back at work today."

"I am sorry I didn't get to see you yesterday. I know you're coming back to visit your girl. Maybe we can hang out then," says Dick.

"Where's you fiancée, Dick?"

"In New York doing a show. Why?"

"Tell her I said hello," I say with a witty tone.

Dick gives me a slight laugh, says good-bye, and hangs up. Evelyn assures me that she will call and give me regular updates on Tam. I get on the plane, arrive in Kansas City by eleven, and I am back on the job by noon. I stop by Sarah's desk to see how the weekend shopping went with Claire. Sarah says that she and Claire spent the entire day buying clothing for themselves and clothing for the baby. She seems to enjoy the lifestyle. I only hope she doesn't mind the constant advice she is going to receive once the baby gets here.

I don't leave work until seven this evening so that I am able to finish my presentation for Friday. I get home, flick on the television, and sit on the futon. It is rare that I watch TV during the week. I usually come home, cook dinner, listen to music or do some writing, and go to bed. However, tonight I am in the mood for a little fiction. I want to be entertained by the stars of Hollywood. I begin to watch an interesting movie on HBO. It's about a girl named Laura who could make wishes for anything she wants and her wishes would come true. However, every wish comes with a consequence, and she doesn't know the sacrifice until the wish is fulfilled. She asks for money and she loses her friends, she asks for a mansion, which costs her a fortune to maintain. Finally she asks for a man who will treat her like a princess and he does. Unfortunately, he treats his other two wives like princesses as well. She could have asked for anything and she never thought to ask for happiness or peace or anything intangible. She assumed happiness and respect from her peers would come with the money, house, and man. Instead happiness and respect are what she sacrifices. As I sit watching the story of Laura, I can't help but feel connected to her. I can't understand how she can ask for anything she wants and still not be happy. Laura and her story linger in my mind as I go to bed. I even put myself in Laura's shoes. I wonder what I would wish for and I wonder if my decisions would be as unwise as hers. She consumes my mind until I become sleepy. I take a shower, slip into my sexy bed attire, a cotton tank and boxers, and fall asleep.

* * *

Today is Sarah's baby shower. I find it hard to believe that
she only has two more months to go. It seems like yesterday
that she and I were on our first date with Wealth and Omar.
Speaking of Wealth, he stills calls me every other week to see
how I am doing. We even went to a party together last weekend. He is a nice guy, just not the guy for me. Yes, I know that
sounds familiar, but I'm serious this time. However, he is a
very well connected man. He is definitely someone who
should stay in my little black book. He can take care of parking tickets, get tickets to any major sporting event, and get me
great deals on real estate. I'll be his occasional arm piece if
that is what keeps me linked into high society. We agree to
remain social buddies.

I pick up Sarah's gift and head to her new mansion in the
country. That baby already has more gifts than I have received
in my entire lifetime. Therefore, I buy Sarah a beautiful baby
book encased in a hand-carved wooden box, which I found in
an antique shop. After her little girl is born, the gentleman
says we can bring it back to have her name and birth date in-
scribed into the wood. Due to her newly found interest in an-
tiques, I am sure she and Claire will approve.

I arrive at the home and the valet parks the car. Although I
am not late, there are a number of cars parked ahead of me.
Sarah greets me at the door and pulls me to the side as soon
as I walk in. She begins to whisper, "She invited all of her
friends and several family members. I don't know these
people. I only wanted a few of my friends."

"Did you tell her that?" I ask.

Sarah shakes her head no.

"Well, you better pray they brought good gifts," I continue
as I walk down the hallway into the main living area.

Claire greets me just before she introduces me to the rest
of the girls. I am used to baby showers with young ladies and

young mothers. These women are old enough to be grand-
mothers. This looks like a bridge convention. Fortunately,
soon after I sit, more of Sarah's friends attend. I really don't
know anyone here except for Sarah. However, Mrs. Fulmore
and Bobbi Fulmore come a few minutes later. Bobbi sits next
to me and yaps about how good men are hard to find and that
I should work things out with Wealth. She is beyond clueless.
The caterer has prepared at least six different appetizers and
we all partake before opening the gifts. We play a few games,
such as name the baby, but the main event is unveiling all of
the elaborately wrapped gifts and I can't wait to see what
she and the baby are getting. I am as excited as Sarah. The
room is covered with gifts. There are twenty-two attendees at
the shower and one-half of them brought at least two gifts.
Claire rings the bell and everyone closes in as Sarah is handed
her first gift. Claire announces the purchaser of each gift as
Sarah begins to unwrap. This is such a big production and I
love it. The first two gifts are from the Fulmores. A hand-
quilted blanket, three sets of cotton crib sheets, and four or
five designer jumpers. What does a newborn baby need with
designer clothing? She will wear the outfit one time and
probably spit up on it, I think to myself. Her second gift is
from a cousin. It's a sterling silver spoon with a gift certifi-
cate to have the name and birth date engraved on the item.
This is appropriate; however, this little girl will never be able
to use the excuse "I wasn't born with a silver spoon." The gift
list continues. Before Sarah finishes, she and her baby have
a year's supply of Pampers, Donna Karan layette sets, walk-
ers, strollers, baby toys, gym memberships for after the baby
is born, a minirefrigerator for the baby's room, lots of nurs-
ing equipment, and believe it or not diamond earrings for the
baby. The earrings are from Claire. I have never had a pair of
diamond earrings and this baby has a pair before she comes
out of the womb. As Sarah finishes unwrapping her gifts,
the crowd thins out and the ladies go back to mingling and

eating. I notice that Sarah's expression is changing. So I take her hand and we step out onto the terrace and talk.

"Are you okay?" I ask.

Sarah places her head on my shoulder and answers, "I wish my mom were here."

In consolation, I rub the back of her head. Sarah's mom died when she was sixteen. She had a heart attack one day while Sarah was at school. Sarah got off the bus, saw the ambulance and paramedics, ran to the house, but it was too late. She told me this a few months after we met, but she hasn't mentioned her mom again until now. I can't imagine how she must be feeling.

"I know, sweetie. It can't be easy, especially now. But look how you found Claire. She loves you like a daughter and she is so excited about her granddaughter. You couldn't have asked for a better situation. You two need each other and it is so beautiful. That is the work of God."

Sarah lifts her head from my shoulder and gives me a small grin.

"So I should be happy, right?" she asks with doubt.

"Would your mother want you to be happy?" I ask.

"Yes."

"Well, there is your answer."

Sarah smiles and walks back into the house. As she steps into the room, Bobbi rushes to her side to ask her about the baby's name. She knows about the Richard tradition and she wants to know if Sarah plans to be the first to break it. Sarah sighs and says she is undecided about the name. Turning to me, she says that she would love to name the baby after her mom, so I ask her mom's name.

"Mary," she replies, making a funny face.

I immediately laugh because I know that Claire will have a stroke if Sarah decides to name her first granddaughter Mary.

"What is her full name?" I ask, hoping for a better response.

"Mary Ann Tether," she says with the same expression.

I sit and think about the name Mary Ann Tether, while looking strangely at Sarah.

"We're from Kentucky," she comments, placing her hands on her hips.

"Okay. Let's see, what was her maiden name?"

Sarah pauses as her eyes roll up into her head in order to pull down the information from her mental Rolodex. Suddenly, she displays a huge smile while grabbing my forearms.

"Carmen!" She beams.

"I believe you have just named your little girl."

Bobbi runs through the house like Paul Revere, telling everyone that Sarah has decided upon a name. She is so annoying. Claire comes rushing to the terrace to hear what Sarah has decided. Once Sarah says the name, Claire kneels and starts speaking to Sarah's belly in gushy, baby talk. Once again, she rings the bell, clears her throat, and makes the grand announcement.

"We have a name for the baby," she yells above the partygoers. "My granddaughter is going to be Carmen . . ." She pauses and looks at Sarah.

Sarah glances at me as she tries to think of a middle name. Finally, she looks up at Claire and speaks. "Leigh."

Speechless, Claire begins to cry. Through the tears, she manages to whimper out the entire name and on December 30 at 2:24 AM, Carmen Leigh Richard is born, weighing six pounds and seven ounces. She is named Carmen after her maternal grandmother and Leigh after her other. I didn't know that Claire's middle name is Leigh, but I have to hand it to Sarah, that was one great power move. The room is filled with flowers and gifts. But the most important gift is that Omar is there for the birth of his daughter. He did come around, just like Claire said. His little girl has his eyes and Sarah's dusty red hair. She is going to be a knockout. Claire is already preparing her granddaughter's career in modeling with Baby Gap. I gently rub her tiny hands and kiss Sarah on the forehead. Finally, I embrace Omar, long enough to whisper a few threats in his ear before leaving.

Sarah went into labor around nine yesterday and I although I did no pushing or breathing, her labor experience leaves me bushed. I walk into my home and crash on the futon. But not before imagining having a little one of my own. I wonder what she or he would look like. Childbirth is incredible. Anyone considering atheism should witness it, because although science is involved, it is nothing short of a miracle.

Good night.

Chapter 37

Starting Over at the End

After a restless night, I awake early in the morning and, lying in the bed alone, I glance over at the empty matching pillowcase. I have been so busy the last few months with Sarah that I haven't had time to feel lonely. She called me last night to thank me for everything, saying that she appreciates all of my help, but that she doesn't want to become a burdensome friend. What she fails to realize is that I need her as much as she needs me. It is going to be a joy watching her raise Carmen and I look forward to being the auntie that lets her get away with everything. I rise and walk downstairs. Once I get into the living room, I forget what I have come downstairs to retrieve. I hate when that happens. I walk into the kitchen and stare into the fridge. I am hungry, but I have no idea what I want to eat and I feel it starting. This is going to be one of those days when everything is frustrating, nothing is satisfying, and I feel the urge to cry, curse, or scream at any given moment. I move to the cabinets and peruse the cereal boxes. I have a houseful of food and yet I can't find a single thing to eat. I sit on the kitchen counter staring into the open icebox. Maybe I can't find what I am searching for because it is not in the kitchen. I grab the Post-it notepad from off the refrigerator door and write.

Why is it that my life feels incomplete when I have no man to love? I have family and friends. Shouldn't that be enough? Most importantly I have myself. If nothing else I should be enough for me. I jump down from the kitchen counter and go upstairs to get showered and dressed. I want to spend the day outside the house, but it is too cold for outside activities, so I decide to go see the new Egyptian exhibit at the museum.

I walk up to the ticket counter to purchase a ticket. The lady looks at me and asks, "How many?"

Now, I know she sees me standing here alone, so why would she ask that? But I figure she is doing her job and I could have some kids straggling behind, so I simply answer her, "One."

"Are you alone?" she continues.

What in the hell is wrong with her? Is she trying to be funny? Why would I ask for one ticket if I were not alone? Just as I am about to answer, I hear a voice behind me speak.

"I hope so."

I turn and find myself staring into a broad chest. I extend my neck upward and see the handsome man attached to the chest. He reaches forward and introduces himself. "I'm Al Sims."

"Hi, Al. My name is Lily."

In the midst of our introduction, the ticket lady clears her throat and repeats her question louder. "Ma'am, are you alone?"

"Yes, I am!" I say with my teeth clenched together.

I take my ticket, smile, and wave bye to Al as I walk into the museum. The Egyptian exhibit is on the far end of the building, so I decide to visit the art collections first. As I walk through the corridors, looking at the oils and pastels of Picasso, Rembrandt, and Monet, I am drawn into their work.

I wonder if these pieces were created from lonely souls. Then again, they could have been created through artistic expressions of love. Nevertheless, these artists have captured their emotions and put them on display for all to see. Of course, some are more personal than others. Some are simple scenic views. But even these scenes evoke deep senses of emotion. I move on through the corridors and finally make it to the Egyptian exhibit. Walking into the mock pyramid, I view the mummies and tombs. While I am walking through the narrator is speaking on each of the mummies, detailing their life and their importance in the structural society of early Egyptian civilization. I find the culture fascinating. These people were intelligent individuals who created healing potions, fragrances, and jewelry. Not to mention the ever-lasting mystery of the pyramids. For me, however, the most interesting fact about their society is the grave importance they placed on the afterlife. In essence they lived their entire lives preparing for the afterlife. I am sure they had day-to-day worries, but I bet they never stressed for long, because they knew that this life is nothing in comparison to what they were preparing for. Sure, they may have gone overboard with the oils, fragrances, and jewels, but they definitely had the right idea.

Our time on earth is so short compared to an eternity. Furthermore, since we have no idea when this time on earth will be over, we should spend each day enjoying life to its fullest. And if this concept is as simple as it sounds, why is it that most people don't apply it? Even as I am saying it, I am wondering how I am going to put it into works. I finish walking through the exhibit and head toward the exit. I would visit the other exhibits, but a few quiet hours in the museum is plenty. Why are museums so quiet, anyway? Everyone whispers as if they don't want to disturb the dead souls of the artists. I love the museum, but museum behaviors are somewhat creepy and three hours is definitely long enough. As I get to the door, I feel a tap on my shoulder. Turning around, I see that it is Al.

"Yes, Al. What can I do for you?"

He hands me his business card and smiles. "Call me," he responds in a baritone voice.

I take his card and without looking at it, I give a hint of laughter while inquiring, "Now, why should I call you?"

"Because I want to get to know this girl named Lily."

"Oh!" I say, as I shake my head.

Upon scratching my cheek I wink and continue. "Well, as soon as I find out who she is, I'll let you know."

I nod a pleasant good-bye to Al and leave the museum. Unenthused, I drive by several shopping malls on the way home; however, I can't stir up the mood to shop, eat, or hang out in the city. I even stop by Blockbusters to pick up a movie, but there is nothing that I want to see. At last, I give up and make my way home.

I walk into the house and sit down on the futon staring at the black television screen. I don't want to watch TV, I don't want to listen to music, and I don't want to eat, sleep, or talk on the phone. It's that type of day. I might as well wait it out and pray for a better tomorrow. Then I remember the proposal I made to myself only an hour ago at the museum. I am going to live each day to the fullest. I am not going to sit here and be depressed because I don't know what to do, I am going to do something and get enjoyment from it. As I think for a second, an idea comes to mind. I lean underneath my futon and pull out three shoe boxes. I open each box and dump out the pictures. The one thing that always brings a smile to my face is memories. I pull out two new photo albums, unwrap the plastic, and begin entering my pictures into the album. I must first put them in some order. Turning all of the pictures faceup, I place them side by side like a completed game of concentration. In total, I have seven rows containing ten pictures and one row containing six. I have pictures of Romance and me, Tam and Evelyn, Stan and Tam, Dick and Tam, Winston and Wealth, and every possible combination of all my friends. I run to my purse and pull out pictures of Sarah and baby Carmen. All of these pictures tell the last few years of my life. Slowly, I begin to put them into the book. I laugh out loud at the situations and predicaments I have managed to get myself into over the last couple of years. This last year alone has been quite a novel. I put the pictures of my girlfriends on one side and the pictures of my dates on the other side. I run my hand across the few pages of men and start to giggle. I have actually had what most women dream of. I have had Romance, Dick, and Wealth. Hell, those three are usually a part of the top five in a perfect mate criteria list. You would think that three out of five should make me a happy woman, but it doesn't. Perhaps I settled for the wrong three. Maybe I should have opted for Humor and Respect. Then again, that's not fair. How often do you meet a man with those names? I wonder if I meet all five, would that guarantee my happiness? Probably not, huh? I am proof that a girl can be romanced, have dick at her disposal and the wealth of the world, and still not be content. For happiness is not found on that perfect mate list. True happiness roots from within.

As I turn the page and look at pictures of Tam and me dressed as men, laughter consumes my body. I begin to laugh uncontrollably. True, the picture is hilarious, but my laugher is more cathartic. All this time, I have been seeking for something that has always been here. It's like I cheated and made an F, because I copied the wrong answers onto my test. I was so anxious to finish, I failed to read the instructions. The test was open-book all along. Lucky for me, I am my own professor and I am giving myself a second chance, but where do I start? Immediately, I think of Al Sims and our brief conversation at the museum. He wants to get to know someone that I need to become reacquainted with: me. I never write about myself. I am not sure if it is because I don't know much about myself or if I am afraid I won't like what I read. Maybe it's a combination of both, yet I must start somewhere. If I want to experience the love Tam has for Stan, Sarah has for Carmen, and Dick has for himself, there is only one way to do it. I need to get to know . . .

Me

I love shoe shopping though I despise shopping for clothing.

I don't spend much time on my hair or nails, but I like to exercise and take care of my body. I have my father's eyes and my mother's hands and smile. I like dark furniture, but I'd prefer as little furniture as possible. I choose cold over hot and feather pillows over foam. My eyes will always resemble my father's, I will shoe shop until the day I die, and my hands will age like my mother's. Right now I have long hair, but who knows? I will probably not always like dark furniture.

I have full lips. I have large feet and strong hips. I like jazz a lot, and Nina Simone I like best. I love to dance and love to write. I curl my tongue when I create. I never argue for long, because I love to laugh. I enjoy making others laugh as well. My feet will always be large, though my hips may not always be strong. My taste in jazz may change, but I hope to always make others laugh.

I enjoy the company of men. I like to flirt, but I despise arrogance. I like to read. I prefer love stories to historical, yet I like suspense the best. I'll see the movie before reading the book. I can dance better than I can sing. But when I sing, I'm an alto. I prefer fresh flowers, and sunflowers are my favorite. Unfortunately, I'm allergic to pollen. One day I may stop dancing, although I will

*always consider myself a dancer. I used to believe in
love. So who knows, I may not always prefer love stories
to historical. However, I will always enjoy the company
of men.*

*And hopefully one day, I will start to believe in love
again.*

I glance over my poem, close my journal, and place it
inside the photo album. Reaching in my closet, I pull out a
new book with crisp white pages. A new beginning deserves
a new journal, right? I sigh, staring at the first page. I have no
idea what to write. Where should I start?

After saying this phrase several times over, I write that
exact question and then read it aloud.

"Where should I start? Where should I start?"

Perhaps . . . I'm not sure . . . then again, maybe . . . I should
start with . . .

A Girl Named Lily?
I don't know
We'll see . . .

Good life.
Lily

Lily's Journal
of Poetry

In Flight

On the wings of a butterfly my mind is in flight.
Here, I have no worry; my tears are joyous.
Pain is nothing more than an ache from the
  abundance of laughter.
With a smile, I deal with day-to-day strife.
With a wink, I deal with day-to-day ignorance.
My mind is light, ever carefree.
Negativity, I have none.
Transcending to a higher plane . . .
In hope.

On the wings of a dove, my soul is in flight.
I find time in an impatient world.
My cup is half-full, no longer half empty.
My pessimistic ways vanish.
I pray for those who spite me as my positive vibes
  uplift those I surround.

My soul is calmed, ever peaceful.
Reaching a higher plane . . .
In faith.

On the wings of an eagle, my heart is in flight.
Although grounded by gravity, I float above all
    others.
There is beauty is the ugliest of creatures.
I see miracles by the minute.
Daydreaming becomes second nature.
I smile, I laugh, I dance, and I play as a child.
Outside opinions hold no merit on my emotions.
My heart is ever so blissful.
To a higher plane I have gone . . .
In love

Are U

When I'm sad and blue for no reason at all
When I can do no more and I need that inner
    strength to come from you
When I need your smile to turn my tears of sorrow
    into tears of joy
When I need your embrace to turn my day-to-day
    strife into pure pleasure
Are U strong enough to be my man?

When I want to be a child, can you control?
When I want to be a woman, can you surrender?
When I want my silence understood and my gabbi-
    ness tolerated
When my Gemini is in rare form
Are U strong enough to be my man?

*When I want nothing more than a walk in the park
    in the dead of winter
When I've given up on happiness can you restore my
    faith in love?
When I need your tender kiss to make me feel beau-
    tiful again
When my imagination carries me away, can your
    reality bring me back?
Are U cool enough to be my man?*

*Leave me alone, but don't wander too far.
Please don't touch me, just be attentive from across
    the room.*

*Hold me as thy woman
Respect me as thy friend
Freak me as thy harlot
Honor me as thy mother
Discipline me as thy child
Spoil me as thy lady
Love me as thy queen
Can U?
When I give you love like no other
Are U man enough to be my man?*

For Him

*He makes me weak.
When he smiles a feeling of warmth comes over my
    body.
I too must smile, for I can't seem to do anything but.
He moves me to a state of bless and when we part,
I immediately miss his smile*

And for a small while, I sadden.
But only for a while, because as my mind replays his
smile,
I get anxious with emotions of a little girl, and I start
to spin in circles.
I literally twirl, around and around and around.
Because I finally found someone who makes me so
happy
and I just get weak, weak for his smile.
And when he laughs, a feeling of joy comes over me.
I too must laugh for I can't seem to do anything but.
He moves me to a state of peace. No matter the
hassle of life.
He is there in times of strife.
No matter the worry or pain, He gives me strength
to gain.
Together we pull through everything.
His laughter eases my soul and I feel like a lady,
pampered and cared for.
So I hold on 'cause I know it's gonna be okay.
And this man makes me feel that way.
And I really feel this; it's not only say.
And I get so weak, weak for his smile.
And when he kisses, my God, when he kisses . . .
A feeling of splendor . . .
Spellbound, I start to quiver 'cause I can't seem to
do anything but.
As if I have been entranced, taken to another plane.
And he's kissing me and kissing me.
Insane, that something so simple could excite so
much.
Earth, as I know, could crumble, glow into a nuclear
dust
The air I breathe could start to rust

And I wouldn't even notice,
Trust, I would not peek,
because he is still kissing me and I am still kissing him.
For real this is how he makes me feel
And I know why God made me a girl, a lady, a
    woman,
to receive love from him.
And I just get so damn weak.
Weak for him.

Chocolate

Your love is better than chocolate
It's better than anything I have ever experienced
Your love is better than walking through wet grass
    on a dewy spring morning
Better than that fresh clean smell after a warm
    summer's rain
More beautiful than a four-color rainbow after a hot
    storm
Sweeter than Grandma's tea in that big Mason jar
    in the back of the fridge.
More breathtaking than a field full of tall, swaying
    sunflowers
Your love is better than chocolate
Godiva!

As We Dance

The love we made last night was perfect. The love
    made was bliss.
I felt the need to write, so as not to be remiss
On every minute detail that evolved into a faint echo.

The night was indeed very so a moment in time of
  absolute divine
You took my hand and danced and smiled
Sade wailed her tune and you began to croon as I
  grooved my head into your chest
In your arms, your arms I rest.
You bowed your head against my face and kissed my
  neck, a tender place
Tonight, I am drawn to your allure
As we dance and dance some more.
Your right hand lifts my face to your lips
and the other wraps around my hips
We kiss like never before as our bodies suddenly
  pound the door.
My feet they lift up from the floor
My blood, your blood begins to soar
The passion so soft, yet so hard-core
My clothes torn apart within the uproar
Tenderly, we dance and dance some more.
As I lie under this shelter of you
You kiss my neck as if to subdue
And we become one, consumed by each other
Much, much more than each other's lover
My arms over yours, yours over mine
Slowly, deeply we take our time
You softly speak into my ear
At the close of my eye rolls out a tear
I can honestly say you replenish my soul
As we stand here clutched detained in this hold
I embody the portal of your love and me you truly
  adore
As we stand here embraced in the dawn of the morn
We dance and dance some more.

Love Is Color

Love Is

> Commonly yellow
> Yellow; Bright sunny; Bright yellow

Love Is

> Orange
> Orange; Spicy hot; Spicy orange

Love Is

> Silver; Cool; Common
> Allowed stolen moments, lighting fire
>   within my heart
> Bright sunny

Love Is

> Passion entering passion, subdue me
> Spicy hot

Love Is

> Sometimes green
> Green; envious careless; envious
> green

Love Is

> Gray
> Gray; cloudy messy; cloudy gray

Love Is

> Golden; Precious; Sometimes
> Allowed stolen moments, burning
>   memories within my heart
> Envious careless

Love Is

> Passion driving passion, crazy me
> Messy cloudy

Love Is

> Rarely white
> White; pure innocent; pure white

Love Is

> *Black*
> *Black; powerful omnipotent; powerful*
>   *black*

Love Is

> *Platinum; Supreme; Rare*
> *Allowed stolen moments burnt craters*
>   *within my heart*
> *Pure innocent*

Love Is

> *Passion becoming passion, you are me*
> *Powerful omnipotent*

Love Is

> *Common; Sometimes; Rare*

Rules

So when am I going to see you again?
Not that I'm excited or anxious. I just want to see
  you again.
So who am I fooling, U or me?
Damn, I dig you, I like you, and I feel you.
I'm excited about the possibility of sharing experi-
  ences with you.
I'm anxious about future memories I will have of
  you.
So when you don't hear from me in a day or two
It's not that I don't want to talk to you. I just can't
  appear that way.
Understand what I say. It's the game.
The game that no one admits they play, but all play,
  just the same.
The game that is as instinctive as blinking. The game
  we all play.

So you see, I can't say I miss you even if I do.
I can't say I want you until after a date or two.
And you know I can't give up the booty, even if I
    want to,
not yet anyway.
That is, unless I don't care if you go or stay.
So if I like you . . . I gotta wait, but if I don't, it's cool.
Now you tell me, these rules were made by what
    fool?
The rules of the dating game that no one admits
    they play,
but they all play
Just the same.
Get his number but wait until he calls you.
When he calls act like you're busy,
but can squeeze in a little time for a date.
Go on a date, but plan a backup just in case.
Have fun, but don't appear to have too much fun.
Wanna have sex, but can't have sex.
Tease and flirt so he knows he'll get some soon, but
    not tonight.
Say it's cool to date other people,
when you know it's not cool to date other people.
Wanna know if he's sleeping with someone else but
    can't ask if he's
Sleeping with someone else.
Won't say I like you until confirmed you are liked.
Can't say I love you until said by the other.
What in the hell is this about?
Miscommunication begets miscommunication.
Soon there is no communication.
So instead of confrontation, I'm going to try honesty.
Honesty is the key to vital information pertaining to
    you and me.

So how 'bout this? I like you, when we are apart I
  miss you.
I want to explore future possibilities with you.
To sum up. I dig you and I hope you dig me too.
I let down my guard.
Got out of the game and into the real.
All I need to know is, baby, how do you feel
About me?

My Stimuli

You stimulate my mind, when your eyes stare into
  mine
I wonder if your thoughts are oft of me, as mine are
  oft of you
Not to say you are all I think of 24-7-365
But in the base of my brain, there you sit and sit and
  sit
And thoughts of you keep reappearing in the after
I have no thought control when it comes to you
An involuntary reflex
No control of my lips as they begin to curl in a faint
  smile as I picture you
No control of my hips as they move to an untimely
  rhythm
as I hold your hand
No control do I have over any of these things
You stimulate my mind

You stimulate my body
Your dreamy eyes paralyze me with passion
Your gentle touch captivates me even more

*Mere chills are nothing in comparison to what you
    send up my spine*
Your hands embracing mine
*Your lips placed upon the base of my neck at the
    origin of my shoulder*
I melt
*Like ice cream spilled on hot pavement, into your
    arms*
I melt
*and as the pavement makes that cold cream puddle
    into hot milk*
You induce my cool milk to stream out as hot cream.
Can you comprehend what I mean
As I say
You stimulate my body?

You stimulate my soul
With you so vivid is my imagination.
*Thoughts of you holding me fill my heart with
    warmth, my spirit with joy*
To know I am yours and you are mine completes me
Yet your thoughts intrigue me, your mind a query
What makes you tick?
What makes me love you so much?
*What makes you the man I don't want to live
    without?*
I don't know
Love?
*Perhaps, you are my destiny, my miracle, least I'll
    say it once again*
You stimulate my soul
Soul, mind, body; Body, soul, mind; Mind, body, soul
No matter the order, you are my love, my passion
My stimuli

Untitled

I feel I have swallowed my heart
And I can't understand.
I have a hole in the pit of my stomach
And I don't know why.
It may be because you and I
Are slowly drifting apart.
Which makes me ask, do I care more than I say?
Do I care more than I know?
So why is it so difficult for me to show my feelings
*   for you?*
The unanimous decision to be friends
The unanimous decision to be lovers
For friends make great lovers, but somewhere down
*   the line*
The honesty of the friendship kills the vulnerability
*   of the love.*
And in time someone gets hurt.
This I know
So I chose to stay in control; my feelings are not for
*   show.*
Trying hard to maintain, I spun uncontrollably
Like a child getting dizzy, I couldn't focus outside
*   spinning to see I was about to fall.*
Attempting to stay in control, I had no time to real-
*   ize I had fallen;*
Fallen into a place I had no desire to be.
And so I spent time with others to conceal my
*   emotions*
But they never satisfied my craving for you.
While I spent time with others I should have known
If I could have opened my eyes and seen it was you
*   all along.*

But now you see another and it's torn me up inside.
'Cause someone's got my man, my lover, my friend
And I can no longer hide this love I have for you.
I love you; I don't want to lose you
And I'm sorry I never told you.
I was holding it back, you see
I want you, my friend, my lover, my man.
I'll take that risk. Will you love me?

Falling (Sand Poem)

The first time you anticipate
you wait, you see
Who will make the first move
first motion, first touch
You must not be too anxious or act as if you want
*   like you want*
don't want to be Mary, can't afford to be Jezebel
Just somewhere in the middle,
where you get the respect but still get the rise
But to my surprise
the rise is not enough; this time
Puzzling as it is, my heart as curious as my mind
Well, there's a first time
for everything, I suppose
It's my turn to fall into that endless spiral of kaleido-
*   scope colors*
Colors so beautiful that reality is unimaginable
so unimaginable that the beauty is tempting as hell
A temptation that always aroused my being
A hell that wasn't worth the price
Will I be turned and turned until my image becomes
*   pleasing to my viewer*

Or will I be viewed more beautiful with each turn of
    my image?
Once in the kaleidoscope
Still hanging on, rope burns and all
As my body grows tired, I want to not want
Yet I want more to let go
Falling into that ocean of colors
Little pools I have conquered, big ones I fear
I could float, I could swim, I could drown
Drowning is finite.
Unfortunately, the outcome is unknown on its way
    down
On a high
Grasping for the walls to slow my speed
Falling . . .

Beauty Part I

I don't care if beauty is in the eye of the beholder, if
    it's not in the hearts of those we behold as beautiful
Well, speaking for me, if the heart is pure, the soul is
    beautiful
And the view of the beholder becomes trivial
For if you live your life attempting to be beautiful
for the sake of the beholder,
You may become enslaved or complacent to society's
    standard of beauty
And honestly speaking, society's standard of beauty
    is not that high.
Yet this is nothing about looking good. If you thought
    so,
you misunderstood.

For you can be fine. Nice pecs, chiseled chin,
    32 straight teeth,
perfect grin. Bald head, wavy hair, or dreads falling
    to the cheek
and just in case the myth is true a pair of big ol' feet
and still fall short of beautiful.
We were told that these things were a prerequisite
of all of that beauty and shit.
And we learned to believe this.
Strong cheekbones, long lashes, and dimples may
    get you a CK 1 ad.
If you feel that counts as beautiful, that's too damn
    bad.
As fine as you may be, if you disrespect your brother,
    if you disrespect your sister, you are not beautiful
    to me and it's just my opinion
But if you spite others to boost yourself, if you belittle
    your ancestors, if you pimp your looks for sex,
    again, you are not beautiful to me.
My beliefs and my opinions I can say.
And since I view these things on beauty, it makes me
    a beholder in a way.
You may not agree and that's fine and that's cool
For no opinion should hold merit to what's deeply in
    your heart,
As I said at the start.
It matters not if beauty is in the eye of the beholder,
    if it's not in the heart of those we behold as
    beautiful.
Don't live you life attempting to be beautiful for the
    beholder.
Be beautiful for you
Forget Webster, become your own definition of
    beauty.

Now, that's a beautiful thang!
My people, that's a beautiful thang!

Dark Chocolate

It's Friday, 5:24 in the afternoon, and what's on my
*   mind?*
Your smooth, dark chocolate that coats your
*   physique.*
So fine are you, when you walk through my door
How I crave for some time alone so that I may adore
Your sexy smooth, dark chocolate masculinity.

It's 8:17, Friday evening, and my imagination runs
*   wild.*
From behind you are wrapping your arms around
*   my body*
Constricting me like a boa.
So tight, so gentle, so strong.
You umbrella my body, as you lean over to kiss my
*   neck.*
Oh how I long for you to cover me with
Your sensuously tender, sexy, smooth, dark chocolate
*   masculinity.*

It's 10:49, Friday night, and I laugh at your humor.
A joke you told, last week, Thursday.
Your humor, in its peculiar ways
Makes me giggle for days and days.
And I smile, as I replay your words for a while.
Please surround me with
Your humble, sensuously tender, sexy, smooth, dark
*   chocolate masculinity.*

*Now it's 12:21 in the A.M. and guess what's on my
    mind.
As I lay me down to sleep
My soul with yours, I'd love to keep.
But if for chance, I do not wake
My love for you, no one could take.
What we have is for eternity
As I dream of
Your ever spiritual, humble, sensuously tender,
    sexy, smooth, dark chocolate masculinity.*

U & I

*Undoubtedly, U . . . Inspire me
Ultimately, U . . . Impact my soul
United with U . . . I become utopian
Divided from U . . . I become unsound
U feel my uproar even if I say nothing
U feel my unhappiness even if I smile
U uncover the truth, with the blink of my I
Unparalleled, U & I
Unclad, I come to U
When they say unusual . . . U say I am eclectic
When they say uncouth . . . U say I am honest
When they say uncertain . . . U say I am free
U come unbiased . . . I can be me
I thank U
I love U
For our undivided, unearthly, unconditional union
U & I*

Those Dark Coils

Those thick dark coils
Tangled ropes of wool enter twined at the roots
The mane, as it is sometimes called
Only worn by the lion, king of the jungle
This jungle of life.
The mane, synonymous with power, which recipes
    1 cup of strength
    1/2 cup of confidence
    1/4 cup of passion
    a teaspoon of mystery
    a dash of vanity, pride, and self-praise
As my lion turns his head and his mane dances
    across his face, he slowly lifts his eyes to me
I smile
I lay my head upon his shoulder and let his mane
    shelter my face.
I feel protected
And as it delicately glides across my skin, he places
    his head in my lap to tell me of his day's struggles
I weaken
They cry stories of years past and tell episodes of
    the future
My brave king
My strong warrior
For him I have nothing but respect, nothing but
    praise

Together we can rise above, conquer all
I elevate him to the highest of all levels
My sweet soldier
My chivalrous knight

I'm your lioness. You place me on a pedestal
But it is there you belong
My confident fighter
My powerful protector

I have only my honor, my loyalty, and my love to give
Worthy of it, you are. And for you
I will give it all

Damn That Thing

I don't know what you've done 2 make me so crazy
I don't know what you've done 2 make me out of my
*   mind.*
Everything inside, all stirred up, agitated.
My heart lies in my stomach, waiting there 2 be
*   digested*
My lungs in my throat, I can't breathe.
My liver in the cavity, where my heart used 2 lie.
Even still, the thought of you and me seems so pure.
Yet life is in disorder, so out of place.
If only I could take you and erase
The last few years of my life, freeze time, start over
*   without you there*
Get you out of my fucking hair
And never look down that road again.
Hindsight is 20/20, my friend.
And I am a victim of that thing called love.

Put your ear 2 my heart and you would hear an
*   ocean*
One so deep and wide, you could swim for an eternity.

*This chasm left by you. In my face you loved me for
    my insecurities*
*In my face, you devoured, digested and shit out my
    insecurities.*
But the sex was the bomb, bordering on phenomenal.
*We could kiss our problems away and fuck them into
    the closet at best.*
But that mess piles up and begins to stink
*And so you thought or so I think, that it was best
    for us 2 part.*
*'Cause see, putting in all of your heart combined
    with most of your dick*
Can only cause you 2 fall in love, sick, with emotion.
But the sex was phenomenal, bordering on magic.
So you came and I came and you came and I came
Back for more,
'Cause sex without love is cool; at least it is 2 a fool
Already a victim of that thing called love.

It's over and it's still on.
*My fantasy has become my reality, my destiny; my free
    will.*
I live 2 love through you, you love 2 live through me
Not healthy still.
Love is not a controlled environment.
*And that mere fact I savor is the same mere fact you
    fear.*
*Hell, guess what, my dear, this thing may suffocate us
    both.*
For you see, you're in my heart,
*I wear my heart on my sleeve, I put your love out
    there 2 soon,*
Just to wallow in its glory and I'm sorry.
Yet I am in your heart,

Unfortunately, you wear your heart under your shirt
  that's under your vest that's under your blazer
  that's under your coat.
You can't appreciate my love, because you can't even
  see it and I'm sorry
I can't stay.
Though I would rather cut off both arms than 2
  leave you behind.
And 2 cut off the limbs of a writer would be death
  twice over.
Yes, to stay would be death, but don't misconstrue
2 leave would be death over, over, and over.
Despairingly caught in the core,
A victim of that thing called love.

Untitled

How can I forget the first time I saw him standing
  there?
Before he extended his hand to greet me.
I thought . . . hmmm . . . kinda sexy . . . I like the
  clothes.
I like the stance, I like the mole. But somewhere
  through the introduction he smiled, and I thought
  Dammnnn! Sexy is an understatement.
This fine man exuded sex appeal from every pore of
  his body.
I'm thinking, I've got to get his number.
Just as he says "Let's keep in touch."
Did he read my mind or what? You've got paper; I've
  got a pen. And I think, he's is not going to call . . .
  just when . . .
he gives me a hug and we part.

*I wonder if this is the end or the start of a beautiful
    moment in life.*

*So how can I forget the first time he called the
    morning after we meet?*

So cool as if a few days had passed.

*What's up? he says. I enjoyed our conversation last
    night.*

*Let's do breakfast or a movie or some sup. Then
    again, we can dance and dance and end with a
    morning breakfast.*

We meet for a meal and an interesting day . . . okay

Just when he grabs my hand to pray

Now, that's what I'm talking about.

Not to talk bad about brothers who don't pray.

*But see, I just don't flow that way. I need his spiritual
    connections to be in the same gray area as mine.*

*And did I mention this man is fine . . . yeah, I thought
    so.*

One date down, how many more to go?

*If any, maybe none, so I'll be grateful for this little
    fun . . .*

but it wasn't over.

*And how can I forget the first time he entered my
    temple?*

*How can I forget the first time he became one with
    my being?*

*My body enveloped his and each and every tiny
    movement created a tidal wave of emotional
    fluid . . . over and over and over*

*And my emotional fluid evolved into true emotions
    for him.*

*So how can I forget the first time I missed him?
    I kept replaying his expressions of our many
    conversations.*

*Dreaming about what I would say if reunited for a
    day.*
I couldn't wait to be in his arms again.
*I can smell him in my dreams, taste his kisses in my
    breath,*
and hear his thoughts in my mind.
Time after time, he became the forethought of my joy
*And all the while, I couldn't wait to get back to this
    boy.*
*How can I forget the moment I felt love for him? I
    can't.*
I say I'll never forget.

Beauty: Guys, What's Hot Part II

*My boys, my brothers, my men, my kings, get in
    where you fit in,*
'cause this call applies to all of y'all.
*You have got to stop judging beauty by what a
    woman has got.*
*Now, let me go back, not to generalize all, for if this
    call doesn't apply to you, please pass this on to
    your boys, one or two, you know with the*
"She Got Blues."
*She got light eyes, she got nice feet, she got dimples,
    she got long hair, she got no kids, she got a slim
    waist, she got sexy full lips, she got long legs, she
    got a "phat" ass.*
Great these things may be, yet they may be not.
*For if these are the only things she got, she ain't got
    much.*

*Not to say she's got nothing to offer, but if you're so
      involved with the physical the true woman gets no
      play.*
So, men, please hear what I'm trying to say.
Go for who she is, not for what she's got.
Stay for how she makes you feel,
don't leave 'cause her look no longer works for you.
*A beautiful woman isn't one with a brick house
      figure,*
but has absolutely no self-respect.
A beautiful woman is not one who is well manicured,
*but has no regard for the next brother, so all she can
      do well is use him.*
*A beautiful woman is not one with an exotic
      appearance,*
store bought I might add.
She seems so sweet, she never gets mad,
'cause she has no identity of her own.
Stop judging beauty by the physical alone.
If you got the "She Got Blues," you will get got.
What you fish out for is what you reel in.
*But no, I'm not saying choose what you aren't attracted
      to,*
or be into her if she does not uplift you.
I'm just saying look deep . . . beyond the shell.
Don't make decisions on bragging rights.
*Use your sight to look into your soul, 'cause I love
      my sistas,*
we are beautiful as a whole.
But there are a lot of stank fish in the sea.
So you good men behold; all that glitters ain't gold.
*If a woman disrespects you, makes you feel like less
      than a man,*

*Don't let her crocodile tears from those bedroom
     eyes*
give you sighs of relief that she is going to change.
If a woman is more worried about what you got,
even if she already has a lot.
*Couldn't care less if you struggle or not. She's using
     you and it's a plot.*
*She will break you down, I don't care if she is fine to
     the ground.*
Beauty she is not.
*And you know how she bats those eyes and gives you
     a smile,*
*used to want dick every day, but lately hasn't fucked
     you in a while.*
*Can't give you a reason, just that time of season. She
     guess.*
*Sweet and innocent she may look. It's the oldest
     cheap trick in the book.*
Look deep.
*That's the way you would want someone to look at
     your little girl.*
*So keep this in mind, but don't sleep on a fine
     woman.*
*She can rock your world upside down, inside out.
     Have you wondering, "What in the hell?*
Focus your eyes deeper than the shell.
*For life would not be hell with a truly beautiful
     woman.*
*Listen to her body, look into her heart, hear her
     thoughts,*
taste her kisses, touch her soul.
Least I say it once again. Look deep.
If the heart is pure, goodness you will reap.

*If you are a beautiful man, you are deserving of a
    beautiful woman.
If you output sincerity from within your heart
You will have room to input beauty.
And that is a beautiful thang, my brothers; A beautiful
    thang.*

Beauty Part III: Women (For Sarah)

*My girls, my sisters, my ladies, my women, my queens.
Get in where you fit in
'cause this call applies to all of y'all.
We have got to stop judging beauty by what a man
    has got.
Now, let me go back, not to generalize all,
for if this doesn't apply to you, please pass this knowledge
    on
to your girls one or two, you know with the
"He Got Blues."
He got a car, he got wavy hair, he got a house, he got
    no kids, he got a good job, he got nice feet, he got
    money, he got bedroom eyes,
he got a big dick.
Perks these things may be, yet they may be not.
For if these are the only things he's got, he ain't got
    much.
Not to say he's got nothing to offer,
but if we're so caught up in the obvious
the hidden truth gets no play.
So, women, please hear what I am trying to say.
Go for who he is instead of what he's got.
Stay for how he makes you feel,
don't leave 'cause he can not do for you.*

*A beautiful man is not one whose big muscles can
    hold us all night long until he gets mad and
    strikes.*

*A beautiful man is not who can drive us around and
    shelter us, until we decide not to give him any,
    and so he takes it all away.*

These are not beautiful men, I say.

If we got the "He Got Blues," we will get got.

What we put out is what we take in.

And just in case you're asking,

I'm not saying choose

*what's not pleasing to the eye or stay true if he does
    not uplift you.*

I'm just saying look deep . . . look deep.

If the heart is pure, goodness you will reap.

*But there will always be a test, for life is nothing but a
    test.*

And if we are trying to live a life of righteousness

Oh, we will be tested.

What's pleasing to the eye may be bad for the soul.

So God gave us five senses,

don't rely on one when it comes to the sexes.

*Hear, taste, touch, see, and smell, use them all and
    we won't fail*

*Being belittled, and disrespected leaves that sour
    taste on our palate.*

Recognize and know that he's not right.

Spit that shit out and keep going.

*Hear what's being said, more importantly hear
    what's not being said.*

Make sure we are being heard from the start,

even if we love his look with all of our heart.

*But the touch, the feel of their hand or the hug is just
    not right,*

If he makes us squirm, fuck the sight.
His fine looks ain't going to get us through the night.
Listen to the signs.
And if we decide to partake in this covenant and one
*   day,*
his scent is just off
That man is not going through puberty.
Confront him and see something is not pure.
We can't look him in the eyes and know for sure.
All five senses won't get us caught up in those tricks.
And if we are really in tune with our womanhood,
*   hell, we got six.*
If we are beautiful women, we are deserving of a
*   beautiful man.*
We can't sell ourselves short, judging beauty by the
*   tangible.*
For it's not what he wears on his back or what he has
*   in the bank.*
Okay, he's fine; okay, he's paid.
But all these things in time shall fade.
Yet beauty is eternal and true beauty is internal.
And if we output sincerity from within our hearts
We will have room to input beauty
And that's a beautiful thang, my sistas
A beautiful thang.

What's His Name

The feeling you give me is so unexplainable,
such an oddity, so novel. I often sit and marvel at the
*   feeling I get*
When you walk into my space, place your hands
*   upon my face, and say*

What's up, little mama?
Nothing special about the quote, it's been heard on
*   an occasion*
Once or twice a day even
But it's your tone, that special quality in that
*   moment's second*
as arms extend and eyes connect and you say
What's up, little mama?
That feeling you give me is inconceivable
But I can't be in love.

The way you arouse my inner being is remarkable
Pure excitement simultaneous peace overwhelms me
*   as you say*
You look sexy tonight; today; this morning; this
*   afternoon.*
The time of the day matters not
For I know the events to follow will contain some
*   mixture between*
My legs wrapped around your back, your body
*   hovered over mine*
Ankle to ears, lips to breast, my back arched over
*   your torso, my back covered by your chest. Nails*
*   embedded into the floor.*
Carpet burns, lips to lips, tongue to clit, my curved
*   back over your legs*
As you gently lift your head to glance,
Thrust it forward and your chance to be the MAN.
Chest to back, hips to ass, you lean over and grab
*   my hair.*
(the male ego is a bitch)
360 degrees, trunk between legs, face to pillow, teeth
*   to neck*
Flip side, mouth to head, teeth to inner thigh

No drugs, not additives feeling high.
Emotions unclad, stripped down to four words
DAMN, YOU FEEL GOOD!
And these words apply for all situations
from your smile to your hug to your mere presence.
They just freely escape during the sexual moment of
*   vulnerability, you see.*
If I say I like chocolate, it doesn't only apply while
*   I'm eating chocolate*
Although I may say it while I partake.
Sweetheart, make no mistake, you are an exceptional man.
But I can't be in love.

The mind is a powerful tool, my thoughts are
*   engulfed by you*
Maybe I'm the fool trying to hoodwink myself.
I relate everything I do to some glance, some phrase
distinguishable only by you.
Maybe it's the similarities between the two; you and
*   me, me and you*
Maybe it's the way you said you know, I could marry
*   you.*
All casual; dead serious, yet not to invoke or suggest
My tactics; not yours.
They way you act hesitantly about seeing me
but show up upon every request
Casual just the same
I don't know if you're coming, you don't know if I'm
*   going*
Are we in it for the love of the game?
'Cause a tear wells up in the corner of my eye at the
*   thought of you making an exit out of my life*
But I can't be in love . . .
Can I?

Poem to My Twin Self

The Perplexity

I don't understand your perplexity, your duality. I'm
the Gemini, not you.
You're on, you're off, you stop, you go.
Your mood swings are not tolerated,
Your vagueness is not validated by me, you see
I need an on or I need an off
A yes or a no, you have to stop, so that I can go on
with my life.
You know the magic is there, you know I want you.
You know that I know you want me as well
but what the hell, is love worth it
if it is indulged in the fear of loving too much
loving too hard, losing yourself to love as such?
I've always dreamed of a love that time will lie down
and be still for
That reason will be quiet for and that inspiration
will live for.
In you, all of those dreams can be a truth.
But, no, I have no proof,
no guarantees that this thing we have can last
forever.
Ironically, everything you seek to find is here in my
heart and mind.
If only we conclude this at the same time, we just
might make it.
But I'm in the game to win and if I win you also win.
Because, you see, it's no sin to love freely, to hurt
deeply.
Just know that one is not always a direct reaction of
the other
As you may think or even as you may wish.

I've been in that sea, catching plenty of fish.
Please keep that in my mind or you may begin to
*   spend most of your time*
Alone.
I've been there. For love waits for no one
And this you know; love waits for no one.
That notion brings your worry, yet brings you
*   comfort*
'Cause for each love that passes, a new one appears.
But the grass that looks greener grows yellow and
*   then brown.*
Variety can be color blinding.
I've been there.
If it's any comfort, I'm scared too.
'Cause even the thought of me and you
Makes my heart skip two beats, sometimes may be
*   even three.*
And you still have to ask what you mean to me.
Maybe I've been too vague, maybe I've been un-
*   clear.*
Maybe I don't understand, because I reside there.
Old habits die hard, now I let down my guard.
I had to step out of myself
To be true to myself and it took a while but now
*   freely I smile*
When I look at love

Beauty: Part IV: What's Love

Love is a beautiful thing. As long as it's a hundred
*   percent pure love*
None of that artificial flavor, concentrate stuff
True love, freshly squeezed

Please, oh please, let it be this love
For this love is beauty, pure love is beauty
A beauty that so many search for yet so few find
Is true love a thing of the mind?
I don't think so, but this one thing I do know
Love is not a thing of pain; love hurts, love stinks
All these things I've heard, is the word on love, some say
But I say, they don't know
For real love only rewards us with a lifetime of gratefulness
Hearts may hurt, hearts are vulnerable, and hearts in love especially
But the beauty of love is that she is not selfish
She lets us deal with her any way we choose
Wail, cry, pout, or have the blues
Rejoice love is gone, no longer do you ache or moan
Or just reminisce in the beauty love left behind.
Avoid, admire, like, or hate, but you can't ignore
Purposely or not, she will change your life for sure.
Yet she gets no profit, she gets no gain
You can't tell me love is a thing of pain
Love is joy
All she asks is that we recognize her presence;
her power is not to be denied
For love is more than that blood rush you get
when you look in the eyes of . . .
Love is more than that nonstop fluttering in your belly when you hold . . .
love is more than that beautiful outlook on life when you're with . . .
Love is more than that high you're on when you're in . . .
Love is all of these things and more.

Not just an emotion, but a state of being
when love adds beauty to your soul
Completing your 360° of life when you didn't know
it was incomplete
Yet so unconditional that you would trade you life
so that the beauty of the other would
Still linger on.
Love is so beautiful, never take it for granted or take
advantage
Just take it for what it truly is . . . love
Not so hard to find, if not tainted by the flesh and the
mind
Be open to love, be open to the miracle of God
Be open to the experience
Don't think love has to end like you choose or else
it's not love at all
For we have no control over love equal to life
It will continue whether we choose to be involved or
not
But please don't plot to trap love
Freedom is the key
If you try to control love's direction, somehow, its
beauty is lost
And true love is never lost
True love is a thing of beauty to witness and to
experience
And you never lose life's experiences
They are with you everywhere you go
In the back of the mind, the heart and the soul
Be grateful if you receive the chance to have such a
gift of love
Know it descended from the spirit above
And give thanks

'Cause admiration for objects come and go, but true
    love lasts forever
Be wise to never, I say never deny one hundred
    percent pure love . . .
Is always a beautiful thing, my people
A beautiful thing.

That Day

Why is reality so unsettling, why is reality so blunt?
I couldn't comprehend why, I hurt so bad
Until that day, I realized I was in love with you
That day you took the company of another
It was supposed to be okay, it was supposed to be all
    right
For we are only friends, right?
Friends who hang, friends who laugh, friends who
    love,
friends who make love?
Is this true or are we two people in love working on
    a friendship?
This question I should have asked before that day
    I realized
I was in love with you
Now over this man, I sit, I lie, I moan
I crawl into a shell
For my heart has been torn all apart
Thoughts of you, I can't rest
Selfishly, I never thought that my actions hurt you
For I know that I've done all of the things that you
    now do
But inside this realm, I couldn't see that those things
I did were out of love not received by you

*I made love to my friend, my friend slept with me
    and said it's all good
So I slept with my boy to not fall in love with my friend
then told my friend about that boy
Just to show it is all good
Not knowing I had already fallen in love with my
    friend
See, it was too late, but a common mistake
And it's not all good
Never meant to play games,
but one was played by Cupid on you and me just the
    same
It was a plan, my plan
But the well-laid plans of mice and men often go
    astray . . . they say
But this is not the way I wanted this to go
'Cause I hurt so bad that day I realized I was in love
    with you
I never meant to hurt you. If I did, you never showed
I didn't know, I didn't know
You are a strong man
I'm a strong woman as well and I still can't sell you
    on my story
Stronger than I thought, you are
But, sweetie, this is the truth by far
No act, no drama, no pity, no jealousy
I love you, man . . . that's it
Can't you be in love with me too?
All of my actions were because of this
all of my reactions were because of this
If it's too late . . . I'll live
but I want you to know you truly inspire me
And I lived for your love, long before that day
I realized that I was in love with you*

Drowning

I am drowning, trying to float in this sea of chaos.
Holding on, survival seemed easy, but my legs grow
* weary*
And faith loses luster
As I see those before me float by lifeless, I don't want
* to give in*
Yet I'm drowning in this sea of turmoil
Where survival once seemed an option
The poison has spread through my body, slowly taking
* my breath,*
slowly taking my life
Thousands have become many, and many have
* become few*
And I amongst the few, I have become tired, tired of
* gasping for air*
I don't want to suffocate
Yet I'm drowning, drowning in this sea of rage.
An emotion that kills slowly
Overruling the shadows of sorrow, pain, and fear
This anger yields me to fight for what's rightfully
* mine.*
Attempting to breathe life into this entity once vibrant,
* now sedated.*
Blood ice cold grows lukewarm. I will not give up.
Even though I'm drowning
In this sea of . . .

As your spell wears off
I don't know whether to laugh or cry
I laugh because I'm no longer drawn to you
I cry because I long for your smile
As your spell wears off

I don't know whether to rejoice or moan
I rejoice because never again will I have to guess
what's on your mind
I moan because never again will I know that I am on
your mind
As your spell wears off
You no longer hold me captive with your sexuality
You no longer hurt me with your callous looks
You no longer have to make those seldom phone
calls
I no longer have to wonder what I meant to you
As your spell wears off
I don't know whether to laugh or cry
I laugh because I'll probably never see you again
I cry because I'll probably never see you again